Dear Reader,

I just wanted to tel~~~~~~~~~~~~~~~~~~~~~~~~~~~~~
my publisher has decided to reprint so many of my
earlier books. Some of them have not been available
for a while, and amongst them there are titles that
have often been requested.

I can't remember a time when I haven't written,
although it was not until my daughter was born that
I felt confident enough to attempt to get anything
published. With my husband's encouragement, my
first book was accepted, and since then there have
been over 130 more.

Not that the thrill of having a book published gets
any less. I still feel the same excitement when a new
manuscript is accepted. But it's you, my readers, to
whom I owe so much. Your support—and particularly your letters—give me so much pleasure.

I hope you enjoy this collection of some of my
favourite novels.

Anne Mather

Back by Popular Demand

With a phenomenal one hundred and thirty books published by Mills & Boon, Anne Mather is one of the world's most popular romance authors. Mills & Boon are proud to bring back many of these highly sought-after novels in a special collector's edition.

ANNE MATHER: COLLECTOR'S EDITION

SPIRIT OF
ATLANTIS

BY
ANNE MATHER

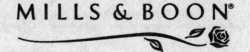

All the characters in this book have no existence outside the imagination of the author, and have no relation whatsoever to anyone bearing the same name or names. They are not even distantly inspired by any individual known or unknown to the author, and all the incidents are pure invention.

All rights reserved including the right of reproduction in whole or in part in any form. This edition is published by arrangement with Harlequin Enterprises II B.V. The text of this publication or any part thereof may not be reproduced or transmitted in any form or by any means, electronic or mechanical, including photocopying, recording, storage in an information retrieval system, or otherwise, without the written permission of the publisher.

This book is sold subject to the condition that it shall not, by way of trade or otherwise, be lent, resold, hired out or otherwise circulated without the prior consent of the publisher in any form of binding or cover other than that in which it is published and without a similar condition including this condition being imposed on the subsequent purchaser.

MILLS & BOON and MILLS & BOON with the Rose Device are registered trademarks of the publisher.

First published in Great Britain 1980 by Mills & Boon Limited
This edition 1997
Harlequin Mills & Boon Limited,
Eton House, 18-24 Paradise Road, Richmond, Surrey TW9 1SR

© Anne Mather 1980

ISBN 0 263 80556 5

Set in Times Roman 10 on 11½ pt by
Rowland Phototypesetting Limited
Bury St Edmunds, Suffolk

74-9711-52461

Made and printed in Great Britain by
Caledonian International Book Manufacturing Ltd, Glasgow

CHAPTER ONE

JULIE made her way down through the trees, her san-
dalled feet sliding on the needled slope. The smell of
pine and juniper was all around her, mingling with
the earthy scents of the forest, and although there were
occasional scufflings in the underbrush, she was no
longer alarmed. After making this particular descent
every morning since her arrival, she was used to the
shy retreat of the small animals that lived in these
woods, and she had no real fear of meeting any human
intruder. Pam and David's cabin-style hotel was situated way off the beaten path, and she doubted any
intrepid motorist would risk the forest track. Their
visitors came by yacht or canoe or motor launch, and
just occasionally on foot, but as no one new had
arrived within the last couple of days, Julie felt safe
in assuming she would not be disturbed.

At this hour of the morning, and it was only a little
after six o'clock, the lake held no appeal for their
predominantly middle-aged clientele, and Julie had
grown accustomed to considering it her private time
of the day. Soon enough, the vast reaches of Lake
Huron would be invaded by speedboats towing sun-
bronzed water-skiers, and paddle steamers giving their
passengers a glimpse of some of the thirty thousand
islands for which the lake was famous. But right now,
it was quiet, as quiet as in the winter, when the lake
was frozen over to a depth of several feet. Then, the

animals had it all their own way, and the summer settlers returned to their centrally-heated homes, and dreamed about the long sunny days at the lake.

Georgian Bay—even the names had a special sound, Julie thought. Beausoleil Island, Waubanoka, Penetang Rock, the Giant's Tomb—she had visited them all in the three weeks since her arrival, and she loved their natural beauty and the timeless sense of space. She was grateful to Adam for giving her these weeks, weeks to recover from the terrible shock of her father's suicide, and she was grateful to the Galloways, too, for making this holiday possible.

She heard the splashing in the water long before she reached the rocky shoreline. It wasn't the usual sucking sound the water made as it fell back from washing against the numerous rocks, but a definite cleaving of the lake's surface, followed by a corresponding insurge of rippling waves right to the edge of the incline.

Julie frowned as she emerged from the trees and saw the dark head in the water. She had half suspected it, of course, and yet she was still disappointed, the more so when she saw the heap of clothes lying on the rocks at her feet. They looked like a man's clothes, but these days who could be sure? Jeans were asexual, and the denim shirt could have belonged to anyone.

Her brain flicked swiftly through a mental catalogue of the guests at present staying at the hotel. Perhaps it was one of them, and yet none of them seemed the type to take an early morning dip. There were the Fairleys, but he was fat and middle-aged, and unlikely to shed his clothes in anything less than a sauna, and she was simply not the type. The Meades? Again she dismissed the idea. They were much younger, but they seldom appeared before noon, and Pam had already speculated on their being a honeymoon couple. So who? Only the Edens were left, and a Mrs and Miss Peters, but she couldn't imagine Richard Eden being allowed to go anywhere without his wife and their two whining children, and neither Geraldine Peters nor her mother would wear anything so inelegant as jeans.

A feeling of intense irritation gripped her. This man, and she was pretty sure he was male, had ruined her day, and she felt vaguely resentful. She was in the annoying position of not knowing what she ought to do, and while it would obviously be simpler to turn and go back to her cabin, she didn't see why she should behave as if she didn't have the right to be there. She probably had more right than he had, even if no one had troubled to put up signs saying it was private land.

She was still standing there, gazing rather morosely in his direction, when he turned and saw her. There was no mistaking his sudden reaction, or the fact that he was now swimming strongly towards her. It made her unaccountably nervous, but she stood her ground as he got nearer. It was only as he got near enough for her to see his face that she realised his appraisal was coolly insolent, and her denim shorts seemed unsuitable apparel for someone who wanted to appear distant.

'Hi!'

To her astonishment she realised he was addressing her, and indignation at his audacity made her gulp a sudden intake of breath. He was obviously under the delusion that she had been watching him out of curiosity, and perhaps he thought she was interested in him.

Ignoring him, she deliberately turned her head, shading her eyes, and making a display of gazing out across the water. Perhaps if she showed him she wasn't interested, he would take his clothes and go away, and she could enjoy the solitary swim she had looked forward to.

'Hi—*you*!'

The masculine tones were faintly mocking now, the familiar salutation suffixed by an equally annoying pronoun. Just who did he think he was? she thought indignantly, and turned glacial green eyes in his direction.

He was treading water a few feet from the shore, making no apparent effort to get out. The lake bed shelved quite rapidly, and he was still out of his depth, but she could see how brown his skin was, and how long the slick wet hair that clung below his nape.

'Will you please stop bothering me?' she exclaimed, unhappily aware that the skimpy halter bra of her bikini was hardly the kind of attire to afford any degree of dignity, and his crooked grin seemed to echo her uneasy suspicions.

'Those are my clothes on the rock beside you,' he called, and she was momentarily struck by the familiarity of his accent. Was he English? Was it possible to meet another English person in this very Canadian neck of the woods, or was it simply his accent didn't match that of the Galloways or any of the other residents staying at the hotel? Whatever, she quickly disposed of her curiosity, and in her most frigid tones, she retorted:

'I can see that. Now will you please put them on and get out of here?'

'I will—put them on, I mean, if you'll be a good girl and go away,' he replied, allowing his mocking gaze to move over her in admiring appraisal. 'Unless you'd like to join me?'

'No, thank you.' Julie was not amused by his invitation. 'And why should *I* go away? This land belongs to the Kawana Point Hotel. You're trespassing!'

'The lake belongs to everyone,' he retorted, pushing back his hair with long fingers. 'Now will you let me get out of here? It's pretty damn cold.'

'I'm not stopping you,' Julie responded coldly, flicking the towel she carried against her legs. 'And no one asked you to swim.'

'No, they surely didn't,' he agreed, his accent sounding distinctly southern at that moment. 'But I don't have no swimsuit, little lady, so unless you have no objections—'

Julie turned away before he had finished speaking, her features burning with indignant colour. How dare he go swimming without a pair of trunks? It was disgusting, it was *indecent*!

'Okay, you can look now.'

The mocking voice was nevertheless disturbing, and she glanced round half apprehensively to find he had put on the denim jeans and was presently shouldering his way into the matching shirt. He had obviously not brought a towel either, and the pants clung in places Julie would rather not look, emphasising his lean hips and the powerful muscles of his thighs. He was tall, easily six feet, with a lean but not angular build, and he carried his height easily, moving with a lithe and supple fluidity as he crossed the rocks towards her.

Julie took a backward step. Somehow he had seemed less aggressive in the water, but now he was all male, all forceful energy, and evidently sure of himself in a way Adam could never be. But then Adam was older, more mature, and infinitely less dangerous, although how she knew this she couldn't imagine.

'Hi,' he said again, holding out his hand. 'My name's Dan Prescott. What's yours?'

Julie was taken aback. 'I don't think that's any of your business,' she exclaimed, in faintly shocked tones, making no attempt to return his gesture. 'I— er—how did you get here?'

'Motorbike,' he said laconically, bending down to push navy canvas shoes on to his feet. 'It's parked up there.' He nodded towards the trees. 'How about you?'

Julie debated whether to answer him, and then decided it would be easier if she could prove her right to be here. 'I'm staying at the hotel,' she declared distantly. 'As I told you, this land—'

'—belongs to the Kawana Point Hotel,' he finished lazily. 'Okay, so I'm trespassing. What are you going to do about it?'

Julie had no answer to that. Glancing up at him, she was intensely conscious of his size and his strength, and she didn't think she altogether trusted him. Perhaps she had been a fool to challenge him. After all, she was at least a quarter of a mile from the hotel. What could she do if he suddenly decided to attack her? No one was likely to be about at this hour of the morning.

'If—if you'll just leave, we'll say no more about it,' she said, with what she hoped sounded like calm assurance, and long thick lashes came to shade eyes that were the colour of the lake on a stormy day.

'And if I don't?' he countered, half amused, and Julie realised she had as much chance of controlling him as she did one of the wild cats that occasionally roamed down to the cabins in search of food.

With a helpless gesture she turned aside. His accent was confusing her again. Sometimes he sounded almost English, but at others he had a definite trans-atlantic drawl. She couldn't make him out, and she was infuriatingly aware that he was getting the better of the discussion.

'You're English, aren't you?' he asked, regarding her intently. 'Are you on holiday? Or do you work at the hotel?'

'You really don't give up, do you?' she flared, giving him an angry look. 'Why don't you just go back to wherever you came from and leave me alone?'

'I'm curious.' He shrugged. 'As to where I came from—I'm staying along there. . .' He indicated the curve of the lake.

'I didn't ask,' she retorted sharply. 'I really don't care who you are or where you're staying.'

'No?' He tipped his head on one side, drops of water from his hair sliding from his jawline to the strong column of his neck. 'That's a pity, because you interest me. Besides,' the grey eyes danced, 'we're almost fellow countrymen. My mother is English, too.'

'How interesting!' Julie's tone was full of sweet acid. 'Now if you'll excuse me, Mr—er—'

'Dan,' he supplied softly. 'Dan Prescott. You never did tell me your name.'

'No, I didn't.' Julie forced a faintly supercilious smile. 'Now, do you mind. . .'

'You want to swim?'

'Yes.'

'Go right ahead. Don't let me stop you.'

The inclination of his head was mocking, and Julie was infuriated. Did he really expect her to step into the water under his insolent gaze? She had no intention of giving him that advantage, and the glare she cast in his direction was venomous.

'What's the matter?' he probed. 'Afraid I may decide to join you?'

Julie tapped her foot. 'Even you wouldn't risk that. I might decide to run off with your clothes. Then what would you do?'

He grinned. 'You have a point.'

Julie sighed. 'Will you go away now?'

'Aren't you afraid I might steal your clothes?'

'I don't swim without them,' she returned sweetly.

'You should.' His lazy gaze dropped down the length of her body. 'Try it some time. There's nothing like it.'

'You're insulting!' she exclaimed.

'And you're over-reacting,' he retorted. 'Where have you been these last ten years? In a convent?'

Julie turned away, and began to scramble up the slope towards the trees. He could not know how accurate his guess had been, but it hurt all the same. Besides, it was obvious she was not going to be allowed to enjoy her swim this morning, and his particular kind of verbal fencing was alien to her.

'Wait. . .'

She heard his feet crunching the shingle behind

her, but she didn't turn, and when his hands suddenly caught her she panicked. No one, not even Adam, had gripped her thighs, and those hard hands encircling the flesh at the tops of her legs seemed disturbingly familiar.

'Let me go!' she cried, struggling so hard that she overbalanced both of them, his feet sliding away on the loosely packed surface, and pulling her down on top of him.

'Crazy!' he muttered, as they slid the few feet down the slope to the rocks, and Julie, trapped by the encircling pressure of his arm, was inclined to agree with him.

'If you hadn't grabbed me——!' she declared frustratedly, supremely aware of the hard muscles of his chest beneath her shoulder blades, and felt the helpless intake of breath that heralded his laughter.

'Okay, okay,' he said, as she scrambled to her feet, lying there looking up at her. 'It was a crazy thing to do. But——hell, what did I do to make you so mad at me?'

Julie pursed her lips. 'I'm not mad at you, Mr Prescott. I——I have no feelings in the matter whatsoever. I wish you'd go.'

'All right.'

With an indifferent shrug he came up beside her, and she smelt the clean male odour of his body, still damp and faintly musky. His nearness disturbed her, not least because he was barely half dressed, his shirt hanging open, his jeans low on his hips, and she could remember how he had looked in the water. He was certainly attractive, she thought, unwillingly wondering who he was. He didn't look like the guests at the hotel, who on the whole had that look of comfortable affluence, and to be riding a motorcycle in a country where everyone drove cars. . . She frowned, feeling an unfamiliar tightness in her stomach, and to combat this awareness she said:

'Goodbye, then.'

He nodded, pushing the ends of his shirt into the belt of his pants, and she waited apprehensively for him to finish. But when he did, he didn't immediately move away from her. Instead he looked down at her, at the nervous twitching of her lips and lower to the unknowingly provocative rise and fall of her breasts.

'Goodbye,' he said, and before she could prevent him, he slipped one hand around her nape and bent his mouth to hers.

Her hand came out instinctively, but encountering the taut muscles of his stomach was quickly withdrawn. She made a protesting sound deep in her throat, but he ignored it, increasing the pressure and forcing her lips apart. She felt almost giddy as her senses swam beneath his experienced caress, and then to her horror she found herself responding.

'*No!*'

With a cry of dismay she tore herself away from him, turning aside and scrubbing her lips with the back of her hand. She felt cheap and degraded, and appalled that just for a moment she had wanted him to go on.

'See you,' he remarked, behind her, but she didn't turn, and presently she heard his footsteps crunching up the slope to where he said he had left his motorbike.

She waited until she heard the sound of a powerful engine before venturing to look round, and then expelled her breath on a shaky sigh as she saw she was alone. He had gone, the receding roar of the motorcycle's engine indicating that he had taken the route around the lake.

Feeling slightly unsteady, Julie flopped down on to a smooth rock nearby, stretching her bare legs out to the sun. Not surprisingly, she no longer felt like going for a swim, and she wondered if she would ever come here again without remembering what had happened.

Shading her eyes, she tried to calm herself by surveying the outline of an island some distance away across the water. Everything was just the same, she told herself severely. Just because a strange man had erupted into her life and briefly disorganised it, it did not mean that she need feel any sense of guilt because of it. He had taken advantage of the situation—he was that kind of man. He was probably camping in the woods with a crowd of similarly-minded youths, all with motorcycles, and egos the size of their helmets.

With a sigh she got to her feet, picked up her towel, and scrambled back up the slope. She would swim later, she decided. Maybe she would persuade Pam's twelve-year-old son to join her. At least that way she could be reasonably sure of not being bothered.

The hotel was set on a ridge overlooking the sweep of the bay. It was a collection of log cabins, each with its own bedroom and bathroom, private suites, with meals taken in the main building close by. Backing on to the forest, with a variety of wildlife on its doorstep, it was a popular haunt for summer visitors, who moored their craft in the small marina below and climbed the stone steps to the front of the hotel. The only other approach was through the forest, but the trails were not easily defined unless one knew the way, and only occasionally did they attract visitors this way.

Pam Galloway's mother had been a friend of Mrs Osbourne, Julie's mother, and the two girls had known one another since they were children. But Pam was eight years older than Julie, and in 1969, when Julie was only ten years old, she had married a Canadian she had met on holiday in Germany, and come to live in this most beautiful part of Ontario.

Julie had missed her, but they had maintained a warm if infrequent correspondence, and when tragedy struck three months ago Pam had been first to offer her a chance to get away for a while. Canada in early summer was an enchanting place, and its distance had seemed remote from all the horrors of those weeks after her father's death. Her friends in England, her real friends, that was, had urged her to go, and with Adam's willing, if melancholy, approval, she had accepted. That had been almost a month ago now, and she knew that soon she would have to think about going back. But she didn't want to. Somehow, living here had widened her perspective, and she could no longer delude herself that everything her father had done had been for her. Returning to England would mean returning to the emptiness she had discovered her life to be, and not even Adam could make up for all those years she had lived in ignorance. She had thought her mother's death when she was twelve had unhinged him. Now she knew that only Adam's money had kept the firm together, and her father's whole existence had been a sham.

Pam and her husband, David, had their apartments in the main building. It was easier that way. It meant they were available at all hours of the day and night, and an intercommunication system connected all the cabins to the small exchange behind the desk. The reception area was already a hive of activity when Julie came in, and Pam herself hailed her from the doorway leading to the spacious dining room.

'Hi,' she exclaimed. It was the usual mode of greeting on this side of the Atlantic, and Julie was getting used to using it herself.

'Hi,' she responded, swinging her towel in her hand. 'Is that coffee I can smell brewing?'

'It sure is.' Pam wrinkled her brow as the younger girl approached her. 'You're back early. No swim?'

'No swim,' agreed Julie, not really wanting to go into details, but Pam was too inquisitive to let that go.

'Why?' she asked. 'You're not feeling sick or anything, are you? 'Cos if you are, I'll phone Doc Brewster right away.'

'No, I'm not sick.' Julie forced a smile. 'As a matter of fact, the lake was already occupied, and as I didn't feel like company. . .' Her voice trailed away, and passing Pam's more generous proportions with a sideways step, she walked across the restaurant to take her usual table by the window.

The dining room was empty, but the waitresses were already about, and one of them, Penny, came to ask what she would like.

'Just toast and coffee,' Julie assured her firmly, aware of Pam's enquiring face in the background, and the girl knew better than to offer the steak or eggs or maple syrup pancakes that so many of their visitors seemed to enjoy.

'Well?' Pam prompted, coming to stand with plump arms folded, looking down at her young friend. She had put on weight since her marriage to David, and having sampled the meals served at the Kawana Point Hotel, Julie wasn't really surprised. Steaks tended to weigh at least half a pound, with matching helpings of baked potatoes or french fries to go with them, while the desserts of cream-filled pastries or mouth-watering American cheesecake simply added inches just looking at them. Julie felt sure she, too, would burst at the seams if she enjoyed their hospitality for much longer, although her own level of metabolism seemed to dispute this anxiety.

'Well, what?' she said now, hoping Pam was not going to be difficult, but the other girl seemed determined to discover the facts.

'Who was occupying the lake? No one from the hotel, I'm sure. I didn't know anyone else knew of that cove.'

'Nor did I,' replied Julie, playing with the cutlery. 'But obviously we were wrong.'

'So who was it?' Pam persisted. 'Not campers? There's barely room to pitch a tent.'

'No, not campers,' Julie assured her resignedly. 'It was just some man, a tourist, I suppose. He said he was staying down the far end of the bend in the lake near the cove.'

'You spoke to him?' Pam was interested, taking the seat opposite her and gazing at her with twinkling eyes. 'Hey, how about that? All these weeks you've rebuffed every introduction we've arranged for you, and now you go and meet some guy down at the lake!'

'It wasn't like that,' declared Julie wearily, wishing she had played invalid after all. 'He was just—swimming, and—well, he spoke to me. It was all perfectly innocent and certainly nothing for you to get so excited about.'

Or was it? Julie couldn't prevent the unwilling surge of some emotion along her veins, and the remembrance of how he had held her and kissed her brought goose-bumps out all over her body. Hoping Pam would attribute them to the chilly air-conditioning of the dining room and not to any other cause, she folded her arms on the table and surreptitiously looped her fingers over the most obvious flesh on her upper arms.

'So who is he?' Pam urged her, arching her blonde brows. 'Did he give you his name?' She frowned. 'I don't know who he might be staying with. The Leytons and the Peruccis have summer places along there, but they don't normally associate with the common crowd.'

'Pam, it was no one like that.' Julie shook her head. 'He was riding a motorbike, or'—she added blushing—'he said he was. He just wasn't the type you think.'

'Ah, older, you mean?'

'No. Younger.' Julie looked up in relief as Penny brought her toast and coffee. 'Mmmm, this is just what I needed. It's quite chilly in here, isn't it?'

Pam waited until Penny had departed and then looked at her impatiently. 'So what was his name? Did you get it?'

Julie sighed. 'Prescott,' she said reluctantly. 'Dan Prescott.'

'No!'

Pam was regarding her in disbelief now, and Julie wished she would go away and stop making a fuss about nothing. It was bad enough having her morning disrupted, without Pam sitting there looking as if she had just delivered her a body blow.

'Pam, look, I know you mean well, but I am going to marry Adam, you know. It's all arranged. Just as soon as I feel able—'

'Julie, did he really say his name was Dan Prescott?' Pam interrupted her, leaning across the table, her hand on the younger girl's wrist preventing her from putting the wedge of toast she had just buttered into her mouth.

Julie pulled her hand free and nodded. 'That's what he said.'

Pam shook her head. 'My God!'

Julie regarded her half irritably now. 'What's wrong with that?' she demanded, popping the wedge of toast into her mouth, and wiping her fingers on her napkin. 'It's a common enough name, isn't it? I mean, he's not an escaped convict or anything, is he?' Her features sobered somewhat at the thought.

'No, no.' Pam shook her head vigorously now, half getting up from her chair and then flopping down again as she realised Julie deserved some explanation. 'Julie, Dan Prescott is Anthea Leyton's nephew!' She made an excited little movement of her hands. 'Anthea Leyton was a Prescott before she got married, and the New York Prescotts *are* the Scott National Bank!'

Julie put down her knife and lay back in her seat. 'So what?'

'So *what*?' Pam licked her lips. 'Julie, don't you realise, you've been talking to Lionel Prescott's son!'

In spite of herself, Julie's nerves prickled at the thought. The names meant nothing to her, but banking did, and judging by Pam's awed expression the Prescotts were no ordinary banking house. New York bankers tended to be immensely rich, and she had no doubt that it was this which had stunned her friend.

Forcing herself to act naturally, she poured another cup of coffee, and taking the cup between her cold fingers she said: 'I rather fancy you might be wrong, Pam. He—er—he said his mother was English, not American.'

'No, she's not!' Pam was really excited now. 'Heavens, that confirms it, doesn't it? Sheila Prescott is English. I think she was only a debutante when they met. You know how these stories get around.'

Julie took a deep breath. 'Well—' She tried to appear nonchalant. 'I've provided a little bit of gossip to brighten up your day.'

'Julie!' Pam looked at her reprovingly. 'Don't say you're not impressed, because I won't believe it. I mean—imagine meeting Dan Prescott! What was he doing here? What did he say?'

Julie put down her cup as David Galloway came into the dining room looking for his wife. He grinned when he saw them sitting together by the window, but before he could say anything Pam launched into an extravagant description of how Julie had made friends with Anthea Leyton's nephew.

'That's not true,' Julie felt bound to contradict her, looking apologetically at David. 'As a matter of fact, I was rather rude to him. I—er—I told him this was private land.'

'Good for you!' David was not half as awed as

his wife, and she adopted an aggrieved air.

'You know how Margie Laurence always talks about the Leytons going into her store,' she protested, getting up from the table. 'Well, I'm looking forward to seeing her face when I tell her about Julie.'

'Oh, no, Pam, you can't!' Julie was horrified, imagining Dan Prescott's reaction if the story ever got to his ears. Pam had no idea what she was dealing with, but she did, and her face burned at the thought of being gossiped about in the local chandlery. 'Please—forget I ever told you!'

'You've got to do it, Pam,' David asserted, shaking his head. 'Besides, if what Julie says is true, the least said about this the better.' He grimaced. 'Just remember, we lease this land from the Leytons, and I'd hate to do anything that might offend them.'

Pam looked sulky. 'You mean I can't tell anyone?'

'What's to tell?' exclaimed Julie helplessly. 'Pam, I'm sorry, but I wish I'd never told you.'

Pam hunched her shoulders. 'But Dan Prescott, Julie! Imagine it! Imagine *dating* Dan Prescott!'

Julie gazed at her incredulously. 'There was never any question of that, Pam. Besides, have you forgotten Adam?'

'Adam? Oh, Adam!' Pam dismissed him with an impatient gesture. 'Adam's too old for you, Julie, and if you were honest with yourself, you'd admit it.'

'*Pam!*'

David was horrified at his wife's lack of discretion, and even Julie was a little embarrassed at the bluntness of her tone. It seemed that meeting with Dan Prescott had been fated from the start, and now she was left in the awkward position of having to accept the apologies

David was insisting Pam should make.

'All right,' she was saying, when he nudged her to continue, 'I know it's not my business, but—well, I'm only thinking of you, Julie. Adam was your *father's* partner, after all, and he's at least old enough to take over that role. Are you sure that's not what you were thinking of when you accepted his proposal?'

There was another pregnant pause, and then, to Julie's relief, the Edens came into the restaurant, the children's voices disrupting the silence with strident shrillness. It meant Pam had a reason to go and summon the waitresses, and David, left with Julie, squeezed her shoulder sympathetically.

'She means well,' he muttered gruffly, his homely face mirroring his confusion, but Julie only smiled.

'I know,' she said, grimacing as one of the Eden boys started doing a Red Indian war-dance around the tables. 'Don't worry, David. I've known Pam too long to take offence, and besides, I have disappointed her.'

'Over the Prescott boy? Yes, I know.' David shook his head. 'Take my word, you're well out of it, Julie. I wouldn't like to think any daughter of mine was mixed up with him. I don't know how true it is, but I hear he's been quite a hell-raiser since he left college, and there's been more scandal attached to the Prescott name. . .'

'You don't have to tell me all this, David,' Julie said gently. 'I'm not interested in Dan Prescott, and he's not interested in me. We—we met, by accident—and that's all.'

'I'm glad.'

David patted her shoulder and then excused himself to attend to his other guests, leaving Julie to finish her breakfast in peace. But as with the swim earlier, her appetite had left her, and despite her assertion to the contrary, she could not help pondering why a man with all the lake to choose from should have swum in her special place, and at her special time.

CHAPTER TWO

JULIE's cabin was just the same as all the other cabins, except that in the month she had been there she had added a few touches of her own. There was the string of Indian beads she had draped over the lampshade, so that when the lamp was on, the light picked out the vivid colours of the vegetable dye; the Eskimo doll who sat on the table by her bed, snug and warm in his sealskin coat and fur cap; and the motley assortment of paperweights and key-rings and ashtrays—chunky glass baubles, with scenes of Ontario imprisoned within their transparent exteriors.

The cabins were simply but comfortably furnished. The well-sprung divans had rough wood headboards, and the rest of the bedroom furniture was utilitarian. There was a closet, a chest of drawers with a mirror above, a table and chairs, and one easy chair. The bathroom was fitted with a shower unit above the bath, and there was always plenty of hot water. Julie had discovered that Canadians expected this facility and remembering the lukewarm baths she had taken in English hotels, she thought they could well learn something from them. Everything was spotlessly clean, both in the cabins and in the main building, and the staff were always ready and willing to accommodate her every need. She would miss their cheerful friendliness when she returned to England, she thought, still unable to contemplate that eventuality without emotion.

Changing for dinner that evening, Julie viewed the becoming tan she was acquiring with some pleasure. She had looked so pale and drained of all colour when she had arrived, but now her cheeks were filling out a little with all the rich food Pam was pressing on her, and she no longer had that waif-like appearance.

Regarding her reflection as she applied a dark mascara to her lashes, she decided Adam would see a definite change in her. She had grown accustomed to seeing a magnolia-pale face in the mirror, with sharply-defined features and honey-coloured hair. Now she had a different image, the thin features rounded out, the hair bleached by the sun and streaked with gold. She had not had it cut for months, and instead of her usual ear-length bob it had lengthened and thickened, and it presently swung about her shoulders, curling back from her face in a style that was distinctly becoming.

She had not troubled much about clothes either since she left England. Most of the time she wore shorts or jeans, adding an embroidered smock or tunic at night instead of the cotton vests she wore during the day. Adam, who had always complimented her on her dress sense at home, would be appalled if he could see her now, she thought ruefully, putting down the mascara brush and studying herself critically. He did not approve of the negligent morals of the younger generation, and in his opinion the casual attitude towards appearance was equally contemptible. Still, Julie consoled herself wryly, she had paid little heed to what she had thrown into her suitcases before she left London, and because what she had brought was unsuitable to her surroundings, she had bought the cheapest and most serviceable substitutes available.

Now she turned away from the mirror, and checked that she had her keys. They were in the pocket of her jeans, and she adjusted the cords that looped the bottom of her cheesecloth shirt before leaving the cabin.

It was a mild night, the air delightfully soft and redolent with the scents of the forest close by. She crossed the square to the main building with deliberate slowness, anticipating what she would have for dinner with real enthusiasm, and climbed the shallow stairs to the swing doors with growing confidence. These weeks had done wonders for her, she acknowledged, and she felt an immense debt of gratitude towards Pam and her husband.

The reception hall was brightly illuminated, even though it was not yet dark outside. Already there were sounds of activity from the dining room, and the small bar adjoining was doing a good trade. Julie acknowledged the greeting of the young receptionist, a biology student working his vacation, and then was almost laid flat by an energetic young body bursting out of the door that led to the Galloways' private apartments. It was Brad Galloway, Pam's twelve-year-old son, and already he was almost as broad as his father.

'Hey. . .'

Julie protested, and Brad pulled an apologetic face. 'I'm sorry,' he gasped. 'But there's a terrific yacht coming into the marina! D'you want to come and see?'

'I don't think so, thank you.' Julie's refusal was

dry. 'And you won't make it if you go headlong down the steps.'

'I won't.' Brad exhibited the self-assurance that all Canadian children seemed to have and charged away towards the doors. 'See you, Julie!' he called and was gone, leaving Julie to exchange a rueful grimace with the young man behind the desk.

'I know—*kids*!' he grinned, not averse to flirting with an attractive girl, so far without any success. 'Did he hurt you? Can I do anything for you?'

'I don't think so, thank you.' Julie's lips twitched. 'I think a long cool drink is in order, and Pietro can supply me with that.'

Pietro, the bartender, was an Italian who had emigrated to Canada more than twenty years ago, yet he still retained his distinctive accent. He had been quite a Lothario in his time, but at fifty-three his talents were limited, and Julie enjoyed his amusing chatter. His wife, Rosa, worked in the kitchens, and their various offspring were often to be seen about the hotel.

'So, little Julie,' he said, as she squeezed on to a stool at the bar. 'What have you been doing with yourself today?'

Julie smiled. 'What do I usually do?' she countered, hedging her shoulder against the press of George Fairley's broad back. He and his wife were always in the bar at this hour, and invariably hogged the counter. 'Yes, the same as ever,' she nodded, as Pietro held up a bottle of Coke. 'With plenty of ice, please.'

'Wouldn't you like me to put you something a little sharper in here?' Pietro suggested, pulling a very expressive face. 'A little rum perhaps, or—'

'No, thanks.' Julie shook her head, her smile a little

tight now. 'I——er——I'm not fond of alcohol. I don't like what it can do to people.' She gave a faint apologetic smile, circling the glass he pushed towards her with her fingers. 'It's been another lovely day, hasn't it?'

Pietro shrugged, a typically continental gesture, and accepted her change of topic without comment. 'A lovely day,' he echoed. 'A lovely day for a lovely girl,' he added teasingly. 'You know, Julie, if I were ten years younger. . .'

'And not married,' she murmured obediently, and he laughed. They had played this game before. But, as always, she saw the gleam of speculation in his eyes, and picking up her glass she made her exit, carrying it with her into the dining room.

She chose a shrimp cocktail to start with. These shellfish were enormous, huge juicy morsels served with a barbecue sauce that added a piquant flavour all its own. When Julie first came to Kawana Point, she had found herself satisfied after only one course, but now she could order a sirloin steak and salad without feeling unduly greedy.

She was dipping a luscious shrimp into the barbecue sauce when she looked up and saw two men crossing the reception hall towards the bar. Her table was situated by the window, but it was in line with double doors that opened into the hall, and she had an unobstructed view of anyone coming or going. The fact that she averted her eyes immediately did not prevent her identification of one of the men, and her hand trembled uncontrollably, causing the shrimp to drop completely into the strongly-flavoured sauce.

Putting down her fork, she wiped her lips with her

napkin, trying desperately to retain her self-composure. What was Dan Prescott doing here? she wondered anxiously. People like the Prescotts did not visit hotels like the Kawana Point. They stayed at their own summer residences, and when they needed entertainment they went into Orillia or Barrie, or to any one of a dozen private clubs situated along the lake shore road.

Her taste for the shrimps dwindling, she picked up her glass and swallowed a mouthful of Coke. It was coolly refreshing, and as she put down her glass again she felt a growing impatience with herself. What was she? Some kind of cipher or something? Just because a man she had never expected to see again had turned up at the hotel it did not mean he had come in search of her. That was the most appalling conceit, and totally unlike her. Was it unreasonable that having discovered the whereabouts of the hotel he should come and take a look at it, but how had he got here this time? She had not heard any motorcycle, a sound which would carry on the evening air, and although he was not wearing evening clothes he had been wearing an expensive-looking jacket, hardly the attire for two wheels.

Appalled anew that she should remember so distinctly what he had been wearing after such a fleeting appraisal, Julie determinedly picked up her fork again. Then she remembered the yacht, the yacht which had aroused such excitement from the normally-laconic Brad. Was that how they had made the trip across to the hotel?

The appearance of Pam in her working gear of cotton shirt and denims, her plump face flushed and excited, did nothing to improve her digestion. Her friend came bustling towards her, and it was obvious from her manner that she knew exactly who was in the bar.

'Did you see him?' she hissed, bending over Julie's table, and the younger girl deliberately bit the tail from a shrimp before replying.

'See who?' she asked then, playing for time, but Pam was not deceived.

'You must have seen them cross the hall,' she whispered impatiently, casting an apologetic glance at her other residents. 'They're in the bar. What are you going to do?'

Julie looked bland. 'What am *I* going to do?' she echoed.

'Yes.' Pam sighed. 'Well, I mean it's obvious, isn't it? He didn't come here just to taste the beer. His cousin's with him—at least, I think it's his cousin. He calls him Drew, and I know Anthea Leyton has a son called Andrew—'

'Pam, their being here has nothing to do with me,' declared Julie firmly. 'If they choose to come—to come slumming, that's their affair. I have no intention of speaking to Dan Prescott, so don't go getting any ideas.'

'But, Julie, you can't just ignore him!'

'Why not?' Julie hid her trembling hands beneath the napkin in her lap. 'Honestly, Pam, I don't even like the man!'

'You said yourself, you hardly know him.'

'All the more reason for keeping out of his way.'

'Well, I think you're crazy!'

'Oh, do you?' Julie stared up at her, half irritated by her insistence.

'Yes.' Pam dismissed the younger girl's objections with an inconsequent wave of her hand. 'Julie, you may never get another chance to meet him socially—'

'I don't want that chance, Pam.'

'Why?'

'Because I'm not interested.'

Pam gazed at her disbelievingly. 'You mean you're afraid.'

'Afraid?' Julie gasped.

'Yes, afraid.' Pam straightened, resting her hands on her broad hips. 'You've had your life organised for you for so long, you've forgotten what it's like to take a risk—'

'So you admit it is a risk?'

Julie tilted her head, and Pam pulled a wry face. 'All right. So he does have a reputation. What of it? You're an adult, aren't you. You can handle it.'

Julie sighed. 'I don't want to handle anything, Pam. I just want to sit here and eat my dinner, and afterwards I'm going to watch some television and then go to bed.'

Pam made a defeated gesture. 'I give up.'

'Good.'

Julie determinedly returned to her shrimp cocktail and Pam had no alternative but to leave her to it. But she shook her head rather frustratedly as she crossed to the door, and Julie, watching her, doubted she had heard the last of it.

By the time she had eaten half a dozen mouthfuls of her steak, she knew she was fighting a losing battle. The awareness of the man in the bar, of the possibility that he might choose to come into the dining room and order a meal, filled her with unease, and she knew she would not feel secure until she was safely locked behind her cabin door.

Declining a dessert, she left her table, walking swiftly through the open doors into the reception area. It was usually deserted at this hour of the evening, most of the guests either occupying the dining room or the bar, and she expected to make her escape unobserved. What she had not anticipated was Brad Galloway, deep in conversation with the man she most wanted to avoid, or to be involved in that discussion by the boy's artless invitation.

'Julie!' he exclaimed, when he saw her. 'Do you remember that yacht I told you about? Well, this is Mr Prescott who owns it.'

'I didn't say that, Brad.' Dan Prescott's voice was just as disturbing as she remembered. 'I said it belonged to my family. It does. I just have the use of it now and then.'

His grin was apologetic, both to the boy and to Julie, but she refused to respond to it. In fact, she refused to look at Dan Prescott at all after that first dismaying appraisal. Yet, for all that, she knew the exact colour of the bluish-grey corded jacket he was wearing, and the way the dark blue jeans hugged the contours of his thighs. His clothes were casual, but they fitted him well, and she realised something she had not realised before. Men like Dan Prescott did not need to exhibit their wealth. They accepted it. It was a fact. And that extreme self-confidence was all the proof they needed.

'What do you say, Julie?'

Brad was looking at her a little querulously now, and she forced herself to show the enthusiasm he was expecting. 'That's great,' she murmured, realising her words sounded artificial even to her ears. 'You must tell me all about it tomorrow.'

'Why not right now?'

The words could have been Brad's, but they weren't, and Julie was obliged to acknowledge Dan Prescott's presence for the first time. Even so, it was almost a physical shock meeting that penetrating stare. The lapse of time had been too brief for her to forget a second of their last encounter, and it was only too easy to remember how she had had to tear herself away from him, breaking the intimate contact he had initiated. Nevertheless, she had broken the contact, she told herself firmly, and he had no right to do this to her. But as his eyes moved lower, over the firm outline of her breasts and the rounded swell of her hips, she felt a wave of heat flooding over her, and nothing could alter the fact that if she were as indifferent to him as she liked to think, it wouldn't matter what he did.

With a feeling of mortification she felt his eyes come back to her face, and then the heavy lids drooped. 'Why not right now?' he repeated, as aware of her confusion as she was herself, and conscious of Brad's puzzled stare Julie tried to pull herself together.

'I—why, I don't have time just now, Brad,' she offered, addressing her apology to the boy. 'Some other time perhaps. . .'

'Okay.'

Brad shrugged, obviously disappointed, and she was sorry, but then, to add to her humiliation, Pam appeared. It only took her a couple of seconds to sum up the situation, and acting purely on instinct Julie was sure, she exclaimed:

'Oh, there you are, Brad. I've been looking for you.' Her smile flashed briefly at Dan Prescott. 'Come along, I want you to help me hang those lamps in the yard.'

'Oh, *Mom*!'

Brad's voice was eloquent with feeling, and after only a slight hesitation Dan said: 'Perhaps I could help you, Mrs Galloway.

Pam was obviously taken aback, but Julie's hopes of reprieve were quickly squashed. 'That won't be necessary, Mr Prescott, thank you,' her friend assured him warmly. 'Brad will do it—he always does. He's such a help around the place.'

'I'm sure he is.' Dan's expression was amused as it rested on the boy's mutinous face. 'Sorry, old son, but there'll be another time.'

'Will there? Will there really?'

Brad gazed up at him eagerly, and with a fleeting glance in Julie's direction Dan nodded. 'You have my word on it,' he nodded, pushing his hands into his jacket pockets, and Brad's demeanour was swiftly transformed.

'Oh—*boy*!' he exclaimed, and grinned almost defiantly at Julie before his mother ushered him away.

But when Julie would have left too, lean brown fingers looped themselves loosely around her wrist. 'Wait. . .'

The word was uttered somewhere near her temple, and the warmth of his breath ruffled the strands of silky hair that lay across her forehead. It was a husky injunction, a soft invocation to delay her while Pam and her son got out of earshot, yet when she tried to release herself his fingers reacted like a slip knot that tightened the more it was strained against. His command might have been mild, but it was a command nevertheless, she realised, and she was forced to stand there, supremely aware that if she moved her fingers they brushed his leg.

'So,' he said at last, when they were alone, the student receptionist having departed to take his dinner some time before, 'why are you running out on me?'

Julie contemplated denying the allegation, but she had no desire to start an argument with him. Besides, he was experienced enough to know if she was lying, and opposition often provoked an interest that otherwise would not have been there.

'Why do you think?' she asked instead, assuming a bored expression, and the long thick lashes came to shade his eyes.

'You tell me,' he suggested, and with a sigh she said: 'Because I don't want to get involved with you, Mr Prescott.'

'I see.' His look was quizzical.

'Now will you let me go?'

He frowned. 'Why don't you like me? What did I do to promote such a reaction?'

'I neither like nor dislike you, Mr Prescott,' she retorted twisting her wrist impotently. 'Please let go of me.'

'Is all this outraged modesty because I kissed you?'

'I'd rather not discuss it.' Julie held up her head. 'I don't know why you're here, Mr Prescott, but I'd prefer it if you'd forget we ever met before.'

'Would you?' The smoky grey eyes drooped briefly to her mouth, and it was an almost tangible incursion. 'Would you really?'

'Yes,' but Julie had to grind her teeth together to say it. When he looked at her like that she found it incredibly difficult to keep a clear head, and almost desperately she sought for a means of diversion. 'I— where is your cousin? Won't he be wondering where you are?'

'Drew?' Dan Prescott's look changed to one of mocking inquiry. 'How did you know I came with Drew?' His eyes narrowed. 'Do you know him?'

'Of course not.' Too late Julie realised she had made a mistake. 'I—er—I saw the two of you come in, that's all. And—and Pam said something about him being your cousin.'

'Pam? Oh—Mrs Galloway, of course.' With a shrug he released her, but as she moved to go past him he stepped into her path. 'One more thing. . .'

'What?'

'I want you to come out with me tomorrow.'

The invitation was not entirely unexpected, but its delivery was, and Julie felt a sense of stunned indignation that he should think it would be that easy.

'No,' she said, without hesitation.

'Why not?'

He was persistent, and she found it was impossible to get by him without his co-operation. 'Because— because I don't want to,' she retorted shortly. 'I've told you—'

'—you don't want to get involved with me, I know.' He pulled his upper lip between his teeth. 'But you don't really believe that any more than I do.'

'Mr Prescott—'

'And stop calling me *Mr* Prescott. You know my name, just as I now know yours—Julie.'

Julie found she was trembling. This verbal fencing was more exhausting than she had thought, and she looked round helplessly, wishing for once that Pam would interfere. But apart from the Meades, who were leaving the dining room with their arms wrapped around each other, there was no one to appeal to, and she could not intrude on their evident self-absorption.

'Why are you fighting me?' Dan's breath fanned her ear as she turned back to look at him, and an involuntary shiver swept over her. 'Come and have a drink,' he invited. 'I'll introduce you to my cousin, and then perhaps you might begin to believe my father wasn't the devil incarnate!'

'You—you're—'

'Disgusting? Yes, you told me. But I can be fun too, if you'll let me.'

The grey eyes had darkened and Julie felt her heart slow and then quicken to a suffocating pace. Oh God, she thought weakly, he knows exactly how to get what he wants, and she didn't know whether she had the strength to resist him.

'I—I can't,' she got out through her dry throat. 'I can't.'

With a laconic shrug it was over. Almost before she was aware of it, he had moved past her, walking with lithe indolence towards the bar where his cousin was waiting, and she was free to go.

With her breath coming in tortured gasps, she practically ran across the hall, dropping down the two shallow steps that led to the swing doors, going through them with such force that they continued to swing long after she had left them. She didn't stop until she was inside her cabin, but even then she did not feel the sense of security she had expected.

although there were other hotels close that she could be
eavesdropping, there was certainly against, probably a mile
away or so further around the lake itself, so she
had lost the route ...

CHAPTER THREE

JULIE did not go down to the lake to swim again for
almost a week. It was foolish because she had no
reason to suppose that Dan Prescott might be there,
but a necessary interval seemed called for, and she
contented herself with going out with Brad in his
dinghy, or taking the controls of his father's power
boat so that he could water-ski. He was quite good at
it, but although Julie tried, she persistently lost her
balance and ended up choking for breath in the
power-boat's wake.

Eventually, however, common-sense overrode her
nervousness, and she returned to her early morning
pastime. Dan Prescott had not come back to the hotel,
and although she had succeeded in evading Pam's
more personal questions about what had happened
between them that night, her continued abstinence was
provoking comment. So she began to make her regular
morning trek to the cove, and after three days of
solitude she began to believe she would never see
him again.

Then, on the fourth morning, he appeared.

Julie was already in the water, swimming vigorously across the mouth of the inlet, when she saw the
tall figure standing motionless on the rocks. As before,
he was dressed in denim jeans and shirt, and even as
she watched, he peeled off his shirt and tossed it on
to the rocks. She turned quickly away before he

unbuckled the belt of his pants. She had no desire to
see him naked, and the awareness that he was coming
into the water with her filled her with trembling anticipation.

There was no way she could get out without passing
him. Around the mouth of the inlet there were currents
she wasn't familiar with, and besides, it was a good
half mile round and into the next cove where David
had built his marina. She was trapped, and he knew
it. No doubt he had planned it this way deliberately.
And she despised him for it.

She heard the splash as he entered the water and
permitted herself a backward glance. He was nowhere
in sight, probably swimming underwater, she thought
apprehensively, and then almost lost her breath when
he surfaced right beside her.

'Hi!'

Julie drew a trembling breath. 'Don't you ever
give up?'

'It's a free country, isn't it?' His eyes mocked her.
'Or are you going to tell me the land is private?'

'I know your uncle owns it, if that's what you
mean,' Julie retorted, pushing back her hair with an
unsteady hand. 'Enjoy your swim. You'll be happy to
know you've spoilt mine!'

The word he said was not polite, and his hands
reached for her before she could defend herself, pulling her down into the water until her nasal tubes were
blocked and she thought her lungs were going to burst.
Then he let her go, allowing her to float up to the
surface, gulping desperately for breath as he came up
behind her.

'That—that was a rotten thing to do,' she got out,

when she could speak again, and he made no attempt to deny it. 'I could have drowned!'

He seemed to consider her protest for a few seconds and then he shook his head. 'I don't think I could have allowed that,' he remarked, in all seriousness. 'Great though the temptation might be.'

Julie pursed her lips. 'You enjoy making fun of me, don't you?'

'I enjoy—you,' he said, slowly and deliberately so that her whole body seemed suffused with heat, in spite of the coldness of the water. 'Or rather I would—if you'd let me.'

There was a brief pause while Julie's green eyes stared in troubled fascination into his, and then with panic quickening her limbs she struck out blindly for the shore. It was useless, she told herself, she could not have an ordinary conversation with him. He persisted in turning every innocent remark into something personal, and her inexperience in these matters made her an easy target. She should have known he would not let her be. He was a predator, and right now she was his prey. And like all hunters, the harder the chase, the more satisfying the kill.

Her feet found the stony lake shore, and she waded up out of the water on slightly wobbly legs. The exertion had been all the more tiring because of her awareness of him behind her, and the fear that at any moment he might grab her flailing feet. However, she made it unscathed, though as she groped for her towel she heard him emerge from the water behind her.

Squeezing the excess moisture from her hair, she tried to ignore him, but he walked across the shingle and sprawled lazily on a flat rock. Almost compulsively, her eyes were drawn to him, and his lips curved in amusement at that involuntary appraisal. It was obvious from the apprehensiveness of her darting glance that she had expected the worst, but to her relief she saw he was wearing thin navy shorts, and although they left little to her imagination, he was decently covered.

'You didn't really think I'd do that, did you?' he enquired, propping himself up on one elbow and regarding her bikini-clad figure quizzically.

'Do what?' Julie was evasive, towelling her hair with more effort than skill, wondering if she could wriggle into her shorts without making a spectacle of herself.

'Swim in the raw,' Dan answered bluntly, knowing full well she was not unaware of his meaning. 'I wouldn't want to embarrass you a second time.'

'You didn't embarrass me, Mr Prescott,' Julie retorted, not altogether truthfully, deciding the shorts would have to wait until she had gained the privacy of the trees. 'Goodbye!'

'Julie. . .' With a lithe movement, he sprang off the rocks and caught her arm as she bent to pick up her belongings. 'Julie, don't go. Look, I'm sorry if I've offended you, but for heaven's sake, what's a guy got to do to make it with you?'

Julie gathered her towel and shorts to her chest almost as if they were a shield, and avoided looking up at him. 'Mr Prescott, I don't know the kind of girls you are used to associating with, but men don't— *make it* with me, as you so crudely put it. Just because you're apparently accustomed to every girl you meet falling flat on her face when you show an interest in them, don't—'

'Why not flat on their backs?' he interrupted her harshly. 'That would facilitate matters, wouldn't it?' and her breathing quickened to a suffocating pace.

'As I said, you're—'

'Forget it!' he snapped. 'I don't know why I came here.'

'Because you can't bear to think you're not irresistible!' Julie retorted recklessly, and then quivered uncontrollably as he tore the towel and shorts from her fingers and jerked her towards him.

When he bent his head towards her, she had no hope of avoiding him and although she turned her head from side to side, he found her mouth with unerring accuracy, fastening his lips to hers and taking his fill of her honeyed softness. His damp body was an aggressive barrier to any escape she might attempt to make, and try as she might, she could not prevent the awareness of her breasts hardening against the forceful expanse of his chest.

It was impossible, too, to prevent him from parting her lips. Choking for breath, she gulped for air against his mouth, but the invasion of his lips robbed her of all opposition. He was devouring her, hungrily teaching her the meaning of the adult emotions he was arousing, and as her lips began to kiss him back, the pressure eased to a paralysing sweetness. His hands released her arms to slide across her back, and her legs trembled as he pressed her body into his. She could feel him with every nerve and sinew of her being, and the growing awareness of what was happening to him made her acutely aware of the fragile barrier between herself and his thrusting masculinity.

He released her mouth to seek the hollow behind her ear, kissing her earlobe and her neck, brushing her hair aside to stroke the sensitive curve of her nape with his tongue. Julie knew she ought to draw back, that this was her opportunity to get away from him, but she was consumed by the urgency of her own emotions, and too aroused to think sensibly about anything.

The bra of her bikini slackened as he released the clip, and a silent protest rose inside her as his fingers found the rose-tipped mounds that no man had ever seen before, let alone touched.

'Don't. . .' he said, as her hands sought to obstruct him. 'Don't stop me. Oh, Julie, you're beautiful!'

'Am I?'

Her breath came in little gasps and his mouth curved in sensuous approval. 'You know it,' he groaned, his lips against her creamy flesh. 'Oh, God, what am I going to do about you?'

'Do about me?' she echoed confusedly, but his mouth covered hers once again, silencing any further speculation. The urgency of his caress drove all coherent thought from her head, and soft arms wound around his neck in eager submission.

Her convent upbringing had not prepared her for this, or for the unexpected sensuality of her own nature, and her instinctive response was all the more unrestrained because of it. She was warm and soft and responsive, her silky body yielding to his with innocent fervour, and Dan almost lost his own grip on sanity as he continued to hold her. She was so completely desirable, so eminently responsive to his every overture, and the urge to lay her on the rocks and submerge himself in her honeyed softness was almost overpowering. He doubted she would oppose him. She was all melting passion in his arms. But if he had been overwhelmed by her artless submission, he was still rational enough to realise that she was not entirely aware of what she was inviting. He could imagine her reaction when she came to her senses, and she would resent him bitterly if he took advantage of her innocence.

For all that, it was incredibly difficult to resist her, and a groan was forced from him as he compelled her away. Then, avoiding her look of hurt bewilderment, he bent and picked up her towel, pressing it into her fingers with a rough insensitivity.

Julie was mortified, as much by the awareness of her own wanton behaviour as by the realisation that he had given her the towel to cover her nakedness. He had taken advantage of her, and she had encouraged him, and what was more humiliating, he had rejected her.

'I'm sorry.' His apology came strangely to her ears, and her averted gaze turned blindly from the shocked realisation that he was no less aroused than before. 'But—well, I guess I lost my head,' he muttered half reluctantly, 'and I guess you did too.'

Julie licked her dry lips. 'Lost your head?' she echoed, as his meaning became clear to her. 'But I wouldn't—'

'Yes, you would,' he retorted harshly. 'We're not children, Julie, and you know I want you. However, aside from other considerations, I don't honestly know what you want.'

Julie blinked, trying to make sense of what he was saying to her. It appeared she was wrong. He had not rejected her because of any inadequacy of her part. He had actually considered the possibility, but because he was more experienced, he had dismissed the idea. There was something horribly cold-blooded about the whole affair, and her head moved helplessly from side to side as she bent to retrieve her discarded bra.

'Julie!' He was speaking to her again, but she refused to answer him. She just wanted to get away, the farther away the better, and she struggled wildly when he endeavoured to detain her. '*Julie!*' he said again, more forcefully this time. 'Julie, listen to me! When am I going to see you again? Today? Tonight? When?'

'Never, I hope,' she choked, throwing back her head, her hair cascading damply about her shoulders. 'Just let me go—'

'No, I won't.' He thrust his impatient face close to hers. 'You're not being sensible, Julie, and I don't intend to let you go until you are!'

'I'll scream—'

'In that state?' His mocking eyes flicked the slipping ends of the towel and her face suffused with colour. But all the humour had left his expression, and he was deadly serious as he said: 'Okay, you want the truth, you got it. When I'm with you, I can't think sanely.' His eyes burned above her. 'But unlike you, I accept that people have feelings, and I didn't want to hurt you.'

Julie faltered. 'To—hurt me?'

'Yes, damn you,' he muttered, unable to prevent himself from pulling her to him again. 'There,' he added hoarsely, 'now tell me you don't know what I'm feeling—you're not that naïve. But I do know you've never been with a man before, even if you do learn fast.'

Julie's tongue appeared in unknowing provocation. 'I—I don't understand. . .'

'Don't you?' His hands slipped possessively around her waist, hard and warm against the cooler skin of her hips. 'Could you have stopped me? Honestly?' He bent his head to her shoulder, his teeth gently massaging the soft flesh. 'But wouldn't you have hated me if I had?'

Julie's face burned. 'You shouldn't say such things!'

'Why not?' Dan lifted his head to gaze intently down at her. 'It's a fact.'

Julie drew an uneven breath. 'Let me go, Dan.'

Her husky request brought a faint smile to his lips. 'At last,' he murmured. 'I wondered what I'd have to do to get you to say my name.'

'Dan, please. . .'

Julie pressed her hands determinedly against his chest, but the hair-roughened skin was absurdly sensuous against her palms, and she stood there helpless in the grip of emotions she scarcely knew or understood.

'Tonight,' he said, his breath fanning her cheek as he bent towards her. 'Have dinner with me, on the yacht. We can serve ourselves—just the two of us.'

'I can't.'

The denial sprang automatically to her lips, and his mouth turned down at the corners. 'Why not?'

'Because I can't.' Julie freed herself from him without too much difficulty, and quickly slipped her arms into the bra, fastening the clip with trembling fingers. Then, gathering up her shorts and the towel, she turned back to him. 'G-goodbye.'

If she had expected him to object as he had done before, she was disappointed. With a weary shrug of his shoulders he bent to pick up his own pants, and thrust his legs into them without giving her another glance. It was as if he had grown bored with the whole exchange, and as on that evening at the hotel, he had abandoned the struggle.

Conversely, Julie was left feeling strangely bereft, and stepping into her sandals she made her way across the shingle with a distinct sense of deprivation.

The feeling had not left her by the time she reached the hotel, but in the sanctuary of her cabin she faced the fact that she had probably had the most lucky escape ever. As her blood cooled, reaction set in, and she sank down on to the bed trembling at the realisation of how near she had come to losing all respect for herself and betraying Adam's trust in her. She didn't know what had come over her, and for someone who for so long had regarded herself as immune from the kind of behaviour gossiped about in the dormitory after lights-out, it was doubly humiliating. She would never have thought she might have reason to be grateful to Dan Prescott, but she was, albeit that gratitude was tinged with anxiety. How long could she trust a man like him, she wondered uneasily, and how long could she trust herself if he persisted in pursuing her?

It was lunchtime before she emerged from the cabin, and Pam intercepted her in the reception hall of the hotel. She had a letter with an airmail postmark in her hand, and Julie guessed it was from Adam before the other girl spoke.

'Where have you been?' she exclaimed, looking with some concern at Julie's unusually pale features. 'I thought you and Brad were going into Midland this morning. He was hanging about like a lost sheep until David went to collect the mail and took him along.'

'Oh, Pam, I forgot all about it.' Julie was dismayed. 'I'm sorry. Where is he? I must apologise.'

'He's tackling a hamburger right now,' Pam assured her lightly, pulling a wry face. 'You know nothing affects his appetite. He did come to look for you earlier with this letter, but you weren't in your cabin.'

'I was.' Ruefully Julie remembered the hammering at her door which she had taken to be the janitor. 'I— well, I had a headache,' she explained. 'I didn't feel like company.'

'And are you all right now?' Pam asked, handing her the letter addressed in Adam's neat handwriting. 'I must say you do look a little washed out. What say we have our lunch together on the terrace? A nice chef's salad with French dressing, hmm?'

Julie nodded. It was easier than thinking up an excuse, but she knew better than to suppose Pam was that easily satisfied. She read her letter while Pam went to see about the meal, but when the salad and freshly baked rolls were set before them, the older girl returned to the attack.

'You've seen Dan Prescott again, haven't you?' she remarked perceptively. 'Did he make those bruises on your arms?'

Julie crossed her arms across her chest, selfconsciously covering the revealing marks just below her shoulders with her fingers. She had been going to pass them off as the result of a fall she had had in the woods, but when Pam made so forthright a statement, she found it impossible to lie with conviction.

'He was down at the lake,' she admitted, avoiding Pam's indignant gaze. 'And that's all I'm going to say about it.'

Pam shook her head. 'The brute!' she exclaimed with feeling. 'I only hope David doesn't notice, or he'll blame me for encouraging you.'

Julie sighed. 'Pam—please, forget it. It's not important—'

'I disagree. If he thinks he can—'

'Pam, it wasn't like that.' Julie could not in all honesty allow her friend to go on imagining the worst. 'He wasn't—violent.' She paused, wishing she had never admitted anything. 'I—I bruise easily, that's all.'

'So what happened?'

Pam was all ears, ignoring completely what the other girl had said earlier, but Julie refused to discuss it. 'I'll take Brad into Midland this afternoon,' she said instead, deliberately changing the subject. 'If he still wants to go, that is.'

Pam was silent for a few minutes, and then she conceded defeat. 'Oh, he still wants to go,' she agreed offhandedly. 'He's looking forward to you treating him to one of those enormous sundaes at the ice-cream parlour. He wouldn't miss that!'

Julie forced a smile. 'I know how he feels. I shall miss them myself when I go home.'

Pam glanced quickly at her. 'You're not thinking of going home yet, though.'

Julie hesitated. 'Well—yes, actually I am. I thought perhaps—at the end of next week—'

'The end of next week!' Pam put down her fork and stared at her. 'Julie, you can't be serious! Why, we're expecting you to stay at least until August!'

Julie bent her head, resting her elbow on the edge of the table and cupping one pink-tinted cheek in her hand. 'I've loved being here, Pam, you know that,' she said uncomfortably, 'but all holidays must come to an end, and I think six weeks is enough, don't you?'

'Not really.' Pam was brusque. 'David and I have discussed this, and we feel three months might be long enough for you to get over everything you've been through. Julie, don't be in too much of a hurry to get back. Remember what you left behind.'

'I do remember, Pam—'

'What is it? Is it Adam? Is he urging you to go back? Is that what his letter says?'

'No. No. At least, not intentionally. He misses me, of course—'

'Then invite him out here,' said Pam abruptly. 'Ask him to come and stay for a couple of weeks. He has holidays, I suppose. Doesn't he?'

Julie's brow was furrowed. 'Well, yes, but—'

'But what? Isn't the Kawana good enough for him?'

'Don't be silly, Pam.' Julie sighed. 'It's not that. I—I just don't know whether he'd come. He—well, he doesn't like America.'

'This isn't America.'

'Well, North America, then.' Julie's flush deepened. 'I don't know, Pam, honestly. . .'

'Invite him. See what he says. At least that way we'd get to keep you a little bit longer.'

'Oh, Pam!' Julie stretched out her hand and gripped the older girl's arm. 'You've been so kind to me. . .'

'And I want to go on being kind,' declared Pam shortly. 'You know what I think? I think you're letting this—this affair with Dan Prescott frighten you away.' She paused, watching Julie's expressive face intently. 'I'm right, aren't I? That's really what decided you to go.'

'No!' Julie could not allow her to think that. 'I—well, I have to go back sooner or later.'

'Make it later,' Pam pleaded gently. 'Please, Julie. Cable Adam. Telephone him, if you like. Explain how you feel. I'm sure he'd come, if you asked him.'

The trouble was, Julie was sure he would, too, despite his reservations. If she really wanted him to come, he would make every effort to do so, but something held her back from making the call. She didn't know why, but she was loath to introduce Adam to the unsophistication of life at the Kawana Point. He wouldn't like it and he wouldn't fit in here. It wasn't that it was not luxurious enough for him; the appointments of the cabins compared very favourably with hotels back home. It was the casual attitudes he would object to, the lack of formality in manner and dress, and the easy familiarity of the other guests.

During the next couple of days she managed to avoid making any decision in the matter. When Pam asked her, she replied truthfully that she was thinking about it, and when she was with Brad she succeeded in putting it out of her mind for hours at a time.

The weather remained hot and sunny, and they swam a lot, though never from the cove where Julie had encountered Dan Prescott. It was easy to put her problems out of her mind when she was spinning across the lake at the wheel of the power-boat, or dodging the swinging sail of the dinghy, but not so easy when she retired to her cabin at night. Then she lay for hours before sleep came to claim her, waking in the morning much later than she used to with the unpleasant throbbing of an aching head.

In spite of herself she was unable to put Dan Prescott out of her mind. She could speak quite off-handedly to Pam whenever she chose to broach the subject, but in the privacy of her thoughts it was a very different matter. However she tried to avoid it, she could not forget the abandoned way she had behaved, and she burned with embarrassment every time she recalled the intimacies she had permitted him. She told herself she dreaded the thought of ever seeing him again, that if she did she would just die of shame—and yet somehow these verbal castigations did not entirely ring true.

This had been made patently obvious to her one day when two new guests arrived at the hotel. The man was tall and dark, and from behind he had looked absurdly like Dan. There was a woman with him, a slim attractive woman in her late twenties, and Julie's stomach had contracted painfully until the man had turned and she had seen he looked nothing at all like her tormentor. Nevertheless, the experience had served to make her realise that she was not as impartial as she cared to think, and she drank three beers that night in an effort to dull her over-active imagination.

By the end of that week she was no nearer making a decision, and on Saturday afternoon she rode into Midland with David and Brad on the motor launch he used to collect supplies. Leaving them at the dock, she sauntered lazily up the main shopping street, looking idly in the shop windows. There was an amazing assortment of goods for sale, and as well as the usual sports and food shops, there were dress shops and leather dealers exhibiting attractive styles for more formal occasions. Midland was not a large town, but it did have a large tourist population, and in summer there were plenty of visitors to the thirty thousand islands.

Julie was looking in the window of a book store when she became aware of someone standing behind her, and swinging round, she came face to face with him. In an open-necked navy sports shirt and the inevitable denims, he looked lean and powerful and disturbingly attractive, and Julie's limbs seemed to melt as she looked up at him. She was glad she had not succumbed to the impulse of not bothering to change before coming into town, and instead of the shorts she had been wearing, she had put on a smock dress of white printed cotton that was square-necked and sleeveless and deliciously cool.

'Hi,' she said, rather breathily, when he didn't say anything, and he inclined his head in acknowledgement. 'Small world, isn't it?'

He glanced up and down the street, and then the smoky-grey eyes returned to her slightly flushed face. 'Are you alone?'

'At the moment,' she replied, pushing her hands into the pockets of her dress. 'I came in with——with Brad and David——that's Pam's husband, but I left them down at the dock.'

'Come and have a coffee with me.'

'A coffee?' Julie licked her lips.

'A milk shake, then,' he said shortly, tucking the parcel he was carrying under his arm. 'Or a beer, if you'd rather. Just so we can talk.'

Julie drew an unsteady breath. 'I don't know. . .'

'Well, I do,' he retorted, and taking her arm, he urged her across the road and into the busy ice-cream parlour where she and Brad had spent many happy hours.

The bartender recognised him. Of course he would, thought Julie, half crossly, acknowledging his family's influence in the town, but she wondered what they thought of her, and whether this afternoon's encounter would reach his aunt's ears through the very efficient grapevine.

After installing her in one of the booths, Dan went to get their order, chatting amiably with the proprietor as he spooned ice-cream into tall glasses and whipped up the milk for their shakes. Milk shakes in Canada tended to be twice the size of anywhere else, and Julie had enjoyed too many in her opinion. They were terribly fattening, but if Dan had them often, he certainly didn't show it. There wasn't any spare flesh on his bones, and she knew from experience how hard and muscular his body really was.

Remembering this brought the revealing colour back to her cheeks, and it didn't help to discover she had already attracted the interest of a group of young people seated in the opposite booth. They spoke to Dan when he came back, carrying the two shakes, and he paused to exchange a few words with them before taking his seat. Everyone seemed to know everyone else, thought Julie uncomfortably, wondering whether they thought she was his latest conquest.

'Good?' he asked, after she had swallowed a mouth-ful through the giant-sized straw they provided, and Julie glanced up at him through gold-tipped lashes.

'Very good, thank you,' she replied politely, and his mobile mouth slanted down rather resignedly.

'So,' he said. 'Do I take it you've forgiven me?'

'Forgiven you?' Her eyes felt glued to the glass.

'Yes.' He pushed his glass aside to rest his arms on the table, regarding her intently across its narrow width. 'Don't pretend you don't know what I mean.' He paused. 'You've given up swimming in the mornings.'

'How do you know?' The words were out before she could prevent them, and darting a look up at his set face, she knew the answer for herself.

'How do you think?' he demanded roughly, and she felt the constriction of quickening pulses. 'I want to see you again, Julie,' he went on in a low voice. 'Don't make me wait too long.'

Julie's throat closed completely. 'Dan—'

'Don't tell me no,' he warned her harshly, casting an impatient glance towards the opposite booth, and then turning back to her with smouldering eyes. 'This is a public place, and I guess you feel safe with me, but don't push it.'

'Oh, Dan, stop it!' With trembling hands she gripped the edge of the table. 'I—I can't see you again. At least, not unless you mean like this.'

'You know what I mean.'

'Yes—well, it's impossible.'

'Why?'

'Why—why, because I'm not—not free.'

'What do you mean—not free? You're not married, are you? You don't wear a ring.'

'I know, I know. But there is someone. We—we have an understanding. He trusts me.'

'Does he?' Dan's eyes regarded her with cold detachment now. 'How foolish of him!'

'That's not fair.'

'Isn't it?' He stifled an oath. 'Was it fair to act the way you did the other morning, knowing you were practically engaged to some other guy?'

Julie's mouth was dry. 'That wasn't how it was.'

'Wasn't it? How was it, then?'

Julie looked at him helplessly, her green eyes wide and troubled, and eloquently appealing. 'Dan, please. . .'

'Don't look at me like that, Julie! So pure and innocent!' He flung himself angrily back in his seat, his mouth pressed together ominously. 'So—who is this guy? Where does he live? And what's he doing letting you run around without him?'

Julie bent her head, her hair falling silkily about her ears. 'He—he lives in England,' she managed to say quietly. 'I've known him all my life.'

'So why isn't he with you?'

Julie sighed. 'Something—happened. Something I needed to get away from. Adam sent me here to—to recover.'

'Adam? That's his name?'

'Yes.'

There was silence for a few moments, and she ventured a look up at him. Dan's face was grim and as rigidly carved as stone. He was staring broodingly into the middle distance, and she wondered anxiously what was going on behind that stony façade.

As the laughing group across the aisle dispersed, Julie looked down into her rapidly flattening milkshake. That was how she felt, she thought miserably, all the lightness evaporating, leaving only the weight of her own guilt inside her. The trouble was, she didn't know which was worse — the guilt she felt towards Adam for having betrayed him, or the equally unsettling realisation that without Dan's self-control the situation could have been far more serious. Was he thinking that, too? Was he chiding himself for not having taken what she had offered when he had the chance?

Taking the straw between her lips, she drew on it rather unenthusiastically. It made a horrible sucking sound as only air was drawn into the tube, and she pushed it aside in frustration, feeling Dan's eyes watching her as she lifted her head. They were dark and disturbing, a mixture of anger and impatience, but after taking in the tremulous uncertainty of her expression they lost a little of their aggression.

'I must be crazy,' he muttered, surrendering his detachment and leaning forward to take one of her hands between both of his. 'You know, in spite of everything, I still want you.'

'No!'

Julie stared at him, half in fear, half in fascination, and he nodded his head, raising her hand to his lips, rubbing the sensitive palm with his tongue. 'Yes,' he insisted, spreading her fingers to slide his between them. 'It was good, Julie, you and me, I mean. That's how I want it to be again.'

'No!' Julie shuddered, and sat as far back in her

seat as his restraining fingers would permit her. 'I—
I can't. And you shouldn't ask me.'

'Why not?' His eyes were narrowed. 'What difference does it make? You're still the same person. So
am I. No one else need ever know.'

Julie gasped. 'That's immoral!'

'Practical,' he corrected her coolly. 'What do you
say, Julie? I want you, you want me. Why shouldn't
we enjoy it?'

Julie's nails dug painfully into the formica top of
the table. 'Is—is this your usual ploy, Dan? Does
nothing have to stand in the way of what *you* want?'

'If you mean do I usually go for girls with complications, then the answer is no,' he retorted without
rancour. 'Married women are bad news, and I avoid
breaking up a good relationship.'

'How generous of you!'

Julie's sarcasm was not lost on him, but his lips
only curved into a mocking smile. 'That's not to say
there haven't been occasions. . .' he drawled, and she
felt an agonising twist of jealousy tear into her. 'So?
What do you say?'

'You know what my answer is.'

'No?'

'No,' she agreed tautly.

'Oh, Julie!' His mockery fled and in its place was
something far more dangerous. 'Julie,' he repeated,
sliding round the banquette until his thigh was pressing
against hers. 'I'm crazy about you! Don't do this to
me. I need you!'

He was too intense, and her heart palpitated wildly.
He was so close she could see every inch of his face,
every pore and every groove, the strong line of his jaw,

the slightly crooked curve of his nose, the shortness of his upper lip and the sensually fuller lower one, the blue-grey eyes, and the long dark fringe of his lashes. His skin was brown, faintly tinged around his chin with the shadow of the beard he had shaved that morning, and his hair lay thick and smooth against his head, long enough to brush his collar at the back and an irresistible temptation to her fingers. His open shirt revealed the upper half of his chest with its light covering of dark hair, and she could remember only too well the feel of his skin against hers. He was right, she thought in consternation, she did want him. And the knowledge horrified her.

His arm was along the seat behind her, his hand closing possessively over her bare shoulder, and her knees shook. When his fingers probed beneath the strap of her dress, however, she knew she could stand no more.

'Dan, don't!' she got out chokingly, unable to look at him but instilling her voice with the urgency of her feelings. 'I—I have to go. David's waiting for me—'

Her words died beneath his mouth, his parted lips covering hers and taking a moist possession. The pressure he exerted was light, but Julie felt her senses swimming.

The sound of voices penetrated her sexually-induced inertia, voices she recognised, and she managed to drag herself away from Dan just in time as David and his son came to occupy the opposite booth.

'Hey, Julie!'

It was Brad who saw her first as his father was about to go to the bar, and she prayed she did not look as disconcerted as she felt. With Dan's fingers still imprisoning her wrist under cover of the table top, and his lazy eyes upon her, she found it incredibly difficult to act normally and had to force herself to listen to what the boy was saying.

'Hi, Mr Prescott.' Thankfully Brad had switched his attention to her companion, and David paused to greet the other man.

'I didn't know we'd find you here, Julie,' he said, and she wondered if she imagined the note of disapproval in his voice. 'I thought you had some shopping to do.'

There was no mistake. David was not pleased, and Julie could hardly blame him. After all, he had warned her about Dan Prescott, and he also knew of the loyalty she owed to Adam.

'I was looking in shop windows when—when I bumped into—into Mr Prescott,' she volunteered. 'We—er—I was just leaving.'

'Oh, don't go!' Brad looked disappointed. 'Say, when are you going to show me the yacht, Mr Prescott. You haven't forgotten, have you?'

'No, I haven't forgotten, Brad,' Dan assured him good humouredly, as the boy's father uttered a word of reproval. 'It's okay, Mr Galloway, honestly. I know what it's like when people make promises they don't keep.' He had to release Julie's wrist to slide out of the booth, and while she ran a nervous hand over her hair he continued: 'I'll come by one afternoon next week, and we'll go for a sail. How would that suit you?'

'Really, Mr Prescott, that's not necessary,' David began, stung by his conscience, but Dan dismissed his objections.

'It's okay, Mrs Galloway,' he assured him, with a grin and transferring his attention to the boy added: 'It's a date. See you, Brad.'

'See you, Mr Prescott,' Brad agreed excitedly, and Julie emerged from the ice-cream parlour with the uneasy feeling that she held his happiness in the palm of her hand.

The sunlight was brilliant after the dimness of the booth, and as she shaded her eyes Dan slipped a possessive hand about her waist. 'Walk with me,' he said, and she had no choice but to accompany him down the steeply sloping street to the dock.

It was quite an experience walking with him. He knew nearly half the people they passed, and their close proximity was not lost on speculatively probing eyes. But Dan seemed unperturbed, and exchanged a word here and there without any apparent embarrassment.

'You can leave me here,' Julie said at last, after they had crossed the railway line and were standing on the dazzling strip of concrete fronting the dock. 'That's David's launch. I'll wait for them on board.'

'Let me take you home,' Dan suggested casually. 'I came on the Honda, and it'll be much cooler riding through the woods.'

And much more dangerous, added Julie silently, shaking her head. 'I don't think so.'

Dan sighed, resting one hand on each of her shoulders, looking down at her in mild irritation. 'You're not going to start all over, are you?' he protested. 'You know it's only a matter of time before— well, let's agree that we attract one another, and where's the harm in a holiday relationship anyway?'

'Are you on holiday?' Julie asked suspiciously.

'Sort of.'

'What's that supposed to mean?'

Dan grinned. 'I'm supposed to be recuperating.'

Julie could not prevent the twinge of anxiety that gripped her. 'Have you been ill?'

'Appendicitis,' he explained dryly. 'D'you want to see my scar?'

'No!' Julie flushed, and then realising he was teasing her, turned away. 'I'd better go. . .'

His hands on her waist prevented her from doing so, and presently she felt his body close behind her. 'When am I going to see you again?' he demanded urgently. 'Tonight? Tomorrow? Promise me you'll come down to the lake in the morning and I'll let you go.'

Julie drew a deep breath. 'And what about your family? Do they know what you're doing? Do they know about me?'

He was silent for a few moments, and then he said quietly: 'Drew does.'

'Your cousin?'

'Yes.'

'And your aunt and uncle?' Julie couldn't prevent herself from going on even though it was like sticking a knife in herself and twisting the blade. 'Pam told me about the Leytons—about your family.'

Dan took her arms and turned her to face him. 'So?'

'So—'Julie pressed her lips together for a moment to prevent them from trembling, 'they don't know about me, do they? I'm nothing to them, just another of Dan's little—'

'Stop it!'

He cut into her words angrily, but she was committed to destroying their relationship and she had to continue.

'They wouldn't approve of our association, would they? I mean—a suicide's daughter and a banker's son! It's just not on, is it? And that's the way it is with you, too, isn't it? All you want from me is an affair. A holiday relationship, as you said. Well, I don't have—affairs, Mr Prescott. So you'd better save yourself for someone who does!'

'You don't know what you're talking about,' he said coldly, but his hands had dropped to his sides, and with a little shiver she turned and walked away— and he let her.

CHAPTER FOUR

THE Boeing 747 landed at Toronto's international airport just before six o'clock, but Julie had to wait another half hour while the baggage was unloaded before Adam was free to walk through to the reception hall. He was among the first to emerge, a porter carrying his suitcase and the briefcase without which he went nowhere, and he looked so dear and familiar that Julie practically threw herself into his waiting arms. His gentle embrace was so soothing after the hectic emotions she had been suppressing, and tears came to her eyes as he drew back to look at her.

'Did you miss me?' he teased, though his shrewd gaze was apt to see more than she either knew or wanted. 'Are you all right? You look a little feverish to me. I thought you said that this climate agreed with you.'

'I did. It does.' Julie urged him impatiently towards the lifts. 'Come along. The car's parked on the sixth level. We can talk after we've left the airport.'

Adam obediently followed her, taking his cases from the porter and thanking him for his trouble. Then they squeezed into the metal elevator and shared the ride with a dozen others all bent on the same purpose.

The traffic was brisk as they joined the parkway, but for once Adam relaxed in his seat beside her. Perhaps the journey had tired him, Julie thought, for usually he objected to her taking the wheel when he was in the car. He did look a little pale, but perhaps that was because she was used to David's weathered appearance, and most of the men she knew were tanned. He seemed smaller, too, his build slimmer, his fair hair lighter and thinner—but again, the larger country seemed to breed larger men, and she had been here more than six weeks. . .

'Did you have a good journey?' she asked, as the traffic began to thin, banishing the unwilling thoughts of Dan Prescott that persistently troubled her. 'At least the flight was on time. I've only been waiting about forty-five minutes.'

'Forty-five minutes!' Adam sounded appalled. 'Why didn't you just book me into an hotel, and let me take a cab into the city?'

'Because I wanted to meet you,' declared Julie swiftly. 'You came here because of me. The least I could do—'

'My dear girl, I came because you needed me,' Adam retorted dryly. 'I've missed you, and when you telephoned I was concerned about you.'

Julie pressed her lips together. 'But you needn't have come out here.'

'I wanted to,' exclaimed Adam forcefully. 'You sounded so—so strung up on the phone. I realised you were not fit to make the journey home alone, so I decided to accept the Galloway's invitation to spend a few days at Georgian Bay.'

'Oh, Adam. . .' She glanced at him affectionately. 'You know you'll hate it. The great outdoors is not really your scene, is it?'

Adam chuckled. 'Perhaps not. If what you're

wearing is a sample of the current fashion, I'm going to be hopelessly out of place.'

Julie laughed too, relaxing for the first time in days, though her mirth was short-lived. She had forgotten Adam's aversion to jeans and in her haste to get to the airport in plenty of time, she had not bothered to change.

'Nobody cares what you wear at Kawana Point,' she told him, sustaining her smile with difficulty. 'But they're very nice, and very friendly, and I know they'll make you welcome.'

Adam nodded. 'But I gather they don't dress for dinner,' he remarked wryly, and she shook her head. 'So I won't be needing my dinner jacket, will I? Unless you and I spend some time in Toronto before going home.'

Julie's expression grew a little doubtful, and she guessed he could sense her uncertainty. 'Perhaps,' she murmured, wishing she had defied him and taken the London flight. 'We'll see.'

It was a long drive to Midland and after leaving the outskirts of the city behind they passed through miles and miles of open land, not unlike England but bigger and flatter. The trees were sparser too, and the houses they saw seemed remote from their neighbours.

'How can anyone live so far from any suburban conurbation?' asked Adam in dismay. 'I hope we're not going to be staying miles from anywhere. You know I like the daily papers, and somewhere to buy my tobacco.'

Julie sighed. 'Well, the Kawana is off the beaten track,' she confessed, 'but I warned you—'

'How far off the beaten track?' he cut in resignedly, and she shrugged.

'David has a motor launch. It takes about thirty minutes to get into Midland.'

'And Midland is what?'

'The nearest town. It's quite a pleasant place. It has hotels, and a cinema, and plenty of restaurants. I like it.'

Adam's note was thoughtful. 'Oh, well, I suppose I can put up with it for a few days,' he conceded. 'But going back to nature doesn't appear to have done you a lot of good.'

'Adam, the Kawana Point is not "going back to nature",' she protested, turning to give him a half impatient look. 'It's a modern, comfortable hotel. The food is out of this world!'

'Well, you do appear to have put on a little weight,' Adam agreed dryly. 'Or perhaps it's just those clothes you're wearing. Where did you get that shirt? Isn't that what pregnant mothers wear?'

Julie contained her indignation. 'It's a smock,' she told him patiently. 'I suppose pregnant mothers do wear them, but they also happen to be very cool and very comfortable.'

'But not very fashionable,' put in Adam shortly, and she decided not to argue. 'So,' he added, when it became obvious she was not going to continue, 'why did you want to come home so abruptly? I thought you were enjoying your stay.'

'I was. I am.' Julie caught her lower lip between her teeth. 'Only—well, I just wanted to come home, that's all. Homesickness, I guess.'

'You guess?' Adam's tone indicated his opinion of

the Americanism. 'And why did you suddenly get homesick? It doesn't appear to have worried you up until now?'

Julie shrugged. 'I suppose I missed you.'

'Well, thank you.' His response was ironic. 'Is that all?'

'What else could there be?'

'You tell me.'

Julie hesitated. 'Did you—did you clear everything up?'

'About your father's estate? Of course. There wasn't much left to do, as you know. You handled most of that before you came away.'

Julie nodded. 'I—is—is Mrs Collins still living at the house?'

'Naturally. Until you decide to sell, she'll continue to do so.'

Julie's fingers tightened on the wheel. 'Would—would he really have gone to prison?'

'Julie, your father knew there was every chance. He wanted to save you that, so he took his own life. That's all that needs to be said. He wrote his own epitaph.'

'If only I'd known him better,' she sighed wistfully. 'I saw more of you than I did of him.'

'Julie, after your mother died—'

'I know.' She sighed again. 'Well, it's over, as you say. Nothing I say or do can bring him back.'

'No.' But Adam's voice was gentle now. 'Let's talk about other things. What have you been doing since you came here? I would imagine there's plenty of scope for swimming and sailing, that sort of thing.'

'There is.' Julie closed her mind against Dan's

image. 'Brad—that's Pam and David's son—he's been trying to teach me to water-ski. He's quite good at it, but I'm just a mess!'

'Water-skiing?' Adam grimaced. 'You mean—in wetsuits and the like?'

'Actually, no. Just bathing suits,' said Julie ruefully. 'It stings like mad when you do a belly-flop!'

'But the lake must be freezing when you get out from the shore,' Adam protested; and Julie nodded in agreement.

'It is. But you get used to it. And when it's hot. . .'

Adam looked as if the whole idea appalled him, and she allowed the topic to lapse. She couldn't expect Adam to appreciate such youthful pursuits. He was a lot older, after all, and she couldn't ever remember him liking to take his clothes off. She remembered a holiday she had had with him and her father at a villa in the South of France. Her father had spent more time in the pool than Adam had, and he had been at least ten years older.

Shrugging, she applied her attention to her driving, and it was Adam who broke the uneasy silence that had fallen. 'Are there any other hotels within reach of Kawana?' he asked. 'Do people live around the lake? Are there villages, settlements?'

'They're mostly holiday homes,' Julie replied a little tightly. 'There aren't any villages, as such, Adam. There are towns, and there are small towns. That's it.'

'Hmm.' Adam was thoughtful. 'But what about the people who live in these holiday homes? Who are they?'

'I don't know, do I?' Julie gave an impatient shrug. 'Do you want to stop for a meal? There's a small town up ahead where we could have some dinner, if you like.'

Adam glanced sideways at her, then he made a negative gesture. 'I don't think so, thanks all the same. You know what it's like on that transcontinental flight—they ply you with food and drink from the minute you get on board. And besides, my metabolism keeps telling me it's after midnight.' He paused. 'Are there many guests at the hotel?'

Julie's fingers tightened over the wheel. 'About a dozen,' she answered offhandedly. 'What film did they show coming over? Did you go and see that French film we were discussing before I came away? I'm probably hopelessly out of touch with everything.'

Once again Adam subjected her to a probing stare, and then, shifting more comfortably in his seat, he replied to her questions, talking about the movie they had shown on the flight, describing the various French and Italian films that were presently playing in London. For a while, he succeeded in distracting Julie's mind from everything else, and her knuckles ceased to show through the creamy brown skin.

Inevitably, however, the conversation shifted back to their destination, and Julie tried to speak casually when she described an ordinary day at the hotel.

'How long do people stay?' enquired Adam curiously, and she replied that occasionally guests had lingered for three and four weeks at a time.

'There's plenty to do, if you like fishing and sailing,' she protested, in response to Adam's grunt of dismay. 'It's a sportsman's paradise, and the scenery is beautiful!'

'Hmm. But I imagine most people commute at

weekends only,' Adam averred. 'These holiday homes you mentioned—I doubt if they're in use all the time. I knew a chap from New York once who had a cabin in the Adirondacks. I suppose this is a similar retreat.'

Why had Adam to mention New York? Julie asked herself despairingly. New York was synonymous with all the things she wanted to forget, and the fact that Dan lived there was prime among them. It was useless to pretend she could forget about him here. Until she got away she would always feel this hollow emptiness every time she let some casual association remind her of the time they had spent together.

'Have you got to know any of the guests personally?'

Adam's query brought her back to the present, but the look she cast his way revealed the blankness in her eyes. 'I—oh, no. No,' she got out jerkily, as her brain comprehended his question. 'I mean, they're usually couples, or families—and I've spent most of my time with the Galloways.'

'I see.' Adam pulled his pipe out of his pocket and began to examine the bowl. 'So who has upset you, Julie? Someone working at the hotel, perhaps? Or David Galloway himself?'

If Julie had not had to concentrate on her driving she might easily have burst into tears at that moment. It was humiliating to feel one was so transparent, and while she applauded his perception, she could not forgive his timing.

'I don't know what you mean,' she lied, keeping her eyes glued to the road ahead. 'No one's upset me, least of all David! If you knew him, you wouldn't suggest such a thing.'

'All right.' Adam tamped his pipe down, and then applied his lighter to the bowl. 'My apologies to Galloway, but someone's upset you, and I'd like to know who it is before we get there.'

'Adam!' Julie glanced indignantly at him. 'I've told you—'

'I know what you've told me, Julie,' he replied calmly, slipping his lighter back into his pocket and drawing comfortably on the burning tobacco. 'But I also know that you're more highly strung now than you were before you went away, and that's not like you at all.'

'You're imagining things.' Julie licked her suddenly dry lips. 'I'm just a little fed-up, that's all. Secondary reaction, I guess. Losing one's father so suddenly and in such a way isn't easy to swallow.'

'I know that.' Adam's tone was compassionate. 'But you were over the worst of it Julie. Believe me, you were on the mend when you left England. That was why I let you come here, because I thought this holiday would complete the cure. You've never been a particularly neurotic girl. You're emotional, I know that, but not abnormally so. Now I come here to find you're on edge and impatient, answering my questions as if I was subjecting you to an inquisition. You're nervous, and touchy. Not like my Julie at all. And I mean to know why.'

'Oh, Adam. . .'

'Don't look at me like that. I know what I'm talking about, Julie. I know you too well to be deceived. Now, something's happened, hasn't it? Are you going to tell me? Or do I have to find out for myself?'

Julie heaved a heavy sigh. She didn't know what

to do. Adam did know her well, it was true, none better, but this was something outside the bonds of their relationship. Indeed, it could destroy their relationship once and for all, and she didn't want that.

'Adam,' she said at last, 'it's nothing, *really*.' She paused. 'If I admit that something did happen, something that did upset me, will you just let it go? Please?'

Adam was silent for a few minutes, drawing on his pipe, and then he said quietly: 'Are you sure *you* want to let it go, Julie? Isn't that what all this is about? Wanting to come home? Your uncertainty? Wouldn't it be simpler if you were completely honest with yourself?'

'But I am being,' she protested, taking her attention from the road to stare at him appealingly. 'Honestly, Adam, it—it wasn't important. And it's all over. Over!'

'Really?'

'Yes, really.' She paused, realising he deserved something more. 'It wasn't—well, like you think. That is, there was never any question of—of it being serious. It was just a brief interlude. Nothing happened, Adam. Nothing at all.'

He frowned. 'I'm beginning to see a little light here. It was someone who stayed at the hotel, wasn't it? Someone the Galloways know about. And that's why you're on edge, why you didn't want me to come here. Because you were afraid they might tell me.'

Julie opened her mouth to deny this, and then closed it again. How much simpler it would be if Adam thought that, she conceded, ignoring the pangs of her conscience. If he imagined it had been a brief holiday romance with someone who had now left the area, she might conceivably be able to relax.

When she didn't say anything for so long, Adam nodded and then stretched out a hand to grip her knee for a moment. 'You don't have to say anything, Julie,' he said quietly, making her feel even worse. 'You're young—and beautiful. It's natural that young men should be attracted to you. And I'm not going to blame you if you enjoyed the experience. Perhaps it's served a useful purpose after all. It's brought us together again, and that's what matters, isn't it?'

Julie forced a smile and covered his hand with one of hers for a moment. If only Adam wasn't so understanding, she thought, taking a determined grip upon her emotions. She might have felt better if he had ranted and raved and blown his top. As it was, she felt a little like a child who has stolen a handful of sticky sweets, who knows he has done wrong, and isn't punished for it. The guilt was not expunged, it remained.

David and Brad were waiting for them at Midland, and Julie handed over the reins of responsibility with some relief. The car, an old Pontiac, was left at the wharf, and they all climbed aboard the motor launch.

'Did you have a good trip, Mr Price?' David enquired politely, as he stowed the luggage, but Brad forestalled any reply by jumping in with his own exciting news.

'He came, Julie, he came!' he exclaimed, almost jumping up and down in his enthusiasm, and the boat rocked alarmingly. 'Mr Prescott, Dan! He said I could call him that,' he added proudly. 'When we were out on the lake.'

Julie's legs gave out on her and she sank down

weakly beside Adam, hoping he would imagine her unsteadiness was due to the upheaval of the boat. David, aware of her suddenly pale face, chastised his son roundly for almost overturning the launch, and then repeated his question to Adam as if nothing more important had happened.

'He took me out on the yacht,' Brad persisted, talking over Adam's moderate reply. 'D'you know what it's called? The yacht, I mean? *Spirit of Atlantis*! Isn't that a terrific name?'

'Brad, will you be quiet?' His father's hand upon his shoulder was a distinct warning, and the boy pulled a sulky face as he subsided on to the engine housing. 'I'm sorry, Mr Price, my son thinks there's nothing more important than sailing at the moment.'

'That's all right.' Adam crossed his legs, the polished toe of his shoe in direct contrast to David's canvas plimsolls. 'I know what boys are like. I have two nephews myself.'

David smiled his understanding, but the look he cast in Julie's direction was more constrained, and catching his eyes upon her, she was puzzled by his expression. He looked both angry and frustrated, but when she arched her brows in anxious enquiry he turned abruptly away, the shake of his head almost imperceptible.

For her part, Julie was desperately trying to regain her self-control. Brad's words had certainly robbed her of the composure she had achieved during the journey from the airport, and her mind throbbed with unanswered questions. Why had Dan come to the hotel? Had it only been to take Brad out? Had he expected to see her? Or was he merely keeping the promise he had made to the boy?

Whatever the answers to these questions, one thing was certain. He would now know all about Adam. Brad was too much of a chatterbox not to have related where Julie was and why, and surely that would curtail any further intentions Dan might have had of continuing their unsatisfactory association. It was four days since that awful scene on the wharf, after all, and Julie had succeeded in convincing herself that she was never likely to see him again. Apart from anything else, the callous way she had thrown her father's suicide at him would have deterred the most ardent suitor, and Dan certainly was not that.

It was a beautiful evening, the sky hazing from lemon yellow to deepest purple, and Julie made an effort to point out the places of interest to Adam. She indicated the deserted crescent of Snake Island and the tangled mass of islands beyond, and then explained that the Kawana Point Hotel was situated at the mouth of one of the many bays that intersected the coastline.

'It's like an inland sea,' exclaimed Adam, in reluctant admiration. 'One could almost imagine getting lost on such an enormous expanse of water.'

'You can get lost among the islands unless you know the channels,' put in Brad, with a hasty glance at his father. 'You can run aground, and Mr Prescott says—'

'That will do, Brad.' Once again, David interrupted him, and Julie couldn't prevent the wave of sympathy she felt towards the boy even if his words did fill her with apprehension. When he looked indignantly in her direction, she gave him a sympathetic smile, and then half wished she hadn't when he scrambled over

Adam's suitcase and came to join her.

Adam was talking to David, asking about the kind of fishing that was available in the area, and Brad took the opportunity to speak to Julie alone. 'You should have been there,' he exclaimed, his eyes wide and excited, and she had no need to ask to what he was referring. 'She's a beauty—the yacht, I mean. There are three cabins and three bathrooms—heads, I should say,' he grinned, glancing surreptitiously over his shoulder to make sure his father wasn't listening, 'and it can do nearly thirty knots!'

Julie tried to assume an interest she was far from feeling. 'Really?' she asked, apparently impressed. 'You'll have something to tell your friends when you get back to school.'

'Gosh, yes.' Brad nodded reminiscently. 'He's nice, Mr Prescott, isn't he? He let me take the wheel. Dad wouldn't believe me when I told him, but Mr Prescott doesn't worry about things like that.' He paused. 'He likes you, Julie. He said so. He asked where you were, and I told him. That's all right, isn't it?'

'Of course.' Julie drew an uneven breath. 'Why not?'

Brad shrugged. 'I don't know.' He cast another doubtful look in his father's direction. 'Dad said you wouldn't be interested in anything Mr Prescott had to say. Not now that your boy-friend's here.' He frowned. 'Is Mr Price your boy-friend, Julie. He looks—old!'

'He's only thirty-eight, Brad,' she retorted impatiently, annoyed to find that she could resent David's assumption even so. 'About the same age as your father.'

'I know, but Dad's been married for years and years!'

'I doubt if your mother would appreciate your sentiments,' remarked Julie dryly, but Brad was unrepentant.

'Anyway, Mr Prescott—*Dan*—said that he expected he'd be seeing you again.' He moved his shoulders offhandedly. 'Only don't tell Dad I told you.'

CHAPTER FIVE

THE invitation came at lunchtime the following day. A man in the uniform of a chauffeur delivered it, arriving aboard a highly-powered cruiser and insisting that he had been instructed to wait for a reply.

Julie saw the man as she and Adam sat at their table in the dining room, and although she had no reason to suspect who he was or why he was here, she could not prevent the tingle of apprehension that rippled along her spine when Pam carried the envelope into the restaurant. She looked uncomfortable as she approached them, and Julie, used to her casual, easygoing manner, was alarmed.

'I'm sorry to disturb you,' she offered apologetically, indicating the envelope in her hand. 'But he—' she glanced over her shoulder, 'he insisted on waiting for a reply.'

'What is it?' Julie tried to sound unconcerned and failed. 'Not bad news, I hope.'

'Not exactly.' Pam was hesitant, and Adam gave her an encouraging smile.

'I'm sure it can't be anything too terrible, Pamela,' he assured her gently. 'The gentleman's not a policeman, is he?'

'Heavens, no!' Pam shook her head and gave a short laugh, and Julie wished she would simply tell them what it was and get it over with. 'It's from— from the Leytons, Julie.'

She gave the younger girl the envelope, and Julie lifted the thick parchment flap with unsteady fingers. Inside was a card, a single card, the edge delicately serrated and tinted a palest rose. It was from Anthea Leyton, inviting Mr and Mrs David Galloway and their two guests, Mr Adam Price and Miss Julie Osbourne, to a barbecue they were holding that evening at Forest Bay.

Julie said nothing. She couldn't. She merely handed the card to David and while he read it, exchanged a look of shaken bewilderment with Pam. The other girl lifted her shoulders in helpless acquiescence and looked at Adam as he spoke.

'Is something wrong with this invitation?' he asked, raising his eyebrows. 'It seems eminently satisfactory to me. Who are these people? Do you know them? Well, of course, you must do, if they're inviting us to dinner.'

Pam sighed. 'I—we—I haven't actually met—Mrs Leyton,' she admitted. 'I—er—I've met her nephew.' She glanced appealingly towards Julie. 'You remember Dan Prescott, don't you, Julie? He came to the hotel a couple of weeks ago.'

'Yes.' Julie's mouth was dry, but she managed to articulate. 'I remember. I—are you—going to accept?'

'Are you?' Pam's meaning was clear, and Julie could only move her shoulders in helpless indecision.

'Prescott, Prescott?' Adam was saying thoughtfully. 'Where have I heard that name before? Oh, yes, it was your son, Pamela. Didn't he say that Mr Prescott had taken him out on his yacht?'

'That's right.' Pam couldn't deny it. 'He came yesterday, Julie. After you'd gone to the airport to meet Adam.'

Meeting Pam's eyes as she said this, Julie felt the tide of embarrassment sweeping up her cheeks. She had gone out of her way to avoid discussing the previous day's events with Pam, but now it seemed it was impossible after all.

'Well,' Adam was speaking again, 'I must say it's very civil of them to invite us. Are they residents in the area?'

Pam hesitated, then she said: 'Forest Bay is the Leytons' summer residence. Mrs Leyton is Lionel Prescott's sister. You may have heard of the Scott National Bank?'

'*That* Lionel Prescott?' Adam was impressed.

'Yes.' It was Julie who answered him, giving Pam an impatient look. 'I expect it's just a—a gesture. People like that do those sort of things.'

'I think we should accept.' Pam made her statement almost belligerently. 'After all, we are their tenants, and I'd hate to offend them.'

Julie stared at her friend incredulously. Pam didn't really believe that, any more than she believed the invitation was genuine. Dan was behind this, it was at his instigation they had been invited—but what his game was she didn't dare to think.

'Yes, I agree.' Adam's words broke into her agitated thoughts. 'It sounds delightful, and it will give me a chance to wear my dinner jacket after all, eh, Julie?'

'What?' Julie was still looking accusingly at Pam, and it was difficult to concentrate on what Adam was saying.

'I said—I'll be able to use my dinner jacket,' he

repeated, and then turning to Pam added, rather doubt-
fully: 'A dinner jacket will be in order, won't it?'

Pam assured him that it would, and then retrieving
the invitation card from Julie's unresisting fingers, she
went to give their reply to the messenger. Julie, unable
to continue with her lunch in her present state, excused
herself on the pretext of fetching a handkerchief, but
after the man had departed she followed her friend
into the small office behind the reception desk.

'And what do you think David's going to say?' she
demanded, closing the door behind her so that their
conversation should not be overheard. 'You know how
he feels about the Leytons—and Dan Prescott, for that
matter!'

Pam shrugged, perching on the corner of the desk
and re-reading the card with annoying deliberation.
'He can't refuse now, can he?' she responded without
heat. 'And I've always wanted to see the inside of
that place.'

Julie did not deign to ask what place. She merely
stood there, pressing her lips together, waiting for Pam
to say something to ease her raw emotions.

After a few moments Pam looked up and seeing
her tension, adopted a conciliatory tone. 'Don't look
like that, Julie,' she exclaimed. 'It'll be fun, you'll
see. And it's not as if you're going alone. Adam will
be with you, and Dan Prescott can hardly come
between you two, can he?'

Julie stared at her for a few minutes more, then her
tension seemed to snap and her shoulders sagged.
'Why is he doing this, Pam?' she groaned, sinking
down on to the chair beside the door, and her friend
regarded her compassionately.

'I think he's more serious than you think,' she admitted, unwillingly. 'Wait and see. Maybe the invitation's as innocuous as it seems.'

'You don't believe that.' Julie sniffed, looking up at her.

'No.' Pam was honest. 'But you shouldn't jump to conclusions.'

'Pam, I'm going to marry Adam!'

'I'm not denying it, am I?'

'No,' Julie conceded with a sigh. 'But Dan Prescott doesn't care about that. He doesn't care about anybody but himself. He practically told me there had been other women. . .*married* women. . .'

Pam sighed. 'Well, I don't know of any.' She grimaced. 'Chance would be a fine thing!'

'Pam!'

'Well!' The other girl was unrepentant. 'He is a dish, isn't he? It would be worth it just for the experience.'

Julie shook her head. 'You're crazy!'

'And you're far too serious for a girl of your age. Take it easy, Julie! Don't worry. Just think—in less than two weeks you'll be back in England, and all this will have faded from your mind.'

Julie wished she could feel as confident. The trouble was she was finding it increasingly difficult to keep Dan's image out of her thoughts, and somehow she doubted even a distance of some three and a half thousand miles would make the slightest difference. She had only to close her eyes to find his face imprinted on her lids, his grey eyes crinkling at the corners, his mouth lifted in that lazy sensuous smile.

As expected, David objected to Pam's arbitrary

acceptance of the invitation, but he was on a fishing trip with two of the guests from the hotel, and by the time he returned it was too late to do anything about it. Besides, as his wife argued, they had a very satisfactory staff, and it was time they had a night out together.

Julie, for her part, had mixed feelings. Despite her fears, she could not deny the purely physical excitement she experienced every time she thought of seeing Dan again, and in consequence she took longer than she should choosing what to wear.

Eventually she decided on a simple black evening gown she had stuffed into her case all those weeks ago in England. She had not expected to need it, but it was easy to pack and crease-resistant, and its plain lines were both flattering and elegant. Boot-lace straps tied on her shoulders above a draped bodice that was cut almost to the waist at the back and fell in soft folds to a few inches above her ankle. It was made of a silky acrylic fibre that clung where it touched, and it accentuated the creamy tan she had acquired. With her hair loose about her shoulders, she knew she would not disappoint Adam, and she felt a little more prepared to face the Leytons.

They used the launch to reach the party, crossing the bay and rounding the promontory to where the Leytons' summer residence was situated. It was a warm evening, and not yet dark as David steered the small craft across the water, and Pam exchanged a conspiratorial smile with Julie.

'You look gorgeous,' she said, looking down ruefully at her own flower-printed cotton. 'I wish I was twelve pounds lighter. I'd wear something sexy too.'

Julie looked a little apprehensive at that. 'Do you

think it is—too sexy, I mean?' she asked anxiously. 'I don't want anyone to—'

'No, of course not!' Pam overrode her protest with an envious grimace. 'Honestly, Julie, you look lovely. Doesn't she, Adam?' She turned to the man who was standing beside David at the wheel. 'Doesn't Julie look stunning?'

'Stunning,' Adam echoed, with an indulgent squeeze of her arm. 'But then she always does,' he added, for her ears only, and she wondered why Adam's compliments always sounded slightly patronising.

There were several boats moored at the breakwater that jutted into the lake below the Leytons' house, some of them as opulently luxuriant as Brad had described the Leytons' yacht to be. A planked jetty was connected to the gardens of the house by a flight of wooden steps, and the whole landing area was illuminated by coloured lights concealed inside swinging Japanese lanterns. The sound of music and laughter and muted voices drifted over the water, and Julie felt her nerves tightening as David tossed the painter on to the jetty and vaulted out after it.

'I'm petrified,' Pam confessed, as she gathered her skirts ready to go ashore, and her husband gave her an aggravated look.

'Don't blame me!' he declared pointedly, uncomfortable in his formal clothes, and his wife pulled a face at him as a uniformed steward came to assist him.

'Let me do that for you, sir,' he insisted, fastening the rope quickly and expertly before offering a hand to each of the girls in turn, and David grumbled gruffly to himself as they all walked along the jetty.

Pam and David climbed the steps first and Julie felt
her heart hammering in her chest as she and Adam
followed them. Now that she was here, she was convinced she ought not to have come, and her hand
tightened uncontrollably on Adam's sleeve.

Their hosts were waiting to greet them, and Julie
didn't know whether to feel relieved or apprehensive
that Dan was not with them. There was no sign of
him, and her tongue came to moisten her dry lips as
she took in the animated scene. There was so much
to see and absorb, and the gardens of the house seemed
full of people in every style and mode of dress, from
the inevitable denims to evening gowns and white
tuxedos. There were so many colours, so much variety,
and the white-coated waiters threading among the
guests carrying trays of champagne and canapés
seemed impervious to the carelessly-placed hands and
feet that impeded their progress. Beyond the mani-
cured lawns she could see a flower-filled patio and
buffet tables, and an enormous charcoal grill smouldering under a huge sirloin of beef.

Many curious eyes had turned in their direction as
Maxwell Leyton took over the introductions. He and
David had met before, although not under these circumstances, and he thanked them all politely for
coming before turning to his wife.

Anthea Leyton was one of the most beautiful
women Julie had ever seen. She was dark, like her
nephew, with the same misty grey eyes and curling
lashes, and her gown of rose-printed silk comple-
mented her olive skin. She wore diamonds in her ears
and at her throat, and the chunky bracelet around her
wrist was obviously worth a small fortune, but if her

appearance was attractive, her manner was not. Her acknowledgement of the Galloways had hardly been polite, and now she turned to Julie with a vaguely speculative hostility.

'So you're Julie,' she said, and the way she said it was hardly flattering. 'My nephew has mentioned you, but I was curious to meet you for myself.'

'Yes?'

Julie's heart seemed to stop and then start again, labouring under the effort. What was this woman trying to say? That she had been responsible for issuing the invitations? That Dan had had nothing to do with it?

'I believe you're English, aren't you?' she continued, apparently unaware of Julie's faltering expression. 'You must tell me what you think of our small country.'

Julie made a helpless gesture, and to her relief Anthea turned her attention to Adam. 'Good evening, Mr Price. I hope you'll enjoy your evening.'

'I'm sure I shall,' he assured her politely, and for once Julie was glad of his very English self-possession, although she wondered what he had made of Anthea's oblique comments. 'This is a beautiful place you have here, Mrs Leyton. An oasis of sophistication for an old epicurean like me.'

Anthea looked as if she wasn't sure whether or not to take him seriously, but at least his remarks had taken the onus off Julie. It gave her the opportunity to scan the crowd once again, but it was impossible to distinguish one tall man among so many. She tried to tell herself she was glad he wasn't around, that she ought to be grateful to Anthea for confirming what she had suspected, and then, just as Adam was leading her away to where Pam and David were waiting, a lazily familiar voice said: 'Hi.'

Julie felt as if someone had just delivered a blow to her solar plexis, and her hand in Adam's arm fell abruptly away. Dan was standing right behind them, casually dressed in light blue trousers and a cream silk open-necked shirt, the only sign of affluence the dark blue velvet jacket that accentuated the width of his shoulders.

'Glad you could make it,' he remarked, giving Adam a swift appraisal before seeking Julie's heated features. 'I'm sorry I wasn't here to meet you, but my aunt insists on utilising every available hand.'

'Er—this is Dan Prescott, Adam,' Julie managed to say hastily. 'Adam Price, Dan.'

'How do you do, Mr Prescott.'

Adam held out his hand and Dan shook it, moving between them to do so, successfully isolating Julie on his right. Then he grinned at Pam and exchanged a word with David before suggesting that he introduced them to some of the other guests.

It seemed the most natural thing in the world that he should walk between them, though Julie sensed Adam's dissatisfaction with the arrangement. However, with Pam and David right beside him he could hardly offer any objection, but Julie guessed he would have more to say later.

Most of the guests acknowledged Dan's introductions with only minor interest. Several of the women gave Julie a critical look and once or twice she sensed the hostility she had felt from Anthea, but for the most part, people were bent on enjoying themselves, and the freely flowing alcohol had oiled the stiffest bearing. There was the hum of conversation, the outburst of laughter, and the musical sounds from the loudspeakers to ensure that no awkward silences occurred. Some of the younger guests were even dancing on the patio, and with darkness falling across the lake the whole scene had the appearance of a stage set.

'Well? What do you think?' Dan murmured in an undertone, bending his head towards Julie as if in answer to something she had said, and she smelt the clean fragrance of his aftershave. 'Did Aunt Anthea make you welcome, or did she give one of her famous impressions of Lucrezia Borgia?'

Julie couldn't say anything in reply, but a faint smile touched her lips as she looked away. He was the same Dan, in spite of everything, she thought, but she wished he would not make it so hard for her.

Glasses of champagne were offered, and Julie buried her nose in the bubbling liquid. Adam was talking to David and a man on his left, who apparently drove formula one racing cars, and Pam wrinkled her nose above the delicate rim of her glass.

'Nectar,' she mouthed, rolling her eyes expressively, and Julie wished she could feel as uninhibited as her friend.

Dan swallowed his champagne without reverence and slipped his fingers around Julie's wrist, twisting it behind her back. 'Dance with me,' he said, all the humour gone from his face, and she felt the familiar pull of her senses as his thumb massaged her palm.

'I—I can't,' she murmured, hoping Pam could not hear them, and his lean face darkened ominously.

'Why not?' he demanded, apparently uncaring of

their surroundings, and she cast an imploring glance up at him.

'Because I can't,' she whispered, her eyes darting in Adam's direction. 'Please, Dan, don't do this. You're making a scene.'

'This is nothing to what I can do, believe me,' he grated, and she didn't doubt it.

'I can't leave Adam,' she insisted in a low tone. 'Try and understand my position.'

'Why should I? Do you try and understand mine?'

'Dan. . .'

'That's my name!'

'Dan, we had all this out before—'

'You wanted to meet my family. Well, you have. What else do you want me to do? You came here. You accepted my invitation—'

'*Your* invitation?'

'What else?'

He was looking down at her as he spoke, and in the fading light she could sense the intensity of his gaze. She could drown in those eyes, she thought, weakening under the physical onslaught of his attraction, and she had to force herself to concentrate on the liquid in her glass as she spoke.

'Your—your aunt implied that she had—offered the invitation,' she said through taut lips, and chanced a glimpse at his expression.

'She did,' he responded, bringing a furrow to her forehead until he elaborated. 'But I asked her to do it.' He paused. 'Will you dance with me now?'

'Dan, she doesn't like me. She doesn't want me here—'

'I do,' he said, and what she saw in his face robbed her of all resistance.

She managed to replace her glass on a passing tray as he drew her after him on to the tiled floor of the patio. She didn't dare to wonder what Adam must be thinking, and presently Dan's arms around her banished all other considerations. She was close against him, her face pressed against the smooth silk of his shirt, his arms encircling her waist so that she was obliged to loop hers around his neck.

'Mmm, I've wanted this,' he muttered, bending his head to nuzzle her ear, and she had to steel herself from resting against him.

'I thought—after that day on the wharf—' she began unsteadily, but his finger across her lips silenced her.

'You didn't think you'd get rid of me that easily, did you?' he mocked gently, and she turned her lips away from the sensual temptation of his.

'How—how did you persuade your aunt to invite me?' she persisted, trying to maintain a detachment she was far from feeling, and he moved his shoulders in a lazy shrug.

'She's not so bad,' he remarked dismissingly, allowing his hand to move from her waist to the silky skin that covered her shoulder blades. 'I like your dress,' he added huskily, 'but I like you better without it. . .'

'Dan!'

Her protest was almost desperate, and for a few moments they turned in silence round the tiny dance floor. It was hardly dancing, and the music didn't help the way she was feeling. It was a haunting melody, all piano and rhythm guitar, and sung by a sexy young singer whose music was full of mood and innuendo. It seduced the mind as well as the senses, and Julie could feel her emotions responding to its insidious appeal. It wasn't fair, she thought frustratedly, but when Dan's fingers probed inside the low back of her dress she didn't try to stop him. On the contrary, she withdrew her arms from around his neck and slipped them about his waist, inside his jacket, close against the fine silk of his shirt. It brought her closer to him, she could feel the warmth of his body through the thin material, and once again she felt the stirring urgency between his thighs.

When the music finally came to an end, Julie felt almost drugged with emotion, and Dan made no attempt to let her go. 'Come on,' he said, resting his forehead against hers, 'I want to show you something.'

Julie looked up at him helplesly. She was aware that the longer they stood there, the more attention they were drawing to themselves, and while the alternative Dan was offering was dangerous, it was also irresistible in her present condition. With a little sound of protest she acquiesced, nodding her head, and Dan released her only so far as the encircling possession of his arm would allow as he walked her towards the house.

Several people saw them go, but no one Julie recognised, and she silenced her conscience with the unconvincing assurance that she was doing nothing wrong. She had wanted to see Dan's home, or at least the place where he was staying, and now she was being given the chance. Even so, nothing she had seen so far had prepared her for the luxury of the Leytons' house and her eyes widened in stunned disbelief as they entered the massive hall-cum-living room.

She supposed it could be called a cabin. The walls were of wood, certainly, but there the resemblance to a hunter's shelter ended. Forest Bay was a tasteful country residence, a millionaire's retreat, that combined all the comfort of a luxury apartment with the plain fabric of simple elegance. There was lots of leather, squashy leather sofas and chairs, and leather-topped tables that supported a variety of Indian relics. The walls were hung with Indian paintings, and over the massive open fireplace, which could surely roast an ox, were a pair of crossed rifles. But overriding everything was the atmosphere of wealth and affluence, evidenced in the fine silk of the lampshades, the lush velour of the curtains, the glittering crystal that ornamented a polished cabinet, and the rich skin rugs upon the floor.

'Uncle Max collects these things,' Dan remarked, indicating the rifles with a wry grimace. 'Sometimes I think it's a sign of repressed masculinity. Aunt Anthea likes her own way.'

'I can imagine,' agreed Julie with fervour, and Dan's arm tightened protectively.

'You don't have to worry about her,' he asserted huskily, turning his mouth against her cheek, and she felt a shiver of anticipation slide along her spine.

'Is there something you want, Mr Prescott?'

A woman in the uniform of a housekeeper was approaching them across the hall, and Dan shook his head. 'That's okay, Mrs Carling,' he assured her politely. 'I'm just showing Miss Osbourne the house.'

'Yes, sir.'

The woman gave Julie an appraising stare before withdrawing again, however, and Julie began to feel uneasy. The compelling spell the music had cast over her was fading, and common sense began to erode her confidence. 'I—what is it you have to show me?' she asked, linking her fingers together. 'Adam—Adam will be wondering where I am. Perhaps it's not such a good idea, after all. I mean, what will everyone think?'

'The worst, I guess,' Dan admitted laconically, but he did not seem perturbed. 'Relax. Enjoy yourself. That's what you're here for.'

Julie sighed. 'Dan—'

'It's upstairs,' he said. 'What I want to show you.' He released her shoulders to take her hand, drawing her resistingly towards the staircase. 'Will you come with me?'

Julie hung back. 'What is it? What do I have to see? Dan, if this is some trick—'

'It's not.' Though his mouth had hardened slightly. 'Julie, trust me.'

'Can I?'

'Well, can't you?'

Her doubts faltered. 'I suppose so.'

'You know so,' he declared harshly, drawing her towards him. Then, when her lips parted in protest, he added: 'Come on. It won't take long.'

The staircase comprised two flights of stairs that led up to an encircling balcony. Julie reached the top and leaned on the rail overlooking the hall below, and Dan rested his back beside her and folded his arms.

'Out of breath?' he enquired, the blue-grey eyes slightly mocking, and she straightened to gaze at him.

'Are you taking me to your room?' she asked,

steeling herself for his reply, but his mouth only curved in lazy humour.

'Miss Osbourne! You surely don't intend some mischief to my body, do you?' he demanded, in a broad Southern accent, and she gave a helpless shrug of her shoulders.

'Dan, please—'

'Follow me,' he interrupted her shortly, and with a feeling of inadequacy, she did so.

A long corridor opened out before them, carpeted in shades of green and gold, with double-panelled doors along its length that were presently closed against them. Wall-lights were set in sconces between the doors, and the silence was barely disturbed by the drifting sounds from the garden. They were alone, and she was completely at his mercy, she thought uneasily, realising that neither David nor Adam knew where she was.

She was about to make some excuse for not going any further when she realised they had reached the end of the corridor. A single door confronted them, set into the woodwork, and totally unlike any of the panelled doors they had passed. A latch secured it in place, and as Julie reached him Dan lifted the latch and the door swung open to reveal a narrow twisting flight of stairs.

Her anxious frown aroused his sympathy, and with a slight smile he said: 'It's not Bluebeard's den, or Rapunzel's tower. Just a room that I want you to see.'

Julie hesitated, and with a sigh Dan went first through the door. After a moment she followed him, curiosity getting the better of her, and they climbed the spiral staircase to the tiny turret room above.

It was still light enough to see that the room was furnished as a den, with specially curved bookcases along its circular walls, and a small desk strewn with an assortment of charts and papers. Dan turned on a small lamp, however, and its mellow light showed the ravages that time had wrought. Now Julie was able to see why there was such a musty smell about the place. The books were old and decaying, and the papers on the desk were sere and yellow with age.

'My grandfather's hideaway,' remarked Dan, watching her reactions. 'He used to come up here to escape my grandmother, I suspect. She was a woman much like Aunt Anthea'.

Julie shook her head. 'It's a—fantastic place.' She moved to the windows. 'And look at the view!'

'I know.' He came to stand behind her, and although he didn't touch her, she was aware of him with every shred of her being. 'That's what I really wanted to show you. Look here. . .'

He indicated an old-fashioned telescope set on a stand near the windows. It was trained on the sweep of bay beyond the promontory, and although it was almost dark, it was possible to see the lights glinting among the trees at the far side of the water.

Julie adjusted it to her eyes, and then made an unexpected discovery. 'I say,' she exclaimed incredulously, 'that's the hotel, isn't it? Look, Dan, those lights shining over there. It's the hotel, isn't it? Heavens, if it was light—'

'—you could see a lot more,' he finished dryly, bending to look over her shoulder. 'Like the cove below, for instance.'

Julie gasped and turned so quickly she almost

knocked him off balance. 'You—you mean, you saw me!' she exclaimed.

Dan straightened, regarding her penitently. 'I'm afraid so,' he admitted, although he didn't sound remorseful.

'You—you trained that telescope on me!'

'Are you shocked?'

Julie could hardly speak. 'But—but I could have been doing anything,' she objected.

'Like swimming in the raw?' He gave a crooked grimace.

'You mean—you came to find me?'

'Hmm—mmm.'

'Oh, Dan!'

'I'd tried for days,' he said wryly. 'That coastline has dozens of inlets, and at first it didn't occur to me that you might be staying at the hotel. I didn't even know there was an hotel until Drew told me.'

Julie bent her head. 'I—I must have been a disappointment.'

'What do you want me to say to that?' he asked huskily. 'Julie, don't make this any harder for me than it already is. You know how I felt when I saw you— how I feel about you still.'

Julie caught her breath. 'We'd better go. . .'

'Do you want to?'

She looked up. 'Do you?'

He shook his head, and with a little gulp she turned aside from him to stare unseeingly through the window. In this small room, it was incredibly difficult to remember her earlier intentions. And discovering that their meeting had been no accident filled her with a reluctant excitement. Imagining Dan standing up here, training his telescope on her small cove, was a tantalising experience, and the sigh she uttered revealed the conflicting uncertainly of her emotions.

'Julie,' he said, and she did not resist when his hands drew her back against him. 'Julie, you're tearing me to pieces!'

'I——I think you're doing the same to me,' she confessed, resting her head against him, and with a groan he sought the worn old easy chair behind him, dropping down on to its scarred leather seat and pulling her down on top of him.

His mouth found hers with unerring accuracy, and she was too startled to object. Warm and insistent and subtly compelling, it robbed her of all resistance, and with his hand cupping her neck and his thumb probing the hollows of her ear, she had no will to avoid the hungry pressure of his lips. Her mouth opened under his like a flower to the sun, submitting eagerly to his searching caress, and her hands slipped around his neck, and tangled in the thick smooth hair at his nape. She was gripped with a mindless ecstasy, submerged in a wine-dark sea of emotion that left no room for doubts, but set her heart pounding at a suffocating pace. His mouth caressed her ears and her cheeks, descending with purposeful sensuality to her neck and shoulder, pushing the boot-lace strap aside and teasing the sensitised skin.

'You don't know what it's been like, staying away from you,' he muttered, threading his fingers through her hair and drawing it across his lips. 'Waiting for Anthea to issue her invitation——dreading the possibility that you might refuse. . .' His mouth sought hers

once again. 'When Brad told me where you were yesterday, I wanted to kill you!'

Julie drew an unsteady breath, but she couldn't
think coherently at this moment. 'He—he said you
had told him to tell me you—you would see me again,'
she whispered. 'I was—afraid.'

'Of me?' he groaned, cupping her face in his hands
and gazing down at her, but she managed to shake
her head.

'Of—of myself,' she confessed helplessly. 'Oh,
Dan, I can't think straight when I'm with you.'

His humour was rueful. 'I know the feeling,' he
conceded dryly. 'I'm not usually so intense,
believe me.'

'I—I expect you usually get what you want more
easily, don't you?' she probed huskily, and his lips
twisted in reluctant recognition.

'If you mean what I think you mean then I don't
think I should answer that question,' he teased,
allowing one tormenting finger to trail pleasurably
from her chin to the hidden hollow between her
breasts. 'But if it's any consolation to you,' he added,
his voice deepening as his own emotions were
aroused, 'I've never been this way with any girl
before.'

'No?'

'No.' His eyes were narrowed and disturbingly
passionate. 'I don't know what you do to me, but I
don't seem able to think of anything else.'

'Oh, Dan. . .' For the first time, she drew his head
to hers, and her lips played with his. 'You do things
to me, too.'

'What things?' he demanded, imprisoning her

mouth beneath his, as her fingers sought the buttons of his shirt, and she pressed herself closer.

'I like looking at you,' she confessed, drawing back to stroke his chest with her palms. 'You're very— brown, aren't you? Very brown—'

'Dear God, Julie, what do you think I'm made of?' he groaned, dragging her hands away from him, and as he did so someone called his name. The sound was insistent, a feminine sound, that echoed hollowly up the spiral stairs. Julie barely had time to struggle off Dan's knees before footsteps accompanied a repetition of the summons. Dan tried to stop her, but she wouldn't let him even though he made no attempt to get up. He just sat there, looking soberly up at her, one leg draped insolently over the arm of the chair, and she wished desperately that she had the right to be here with him.

The girl who erupted into the tiny turret room dazzled Julie. Tall and slim and willowy, with Afro-curled hair tinted a startling shade of red, she was wearing a scarlet jump-suit that somehow just failed from clashing madly. The jump-suit was made of satin, and clung to every line of her slender body, and it was obvious even to the least perceptive of eyes that she wore nothing beneath it. Blue eyes surveyed them from beneath artificially-long lashes, and black mascara had been used to elongate them to good effect. Combined with shiny red lip-gloss, her make-up was perfect, and Julie wondered who on earth she could be.

'Darling,' the girl exclaimed, as soon as she saw Dan. 'There you are! I've been looking everywhere for you.' Her eyes flickered scathingly over Julie before she continued: 'Mommy's simply livid, darling.

You've been neglecting your duties. You know how she depends on you to keep all the little ladies occupied.'

'Go away, Corinne, there's a good girl.' Dan's words were mild, but no one could doubt the menace behind them. 'Tell your mother I'm busy.'

Corinne Leyton, for Julie could only assume that this was Dan's cousin, made a sound of frustration. 'Don't be a meanie, Dan,' she protested, approaching his chair and stroking his sleeve with scarlet-tipped fingernails. 'Darling, you know what Mommy's like,' she added wheedlingly, finger-walking her way up to his neck. 'If she doesn't get her own way, she'll blame me, and I might have to tell her where you are and who you're with. . .'

Julie was feeling a little sick now. The recklessness of her own behaviour was hard enough to justify without being made to watch Dan being mauled by this female predator. It was obvious from Corinne's attitude that she considered she had some prior claim to his attentions, and judging from the way she was leaning over him, she did not consider Julie any competition.

'If you'll excuse me—' she began, only to halt uncertainly as Dan sprang up from the chair, brushing his cousin aside and grasping her arm with possessive fingers.

'You don't have to go,' he muttered, his eyes still smouldering with emotion, and for a moment Julie wavered.

But then the recollection of where she was and how she had got here came to sober her. 'Oh—yes, I do,' she got out unsteadily. 'Adam—Adam will be looking for me—'

'To hell with Adam!' he snapped, apparently indifferent to Corinne's shocked disapproval. 'I want you, Julie, no one else!'

'Dan!' It was Corinne who interposed herself between them then, pressing her fist against his shoulder. 'Don't be a fool!'

'Get out of my way, Corinne!'

There was no mistaking his accent now. It was not his polite English heritage that faced his cousin with ice-cold aggression, and Julie felt her hold on reality slipping. This couldn't really be happening to her, she thought disbelievingly. It was some awful dream she was having and very soon she would wake up to the warm security that Adam represented. Dan did not offer security. He only offered himself, the disturbingly sensual man he was, and that only on a part-time basis.

With a twist of her wrist she broke free of him, and he was baulked by Corinne's clinging fingers as he tried to go after her. Julie's heels clattered noisily on the stairs, as Corinne's had done on the way up, but soon enough she had reached the long strip of carpet that led to safety and sanity, and she walked swiftly along it.

'Julie!' She heard his voice behind her, but she didn't turn, although his quicker stride easily brought him abreast of her. 'Julie, for heaven's sake,' he muttered savagely, 'stop and listen to what I have to say!'

'No.' She shook her head and continued to shake it as she reached the head of the stairs, pressing her palms to her ears to silence his bitter protests. 'Don't say anything else, Dan, please. I don't want to hear it. I don't want to listen to you—'

'Julie!'

The torment in his voice was almost her undoing. Her head jerked helplessly in his direction, and she was torn by the anguish in his face, but she couldn't stop now. Somehow she had to destroy the feelings he aroused inside her, and so long as she was with him that was impossible to do.

She was partway down the second flight when she realised he had stopped at the halfway landing, and blinking she saw the reason why. As she self-consciously removed her hands from her ears, she saw the hall below was now milling with people, all sheltering from the sudden shower of rain that had driven them indoors. And watching her descent with varying degrees of hostility were Pam, David, Adam—and Anthea Leyton.

CHAPTER SIX

THE remainder of the evening was a disaster. How could it have been anything else? Julie tormented herself later that night, lying sleepless in her cabin. The worst that could happen had happened, and the emptiness of her future stretched ahead of her in cold isolation.

She didn't know which had hurt most—suffering the censuring silence of her friends, or having to watch Dan making himself amenable to his aunt's other guests. It had been bad enough knowing her behaviour had been unforgivable without being made forcibly aware that Dan appeared to have recovered himself remarkably quickly. Observing his easy conquest of men and women alike, watching that quizzical smile come and go, she had been torn by the growing conviction that he had been lying to her all along, that he had not been as distracted as he had pretended, and when he took his cousin on to the dance floor, Julie had turned so that she could not even see him.

Of course, that had been after the icy reception that had greeted her return. She had wanted to apologise, to try and explain to Adam that what had happened would never happen again, but neither he nor David appeared to be speaking to her, and it was left to Pam to suggest they might visit the powder room.

Once there, Julie had realised why the two men had looked at her so contemptuously. She had Dan's mark all over her, from the tumbled curtain of her silky hair to the shiny bareness of her mouth. She could imagine what they had thought of her, what everyone here must be thinking of her, and she had cringed at the thought of returning to the party. Did they imagine she and Dan had been to bed together? They had had the time, goodness knows, and her flesh crawled at the humiliation he had wrought.

'Couldn't you at least have repaired your make-up?' Pam exclaimed, speaking for the first time since she had suggested they left the two men, and Julie sank down weakly on to the padded stool before the vanity mirror. Fortunately the powder room was almost empty, and the two other occupants were more interested in their own conversation than in Julie's ravaged features.

'No,' she said now, moving her shoulders helplessly. 'Pam, I—'

'Don't try to explain yourself to me,' the older girl interposed swiftly. 'Really, Julie, I wish you wouldn't. This whole outing has turned into a fiasco, and I wish I hadn't come.'

'You wish!' Julie reached for a tissue and began massaging the skin around her nose and mouth. 'Pam, might I remand you, *you* wanted to come!'

Pam sighed, and as if giving in, she sank down on to the stool beside her. 'All right,' she said. 'So I'm to blame. But, for heaven's sake, why did you go off with him?'

Julie bent her head. 'You wouldn't understand.'

'Try me.'

Julie sighed. 'What if I told you I loved him? What then?'

'Julie!' Pam was aghast.

'I know. Crazy, isn't it?' Julie indicated Pam's evening bag. 'Do you have any powder base or lipstick? I didn't think to bring anything with me.'

Pam rummaged in her bag and brought out a comb, a compact and a lipstick. Then, while Julie endeavoured to keep her hand steady enough to apply the make-up, she said desperately: 'I never expected this to happen, Julie, believe me! Oh, I know what I said about dating Dan Prescott, but I never intended you to take him seriously. I—I just wanted you to see that there were other men in the world besides Adam.'

Julie shrugged. 'Well, you certainly succeeded.' She paused to give her friend a half sympathetic glance. 'Don't worry, Pam, I'm not blaming you. It's all my own fault, and I should have known better. I will in future.'

Pam bit her lip. 'Did—did anything happen? I mean, you looked so—so—'

'Dishevelled?' suggested Julie tautly, but Pam shook her head.'

'No. No—dazed! Julie, did he—'

'No.' Julie's tone was flat now. 'He hasn't seduced me, if that's what you're thinking.'

'Thank God for that!' Pam was fervent. 'Oh, Julie, I thought David was going to blow his top when Anthea Leyton asked where you were.'

Julie frowned. 'She asked where I was?'

'Yes. About fifteen minutes ago.' She shivered. 'Oh, Julie, I don't like that woman. She's horrible!'

'Why? What did she say?'

'Well, at first she was very polite.' Pam paused to replace her compact in her bag. 'She asked if we were enjoying ourselves, you know the sort of thing—isn't it a warm evening—have you had some champagne—so pleased you could come, etc. Then she asked where you were. I had to tell her the last time I'd seen you, you'd been dancing with her nephew, and her whole manner changed, just like that.' She snapped her fingers, and then looked away in embarrassment as she realised she had attracted the attention of the women at the other end of the room.

'Was she rude?' Julie applied the lipstick with trembling fingers.

'She was—insulting. She said she hoped you were not going to make a nuisance of yourself, that Dan spent his time extricating himself from relationships with girls who persisted in imagining he was seriously interested in them. She laughed—you know, one of those supercilious sophisticated laughs, saying that it was just as well her stepdaughter had a sense of humour, otherwise she might choose to give Dan a taste of his own medicine.'

Julie tasted the sourness of bile in the back of her throat. 'Her—stepdaughter?' she echoed faintly. '*Corinne* Leyton?'

'That's right. Have you seen her? She's wearing a jumpsuit that's practically indecent—'

'I've seen her,' Julie put in flatly, and Pam nodded in sympathy.

'Anyway,' she went on, apparently unaware that Julie was paler now than she had been before, 'David got really mad. He said he didn't know about any of the other girls Dan's supposed to have dated, but that he—*Dan*—was making all the running so far as you were concerned. Of course, that didn't suit her, and

Adam finished it off by saying that you and he were
going to be married in the fall.'

'Oh, Pam!'

Julie closed her eyes in agony, and with reluctance
Pam concluded what she had to say. 'She had to accept
it,' she said doggedly. 'What else could she do? Then,
ten minutes later, you came down the stairs like he'd
been all over you, and I guess we all felt pretty
foolish!'

'Oh, God!' It was worse than she had imagined,
and all she wanted was to run and hide, somewhere,
anywhere, away from here, where she could lick her
wounds in private.

But she had had to go back to the party, and the
only way she could do that was by adopting an air of
indifference she found almost impossible to sustain.
Nevertheless, it enabled her to meet the eyes of Anthea
Leyton and her friends without flinching, and if she
wavered a little every time Dan looked in her direction,
that was easily remedied by avoiding him altogether.
Certainly, he made no further attempt to come near
him, and she guessed his aunt's warning had been
sufficient to deter him.

It was harder coping with Adam and David. David
was brusque and abrupt, speakingly only when obliged
to do so, but over the plates of steak and salad that
were served by the uniformed staff, Adam unbent sufficiently to ask whether she was all right.

'Of course. Why shouldn't I be?' she had countered
stiffly, unable to relax even with him in case her whole
façade of composure should collapse; and he had
shrugged his slim shoulders in confusion, obviously
bewildered by this unexpected turn of events.

They were all relieved when they could reasonably make their escape. Maxwell Leyton wished them farewell, without the inimical presence of his wife, and Julie climbed into the launch eagerly, desperate to put some distance between herself and the man standing watching them from the top of the steps. He must have heard them saying their goodbyes, she thought bitterly, and turned her head as a shadowy figure blended itself with him, a slender wraith outlined in scarlet.

At the hotel, when she might have spoken to Adam, he took himself off to his cabin with only the briefest of goodnights, and left with Pam and David, Julie could only offer her apologies.

'Forget it,' David advised brusquely, his expression more sympathetic than it had been earlier. 'I warned you about Dan Prescott. Perhaps now you'll believe me when I say he's bad news!'

'Yes, David.'

Julie conceded the point and wished them good-night, but she knew it wasn't going to be that easy to put Dan out of her thoughts, in spite of his duplicity.

In the morning she awakened with a muzzy head, due no doubt to the amount of champagne she had consumed the night before. She was not used to such high living, but she had used the wine to dull the sharp edge of vulnerability. Now, she wished she could do the same again, and exist in a numb, unfeeling state until the rawness of her emotions began to heal. Perhaps after she got back to England, she thought, clutching blindly for a lifeline, and then realised she might well have forfeited that security once and for all.

She was drinking coffee at her table in the dining

room, both hands cupped protectively round the cup, when Adam joined her. He slipped into the seat opposite with the least amount of fuss, and then looked at her with wary eyes. Julie returned his stare rather nervously, her smile only tentative, but Adam broke the ice by leaning towards her and saying:

'I thought you might not want to talk to me—after last night. I let you down, I know, going to bed like that, but I needed to think. Now I have to know where I stand.'

Julie put down her cup with careful precision, then clasped her fingers together. 'Where you stand?' she said, echoing his words. 'Where do you stand, Adam? Am I beyond absolution?'

'No!' Adam's response was sure and firm. 'At least, not if you don't want to be. Look, Julie, I realised something was wrong on the way up here—I told you that. Why couldn't you have been honest with me then?'

Julie shrugged. 'There was nothing—there is nothing—to be honest about.'

'But you can't deny that you went off with Prescott last evening, that you—well, had some—contact with him.'

Julie bent her head. 'No, I can't deny that.'

'So tell me about it. Tell me what he means to you.'

That was more difficult. Julie looked up. 'You won't like it.'

'I don't particularly like any of this, Julie.'

She sighed. 'I'm attracted to him.'

'Are you in love with him?'

'Perhaps.'

'I see.' Adam did not sound entirely surprised.

'And what about him? How does he feel?'

'It's not the same.' Julie could be certain of that. 'You heard what his aunt said—Pam told me. I think she outlined the situation pretty well.'

'Yes.' Adam was thoughtful. 'It's not a relationship the Prescotts would welcome.'

'Do you think I don't know that?' Julie clenched her fists.

'So how far has this relationship gone?'

'I haven't slept with him, if that's what you're suggesting.'

'I'm relieved.' He made a dismissing gesture. 'It's better if these things can be kept simple.'

Simple! Julie's heart contracted. If only it was simple!

'And what about us?' Adam asked now. 'You know how I feel about you, how I have always felt. Our relationship—well, it's always meant more to me than anything else, and—and I think your father knew that and depended on it.'

'Oh, Adam. . .'

'Let's get something straight, shall we?' He reached across and covered one of her hands with his. 'So far, I've made no demands upon you. Ever since I came to fetch you home from St Helena's, I have considered you—respected you—endeavoured to give you time to regain your balance.'

'I know that, Adam.'

'But that's not to say, I don't love you, or desire you, just as much as any younger man. I know I'm almost twenty years older than you are, I know that must seem a terrible gap to someone of your age—'

'No, Adam!'

'—but I've always considered you a mature and capable young woman, perfectly able to share my life, my work, and my love. To be the only woman in my life, the hostess in my house, the mistress of my fate—this is what I'm offering you, and it's still yours, if you choose to take it.'

'Adam. . . Adam. . .' She turned her hand so that she could squeeze his. 'I know how kind you've been, I know I couldn't have managed these past weeks without you, even here, knowing you were always there, always waiting, caring. . .' She sighed. 'I don't think I have changed. I think this—this affair with—with—well, you know—it hasn't altered my opinion of you, it's—it's strengthened it. I don't want to change anything. We—we are still the same people, aren't we?'

'Of course we are.' Adam's doubts had cleared away, and his smile was confident. 'Oh, Julie, I'm so relieved. You don't know what a terrible night I spent!'

'I do.' Julie's smile was tremulous. 'Mine wasn't too great either.'

Adam nodded. 'You know what I think? I think we should get away from here, right away. And I don't just mean Toronto. Let's pack our bags and leave anyway. We could go to the coast. California! Spend a couple of months travelling. I need a break, too. We might even get married before going home.'

Julie couldn't prevent the sudden surge of despondency that gripped her at his words. It was what she had wanted to hear, she told herself fiercely, of course it was! So why did her spirits abruptly sink so low, and misery envelop her at the thought of leaving this place?

'What do you say?'

Adam was waiting for her answer, and she knew she had to make a decision. Who was she fooling, after all? There was nothing for her here. Nothing but pain and unhappiness and humiliation.

'If—if that's what you want, Adam,' she answered, picking up her coffee cup again, hiding her uncertainty behind its sheltering thickness. 'You know I wanted to leave days ago.'

'Good. That's settled, then. We'll leave this afternoon.'

'*This afternoon!*' Her cup clattered into its saucer again at that.

'Why not? I'm sure your friend Galloway won't object to driving us to the airport. And first class seats are usually available.' He consulted his watch, and then went on: 'I happen to know there's a flight from Toronto to Vancouver at eight. That gives us plenty of time.'

Julie was in a state of shock. She had expected Adam to make arrangements for them to leave tomorrow, or even the next day, but today!

'Don't you think that's rather—rushing things?' she ventured. 'And it's very short notice for Pam.'

Adam looked at her squarely. 'A clean break, that's what I always recommend,' he declared. 'A clean break, and a fresh start. We can always invite the Galloways to stay with us in England after we're home. You know your friends will always be welcome.'

Julie couldn't take it all in. Half of her was applaud-

ing his single-minded strength of purpose, but the
other half of her was holding back, protesting at the
impulsiveness of his action, clinging to the present
with clenched fists.

'Not today,' she said at last, unable to meet him all
the way. 'Adam, I need time—time to pack, time to
say goodbye to people. To say goodbye to Brad!
We've been such good friends. I can't just run out
on him.'

'Oh, very well.' Adam gave in with good grace,
aware that he had won a minor victory nonetheless.
'Tomorrow, then. Tomorrow afternoon. I promise you,
you won't regret it. I'll make you happy, Julie. It's
all I ever wanted to do.'

Julie smiled, but it was a fleeting illumination, and
when the waitress returned to take Adam's order, she
excused herself to go and start packing.

'I'll come to your cabin after breakfast,' Adam
called as she reached the door into the hall, and she
nodded a little absently as she went out.

Crossing the tree-shaded square to her cabin, however, she was struck again by pangs of homesickness.
It was curious, but this place had come to mean that
to her, and England and the house in Hampstead,
seemed a long way away. She had to leave sooner or
later, she told herself fiercely, but the suddenness of
Adam's decision had left her cold and strangely bereft.

Her cabin seemed shadowy after the brilliant
sunshine outside, and as usual it took her eyes a few
moments to adjust. Closing the door, she leant back
against it wearily, allowing her lids to droop against
the prospect ahead of her. In a minute she would have
to start dismantling her occupancy of the cabin, and

all the little mementoes she had collected would all have to be stowed in her suitcases. It was not a task she looked forward to, particularly as she instinctively knew that Adam would not want them cluttering up any room he had to live in.

'Hello, Julie!'

The low, distinctive masculine voice was shatteringly familiar, and her eyes opened wide, darting disbelievingly across the room. It was too early in the morning to be hallucinating, she thought, but the man propped negligently against the end of her bed had to be a figment of her overactive imagination, and she blinked rapidly in the hope that he might disappear. But he didn't. He straightened from his position and came towards her, and sheer unadulterated panic gripped her.

Her fingers groped desperately behind her, searching for the handle, but she couldn't find it, and before she could turn Dan had imprisoned her where she was, his hands resting against the door at either side of her.

'Oh, Julie,' he said, and there was a driven note in his voice now. 'What am I going to do about you?'

'How—how did you get here?' she stammered, avoiding his eyes, concentrating on the column of his throat rising from the unbuttoned neckline of his shirt.

'Brad told me which was your cabin,' he conceded flatly. 'Don't blame him—I bribed him to tell me. I can be unscrupulous if I have to.'

'Don't I know it?' she got out unsteadily, pressing her palms against the cool wood at her sides. 'Did— did you and—and Corinne enjoy yourselves after I left?'

He didn't answer her, and her eyes darted upward

to find him watching her with weary resignation. 'Do you expect me to answer that?' he asked. 'What do you think we did? Went to bed together?'

'It—it wouldn't be unreasonable in the circumstances, would it?' she demanded jerkily, and he expelled his breath on a long sigh.

'What circumstances?'

'You and she. Your aunt told Pam and David and—'

'I don't care what the hell my aunt told anyone,' he cut in savagely. 'Corinne and I mean nothing to one another. We never have. And if you think it's on offer, then you'll have to take my word that I've never sampled the merchandise.'

'Then why did your aunt—'

'Why do you think?' he snapped, his temper giving way. 'She knows the way I feel about you—she's not stupid. She's just using every weapon in her power to drive you away.'

'And she's succeeded,' declared Julie tremulously. 'I—we—Adam and I are leaving tomorrow.'

'Leaving?'

'For California. He wants us to have a holiday together before we go home to England—to the house my father left me.'

'William Osbourne,' muttered Dan broodingly.

'Yes, I know.' Then he shook his head. 'But you can't leave, Julie. I won't let you.'

'How are you going to stop me? I'm going to marry Adam.'

'Are you?' With a lithe movement he closed the space between them, crushing her back against the door with the weight of his body. 'And does he know how you feel about me?'

'As—as a matter of fact, he does,' Julie got out breathlessly, finding it difficult to draw any air into her lungs. 'Dan, take your hands off me! I'm not your possession. Just because—'

'What did you tell him?' he demanded harshly. 'Did you explain how we met? I can imagine he would find that very amusing. And what did you say in your own defence? That I chased you, that I forced you to do things you wouldn't otherwise have thought of?'

'No! No!' Julie jerked her head back. 'I—I just told him I—I was attracted to you—'

'Attracted to me?' Dan shook his head. 'Well, okay. That's one way of putting it, I guess. And he'll marry you, knowing that?'

'Of course.'

'*Oh, God!*'

'Dan, Adam's not like you—'

'That's the truth. He's not,' he conceded harshly, his hands at her waist tightening painfully. 'Julie,' he bent his head towards her, and she was disturbingly aware of the parted invitation of his mouth. 'Julie, don't do this to me—*to us*! We're so good together!'

'And is that all you think matters?' she got out unsteadily. 'Be-being good together? There—there's more to life than—than—'

'Sex,' he interposed smoothly. 'Why don't you say it? Or is that word not part of your vocabulary?'

Julie pursed her lips, pressing her fists against his chest. 'Just let me go, Dan,' she pleaded. 'Adam will be here soon. He—he's just having his breakfast, then he's coming to help me pack.'

'To leave.'

'Yes.'

Dan's lips curled. 'Well now, why don't I just hang around until he comes? Perhaps I can give him some pointers about you—'

'You wouldn't!'

Julie's words were torn from her, her head tipped back in dismay, eyes wide with consternation. She had never looked more desirable, and Dan's expression softened slightly.

'Kiss me, Julie,' he said roughly. 'Just one more time. Then I'll go, I promise.'

'You—you promise?' she whispered, not altogether convinced of his sincerity, and he nodded.

'Scouts honour,' he agreed mockingly, and cupped his hand possessively around her throat.

She had hoped to keep it brief, but when she reached up to touch his lips and his mouth parted over hers, she knew that was not his intention. Her breathing seemed suspended as he moved his head from side to side against the resisting barrier of her lips, arousing a response she had to fight to overcome. He did not force her, and although her fists were still balled against him, they offered little opposition as he continued to hold her.

'Coward,' he said at last, his voice muffled against her cheek, and soon as she opened her mouth to protest, she knew she had lost. Her senses were already swimming, and when his lips touched hers, she had no more strength to combat her own desires. Weakness overwhelmed her, and her hands uncurled to spread against his shoulders.

When Dan finally lifted his head, his face was pale beneath his tan, but he stepped back from her abruptly and pushed both hands through the virile thickness of his hair. 'Okay,' he said, as she endeavoured to gather her scattered senses, pulling the lapels of her denim jacket together, checking the zip of her jeans, anything to avoid the inevitability of their parting. 'Walk me down to the marina.'

'That—that wasn't part of our bargain,' she objected, and then submitted when he turned bruised eyes in her direction. 'All—all right. But I'll have to be quick or Adam will wonder where I am.'

'Right.'

Dan waited until she had straightened and then wrenched open the door, blinking as the brilliant sunlight flooded into the room. He allowed her to precede him, and then closed the door behind them and matched his lean stride to hers as they walked to the head of the steps that led down to the small breakwater David had built.

She saw the yacht Brad had gone into such raptures about as they walked along the jetty. It truly was a magnificent craft, all cold steel and mahogany, its sleek racing lines combined with big-boat luxury. The afterdeck was furnished with cushioned basketweave chairs and tables, and steps led down to the cabins below which Brad had described in enthusiastic detail, while the wheelhouse possessed two squashy leather armchairs for the pilot and a companion.

'So that's the *Spirit of Atlantis*,' Julie observed tautly, needing to say something to break the uneasy silence between them, and Dan inclined his head.

'That's right. D'you want to look around?'

'Oh, no—no,' Julie shook her head vigorously, trying to remain cool, when the knowledge of how he could make her feel was turning like a screw inside her. 'I—it's beautiful, isn't it? No wonder Brad was so impressed.'

'Come aboard,' Dan urged tersely, glancing round at the other vessels rocking on their moorings, and she felt the devastating pull of his attraction.

'I—I can't—'

'Why not?' He bent to untie one of the ropes that kept it steady. Then he straightened and looked into her eyes. 'Julie, don't make me say goodbye to you here on the jetty.'

'Dan, that's not fair,' she protested. 'We said goodbye up there.'

'Did we?' He held her gaze. 'Are you going to deny that you'd like to repeat it?'

'Oh, Dan. . .'

'At least step on to the deck,' he suggested, possessing himself of one of her hands. 'Look, it's easy. Just step across the gap—'

'I know how to get on board,' she exclaimed, inhaling indignantly. 'Dan—'

'I'll help you,' he said, ignoring her objections, and before she realised what he was doing, he had picked her up and deposited her on the afterdeck.

'Dan—' she began again, as he bent to release another rope, but he continued to ignore her, and she realised with a mixture of dismay and excitement that the yacht was definitely breaking free of the mooring. 'Dan, this is crazy!'

'I know,' he answered, but his face had recovered a little of its colour. 'However, we can't all live by the book, can we? And I have no intention of letting you spend today with Price.'

CHAPTER SEVEN

JULIE supposed she could have swum ashore if she had wanted to. After all, Dan had to go for'ard to start the two powerful engines, but the jeans and denim jacket she was wearing were a definite deterrent, and she doubted she could strip in the time she had. Instead she stood at the rail, one hand gripping the steel pillar that supported the upper deck, and watched the little harbour receding swiftly behind them.

'Are you mad at me?' her captor demanded softly, his breath fanning her ear, and she turned swiftly to face him.

'What do you think?' she exclaimed, emotion bringing a break to her voice. 'Adam will know where I've gone. Brad is bound to confess when I go missing.'

'So what?' Dan's lean face was sombre. 'You're not Adam Price's possession.'

'I'm not yours either!'

'Is that right?'

'Yes,' she declared fiercely, and he shrugged his broad shoulders.

'Well, we'll see,' he averred flatly, and turned back towards the wheel.

Julie took another anxious look over her shoulder and then sank down weakly on to one of the cushioned loungers. She wasn't really afraid, only apprehensive, but she couldn't help wondering what Dan intended doing with her, and what Adam's reactions might be.

He was probably only taking her for a sail, she told herself firmly. It was not as if he was abducting her, and once they got back she would explain to Adam how it had happened. Whether or not he believed her was not in question. Adam knew she would not lie to him.

With the cool breeze off the lake fanning her cheeks, it was not unpleasant sitting there, and she half wished she could relax and take off her denim jacket. She had put the jacket on over a cotton vest deliberately because she knew how much Adam deplored bare arms, but now her skin prickled in protest against the coarse fabric. Dan had no such problem. In his usual narrow-fitting jeans and a collarless sweat shirt that exposed every muscle of his hard body he looked cool and controlled, and very much in command of the situation. He was lounging lazily on one of the leather chairs at the wheel, casually studying a map he had spread out on the control panel in front of him.

Now that Julie noticed it, she could see the yacht was very comprehensively equipped with instruments. Various dials and gauges indicated a sophisticated communications system, and most significantly of all, there was a slim radio telephone.

Pressing down on the arms of her chair, she pushed herself to her feet and strolled with assumed indolence towards him. He noted her movements out of the corner of his eye, but he didn't make any move towards her, and she pushed her hands into her jacket pockets to hide their agitation.

'What—what are all these dials?' she asked at last, forced to say something, and he moved his shoulders in an offhand gesture.

'Oil and gas pressures, temperature gauge, echo-sounder, auto-pilot, radar—'

'*Radar*!' She was astounded.

'It's a sophisticated boat,' he remarked expressionlessly, and she nodded helplessly.

'I believe it.'

Unable to resist, she leaned over his shoulder to study the dials more closely, and he turned his head to look at her. He was too close, narrowed eyes focused on her mouth, and she quickly straightened again and ran a nervous finger round the inside of her collar.

'Take it off,' he advised, observing her discomfort. 'And those, too,' he added, indicating her jeans. 'Or you're going to be pretty hot by this afternoon.'

'This afternoon!' Julie was aghast. 'You can't mean to keep me out all afternoon!'

'Why not?' He tipped his head on one side, but there was no humour in his expression. 'Don't you think I'll do it? I can assure you I will.'

'You're mad!'

'Just desperate,' he conceded dryly. 'Now, if you'll give me a few minutes, I'll finish plotting our course—'

'Your course!' she burst out frustratedly, and without really considering the futility of what she was doing, she snatched at the radio telephone.

Of course, he removed it from her resisting fingers without too much effort, and she realised she had probably destroyed her only chance of thwarting him. He would be on his guard now, and she might never get the opportunity again.

'Adam will come looking for me,' she warned,

clutching at straws, and Dan gave her an old-fashioned look.

'In what? A helicopter?' he enquired. 'I doubt he'll find us in anything less. He doesn't know these islands. I do.'

'You—you arrogant devil!'

'Relax, why don't you? Go make us a cup of coffee, if you want something to do. Or there's beer and Coke in the freezer, and ice, too, if you want it.'

Julie stared at him resentfully for a few seconds longer, then she turned away. 'You'll make me hate you,' she declared childishly, and he made a sound of indifference.

'That's better than nothing,' he remarked, bending his head to the map once more. 'Oh, and by the way, you'll find a bikini in the locker. I'd put it on, if I were you. It might cool you down.'

She was tempted to defy him, but she was beginning to feel really uncomfortable, and tossing off the jacket with ill-grace, she swung herself down the steps.

The cabin below was just as impressive as the control panel above. Sheathed teak panelling, wall-to-wall carpeting, matching velvet curtains—it was a luxury apartment in miniature, and unable to resist the temptation to explore, Julie ventured forward into the two double cabins, one with an enormous double bunk, and the other with two singles. Each of the cabins had its adjoining shower and toilet compartment, and she discovered a third bathroom next door to the kitchen, with a real bath in it, and not just a shower.

There were fitted cupboards in the cabins, and deciding that Dan's suggestion had given her justification to open them, she looked inside. They were disappointingly empty. Just a pair of canvas shoes had been tossed in the bottom of one tall cubicle, and another produced a leather wet-suit and some oxygen cylinders.

Shrugging, she went back into the second cabin, and on impulse opened a locker set high on the wall above one of the single bunks. This was more successful. The locker contained a pair of jeans, several thick sweaters, and a pair of men's pyjamas. It encouraged her to look in one on the opposite wall, and here she found what she was really looking for, a cotton shirt—and two bikinis.

The bikinis were much more daring than anything she had ever possessed, and she guessed rather unwillingly that they probably belonged to Corinne. One was yellow, a rather repulsive shade, Julie thought, and she could imagine how it looked with Corinne's red hair. The other was brown and delightfully simple, but she viewed it with some misgivings. Despite the discrepancies in their height, and the fact that Corinne was obviously slimmer, it would probably fit her, but she shrank from the possibility of Corinne's reactions if she ever found out who had been wearing her swimsuit.

Realising that she was wasting time, she carried it into the double-bunked cabin and quickly stripped off her clothes. There was no lock on the door, and she wondered apprehensively what she would do if Dan got suspicious and came looking for her. But he didn't, and she put the bikini on, grimacing at her reflection in the long narrow mirror beside the vanity unit.

As she had expected, it was a perfect fit, and very becoming. More becoming than her own, she acknowledged reluctantly, allowing for the fact that it was a little too brief. It revealed the swell of her hips and the curving length of leg below, and she wondered if she really wanted to display herself like that. With a feeling of resignation, she reached for her jeans and put them on again, over the briefs. The bra would suffice, she decided, remembering that scene by the lake. It would be foolish to affect modesty after the intimacy of their embrace, and without giving herself time to change her mind about that too, she walked quickly through to the living area.

The galley was equally as well equipped as the rest of the craft. As well as the cooker and freezer, there was a dish-washer and sink-disposal unit, and a variety of gadgets for peeling, dicing and liquidising food. The cupboards were well stocked with tinned and other convenience foods, and Julie paused to wonder who spent time aboard.

She found the coffee beans without too much difficulty, and a percolator, but after a moment's hesitation she decided not to make a hot drink. It was hot enough already, and instead she extracted a couple of cans of Coke from the fridge, and clutching them against her, she climbed the steps once more.

The yacht was plunging a little as it rode the waves, and she saw with concern that they were well out from the shore now, and in deeper waters that she had hitherto sailed. The cluster of islands she had explored were away to their right while on their left was the mound of the island known as the Giant's Tomb. This was obviously not their destination, however, and her heart flipped a beat as she saw the great expanse of water ahead of them.

'Here's your Coke,' she said, approaching Dan reluctantly and offering him a can, and he took it with a wry smile.

'Coke! How nice,' he acknowledged mockingly, and she realised he would probably have preferred beer. But before she could offer to change it he had peeled off the cap and raised the can to his lips, and she shrugged rather awkwardly as he wiped his mouth on the back of his hand. 'That's cute!' he remarked, waving the can towards her outfit. 'A bra but no briefs! I wonder what happened to them.'

Julie tugged aggravatedly at the ring screw of the can. 'Unlike your cousin, I'm not used to going around half naked,' she declared rightly, and glimpsed his smile before he turned back to his charts. 'Anyway, where are you taking me? Don't I have a right to know?'

'Sure.' He jabbed a finger at the parchment. 'Here. That's where we're going.'

Julie stepped forward warily and took a hasty look at where he was pointing. Then she gasped. 'But— but that's right over there!'

'That's right.' He finished his Coke at a gulp. 'They're the islands that used to be used as lookout points by the Hurons.'

'The Indians?' Julie was impressed in spite of herself.

'You got it.' Dan turned to look at her again. 'So why don't you just stop fighting me and enjoy yourself?'

'I have packing to do—'

'The hell with that!' Dan's mouth thinned. 'You're not leaving, Julie.'

With a feeling of impotence she turned away, unwilling to argue with him further. What was the point of making him angry? Until she could get off this boat, she was in his hands.

She returned to the afterdeck and after a few restless moments leaning on the rail, watching the places she knew and recognised recede into the distance, she put down her Coke and climbed the ladder to the upper deck. It was more breezy up here, but she found that if she stretched out on the deck itself she was sheltered by the low metal barrier that surrounded it. It was a sun-trap, and she moved sinuously, finding a more comfortable position.

She had been lying there perhaps fifteen minutes when Dan came to find her. She was unaware of his approach until he spoke, and then she jack-knifed into a sitting position, staring at him resentfully.

'Having fun?' he enquired dryly, and she tilted her head aggressively.

'Oughtn't you to be steering this thing?' she demanded, and he shrugged indifferently.

'There's the wheel, if you want to take charge of it,' he remarked, stepping over her legs, and she noticed the secondary steering mechanism. 'But no sweat. It steers itself pretty satisfactorily.'

'You think you're so clever, don't you?' she accused him bitterly, resentful that he had shed his jeans and shirt and was now wearing only navy cotton shorts. The fact that the shorts displayed the muscular length of his legs to good advantage was an additional source of irritation, particularly when he caught her looking at him, and she deliberately turned on to her stomach and buried her face on her folded arms.

It wasn't a happy solution. She couldn't see him, and consequently she didn't know where he was or what he was doing, and she almost jumped out of her skin when a chord on a guitar was struck near her ear. She rolled protestingly on to her back, and then felt a reluctant surge of interest when she saw Dan seated with his back to the wheel strumming the instrument. His legs were crossed, one ankle resting on his knee, and the guitar was draped lazily across his thighs. As she continued to watch him he flicked a mocking glance in her direction before beginning to play a taunting Country and Western tune, the lyric of which was in no way complimentary to an independent woman.

'Do you sing, too?' she enquired, propping herself up on her elbows, and as if in answer he changed to an instrumental that had topped the singles charts some weeks before.

With a sigh, Julie sat up, crossing her legs and facing him with some impatience. 'All right, you're good,' she said caustically. 'What is this—music to soothe the savage beast?'

'The word is breast,' he mocked, playing a final chord and putting the guitar aside. 'Music to soothe the savage breast! Which reminds me, there's another bikini below with both pieces intact.'

Julie's face burned, and she bent her head angrily, annoyed with her own inability to control her emotions where he was concerned. 'You know I'm wearing the briefs,' she told him moodily. 'I—I just didn't feel like—like making an exhibition of myself, that's all.'

Dan shrugged and stood up, but although she felt a moment's apprehension he only stepped over her legs again and went down the ladder, his bare feet soundless on the rubber-encased rings.

Her solitude destroyed, Julie decided to follow him, and found that they were approaching an island. There was a bay, set within the sheltering curve of the headland, and she gazed at it with undeniable interest as Dan handled the controls.

The powerful engines were slowed to a snail's pace, and the yacht moved slowly through the channel and into the bay. Then, some distance out from the sandy shore, he cut the engines altogether and dropped anchor, and the sudden silence was almost unnerving.

'Iroquois Bay,' he remarked, turning from the wheel and looking at her. 'The Huron Indians were practically wiped out by the Iroquois, even though they were both technically from the same linguistic family. But people are like that, aren't they? They always see enemies where there are none.'

'I imagine they had a reason,' replied Julie tautly, concentrating on the pine-covered slopes that climbed above the bay, and Dan inclined his head.

'Oh, sure. They were bitter enemies in the fur trade, but the Hurons were far the more civilised tribe. They made friends with the French, and the Jesuits made quite a number of converts. But the Iroquois were a bloodthirsty crew and I guess they didn't want to be civilised.'

Julie shrugged. 'Why are you telling me all this?'

He grinned. 'Just to prove that constant hostility prevents the development of a good relationship.' He made a final examination of the instrumentation, and then came aft to where a small dinghy was suspended just above the waterline. 'Now, do you want to swim ashore, or would you rather take the dinghy?'

Julie sighed. 'I'd rather not go ashore at all.' She examined the narrow watch on her wrist. 'It's almost noon. Oughtn't we to be turning back?'

Dan just gave her a resigned look and waited with folded arms for her to make her next move. It was obvious she was going to have to go ashore one way or the other, and with an impatient sound she said:

'I suppose we might as well use the dinghy.'

'Okay.'

He released the cradle and the small craft splashed down on to the water, bobbing about unsteadily on the swell, making Julie feeling slightly sick just watching it.

She refused to accept the offer of Dan's hand to get into the boat, however. Touching him was apt to create difficulties she would rather avoid, so she lurched into the dinghy with more determination than grace. She saw to her relief that it had an outboard motor, and she waited impatiently for Dan to join her. The sooner they were ashore the better, as far as she was concerned, and she concentrated on the island, trying not to think about the heaving craft beneath her.

Dan climbed in easily, used to the unpredictability of the boat, and leaning over, pulled the cord that started the motor. It took a couple of jerks before it actually fired, however, and by the time they started out towards the shore Julie was feeling decidedly green.

'What's wrong?' Dan enquired, noticing her pale face. 'You're not feeling seasick, are you?' He grinned. 'You're probably hungry. Did you have any breakfast this morning?'

'You have no sympathy, do you?' she choked, turning away from him. 'No, as a matter of fact, I've had nothing since last night, but don't let it worry you!'

Dan said nothing more, and a few minutes later the dinghy grounded on the shingly shore. Julie got up at once, eager to get out on to dry land, and in so doing lost her balance. Her head was spinning, and groping helplessly for the side, she tumbled out into the shallows. Her jeans were soaked in seconds, and before she could pull herself upright Dan had vaulted out beside her and hauled her up into his arms.

'Stupid,' he muttered, swinging her off her feet, and she had no strength left to protest as he carried her up the beach. He set her down on the sand some distance from where he had beached the dinghy, then reached for the fastening of her jeans as she lay weakly back on her elbows.

'What do you think you're doing?' she demanded in horror, clutching at her waist, but he brushed her hands aside.

'Hold still,' he said, compelling the zip down and releasing the metal button. 'You can't lie around in wet clothes, but I'll go get you a spare pair of mine if you're so desperate.'

Julie's lips quivered. 'You have no right—'

'Don't I?' he asked, looking at her quizzically, and she had to tear her gaze away before she permitted something irrevocable to happen.

In actual fact, his hands on her body were a pleasurable experience, but she wondered bitterly how many girls he had undressed in this way. He was certainly adept at it, although perhaps she was being unjust. Jeans were jeans, no matter who was wearing them.

With the jeans removed, he stood up, looking down at her with disturbing eyes as he wrung them out. 'Well?' he said. 'How d'you feel? Do you want me to get you a sweater or something?'

'No.' Her eyes were sulky, and she was scooping up handfuls of sand, allowing the grains to filter through her fingers. She knew it would be silly to get dressed again now. She was just beginning to feel cool, and he had seen her anyway. 'I'm all right. Go and do what you have to. I'm fine here.'

Dan grimaced. 'I don't have anything to do,' he told her patiently. 'Come and swim! The water's fine.'

'You swim,' she retorted, not looking at him. 'I want to sunbathe. Or at least, that's all I intend to do. Until it's time for us to go back.'

Dan sighed. 'Look, it's more sensible to swim on an empty stomach, and as we'll be having lunch in a half hour—'

'Will we?'

'Julie, don't bait me,' he warned, an edge sharpening his tone. 'Now, do you walk into the water unaided, or do I carry you?'

She was on her feet in a second, brushing the sand from her thighs, gazing up at him in resentful silence, and with a shrug he left her. She watched him walk away, moving with the lithe fluidity that was so unusual in a man of his size and build, and her pulses quickened. There was a disruptive excitement in just being with him, she thought helplessly, but then she remembered Adam, and how concerned and angry he must be feeling, and the weakness left her.

She walked some distance along the beach before venturing into the water, but she might as well have saved herself the effort. Dan kept pace with her, several yards out from the shore, and when she waded into the water, he approached her with a purposeful crawl.

'Keep away from me!' she exclaimed, pursing her lips, but he only turned on to his back, kicking his legs lazily and making no attempt to do as she asked.

Shaking her head, she took the plunge, gulping as the cold water assaulted her overheated body. But it was delightful, and she couldn't remain angry for long when Dan started to fool around. He kept disappearing, surfacing right behind her so that she was startled into sudden flight. Then he would just sink below the waves for minutes at a time, and just as she was beginning to panic he would appear again, his grinning expression evidence of his awareness of her anxiety.

'Better?' he suggested, turning on to his back beside her and kicking water over her, and after a moment she nodded.

'I suppose so.'

'Aren't you enjoying yourself?'

'Maybe,' she shrugged. 'But I shouldn't be.'

'Why not?' His eyes had darkened. 'No, don't answer that. I don't want to hear it.'

Julie sighed. 'Won't your—your aunt wonder where you are?' she ventured, and he grinned.

'She knows exactly where I am,' he stated dryly. 'Well, maybe not the exact location, but she knows who I'm with.'

'How could she know that?' Julie frowned.

'Would you believe—I told her?'

'You mean—you mean—' Julie gazed at him incredulously. 'Why, you—you—'

'Race you to the shore!' he challenged laughingly, and needing something to expunge the frustration she was feeling, Julie lashed out at him angrily before threshing madly towards the beach.

She stumbled out on to the sand exhaustedly, and looked round for him with angry eyes. He was nowhere in sight, and she blinked and wrung out her hair, waiting for him to appear. He must have planned the whole trip, she thought resentfully, and if she could have handled the dinghy she would have set out for the yacht and left him to swim for it.

As the minutes passed, however, her anger quickly dissipated. Where was he? she wondered anxiously. Surely the blow she had delivered had not been that powerful. Even so, the doubts persisted, deepening as the water rippled shorewards without any sign of a swimmer's head.

'Dan!'

Her first attempt at calling his name was a tentative cry, barely reaching beyond the beach, and she repeated it a second and third time, projecting her voice a little further. Oh, please, she begged, let him be safe! She doubted she could bear it if anything had happened to him.

'Did I hear my name?'

The unexpected enquiry behind her brought her round with a start, her eyes widening in sudden relief at the sight of his familiar form. For a moment she gazed at him unguardedly, her feelings plain for anyone to see, and then anger banished all other emotions as she realised he had not *just* come out of the water.

'Where were you?' she gulped, her chin wobbling

ignominiously, and he gestured back towards the rocky slopes above the beach.

'I just wanted to see if you'd miss me,' he remarked, grinning irrepressibly, and she swung her fist against his chest in angry retaliation.

'You let me think you'd drowned!' she accused him, unable to keep the tremor out of her voice and all the humour drained out of his face.

'Hey,' he exclaimed disbelievingly, 'you were really worried, weren't you?' He shook his head, taking hold of her by the shoulders and staring down at her. 'Julie—honey! I wouldn't frighten you deliberately. Hell, I'm sorry. I'm a louse! I don't deserve for you to be concerned about me.'

'No, you don't,' she concurred with a sniff, and with a muffled oath he pulled her into his arms, pressing her close to him, and burying his face in the hollow between her neck and her shoulder.

'I wouldn't hurt you, Julie,' he groaned, and she realised he had no idea how much he had done so already. But that was not his fault. It was hers—for allowing herself to fall in love with him.

'Did—did you say something about—about lunch?' she got out jerkily, as the compulsive warmth of his body began to penetrate hers, spreading tentacles of flame along her veins and weakening her already strained resistance, and he sighed. She thought at first he was going to ignore her, but after a moment he lifted his head and presently he drew back to look at her.

'Lunch,' he said, and his eyes were narrowed and softly caressing. 'Okay, let's have lunch. We have plenty of time, don't we?'

CHAPTER EIGHT

THEY ate on the yacht, though not in the cabin as
Julie had expected. Dan installed her in a chair on the
afterdeck, and then he went below to prepare the food.
Julie felt a fraud, allowing him to do it, but she was
not sufficiently familiar with him to insist on partici-
pating, and only when the delightful smell of grilling
meat drifted up the steps did she venture to investigate.

Dan was at the stove, turning the succulent
hamburger steaks on the grid, and there were sesame
seed rolls and salad waiting on a tray. It made her
realise how hungry she was, and by now completely
at ease in the skimpy swimsuit, she crossed the floor
to stand watching him.

'Forgiven me?' he asked, without looking at her,
and she moved her shoulders in reluctant assent.

'Of course.'

'Of course?' His grey eyes met hers and she
coloured.

'Something smells good,' she said evasively, and
he turned back to what he was doing with more
enthusiasm.

They ate lunch on the afterdeck, seated across from
one another in the easy chairs, forking up pieces of
steak and salad, munching on the sesame rolls. Dan
had produced a bottle of red wine to drink with the
meal and it added to the flavour of the meat. It also
made Julie feel deliciously drowsy, and she relaxed

140

completely under its influence. It was impossible to sustain hostilities anyway in such idyllic surroundings, the boat rocking gently on its mooring, the sky an arc of blue above. So they talked, about anything and everything, and Julie discovered what an entertaining companion Dan could be when she was not trading insults with him. He had been so many places and done so many interesting things, and she was fascinated by his stories of gold mining in South Africa and drilling for oil in the icy wastes of Alaska.

'My father believes it's important to know something of the real world before entering the cloistered halls of banking,' he explained, with a wry grimace. 'He says it's no use handling money if you have no conception how it's made. He thinks there are too many people in finance who come to it cold—straight from business school—without any background knowledge. Economists deal with paper assets, they handle millions of dollars, but it's only paper money. Even the gold standard is a man-made institution. Gold itself is worthless—it doesn't have the properties of uranium or the cutting power of a diamond. But in 1812 the UK adopted it as a monetary system, and since then it's achieved international status, but what does it really mean? The ordinary man in the street isn't allowed to own gold in any quantity, there aren't even any gold coins any more, and even the standard itself is open to criticism. For one thing it makes it difficult for any single country to isolate its economy from depression or inflation in the rest of the world, and it's terribly easy to forget, when you're handling such enormous amounts of money, exactly whose sweat and toil have gone into making it.'

Julie smiled. 'So you did some sweating and toiling yourself?'

'You better believe it,' Dan grinned. 'I'm sorry if I'm boring you, but it's something I feel strongly about.'

'You're not boring me,' Julie protested vehemently. 'I'm fascinated, honestly. I didn't know there was so much to learn.'

'God!' Dan gave her an indulgent look. 'My father's going to love you. If he can get someone to listen to him, he's happy, and I don't know anyone who knows more about finance than he does.'

'Oh!'

Julie bent her head, disturbed by his careless statement. It was obvious he was speaking hypothetically. There was no earthly chance of her meeting his father, and she wished he had not said it. It destroyed the harmony they had achieved, and restored the obvious barriers between them.

'So, tell me about you,' he invited, after she had been silent for several minutes. 'Tell me how you've spent the last—what? Eighteen years?'

'Nineteen, actually,' admitted Julie in a low voice. 'Oh, I'm not very interesting, and I certainly haven't done any of the things you've done.'

'That's a relief,' he remarked dryly, and she felt a reluctant smile lifting her lips once again. 'Come on, Julie, tell me about your father. I want to know.'

Julie sighed. 'You said you knew. . .'

'I've heard the story. But I want you to tell it, the way it is.'

Julie put down her wine glass and lay back in her seat, studying the ovals of her toenails. 'Well,' she said slowly, 'he shot himself. He put a gun in his mouth and shot himself. That's it.'

'No, it's not.' Dan was serious now, leaning forward in his seat, knees apart, hands hanging loosely between. 'I want to know what was behind it. Where you were at the time. And what Price's part in it all was.'

Julie hesitated. The mention of Adam's name had reminded her of where she was and to whom she was speaking, but Dan's earnest expression dispelled her momentary reluctance.

'All right,' she said. 'I was at school, at a finishing school in France, when it happened. Adam brought me home.'

'And before that?'

Julie licked her lips. 'Well, as you probably know, my father and Adam were partners in a law firm. . .'

'Yes.'

'Daddy had originally been in partnership with the man who founded the firm, and when Mr Hollingsworth died Adam joined him. I suppose that was about—fifteen years ago now.'

'Go on.'

Julie frowned. 'Daddy used to deal with all the work concerning probate and the administration of deceased estates. He handled clients' investments, trusts, that sort of thing. Anyway. . .' She paused, composing her words carefully, 'when my mother was taken ill, there were apparently a lot of medical expenses. Daddy didn't have the money.' She took a deep breath. 'You don't need me to tell you what happened.'

'I guess he borrowed from clients' resources?'

'Not initially,' she confessed quietly. 'He—he borrowed what he could from the bank, and when that was overdrawn he went to a credit agency.'

'I see.'

Julie shook her head. 'I knew nothing about it, of course. I was only about seven at the time, and when Mummy died he sent me away to a convent school, and I only used to see him in the holidays, and not always then. It was Adam who came to speech days and sports days and replied to my letters.'

Dan hunched his shoulders. 'I guess that's what makes him think he has the right to look after you now.'

Julie shrugged. 'Adam was always very fond of me. Even when he and Daddy—what I mean is, he was always the same with me.' She caught her lower lip between her teeth. 'I think sometimes Daddy resented Adam's affection for me, but I don't think he really cared about anything after Mummy died,' she added, unable to disguise the break in her voice.

'Oh, honey. . .' Dan stretched across the space between them and captured her hand in both of his. 'Was it very bad?' He shook his head. 'I didn't mean to upset you, I just wanted you to talk about it. To get it out of your system.'

Julie bent her head. 'I'll never do that.'

'Why not? It's over.' Dan squeezed her fingers until they hurt. 'Baby, believe me, you have your own life to lead now. The past is over. Dead! And you can't resurrect it.'

Julie's faint smile revealed her lack of conviction in this statement, and as if realising she was becoming too morose, Dan stood up and pulled her up with him.

'Come on,' he said, releasing her almost immediately. 'We'll load the dishes in the washer and then we'll go ashore again. Okay?'

Julie acquiesced, as much from a desire to dispel the mood of dejection which was gripping her as from any obligation to obey him. For the present he had successfully banished any inclination to return to the hotel. Adam was at the hotel, and right now Adam represented too many things she wanted to forget. She refused to consider the eventual outcome of this reckless abduction. She would face that when she had to, but for now she wanted fun and freedom and escape—though from what she hardly knew.

Dan took his guitar ashore, and she stretched lazily on a towel beside him, enjoying the undemanding refuge of his music. It was so easy to forget time and consequence lying there, to lose oneself in abstract pleasure, and exist only for the moment. The only intruders were the wild geese who considered these islands exclusively theirs, and who uttered their mournful protest as they rose gracefully into the air.

After a while Dan put the guitar aside and relaxed beside her, closing his eyes against the unrelenting glare of the sun. Julie, already sleepy, felt her eyes closing, and for a time there was utter silence.

Julie stirred first, her skin protesting against the unremitting heat, and leaving Dan lying on the sand, she went to submerge herself in the cooling waters of the lake. It was a delightful release, and when she walked back up the beach she felt better than she had done for weeks.

Dan was still asleep, flat on his back, one arm raised to protect his face. He looked young and disturbingly attractive, and Julie felt her senses stir just looking at him. This was what he would look like in the mornings, she thought, picturing him in bed, in *her* bed, and she wrapped her arms about herself tightly, as if to ward off the dangers he represented.

But after a few moments she realised the futility of that and sank down beside him. Crossing her legs, she adjusted them to the lotus position, and then unwound herself again and rested back on her elbows. She was restless, and almost compulsively her gaze turned in Dan's direction.

The uplift of his arm had shifted the waistband of his shorts lower on his stomach, and she noticed how well the cuffs fitted his brown legs. They might have been made for him, she reflected reluctantly, her eyes moving up over the flat stomach to the waistband once more. There was a darker mark on his stomach, she noticed now, and leaning forward she realised it was the start of his scar. Although it had healed, there was still a puckering of the flesh around it, and her fingers moved almost involuntarily towards it, curious to see more.

'I said I'd show you if you wanted to see it,' Dan remarked huskily, and her hand was withdrawn without making contact.

'I—I was curious, that's all,' she explained, embarrassed at being caught out, but he only pushed the waistband lower until she could see the whole of the scar and the arrowing of hair below his navel.

'Ugly, isn't it?' he observed with a grimace. 'Scarred for life!'

Julie dragged her horrified gaze away, seeking the lazy indulgence of his, and his fingers reached up to curve around her nape, under the weight of her hair.

'Don't look so worried,' he taunted gently. 'It doesn't hurt. It's six or seven weeks since it happened. I'm not about to break open, you know.'

Julie shivered, but her eyes drifted irresistibly back to the scar. Then, almost involuntarily, she bent and put her lips to the narrow ridge of hard tissue than ran diagonally across his body, and felt his convulsive response.

'Julie,' he groaned, grasping a handful of her hair, and lifting her head up to his. 'Julie, have some sense!' he muttered hoarsely, but right then she didn't feel particularly sensible. His lips parted almost tentatively beneath the tremulous exploration of her mouth, and she knew this was what she had been waiting for.

It wasn't enough just to look at Dan. She wanted to touch him. She wanted him to touch her. And there was an aching need inside her that she sensed only he could fulfil. She wanted to be close to him like this, closer than even his shorts or her bikini would allow, and her legs curled seductively between his, unconsciously alluring in her search for satisfaction.

'God, Julie,' he muttered, rolling her over on to her back and covering her damp body with his. 'Let me go and cool off in the water or I won't be responsible for the consequences.'

'Isn't it good?' she breathed, her silky arms entwined around his neck, and he took possession of her mouth with hard urgency before pressing himself away from her.

She watched him plunge into the lake, the ripples his entry made spreading unevenly along the sand. He wasn't visible for several seconds, but when he did emerge, he was several yards out from the shore, swimming strongly against the current.

With a sigh Julie sat up, realising dully that already the sun was sinking in the west, and soon they would have to go back. This had been a day out of time, but it was almost over, and in a very short while she would have to see Adam and explain where she had been and why. Tomorrow she was leaving, and eventually she would have to go back to England and the trailing threads of the life she had left behind. There was no point in railing against an established fact. It was there. It was irrevocable. And she had to accept it.

She had gathered the towels and Dan's guitar into the dinghy by the time he returned, and he gave himself a quick rub down before piloting them back to the yacht. Once on board she expected him to start the powerful engines, but he didn't, he went below, and she fretted about on deck waiting for him to reappear.

He didn't, however, and beginning to feel slightly chilled in her damp bikini, she ventured down the steps. To her astonishment, she found Dan heating soup on the stove, dressed now in the jeans and sweat-shirt he had been wearing earlier. He was aware of her approach, and noticing the goosebumps on her skin, he said:

'If you're cold, get dressed. The soup won't be long.'

She hesitated, tempted to ask when they were leaving, and then bit on her tongue. She would know soon enough, and the idea of getting dressed and sharing a bowl of soup with Dan was too attractive a prospect to spoil.

She found her vest and jeans in the cabin where she had left them, and quickly towelled herself completely dry. Her hair was still damp, of course, but she secured it with a piece of string she found in one of the drawers, and emerged feeling infinitely warmer.

Dan had laid two places on the table in the cabin, and she paused a moment to admire the silver cutlery and slim crystal glasses. Everything was suited to its surroundings, she thought, not least Dan himself.

As well as the soup, there was some cold ham and chipped potatoes, or crisps, as Julie was used to calling them. There were more of the sesame rolls, and a bowl of salad, and another bottle of wine, white this time.

'It will be dark soon,' she ventured, as he joined her on the banquette, and he nodded his head. Since that disturbing moment on the beach he had said almost nothing to her, and her skin prickled at the awareness of feelings suppressed.

'Have some wine,' he said, uncorking the bottle, and she held the delicate glass for him to fill. 'It's hock,' he added, as her tongue circled her lips in anticipation, and her eyes smiled at him across the rim as she tasted its slightly dry flavour.

'It's delicious,' she averred, in answer to his unspoken question. 'But so was the wine at lunchtime,' She paused. 'Everything's been—wonderful.'

Dan averted his gaze and concentrated on spooning soup into his mouth, and Julie put her glass down and applied herself to the food. She was hungry, but the prospect of what was ahead of her tended to inhibit her appetite, and after a few spoonfuls she had had enough.

If Dan noticed that her dish was almost full when he returned it to the sink, he said nothing, and she endeavoured to make a better effort with the ham. But it was no good. Her throat seemed to close up every time she allowed herself to think that this time tomorrow she would be aboard the 747, and she pushed her plate aside with a feeling of desperation.

'Don't you like it, or aren't you hungry?' Dan enquired at last, and she gave him a sideways look before getting up from the banquette and wandering aimlessly round the cabin.

'We ought to be going back,' she said, gripping the edge of the sink and staring broodingly through the porthole at the rocky headland. It wasn't what she wanted to say, but it had to be said, and maybe she would find it easier once it was over. 'We have a long way to go, don't we?'

There was silence for a few minutes, and then Dan said quietly: 'Are you so desperate to leave me?'

Julie swung round, still holding on to the sink behind her. 'That's not the point, is it?' she demanded, her face flushed. 'Oh, I know I haven't any room for complaint regarding your behaviour. Apart from the fact that you tricked me into coming with you, you— you've behaved commendably. I know I haven't. But you—I've never denied I find you—attractive.'

'Oh, Julie. . .' Dan spoke slowly, shaking his head as he did so. 'Stop trying to find excuses. We're good together, we knew that before today.' He regarded her with lazy indulgence. 'But it's more, isn't it? I think we both know that today can't end. Not in the way you're envisaging anyway.'

Julie stared at him, her lips parting anxiously, and he got up from the banquette and came towards her. His feet were bare, but he was still several inches taller than she was, and in the lengthening shadows of the cabin he seemed absurdly menacing.

'Dan. . .' she murmured, putting out a hand as if to ward him off, but he just used it to pull her towards him, hauling her close into his arms. 'Dan, don't touch me. . .'

'Touch you?' he groaned, burying his face in her hair. 'Julie, I've got to touch you. I've got to hold you.' He lifted his head to look down at her. 'I love you, Julie, I love you!'

'You—love—me?'

It was a disbelieving squeak, and for a moment, humour deepened the lines beside his eyes. 'Yes, I love you' he repeated, probing the contours of her lips with his thumb. 'I love you, and I want to make love to you.' His eyes darkened passionately. 'I want to be part of you, Julie. Don't tell me you don't want that too.'

His husky confession had left her weak and confused and totally incapable of fighting him. When his mouth found hers with sensual sureness, she could only cling to him urgently, returning his kisses in helpless abandon. All day she had been aware of the tumultuous craving inside her, and his lips ignited the flame she had tried to subdue. Released from the bonds of inhibition, it burned like a forest fire, eating away her resistance, engulfing her in a blaze of passion. If Dan had had any doubt about her feelings, they were consumed by the eager submission of silken arms and seeking lips, and his own emotions ran wildly in concert with hers.

Swinging her off her feet, he carried her through the twin-bedded cabin to the double bunk in the master cabin. With his mouth still clinging to hers, he deposited her on the damask cover and subsided on top of her, the muscular weight of his body a potent intoxicant to her already enflamed senses.

Kisses were rapidly becoming not enough, and with a groan he drew back to tug the sweatshirt over his head, exposing the brown expanse of his chest. Then, when his fingers would have gone to the belt of his jeans, she forestalled him, unfastening the buckle herself, holding his eyes with hers as she did so.

'Julie,' he moaned, half in protest, but she seemed to know instinctively how to please him, and pleasure overcame all else.

With quickening passion Dan undressed her, his mouth hard and persuasive on hers when she felt the muscled hardness of him against her for the first time. It was a disturbing experience, but wonderfully satisfying, though her face flamed when he drew back to look at her.

'Don't be coy,' he said huskily, when she withdrew her arm from around his neck to cover herself. 'We have no secrets from one another. And you're much better to look at than I am.'

'I—I wouldn't say that,' she breathed, drawing his mouth back to hers, and he crushed her beneath him as the urgency of his own needs made anything else impossible.

It was odd, but she wasn't afraid.

Years ago, in the convent, when she had heard girls whispering about the things that happened between a man and a woman, she had been. Even the practicality of biology lessons had not persuaded her that anyone could find enjoyment in such pursuits, and she had determinedly put such thoughts from her mind.

Even later, at the finishing school in France, she had felt apprehensive of that side of marriage, but Adam had always been so retiring in terms of a physical relationship that she had assumed she would get used to it when she had to.

But since meeting Dan, all those preconceived notions had gone out the window. She had suspected from the first time he held her in his arms that a girl might feel differently with him, and she was right. Being close to somebody, becoming a part of them, was not something one contrived. With the right person, it was a natural extension of their love for one another, and with Dan she wanted to experience everything. It wasn't enough to lie in his arms—she needed to know all there was to know about him. . .

It happened so naturally that afterwards she scarcely remembered the sharp stab of pain that heralded his invasion of her innocence. The sensual possession of his lips left her weak with longing, and she instinctively arched herself against him, inviting the penetrating thrust of his body.

But even then, she had had no conception of how it might be. Her timid expectations had been limited by a physical reality, and she had had no idea of the sensations Dan could arouse inside her. She had wanted to please him, to give him pleasure, to drive away the look of strain he had worn when he left her on the beach; but instead he was pleasuring her, exciting her, invoking feelings that demanded a full and consummate expression. When the crescendo began to build inside her, she heard the moans she was emitting and hardly recognised herself. Her nails were digging into Dan's shoulders, raking the smooth brown skin, and when the release came she would not let him go. Instead, she wound herself about him, her mouth clinging to his, and minutes sank into oblivion as the world slowly steadied and righted itself.

Dan lifted his head with reluctance some minutes later, his eyes still dark and glazed with emotion. He looked down at her intently, just visible in the fading light, and then he said huskily: 'It was good, wasn't it?'

Julie reached up to touch his cheek with her fingers, and when he turned his lips into her palm she whispered: 'I love you, Dan. But you know, don't you? I'm not very good at hiding my feelings.'

'Thank God for that!' he murmured fervently, and took possession of her mouth again, tenderly now, and eloquent with emotion.

Some minutes later he aroused himself sufficiently to add gently: 'In answer to your question, I did suspect you didn't altogether object to my attentions.' He gave a wry smile. 'Even though you have given me some bad moments.'

'I have?' She brushed the thick swathe of dark hair back from his forehead with soft fingers and he nodded.

'Like at the party, for instance,' he averred huskily. 'When Corinne broke in on us. I didn't sleep well last night, Julie. I didn't sleep well at all.'

'But you will tonight,' she murmured breathily, and he nodded.

'With you,' he said, his voice deepening. 'We'll go back in the morning, hmm? Then we'll tell them we're going to be married.'

'Married?' Julie gazed up at him.

'Don't sound so surprised,' he teased. 'Or have you had lots of lovers?'

She flushed. 'You know that's not true.'

'Mmm—mmm.' He grinned with satisfaction. Then he bent his head to kiss her once more. 'But you will marry me, won't you?' he breathed, against her lips. 'Just as soon as I can get a licence?'

Julie caught her breath. 'Oh, Dan, you know I want to, but—'

'But what?' He propped himself up on one elbow to look down at her. Then his expression hardened. 'Don't tell me you're still going to marry Price?'

'No.' She sighed. 'No, of course not—' She broke off as he stroked her lips with his tongue. 'But Dan, your aunt—your family—'

'—will love you as I do,' he interrupted her roughly, and there was silence for a while as he explored her mouth with his own. 'Julie, I've never asked any girl to marry me before. Don't tell me no.'

'Oh, I'm not,' she confessed eagerly. 'Of course I'll marry you, Dan. Tomorrow, if it was possible. Only—only please—'

'What?' His smoky eyes were narrowed.

'—make love to me again!' she finished huskily, and with a muffled groan, he complied.

They drank the remains of the wine at midnight, curled up in the comfortable double berth. They had

had a shower together earlier, and now Julie was pleasantly sleepy and utterly at peace.

'I'm so glad you kidnapped me,' she murmured, burrowing against him, and Dan relaxed on his back, gazing contentedly up at the ceiling.

'You didn't think so this morning,' he mocked, slanting a look down at her, his expression indulgent in the mellow lamplight, and Julie pummelled her fists against him, pressing her nose against his chest.

'I guess I was afraid of you—or of myself,' she admitted soberly. 'I was afraid to get involved. I was afraid of being hurt.'

'And did I hurt you?' he asked, rolling over on to his stomach beside her, and she wound her arms around his neck.

'Some,' she confessed softly. 'Oh, Dan, this is real, isn't it? I'm not going to wake up and find it's all just a dream, am I?'

'Nope.' He stroked her hair back from her face with tender fingers. 'You're stuck with me,' he conceded gently. 'Now, do you want any more wine, or can I put out the light?'

'Put out the light,' repeated Julie happily. 'Hmm, that sounds nice. Put out the light, darling.'

Dan was not proof against such endearments, and in the ensuing darkness his mouth sought and found hers with increasing urgency.

CHAPTER NINE

THE radio telephone disturbed them at six in the morning.

Julie awakened from a sound slumber to find Dan already stirring, squinting at the dial of his watch with impatient eyes. It was already light outside, but the drawn curtains made the cabin shadowy, and it took some seconds for him to focus. Then he groaned as he pushed back the sheet that was all that covered them and thrust his long legs out of bed.

'What is it?' Julie asked drowsily, not recognising the distinctive buzz, and Dan paused a moment to bestow a warm kiss on her parted lips.

'Just the telephone,' he murmured, tucking the covers about her again and reaching for his jeans. 'I won't be long.'

She watched him walk through the cabin beyond to the living area, zipping himself into his jeans as he went, and a feeling of cold apprehension gripped her. She guessed only his family knew how to reach him, and her lips felt dry as she passed her tongue over them. After all, the Leytons must be wondering where Dan was and whether he was all right, and her conscience stung her at the realisation of how little thought she had given to whether anyone might be worried about her.

It seemed ages before he came back and by then she was sitting up in the middle of the wide mattress, the sheet tucked anxiously under her chin. With her silky hair loose about her shoulders, she was unknowingly provocative, and Dan's eyes darkened as they met the troubled depths of hers.

'Who was it?' she asked, gazing up at him, and unable to resist the artless temptation she represented, Dan sank down on to the bed and tugged the protective sheet aside.

'Would you believe—Aunt Anthea?' he murmured, against the creamy flesh of her breast, and she slid her fingers into his hair to pull his head back and look at him.

'Yes?'

Dan shrugged, his eyes drowsy with emotion. 'Can't it wait?' he suggested huskily, seeking the curve of her ear, and although she wanted to give in she had to know the worst.

'Dan, please. . .'

'Okay, okay.' He drew back from her completely and took a deep breath. 'Apparently your friend— friends—have been concerned about you.'

Julie's brows drew together. 'Do you mean Pam and David? Or Adam?'

Dan shrugged, his shoulders smooth and bronzed in the early morning light. 'I'd guess the latter, but I don't know.'

'So what happened?'

Dan sighed. 'Well, when you didn't get back by midnight, he—they—phoned Forest Bay.'

'Oh, *lord*!'

Dan shook his head. 'No sweat. Max told them you'd be okay with me.'

Julie could imagine how Adam—*how all of them*—

would have taken that. 'Is that all?'

'No.' Dan pushed a weary hand into his hair. 'They phoned again around two a.m. and insisted Max got in touch with us—Brad must have told them about the radio link. But Max refused to phone at that hour of the night, so Anthea waited until it was light and—that's it.'

'Oh, Dan!' Julie sat cross-legged facing him, anxiety darkening her delicate features, like a slim naiad in the pale illumination filtering through the curtains, and she felt his senses stirring urgently. 'We must go back.'

'I know it,' he said huskily. But not yet. Not yet—'

It was a little after nine when the *Spirit of Atlantis* sailed in to the mooring below Kawana Point. Dan was seated at the wheel, with Julie on the seat beside him, her arm around his neck and looped to the other arm that circled his chest.

In spite of the apprehension she felt at seeing Adam again, she was supremely content in the knowledge of Dan's love for her, and he was already talking of taking her to New York to meet his parents. So far as he was concerned, he saw no reason why they shouldn't be married almost immediately. He didn't like bringing her back to the hotel, and he showed the first trace of anger towards her when, after he had manoeuvred the yacht into the marina, she said she would rather speak to Adam alone.

'Why?' he demanded, his expressive eyes steel grey in his tanned face, and she almost succumbed. He looked tired this morning, she thought, smoothing back the hair from his temple, and then smiled when she recalled the cause of his weariness. 'What's so funny?' he added harshly, his hands hard on her hips, and she quickly put her fingers across his lips.

'Darling, I was just thinking how handsome your haggard look is,' she protested, evading his urgent response. 'When will I see you again? Later this morning? This afternoon?'

Dan sighed. 'You'd better make it this afternoon,' he said heavily, 'if you insist on going through with this alone. I'll spend the time making the arrangements for our trip to New York. I guess you don't have a visa, do you?'

Julie shook her head, and with a groan he gathered her close to him again. 'You won't let Price change your mind, will you?' he muttered. 'I think I'd go out of my mind if you left me now.'

'Oh, Dan. . .' Julie's voice was shaken, too. 'These last twenty-four hours have been the most wonderful in my life! I love you. How could I change that?'

Dan let her go unwillingly, retaining a hold on her hand as she prepared to step ashore. 'I'll come by after lunch,' he said. 'We'll spend the afternoon on the lake. At least that way I can be sure of having you all to myself.'

Julie glanced at him adoringly, aware of the meaning behind those simple words, and he took the opportunity to kiss her once again. 'I love you,' he said, in a strangled tone, and then turned away as she stepped on to the jetty.

Julie guessed the yacht had been sighted coming into the marina, but there was no one to meet her. She did gain a casual salutation here and there from the yachtsmen who were staying at the hotel and who were down attending to their craft, but there was no sign of David or Adam, and Pam was no doubt involved with her regular morning routine.

She was halfway up the steps when she saw Brad lounging at the top of the flight waiting for her. He was propped against the rail, and as she came abreast of him he offered her an awkward grin.

'Hi!'

'Hi,' she answered, glad to break the ice with him. 'Isn't it a lovely—'

'Mr Price is real mad with you!' the boy broke in urgently. 'And Mom and Dad, too. Where've you been? Did you spend the night on the yacht?'

Julie sighed. 'Yes.'

'With Dan?'

'Yes.'

'Gosh!' Brad shook his head at this, and she realised that for the moment he was more envious of her good fortune than anything else. 'I bet that was terrific!'

Julie smiled. 'It was rather.'

Brad gazed at her admiringly, then shoved his hands into the pockets of his jeans. 'You know, I'd really like to do that,' he exclaimed, entirely diverted now at the prospect. 'I've never slept on board a boat before. Did you have meals, too? There's a proper stove, isn't there, and a freezer—'

'That's enough, Brad!' David's brusque tones interrupted them, and Julie saw that Pam's husband had approached them without either of them being aware of it. 'Go find Pietro. Tell him I want some more cases of beer up from the cellar.'

Julie stopped Brad, however, before he could dart away, taking hold of his firm young arm and saying gently: 'You know, I might be able to arrange something, about the yacht, I mean. If your parents don't object.'

Brad gulped. 'Hey, do you mean it?'

'I said that's enough, Brad,' David intervened once again. 'There'll be no yachting trips for you. Julie's going away. She won't be able to arrange anything.'

Julie let the boy go, as much to save him the humiliation of arguing with his father as through any desire to protect him from what she had to say. But as he charged away across the square she turned to David fearlessly and in cutting tones she said:

'I think you've got it wrong, David. I shan't be leaving, after all. Not crossing the Rockies, anyway. I'm going to marry Dan Prescott.'

David could not have looked more stunned, but he recovered quickly, and gave an impatient shrug. 'Perhaps you ought to wait and see what Adam has to say about that,' he muttered, indicating the hotel behind them. 'Come along. He's in the. apartment. He's waiting to speak with you.'

Julie sighed. 'He won't make me change my mind, David. It's quite made up already. And nothing he— or any of you—can say will alter it.'

Pam met them in the reception hall, her face flushed from the kitchen, and she avoided her husband's eyes as she asked if Julie was all right.

'I'm fine.' Julie returned the kiss the other girl offered her with warmth. 'Honestly, Pam,' she insisted, looking compassionately at her friend. 'I've never been so happy in my life.'

'What—what do you—'

'Don't you think we ought to be saying all this in front of Adam?' David suggested curtly, gesturing towards the door to their apartment. 'He is most involved, isn't he?'

'I just wanted to—'

'I think you've done enough, Pamela,' her husband cut in coldly. 'If you hadn't filled Julie's head—'

'No, that's not true!' Julie couldn't let Pam take the blame. 'David, I was attracted to Dan from the minute I first saw him. He knew that, and so did I. I've just been—fighting it, that's all.'

'You mean—he cares about you?' Pam stared at her in astonishment, and Julie nodded.

'He wants to marry me,' she said gently. 'Honestly. We're going to New York tomorrow or the day after so that I can meet his parents.'

'Oh, Julie!'

Pam was obviously overcome, but her husband only flung open their living room door and urged both girls inside without making any comment. His face was grim, and Julie passed him with a feeling of resignation.

Adam was standing by the window, staring out broodingly at the tennis courts where a good-natured mixed doubles was taking place amid gales of laughter. He turned at their entrance, however, and the pitying expression on his face aroused a curious fluttery feeling inside her. In a light grey lounge suit, he looked austere after the casual attire normally worn around the hotel, and she dropped the jacket she was carrying, deciding it didn't really matter what he thought of her vest and jeans now.

'Good morning, Julie,' he greeted her, almost as if he hadn't been up half the night trying to discover her whereabouts. 'I'm pleased to see you're obviously unharmed.'

His severe tone made David shift awkwardly from one foot to the other, and after giving Julie an assessing look he turned to his wife. 'I think we ought to leave them to it Pam,' he said abruptly. 'After all, now that we know Julie's safe, it's really not our affair.'

Pam looked reluctant to leave and truthfully Julie would have been glad of her support, but she could see how difficult it was for them, and with a smile she said:

'I'll see you later, Pam. We can talk then.'

'All right.' Pam made an offhand movement of her shoulders. 'If—er—if you need me, Julie, just give a call.'

Julie appreciated the gesture, and after they had gone she sought refuge in helping herself to some coffee from the tray on the bureau. Then, when it was impossible to continue avoiding the inevitable, she said:

'I'm sorry, Adam. I'm sorry you were worried about me, and I'm sorry this had to happen.'

Adam folded his hands behind his back. 'Brad told us where you'd gone, of course.'

'I guessed he would.' Julie took a nervous mouthful of her coffee. 'I'm sorry.'

Adam shrugged, apparently as calm and unflappable as ever. 'It's over now. I just hope it's brought you to your senses.'

Julie's cup clattered on to the tray. 'What do you mean?'

'Isn't it obvious?' Adam spread an expressive hand.

'I'm not naïve, Julie. I can see what's happened between you two. And I can't deny a certain amount of—irritation, that things had to go so far. But,' he hastened on as she would have interrupted him, 'perhaps you needed the experience. Perhaps you needed to be brought face to face with reality. Obviously, my words on the matter had little effect, but it must be apparent to you now the kind of man you're dealing with—'

'Adam, it wasn't—it *isn't*—like that!' Julie tried to explain. 'We—we love one another, Dan and I. He—he wants to marry me.'

'Oh, does he?' Adam did not sound at all surprised, and Julie wondered with a sense of bafflement what she had to say to disconcert him. 'And what does his family have to say about that?'

'I—we—don't know, do we?' Julie shook her head. 'I'm sorry, Adam. I know this must come as a great shock to you, but I—I am going to marry him. I'm going to meet his parents within the next few days.'

'Really?' Adam's lip curled. 'I shouldn't be too hopeful of that, if I were you.'

'Why not?' Julie stared at him.

'Simply that Anthea Leyton assured me last night that there was not the slightest chance of Dan marrying anyone but his cousin. His *step*-cousin, that is. Corinne. You may remember, you met her at—'

'Dan's not going to marry Corinne!' Julie's tone rang with conviction. 'Why, he doesn't even like her!'

'Liking is not a necessary attribute to marriage,' retorted Adam calmly. 'Suitability; convenience; *expediency*. These are the factors people like the Prescotts and the Leytons take into account.'

Julie squared her shoulders. 'You're wrong.'

'I know these people, Julie.'

'Well, even if you're right about what Anthea Leyton told you, you're wrong about Dan and me.' Julie took a deep breath. 'I realise this must be distressing for you, Adam, but you wouldn't want to marry me, would you, knowing I loved someone else?'

Adam hesitated, his brows drawing together across the narrow bridge of his nose. Then he came towards her. 'Julie,' he said, placing his hands on her shoulders, 'I know how you feel, believe me. And I believe you when you say you love this man. But he's not worthy of you—'

'Don't say that.' Julie twisted away from him. 'Dan's the most marvellous—the most sensitive man I've ever known.'

'And how many men have you known, Julie?' asked Adam quietly. 'A handful, that's all.'

'You expected me to marry you, knowing the same,' she countered, and Adam sighed.

'How long have we known one another, Julie? Fifteen years? A little different from three—maybe four weeks, isn't it?'

'I know Dan,' she insisted.

'You know what he's told you,' corrected Adam evenly. 'You don't know his home, his background—'

'I intend to.'

'And this is what he intends as well?'

'Yes.'

Adam shook his head. 'You know what I think? I think he realised the kind of—fanciful, romantic girl you are. I think he knew that you'd never agree to an—affair. There had to be something more. Something concrete, for you to build your hopes and dreams upon. So he came up with this idea of marriage—'

'That's not true!' Julie's eyes were wide and indignant. 'You don't know how it was. You have no idea. If—if Dan had wanted an affair, he—he could have had one.'

Adam's lips thinned. 'What are you saying?'

Julie flushed. 'I'm saying that—that it was—Dan who held back.' She sighed. 'And he didn't ask me to marry him—before. It was after.'

Adam showed the first signs of crumbling dignity. 'You don't expect me to believe that?'

'It's the truth.' Julie pressed her palms together. 'Oh, Adam, I don't want to hurt you. I don't want to lose your friendship, but you have to believe this is the most wonderful thing that's ever happened to me.'

'And what about his feelings when he discovers your father took his own life?'

Julie bent her head. 'He knows.'

'He knows?'

'Yes. I told him.'

'I see.' Adam was finding it difficult now to maintain his air of detachment. 'But no one else knows, do they? Not his aunt and uncle, or his parents?'

'I suppose not.' Julie felt a faint twinge of unease. 'But if Dan doesn't care—'

'Oh, Julie. . .' Adam seemed to recover a little of his composure. 'What an innocent you are, aren't you?'

There was nothing to say to that, and with a helpless movement of her shoulders she would have left him then had not Adam chosen to ask one last question.

'Your plans?' he said. 'Am I permitted to know what you intend to do now?'

Julie turned, her tongue moistening her upper lip. 'Dan's coming back this afternoon. He—well, he's making arrangements for us to fly to New York, so that I can meet his parents.'

'I see,' Adam nodded. 'This afternoon. Very well, I'll delay making any decision about my own arrangements until tomorrow.'

Julie didn't know why, but she was apprehensive of his consideration. It was as if his concern for her weakened her belief in what Dan had told her, and she didn't want to feel this sense of marking time.

'There's no need,' she said now, forcing a note of lightness into her voice. 'I—we—we'll probably be leaving for New York tomorrow. There's no need for you to delay your trip because of me.'

'But I want to,' said Adam firmly. 'It occurs to me that Prescott might well be leaving for New York tomorrow. But whether you will be with him or not. . .'

Julie didn't wait to hear the end of his supposition. Snatching up her jacket, she left the room and stood for several seconds in the hall outside, trying to recover the feeling of conviction she had had when she came here.

Pam was looking out for her when she crossed the reception hall, and realising she owed it to her friend to explain, Julie followed her into the almost empty dining room.

'I've caused a lot of trouble, haven't I?' she said ruefully. 'Is David very angry?'

Pam grimaced. 'He's just suspicious-minded,' she declared, drawing Julie down into the chair opposite. 'Now, tell me: has Dan really asked you to marry him?'

'Really,' said Julie, and wondered why it didn't sound as convincing as it had. 'Is that so unbelievable?'

'No.' Pam sounded defensive. 'Why should it be?'

'Oh, I don't know. . .' Julie propped her head on her knuckles. 'Adam seems to think so.'

'Well, he would, wouldn't he?' suggested Pam reasonably. 'Mind you, I don't think he was so sure of himself last night.'

'No?'

'No.' Pam shook her head. 'We think he thought you might have eloped together. He was pretty sick, I can tell you.'

'Sick?' Julie stared at her friend. 'I can't believe it.'

'I know. He seems so emotionless, doesn't he? But you know, there are emotions there—beneath the surface.' Pam hesitated. 'Quite honestly, Julie, I'm glad you're not going to marry him—'

'Because he's too old—I know!' Julie humoured her, but Pam gestured her into an unwilling silence.

'No,' the older girl insisted, 'it's something else. Something I can't really explain. A—a kind of—gut feeling.'

'Oh, Pam!'

'No, listen to me. I know what I'm talking about. I don't think your Mr Price is half as—as nice as you think him.'

'Pam, he's been like a father to me—'

'That's just it.' Pam pressed her palms on the table. 'He's like a father, but he's not. He wants you, Julie—'

'I know that.'

'—and I think he means to have you, no matter what.'

'Oh, honestly!' Julie was staring at her friend impatiently now. 'You're letting your imagination run away with you, Pam. Of course Adam wants me. He hasn't made a secret of it.'

'And did your father approve?' asked Pam urgently, then put her hand across the table to grip Julie's arm sympathetically. I'm sorry. I shouldn't have asked that.'

'Why not?' Julie looked at her squarely. 'I can talk about it now. I—Dan asked me about it, and I told him.'

'That's good.' Pam was approving. 'So—did your father want you to marry Adam?'

Julie hesitated. 'I think so. He never said he didn't.'

'But did you discuss it?'

'No—o.' Julie was trying to remember what her father had said about Adam. 'I think he just took it for granted. As Adam did—as *I* did.'

'Mmm.' Pam sounded thoughtful. 'I wonder.'

'What do you wonder?'

Pam shrugged. 'I'm not sure. I just wish your father was still alive, that's all.'

'So do I!' Julie spoke fervently, and for a few moments there was silence between them.

They were still sitting there, each involved with their own thoughts, when David came striding into the room. His square-cut features were set in dour lines, but they lightened somewhat when he saw Julie.

'The phone,' he said brusquely, approaching their table. 'You're wanted on the phone, Julie. I think it's Prescott.'

'Oh!' Julie sprang up from her seat and stood for a moment looking at him. 'I—where can I take it?'

'Go into the office,' directed David shortly. 'I'll wait here until you're finished.'

'Thanks.'

With an apologetic smile that encompassed both of them, Julie fled across the dining room, hurrying into the small office and closing the door firmly behind her. Then, controlling the unsteady tremor of her hand, she lifted the receiver David had left lying on his desk.

'H-hello?'

'Julie!'

Dan's voice was so endearingly familiar that she sank down weakly on to a corner of the desk, grasping the receiver tightly in her fingers. 'Dan? Oh, Dan, I'm so glad you called!'

'Why? What's wrong?' Almost intuitively he sensed her anxiety, and she had to force herself not to blurt the whole story of the morning's events into his waiting ear. It could wait until later. He had not rung to hear her troubles—particularly not when she had prevented him from accompanying her.

'Oh, nothing,' she managed now, hiding the tension she was feeling. 'W-why did you ring?'

'Would you believe to hear your voice?' he asked huskily, and when she didn't immediately respond he added: 'No, actually, it wasn't just for that. Julie, I've got to leave for New York this afternoon. I won't be able to keep our date after all.'

Julie heard what he had to say, but she couldn't believe it. Dan? Leaving for New York? Without her? There had to be some mistake. But there wasn't. The words had been said, and everything Adam had hinted washed over her in humiliating detail.

'Julie? Julie, did you hear what I said?'

She heard his words through the mists of disbelief, and realising he must never know the blow he had dealt her, she summoned all her fortitude to say: 'I heard.'

'Julie!' Dan's voice was low now, and filled with the impatience she remembered so well. 'You don't imagine I planned this, do you?'

Julie took a deep breath. 'P-planned what?' she got out jerkily, and heard the oath he muttered half under his breath.

'Julie, my father is not well. I *have* to go, do you understand? It's not a social visit.'

His father was *ill*? Julie absorbed this without conviction. She could imagine Adam's reaction to that. And why not? It had certainly come at a most convenient time.

'I'm sorry,' she said now, stiffly, but she sensed he was not satisfied with her answer and his next words confirmed it.

'What has Price been saying to you?' he demanded. 'I knew he'd try to poison your mind against me. You don't believe me, do you? You think this is some clever ploy arranged by my aunt and my father to get me away from Forest Bay, from the lake, from *you*!'

'And isn't it?'

Julie heard herself asking the words and heard his angry denial. 'No, goddammit,' he snapped. 'I wouldn't do that. I love you, Julie. But I can't help wondering what kind of love you feel for me that can be put in jeopardy with so little provocation!'

Julie gasped. 'That's not fair—'

'And is it fair to convict me without any evidence? To take another man's word before mine?'

'No, but—'

'Either you believe me or you don't.'

'Dan, Adam says you're going to marry Corinne.'

'Do you believe it?'

'I. . .I didn't. . .'

'Past tense?'

'I want to believe you, Dan.'

'Then do it.' He sighed. 'Julie, this is a hell of a time to do this to me!'

'Oh, Dan. . .'

'I have to go. I'm flying from Barrie in less than an hour to connect with a flight to Kennedy, and I don't have time to come see you.'

'It's all right.' Somehow Julie managed to squash her fears. I—when will you be back?'

'Tomorrow, the day after—how can I be sure!' Dan sounded distrait. 'Wait for me, Julie. Don't let anyone persuade you otherwise. Promise me!'

Julie licked her dry lips. 'I—I'll wait,' she agreed huskily. 'I'll wait. But please—don't make me wait too long. . .'

Putting down the receiver was the hardest thing she had ever done, and even after the bell had rung signifying the connection had been broken, she sat for several minutes more just staring at the grey instrument. Then, when it became obvious that she couldn't stay in David's office any longer, she rose from the desk and let herself out of the room.

She didn't want to have to explain what had happened to Pam, but she had no alternative. The Galloways were waiting to hear what Dan had had to say, and she couldn't avoid the inevitable. However, she refused to let them see how shattered she was feeling, and she adopted a confident manner as she rejoined them in the restaurant.

'Dan's father's been taken ill,' she exclaimed, assuming an anxious tone. 'Isn't that a shame? Just at this time. Dan's terribly upset.'

Pam exchanged a glance with her husband, then said sympathetically: 'What rotten luck! Is it serious? Does this mean you won't be going to New York after all?'

Belatedly, Julie remembered she had not asked exactly what was wrong with Lionel Prescott, and flushing a little she avoided a direct answer. '*I* shan't be going to New York,' she replied, endeavouring to keep her tone light. 'Not yet, anyway. Dan has to go, of course. It is his father, after all.'

'Of course,' echoed Pam, but there was another of those significant exchanges with her husband, which Julie recognised as a plea for sympathy. 'Oh, well. . .' she continued. 'That means we'll be able to keep you for a little bit longer, doesn't it?'

It was Adam Julie dreaded to face, and the encounter came at lunchtime. She had had to go into the dining room to take her meal. Anything else would have prompted the suspicion that all was not as it should be, and she wanted to allay those kind of doubts. So she took her seat as usual, ordered an omelette and a side salad, then started nervously when Adam came to take the seat opposite.

'You don't mind if I join you, do you, Julie?' he enquired, pulling out the chair, and she shook her head quickly as he sat down. 'So,' he went on, 'they tell me the spare ribs are very good here. What would you recommend?'

Julie shrugged. 'I don't know your preference, do I?' she returned shortly.

'I think you do,' he averred, but he let it go. 'What have you ordered? Perhaps our tastes concur.'

'I'm just having an omelette,' said Julie, shaking out her napkin. 'And I know you don't like them.'

'Ah, you know so much about me, don't you, Julie?' he remarked, leaning back in his chair. 'My tastes in food, in clothes, in hotels—in women—'

'Please, Adam—'

'—and I know you,' he finished dryly. 'I know when you're happy and sad, when you're worried and anxious, or when you're apprehensive, like now, aware that I predicted exactly what Prescott would do!'

'Adam—'

'What's the matter, Julie? Can't we talk any more? Can't you confide in me? You always have. And I've always respected those confidences. Why is it suddenly so hard for you to discuss your problems with me?'

'You know, why, Adam.'

'Because of Prescott? Why should that be so?'

'You're biased, Adam.'

'Am I? Well, perhaps a little. But if I thought he was the right man for you, do you think I'd stand in your way?'

Julie bent her head. 'I'd really rather not talk about it.'

'Why not? Because you suspect I'm right, and you're afraid to accept the truth?'

'*No!*' Julie lifted her head to look at him. 'Adam, Dan loves me, I *know* he does.'

'But he's gone away.'

'How do you know that?'

Adam shrugged. 'I could say your face says it all. But I won't. I'll admit, I asked Galloway.'

Julie sighed. 'Adam, Dan has gone to see his father who is unwell, that's all. He'll be back tomorrow, so you have no need to concern yourself about me.'

'Oh, but I do, Julie.' He toyed thoughtfully with the knife beside his plate. 'You see, I know a little more about the Prescotts than you do, and I also happen to know that Anthea Leyton was speaking to her brother yesterday on the phone, and he was perfectly healthy then.'

Julie had expected him to say something like this, so she was prepared for it, but that didn't prevent the twisting pain that tore into her heart at this news. Adam would say anything to make her believe the worst of Dan, she told herself fiercely, but it still hurt.

'Look,' she said, trying to speak slowly and succinctly, 'I'm not a fool. I know that this—this marriage—is going to cause problems. We both—Dan and I, that is—know that. But if we love one another—'

'You're a romantic, Julie,' exclaimed Adam scornfully. 'My God, I'm beginning to wonder if I ever knew you. I thought you were a sane and sensible girl, not a sentimental fool with her head filled full of pipe-dreams! Come down to earth, Julie. It's money that makes the world go round, not *love*, and the sooner you realise that the less painful it's going to be for you.'

The arrival of the waitress with Julie's omelette interrupted his remonstration, and Adam hastily ordered a steak to get rid of her. But to Julie's relief, Pam had noticed her flushed cheeks, and ignoring Adam's sour look of disapproval, she carried a cup of coffee to their table and sat down.

'Can I join you?' she asked, fanning herself energetically. 'I've been run off my feet since breakfast, and I must sit down or I'll collapse!'

CHAPTER TEN

THE rest of the meal passed without incident, Pam's presence preventing any serious conversation. Adam hardly spoke at all, except when Pam addressed him directly, and Julie was grateful for the other girl's perception. She had a lot to thank the Galloways for, she thought ruefully, but she couldn't help wondering whether she would always feel that way. If Dan let her down. . .

But she refused to allow such negative thinking to ruin the day. Nothing had changed. She was still the same girl, and Georgian Bay was still as beautiful as ever. She would find Brad and ask him whether he'd like to go swimming. Twenty-four hours would soon pass, and she would prove to Adam that she was not as disillusioned as he imagined.

However, before she could put her plan into operation something else happened. She was still standing in the reception hall, waiting for Pam to find her son, when Corinne Leyton strolled through the swing doors. Today the other girl was wearing a purple thigh-length tee-shirt over white cotton trousers, her vivid hair confined beneath a silk scarf tied turban-wise around her head. As on the night of the barbecue, she managed to look startling, and the long curling lashes swept the reception area in mild disdain before alighting on Julie.

'What a coincidence!' she drawled, sauntering

towards her. 'You're exactly the person I wanted to see.'

Corinne was exactly the person Julie *least* wanted to see, but she stood her ground and surveyed the other girl with what she hoped was equal composure.

'You wanted to see me?'

'Well, not me, actually, darling. Mommy. She asked me to come over and invite you to Forest Bay for tea. You do take tea, don't you, Julie? All English people take tea.'

Julie expelled her breath on an uneasy sigh. 'It's very kind of your mother to invite me, but—'

'Oh, don't say no.' Corinne puckered her lips. 'Mommy will be so disappointed. She so much wants to get to know you. And I mean—if you're going to become part of the family. . .'

Julie's face suffused with colour. She didn't believe for the smallest instant that Corinne really meant what she said. This was the girl who had expected to marry Dan, if all the portents were true. And whether or not he intended to marry her, she was hardly likely to offer the hand of friendship to a rival.

'I don't think having tea with your mother would be a good idea, Corinne,' she said now, refusing to address her as *Miss* Leyton. 'If you'd thank her for me, and—'

'Would you like her to come here?' suggested Corinne mildly. 'She will, you know, if you refuse. And somehow I don't think your friends would appreciate the gesture. I mean, Mommy can be a good friend—or a bad enemy.'

'Are you threatening me, Corinne?' Julie was appalled.

'No.' The girl shook her head, giving the student behind the reception desk a considering look as she did so. 'I'm only saying that Mommy is the wrong person to cross. Remember, the Galloways have to live here after you've gone.'

Julie bent her head. 'That's blackmail!'

'Oh, no!' Corinne uttered a light laugh. 'You English are so serious, aren't you? You take everything so personally. All you're being offered is an invitation to tea. Now that's not so bad, is it?'

Julie shook her head. 'I'm not so naïve, Corinne. Your mother wants to talk about Dan, doesn't she? About our love for one another. She thinks now that Dan's gone away. . .'

'You know about that?' Corinne sounded surprised, and Julie stared at her.

'Of course I know. He rang me and told me, this morning.'

Corinne grimaced. 'Oh, well. I expect he had his reasons. But I wouldn't like to think any guy who professed love for me would take off for Miami without me.'

'For Miami?' echoed Julie disbelievingly, then pulled herself up. This was just another ploy, she thought incredulously. Now they were going to tell her that Dan hadn't gone to see his father at all. That having achieved his objective so far as she was concerned, he was now in pursuit of other amusement.

'Didn't you know?' Corinne asked now, arching those ridiculously dark brows. 'Mommy said that probably you wouldn't. But then she didn't know Dan had rung you. That was really something, wasn't it? I guess I have to give him full marks for initiative.'

'Will you go away, Corinne.' There was just so much that Julie could take, and right now she was coming to the end of her tether. 'I don't want to listen to any more of your lies, or your mother's lies either, for that matter. I believe Dan. I believe he loves me. And wherever he's gone and for whatever reason, he will come back. I know it.'

Corinne's lips twisted. 'You really cling, don't you, Julie? Dan said you would, but I didn't believe him. I mean, I'd die before I'd do what you're doing. You know he doesn't have any intention of marrying you, but still you hang on with those sharp little claws of yours. Go home! Go back to England where you belong. Go marry that smarmy lawyer of yours, and save yourself a lot of pain and humiliation!'

Julie turned away, almost stumbling as she went down the steps that gave access to the tree-shaded courtyard beyond. The air briefly revived her, but she hurried as she made her way to her cabin, pushing open the door and closing it behind her with hands that shook as she fumbled with the lock.

Then she flung herself on her bed, burying her face against the hand-worked coverlet, and letting the tears she had been suppressing since Dan's phone call give her the release she needed.

It was early evening before she lifted her head. The exhaustion of her tears had given way to sleep and she awakened from a heavy slumber feeling hollow-eyed and desperate.

Getting up, she sluiced her face under cold water and then surveyed her reflection in the mirror above the basin. She looked awful, she thought wearily, but then no one was going to care about that. All the same, she couldn't allow herself to remain in that state, and she spent time reapplying her make-up to hide the worst ravages of her grief.

Brushing her hair, she tried to think positively, but it was difficult when she knew so little of the facts. Dan had told her his father was ill. Adam said that the previous day Lionel Prescott had been speaking with his sister. She sighed. Dan had said he was going to New York. Corinne had said it was Miami, and while she didn't trust the other girl, she doubted she would tell an outright lie. And yet why not? If it was true, Dan had, and they were members of the same family.

Her head ached with the effort of trying to make some sense of what she ought to do. Dan had said stay, she kept telling herself, but what if he didn't come back? How long could she suffer Pam and David's sympathy? How long before humiliation forced her to pack her bags and leave?

Putting down the brush, she walked across to the windows, staring out disconsolately at the lengthening shadows. It was evening; it would soon be night. What kind of a creature was she if she couldn't give him the benefit of the doubt? He had said he would be back tomorrow or the day after. Until that time, she had to *believe*. . .

She ate dinner alone, Adam apparently deciding to give her a breathing space, and then retired to her cabin early to watch television. But the constant interruption of the advertisements irritated her, and presently she turned the television off again and stared broodingly into the gathering dark.

Morning brought a respite from her tortuous thoughts. Brad joined her for breakfast, and with him she could briefly forget the problems that were troubling her.

'You want to go water-skiing, Julie?' he suggested hopefully, watching her with anxious eyes, and she hesitated only a moment before nodding her head.

'Water-skiing it is,' she agreed, her smile bringing animation to her pale features, and Brad whooped his delight to the restaurant in general.

Changing into her bikini in the cabin, Julie couldn't help but remember the last occasion she had put on a swimsuit. That day, the day she had spent with Dan, had assumed a state of unreality already, and she wondered if she had only imagined his tenderness and sensitivity.

Brad offered no such soul-searching. His was a simple companionship, an undemanding friendship, that had no hidden significance, that held no traumatic threat. Being with Brad was like being with a favourite younger brother, and she wondered how much different her life would have been if she had had a brother or a sister.

Her own attempts at water-skiing were no more successful than before, and she returned to the hotel at lunch-time exhausted by her efforts. Still, she had provided Brad with a lot of amusement, and they were laughing together as they climbed the steps to the hotel and found Adam waiting for them at the top.

'Ah, Julie,' he said, dismissing the boy with a patronising gesture. 'I've been waiting for you. I have a message—from Forest Bay. I thought you should see it right away.'

'A message? From Dan?' Julie was instantly alarmed. 'What is it? Where is it? Let me see it!'

'It's here, it's here.' Adam was annoyingly unperturbed. He handed her the envelope calmly. 'It came just after you left. That chauffeur person brought it.'

'How do you know it's from Dan?' Julie exclaimed, tearing open the flap with frantic fingers, and Adam shrugged.

'I never said it was from Prescott,' he retorted mildly. 'I said it was from Forest Bay. Is it from him?'

Julie scanned the note she had extracted with anxious eyes, seeking the signature first. It was from Dan, and her heart flipped a beat as she turned back to the beginning. It was brief and to the point. He had written it before he left the previous day. It said simply that he was sorry he had lied to her, but he had not wanted to hurt her, and perhaps this letter would make it easier for her. He did care for her, but not deeply enough to oppose his parents' wishes, and while she might imagine they could make a good life for themselves, he knew it would never work. He knew if he had tried to tell her she would have tried to persuade him otherwise, and there was no point in continuing a relationship that had never been intended as a lasting one.

Julie swayed a little as the last words swam before her eyes. Words of love and affection, and of his hope that she would be happy with Adam if she chose to marry him. She felt sick and empty, and totally devastated, and she just wished she could crawl into some corner and die.

'Is it bad news?'

Adam was looking at her strangely, and she didn't

like the avidity in his expression. It was as if he knew
exactly what was in the letter, and she was loathe to
tell him and satisfy that speculative gleam. She bent
her head, crushing the parchment between her fingers,
and then looked up to find his eyes were unexpec-
tedly gentle.

'You don't have to tell me, you know,' he said
quietly. 'I can always tell what you're thinking. Come
away with me, Julie. Leave this place. Let's go now—
this afternoon. Before anything else happens.'

'What else can happen?' asked Julie dully, looking
down at the envelope in her hands. 'But—all right,
Adam, I will go away with you.' *Anything to escape*!
'Just leave me alone now. I—I need to think.'

'Of course.' With a brief smile he turned away, and
she watched him stride firmly across the square.
Beside the broader Canadians he seemed thin, slight—
and older than she could remember.

Her own passage to her cabin was less confident.
Once there, she sank down on the bed and re-read the
note, noticing inconsequently what an unusual hand
Dan had. She would have expected his writing to be
like him, firm and aggressive. Instead it was almost
tentative, the ts and Is looped with a feminine attention
to detail. Something else she realised, too. Once again
she had only Adam's word that the note was from
Dan. She had never seen his hand-writing, so how
could she be sure this was it?

Her head began to throb. Surely, surely Anthea
Leyton would not sink to this! Was this why she had
asked to see her the previous afternoon? Had she
devised this letter—this very carefully written letter?
How could she find out? There was no way.

Getting up from the bed again, she stared at her reflection in the mirror. Was she a fool to suspect anything? Was the letter genuine? Was she clutching at straws in this attempt to hold on to her beliefs? Or was she, as Corinne had said, clinging to a dream, a state of unreality, becoming one of those girls that his aunt had deplored to Pam and David?

She didn't know what to do, who to turn to. Pam could tell her nothing, nor could David. They would probably accept the letter at its face value. Obviously Adam would. It confirmed everything he had said.

Shaking her head, she picked up the envelope and smoothed it out, and as she did so she saw something she had not noticed before. The envelope was not addressed to her, not to her personally, that was. It was addressed to the Kawana Point Hotel, just as the invitation had been three days ago.

Blinking, she stared at it in disbelief. Were she to give in to her vivid imagination once again she would say that it was the *same* envelope. But it couldn't be. If that were so. . . *if that were so*, it would mean someone here had written the letter, someone at the hotel. . .

With her breathing quickening in concert with her agitation, she examined the handwriting once again. It wasn't like Adam's handwriting, but then, if it was he who had written the letter, obviously he would have disguised it. And perhaps that was why it looked so detailed, why the loops were so carefully drawn. Had someone invented the style just for the purposes of disguise?

She sank down again weakly. Would Adam do such a thing? she asked herself half impatiently. He was upset with her, that was true, but inventing a letter like this. . . It didn't make sense. He must know that sooner or later he would be found out. All the same, it did occur to her that they could well be married by that time. He had already suggested getting married in the United States, travelling around, moving from place to place. It could be weeks before any communication from Dan reached them. . .

Trembling now, as much from inner cold as an outer one, she went quickly into the bathroom and took a shower. Then, without giving herself time to think or change her mind, she dressed in the fringed suede suit she had worn to travel in, collected her bag and passport, and left the cabin.

David's motor launch was waiting at the jetty, and she was glad she knew how to handle it. The engine fired at the second attempt, and with slightly unsteady fingers she steered it out of the marina and across the expanse of blue water towards the dock at Midland.

She spent a frustrating twelve hours trying to get to New York. She had no visa, and she was forced to spend a long time at the United States Consulate in Toronto to get one. This took valuable time, but at least she was able to fly direct from there to New York, and she arrived at Kennedy airport very late in the evening.

The time that had evolved since those moments in the cabin when she had conceived the idea of coming to New York and confronting Dan herself had had a debilitating effect on her nerves, and sitting in the airport building, waiting for a cab to take her into the city, she felt isolated from everything—and every-one—she had ever known and loved. It was as if she was in limbo, between the world she knew and the world she didn't, and indeed the world which might not want to know her.

Because she knew the names of few hotels in New York, she asked the driver to take her to the Pierre, then sat back enthralled to watch the encroaching lights of the city. In spite of her anxiety, it was impossible not to be thrilled at this her first sight of that most famous of skylines, and she gazed through the car window in fascination as they crossed the Triborough bridge and ploughed through the suburbs of Manhattan.

The Pierre stood at the junction of Fifth Avenue and Sixty-First Street, and Julie was soon standing at the window of her allotted room looking out on the sleeping city. Only it didn't appear to be sleeping, she thought wryly, hearing the curious whooping of a police car from beyond the tree-shrouded mass of Central Park.

Still, she had to have some sleep, she thought, before facing whatever ordeal was facing her, and after washing her face and using soap on her teeth, she sank wearily into the comfortable bed.

She must have slept, because when she opened her eyes the room was bright and sunlit, and from below her windows there was the increasing hum of the traffic.

She rang room service and ordered toast and coffee, then took another shower before putting on the suede suit once more. At least the slim skirt was not creased, she saw with relief, and by the time her tray was delivered she had examined the telephone directory and discovered, to her dismay, exactly how many

Prescotts there were in the inner city area.

Drinking black coffee, she decided gloomily that she would have to ring the bank. Whether or not they would be prepared to give her Dan's address was another matter, but at least she had to try. Other than that, she could only visualise making calls to every Prescott listed in the book.

The main branch of the Scott National Bank appeared to be on Sixth Avenue, the Avenue of the Americas, and she dialled their number first, waiting impatiently for them to answer. But there was no reply, and glancing at her watch, she realised why. It was only a little after nine o'clock, and the bank wouldn't even be open yet.

Finishing her breakfast, she left the hotel and walked restlessly along Fifth Avenue, looking in shop windows. The layout of the city was in squares, or blocks, and the numbering of the streets and avenues made it a simple matter to work out how far it was to any particular junction. She understood now why Americans denoted distance in blocks. The city was built like a gigantic crossword puzzle.

Despite what she had heard, she was not accosted on her walk, and she was pleasantly surprised by the cleanliness of the city. She liked the banks of fountains, too, that provided the constant sound of running water, and the sometimes crazy antics of the cabs, that each possessed the inevitable ravages of constant competition.

It was after ten-thirty by the time she returned to the Pierre, and the doorman greeted her politely. 'Did you enjoy your walk, ma'am?' he enquired, opening the door for her, and she thanked him as she assured him that she had enjoyed it very much.

This time a telephonist responded to her call to the bank, but when she asked whether it was possible for them to give her Mr Daniel Prescott's address, there was a flurry of activity.

'Mr Daniel Prescott, Miss Osbourne?' the girl asked after ascertaining her name, and Julie said: 'That's right,' in faintly breathless tones.

The line went dead for a while after that, and she suspected she had been disconnected. After all, she could be anyone calling to ask for Dan's address, but she continued to hold on and hope for the best.

Eventually another female voice came on the line: 'Miss Osbourne?'

'Yes.' Julie swallowed with difficulty. 'Who am I speaking to, please?'

'I'm Mara Elliot, Miss Osbourne. Mr *Lionel* Prescott's secretary. Would I be right in thinking you are a Miss *Julie* Osbourne?'

Her voice had definitely Southern overtones, but Julie was hardly in a state to register anything. 'I— why, yes,' she got out chokingly. 'Do—do you know about me?'

'Mr Prescott isn't here right now,' Mara Elliot continued, without answering her question, 'but I know he'd surely like to meet you, Miss Osbourne. So if you could come by at say—twelve-thirty, I could try to arrange for you to see him then.'

Julie licked her dry lips. 'To—to see *Dan*?'

'No, Miss Osbourne. For you to meet Mr Lionel Prescott, Dan's father.'

Julie was stunned, as much by the realisation that this girl seemed to think Lionel Prescott would want to meet her as by the knowledge that Dan had been lying to her.

'I—er—I thought Mr Prescott was—was unwell,' she got out unevenly.

'Not to my knowledge,' Mara Elliot denied smoothly. 'Will twelve-thirty be all right with you?'

'Twelve-thirty? Oh—no, no.' Julie couldn't even think straight. 'That is, it doesn't matter, thank you. I've made a mistake. I'm sorry I troubled you—'

'Wait!' the other girl sensed she was about to ring off and interrupted her. 'If—if I could get in touch with Dan—'

'That won't be necessary.' Julie's words were clipped and tense. 'Thank you for your assistance.'

'And if Dan comes into the office? Where shall I tell him he can get in touch with you?'

'He can't,' said Julie tightly. 'G'bye.'

Of course she cried again, more bitterly now, but sufficiently energetically to obliterate her make-up and leave her eyes all red and puffy. She was a mess, she thought miserably, surveying herself in the mirror above the chest of drawers. She *was* a mess and she had *made* a mess of her life. Were the Osbournes fated never to find happiness?

She didn't feel like any lunch, so she remained in her room, lying on her bed, trying to plan what she should do now. The letter had faded into insignificance beside these latest revelations, but if Adam had written it, he had destroyed the last links between them.

She must have dozed because she awakened with a start to the phone's ringing. She was slightly dazed, but she couldn't imagine who might be ringing her here, and guessing it must be the concierge, she groped for the receiver.

'Miss Osbourne?' It was the receptionist. 'We have a visitor for you, waiting in the hall. Would you like me to send him up?'

'*Him?*' Julie swallowed convulsively. 'Who—who is it?'

'A Mr Prescott, ma'am.'

'Oh!' Dan? Julie blinked rapidly. 'Oh, no! That is—ask him to wait. I—I'll come down.'

How had he found her?

Scrambling off the bed, she stared in agony at her reflection. Pale cheeks, hollow eyes, traces of puffiness around the lids—how could she face him like this? And why had he come here? What could he possibly have to say to her now?

With trembling fingers she rinsed her face and then applied her make-up. Blusher only made her look hectic, like a painted doll, so she had to be content with looking pale, though hardly interesting, she thought unhappily. At least her hair was soft and silky, and if she brushed it forward it tended to distract attention from her sallow features.

The suede suit would have to do, she had no alternative, and picking up her handbag, she gave herself one last dissatisfied appraisal before walking the carpeted corridor to the lift.

Downstairs in the lobby she looked about her anxiously, wanting to be prepared for this meeting. She didn't want him to come upon her unannounced, and she hurried across to the reception desk to find out where he was waiting.

'In here, ma'am,' the young man behind the desk

directed smilingly, and Julie stepped hesitantly into the discreetly-lit atmosphere of the bar.

It took her a moment to adjust her eyes, but before she could assimilate her surroundings a light hand touched her arm and an unfamiliar male voice said: 'Julie?'

She looked up, startled, into eyes she recognised in a face she didn't. And yet the similarity was there, the way his hair grew back from his temples, although in this case it was liberally streaked with grey, and the faintly sensual curve of his mouth. It had to be Dan's father, and she panicked.

'I—*no*,' she said foolishly, realising her accent was giving her away, and then heaved a heavy sigh. 'That is, I am Julie, yes, but I didn't—want—*expect* to see you, Mr Prescott.'

'That's good,' he said mildly. 'You know who I am. Now shall we stop all this jittering and sit down?'

'Oh, but I—'

Julie glanced back longingly over her shoulder, then realising there was no escape, she acquiesced. Lionel Prescott saw her comfortably ensconced on the banquette, and ordered two Martinis before seating himself beside her. Then, when their drinks were set before them, he gave her a slightly rueful smile.

'So,' he said. 'At last we get to meet.'

'How did you find me?'

The words were out before she could stop them, but Lionel Prescott didn't seem to mind.

'Well, I could say I hired a gang of private eyes to do the work for me,' he remarked dryly, 'but I don't want to worsen the impression you probably have of me, so I'll admit that Dan told me.'

'*Dan told you?*'

'That's right. He got the information from the Consulate in Toronto, would you believe?'

Julie blinked, and then she remembered that when she applied for her visa she had had to state where she intended to stay in New York. But if Dan had found that out, it must mean he had returned to Georgian Bay. . .

CHAPTER ELEVEN

SHE was staring blankly into space when Lionel Prescott spoke again. 'It doesn't really matter how I found you. The fact is, I have, and I can't deny I'm relieved. My son means everything to me, and while I may have many faults, interfering with his life is not one of them.'

Julie's brows descended and she turned to stare at him in disbelief. 'You mean—you mean Dan has—has told you—about—about us?'

'You didn't know?'

Julie shook her head. 'I—I didn't know what to think.'

'But I understood him to tell me that—'

'He said you were ill, Mr Prescott,' Julie broke in defensively. 'And you're not, are you?'

'Ah. . .' Lionel Prescott nodded slowly. 'You found out about that. Who told you? Anthea? Corinne? Dan guessed the minute he was out of sight they'd try to interfere.'

'Then why didn't he warn me?' exclaimed Julie half tearfully, not fully recovered from the emotive upheaval she had suffered. 'And—and why didn't he tell me the truth?'

Lionel sighed. 'That was my fault, I'm afraid. I asked him not to.'

Julie couldn't take this in, and with a sympathetic shrug Lionel added: 'This isn't really the place to discuss such things, but it will have to do. I asked Dan to come and see me because of a message I'd received.'

'A message?' Julie stared at him.

'From a Mr Price?'

'Adam?'

'I guess that is his name.'

Julie put a hand to her head. 'But—but why would Adam send a message to you? What could he possibly have to tell you?'

'Can't you guess?'

Julie's throat closed up. 'Oh, God!' Then she shook her head. 'But I told Dan!'

'I know it.'

'But why would Adam do such a thing?'

'I imagine because he thought it might influence us against you.'

Julie hesitated. 'And—and that was why you sent for Dan?'

'Partly.'

'Then I'm afraid I don't understand. Where is Dan? Why are you here? What are you trying to tell me?'

'Be patient,' he advised gently. 'At this moment in time,' he consulted the gold watch around his wrist, 'Dan ought to be in the airplane bound for Kennedy. He'll be here in a couple of hours. And I'm here to prevent you running out on him again.'

Julie was confused. 'You knew I called your office?'

'Or course. Mara rang me at once, and as I'd already had Dan on the phone from Forest Bay explaining that you'd disappeared. . .' He grimaced. 'We were all very relieved, believe me.'

Julie shook her head. 'If Dan had only explained. . .'

'What about? Price's message? Or the publicity his actions are likely to promote?'

'Whose actions? What publicity?' Julie was bewildered. 'Mr Prescott, if there's something more to this, something I should know. . .'

'I don't think it's my place, Julie,' he said quietly, and she gazed at him in bafflement. And then, as if responding to her evident consternation, he added: 'You'll find out soon enough, I guess.'

'Mr Prescott, please. . .' Julie was almost beside herself. 'Has this to do with Dan and me? Did he tell you he'd asked me to marry him?'

'He did.' Lionel Prescott nodded.

'And—and you don't—disapprove?'

'Julie!' He took one of her hands in both of his. 'Dan has his own life to lead. You want me to be honest with you? All right, I'll tell you. His mother and I, we did hope he would marry a nice American girl. But I didn't, so why should I expect him to?'

Julie shook her head. 'Your sister—Corinne—'

'I know, I know. But although I have three daughters, I have only one son, Julie, and I don't intend to lose him. And I know I would if I tried to stand in his way. He's a pretty easy-going guy normally, but then so am I. However, if you cross him. . .' He shrugged. 'You know what I mean?'

Julie nodded, rather tremulously. 'I know.'

'So that's cleared that up. I'm not saying Dan's mother's going to greet you with open arms—that's not her way. But she respects Dan's wishes, and you know—I think she just might admire your spirit.'

Julie pressed her lips together. 'So—so if it's not

to do with Dan and me, why did you mention Adam—
and publicity?'

Lionel sighed. 'Julie—'

'It concerns me, doesn't it? Don't I have a right
to know?'

'A right to know?' echoed Dan's father reflectively.
'Yes, I guess you do at that. But Julie, these things
are better handled by lawyers, you know. I'm just a
banker. I wouldn't know how to tell you.'

'Then just say it,' she exclaimed. 'Is it about—
Daddy? He—he wasn't murdered or anything,
was he?'

'No.' Lionel pressed her hand once more and
released it. 'No, I'm afraid your father took his own
life. However, I can tell you it has to do with—why
he died.'

Julie stared at him. 'Did Adam have something to
do with that?' She shook her head. 'But they were
friends! And in any case, how could you find out a
thing like that?'

Lionel studied her pale cheeks for several seconds,
then he seemed to come to a decision. 'All right,' he
said. 'I'll explain what happened, at least so far as I
am concerned.' He paused. 'I told you I had a message
from Price, didn't I? It was—let me see—four days
ago now. The day you and Dan spent on the yacht, is
that right?' Julie nodded, and he went on: 'I got this
telephone message, relayed via Anthea, to the effect
that—well, that I ought to be warned there was insta-
bility in your family.'

'I see.'

Lionel frowned. 'Up until then, I hardly knew of
your existence. Dan's mother and I have been

in Miami for the past three weeks—'

Miami!

'—and although Anthea had phoned a couple of times complaining that Dan was getting mixed up with some English girl, we hadn't taken her seriously.'

Julie quivered. She could still scarcely believe that Dan was serious!

'Anyway, your father's name was familiar to me, and really almost—accidentally, I learned of Price's involvement.'

'He was my father's partner.'

'Yes, my dear, I know.' Lionel looked solemn. 'Exactly how well do you know him?'

'Very well. I've known him since I was tiny. And—and after my mother died and Daddy became—sort of withdrawn, he used to try to take his place.'

'Mmm.' Lionel sounded doubtful. 'Your father was in debt, I gather.'

'That's right. Only Adam's money saved the firm from bankruptcy.'

'Is that so?' Again there was a pregnant pause. 'How do you know all this?'

'Adam told me. After Daddy was dead. He—he had got into difficulties with interest payments. There was a considerable sum of money involved. Several thousand pounds, I think. He couldn't face prison, so he took his own life.'

Lionel was watching her closely now as he said: 'Just how did taking his own life solve anything?'

'Oh. . .' Julie shrugged: 'There was insurance. Adam dealt with all that. He said Daddy had done the only thing left to him, in the circumstances.'

'I see.' Lioned sighed. 'And you never questioned that?'

'Questioned it? No. Why should I?' Julie was puzzled.

'Julie, insurance companies don't pay out in cases of suicide.'

'Oh, I know that, but Adam said this was a special case.'

'A special case?'

'Yes.'

'Julie, there is no such thing as a special case. Not where suicide is concerned. Can you imagine? Every guy who got into financial difficulties and thought of suicide would insure himself several times over. It's just not on, honey. Insurance companies are not benevolent societies. Believe me, I know!'

Julie stared at him. 'But if there was no insurance money. . .'

'Exactly. Where did the money come from?'

'Yes.'

'Would you believe Price?'

'Adam?' Julie blinked. 'But if he could do that. . .'

'—why didn't he do it sooner?'

She swallowed. 'Yes.'

Lionel sighed. 'I don't know how to tell you this, honey, but the way I hear it, Price had bought up all your father's debts long before the crash came.'

'No!'

'That's the way it's looking.'

'But how do you know all this?'

Lionel hesitated. 'I have friends. Friends in England. Relatives, moreover. I made a couple of phone calls, that's all.'

'After—Adam contacted you?'

'That's right.' He shrugged. 'I'll admit, I wanted to know more about this girl that Dan was getting involved with.'

Julie shook her head. 'But what did you mean about publicity?' She moved her shoulders helplessly. 'How did anyone get to know?'

'These things invariably come out, Julie. I suspect that Price got careless when he thought he'd gotten away with it. Whatever, it must suit his purpose to be out of England right now.'

Julie tried to make sense of her thoughts. It was true, Adam had been unusually willing to leave his beloved apartment and come to Canada, and he had deterred her from coming home. But could it be true? Could he have professed friendship for her father and stabbed him in the back like that? It didn't make sense. They had been partners for so long. . .

'But why?' she murmured now, hardly aware she was voicing her thoughts aloud, and Lionel said softly:

'Perhaps you were the catalyst. Have you thought of that?'

'*Me?*'

'Yes, you. Didn't Dan tell me that Price wanted to marry you?'

'Well, yes. But Daddy knew all about that.'

'Did he approve?'

Julie hesitated. 'I—I think so.'

'Didn't he think the man was too old for you? Dan says he's at least twenty years your senior.'

'Well, he is, I know, but—' Julie broke off helplessly. 'It was just taken for granted.'

'By Price?'

'And—and me,' she admitted, unable to absolve herself of all blame.

Lionel reached for his Martini. 'Oh, well, maybe we'll never know the truth. The fact remains, he seems a pretty contemptible guy. Don't you think so?'

Julie said nothing. She couldn't. She was too shocked to make any judgment. But one thing more needed to be confirmed. Opening her handbag, she extracted the letter she had stuffed there the previous morning and handed it to him.

'I—I received this,' she said jerkily, realising now that Dan could have had nothing to do with it.

Lionel studied the letter disbelievingly. 'My God! You don't imagine Dan wrote this, do you?'

Julie licked her dry lips. 'I didn't know what to think at first. He'd signed it. I couldn't tell whether it was his handwriting or not. . .'

Lionel nodded. 'It's not, I can tell you that.' He paused. 'And if it had been writen at Forest Bay, the notepaper would have been identifiable. Anthea has everything monogrammed.' He frowned as he examined the envelope. 'This is monogrammed!'

'I know.' Julie heaved a sigh. 'I think it's the envelope our invitation to your sister's barbecue came in.'

Lionel turned it over in his hands. 'So you're suggesting someone else wrote this letter. Who? Price?'

Julie shrugged. 'Perhaps.'

'Is this why you came to New York?'

She nodded again. 'I had to know, one way or the other. I had to speak to Dan. But when I discovered you hadn't been ill—'

'You thought the worst?'

'Yes.'

'Oh, Julie!' He touched her cheek with a gentle hand. 'You've had a hard time. And it's all been my fault. I told Dan to make that excuse. I wanted to warn him about Price, and I didn't know what your reaction might be. I had to speak with Dan alone.'

Julie felt too dazed to think coherently. So much had happened in such a short space of time, she couldn't absorb it all, and all that was real was that Dan loved her and wanted her, and she could believe in him.

Towards Adam she felt an intense feeling of incredulity. Even now, without Lionel Prescott's words ringing in her ears, she could hardly accept what she had learned. And yet she had the evidence in her own hands. The letter—which he had delivered so callously—he must have banked on her lack of confidence in herself to swing the balance. And it almost had, let's face it, she thought deploringly. Without the strength of her love for Dan, she might well have taken the easy way out, and once she and Adam had left Georgian Bay it would have been incredibly difficult to find them.

She shivered a little in the wake of this conclusion. Everything could have gone so badly wrong for her, just as it had for her father, and thinking of those debts William Osbourne had run up, she realised the torment he must have gone through. She tried to recall whether he had shown any opposition to Adam's plans, but all that she remembered was his indifference towards her, which she had attributed to his grief after her mother's death.

Noticing her drawn features, Lionel exclaimed: 'I wish I'd insisted that I should take you home with me, Julie, but as Dan said, I guess you two young people need to be alone together.' He sighed. 'I know, what say we take a ride down to the Prescott building? We've got plenty of time,' he smiled, 'and we can always leave Dan a message. A genuine one this time.'

Julie agreed. She needed the break from her own thoughts, and they rode the Avenue of the Americas to the giant skyscraper where the Prescott group of companies had their offices. The offices were closing, but walking the plate-glass walled halls and riding in the high-speed elevators, Julie gained a little impression of the efficiency which had made the Prescott name so famous.

'You know what Mark Twain said, don't you?' Lionel remarked, as she surveyed the sumptuous appointments of his huge office, and when she shook her head, he went on: 'He said "In Boston they ask, how much does he know? In New York, how much is he worth?" ' He grinned. 'I guess this place appals you, doesn't it?'

Julie made an awkward gesture. 'Not exactly—'

'But you don't find it impressive?'

'Mr Prescott, I realise you expected Dan to marry a rich girl—'

'I expected him to show good judgment, and you know something? I think he has.'

She stared at him. 'Were you testing me, Mr Prescott?'

He shrugged. 'I admit, I was curious to see how you would react to this place.'

'And if I'd reacted differently?'

'But you didn't,' said Lionel, tucking his hand under her elbow. 'And I'll be complacent and say that I

knew it all along. After all, I taught Dan everything
he knows.'

Not everything, thought Julie dryly, but she didn't
contradict him.

Back at the hotel, Julie entered the lobby half apprehensively. She was tired, more tired than she had
realised, and she had yet to learn whether Dan had
forgiven her. His father had been kind, but was she
not expecting too much of their relationship? Had the
time and the place not distorted their real feelings for
one another?

She crossed the carpeted hall on leaden feet, and
then saw Dan himself, standing beside the display
cabinets, impatiently contemplating their contents. It
was a different Dan, and yet the same, his casual
clothes having given way to a dark grey lounge suit,
the usual open-necked shirts replaced by a pristine
white one, a dark tie slotted neatly beneath the collar.
It accentuated his tan, and his hands pushed carelessly
into the pockets of his pants drew her attention to the
muscular length of his legs. Oh, God, she thought
helplessly, I do love him, *I do*, and then faltered in
mid-step as he turned and saw her.

'Julie. . .'

The word was uttered half under his breath, but she
read her name on his lips as he strode eagerly towards
her. Ignoring everyone, including his father behind
her, he pulled her almost roughly into his arms, and
his mouth on hers erased all the horrors of the last
three days.

The kiss was not long, but it was hard and passionate, and their intimacy was in no doubt when he lifted
his head. 'I've been nearly out of my mind,' he told

her with barely suppressed anguish, and she touched his face almost wonderingly as she said:

'So have I.'

His eyes narrowed, returning to the parted sweetness of her mouth, and then realising they could not continue this conversation satisfactorily here, he forced himself to look beyond her to where his father was assuming a feigned interest in an enormous bowl of flowers occupying a central plinth.

'So you made it,' he said, addressing the older man, and Julie turned half tremulously to face her future father-in-law.

'Don't I always?' Lionel enquired dryly, giving Julie a conspiratorial smile, and Dan's hand on her shoulder tightened.

'Where were you?' he demanded. 'I've been waiting almost twenty minutes.'

'Didn't you get the message?' asked Lionel, frowning, and Dan nodded.

'Yeah, I got it,' he agreed, drawing Julie back against him, as if he couldn't bear for them to be apart. 'But what took you so long?'

'I was just showing your—Julie—your grandfather's office.'

'Oh,' Dan nodded, 'I get it. To see if she was impressed, right?'

Lionel shrugged. 'Julie and I—understand one another, I think.' He smiled again. 'You don't begrudge me that, do you?'

Dan looked down at Julie with lazily mocking eyes. 'I guess not,' he admitted. 'Just so long as you don't expect me to invite you to join us for dinner. We have a lot to say to one another.'

'My dismissal,' remarked Lionel wryly, grimacing at Julie once again. 'You'll come over to the house later?'

'Tomorrow,' said Dan firmly, and Julie quivered. 'Tell Ma not to worry. We won't elope. I promised her a proper wedding, and that's what she shall have. And you can tell her that she can arrange it, hmm?' This as he looked down at Julie. 'We're your family from now on,' he added huskily. 'And we want to do it right, don't we?'

Julie nodded, too full of emotion for speech, and Lionel decided the time had come to make his departure. 'Tomorrow, then,' he said, and after a moment's hesitation he leant forward and touched Julie's cheeks with his lips. 'We'll look forward to that,' he said gently, and left them.

With his father's departure, Dan swung her round to face him again, his face a little strained in the artificial lights of the lobby. 'Do you have a suite?' he demanded, and in breathless tones she explained she had a *room*. 'Okay,' he said. 'Let's go there, shall we?'

The look in his eyes was unguarded, and her lips parted in nervous anticipation. Nodding her head, she led the way along to the lifts, and suffered the bell-boy's cheerful patter as they ascended to the fourteenth floor.

Walking along the corridor, Dan didn't touch her, and she fumbled in her handbag for her key, pulling it out and dropping it, and having him retrieve it for her as they reached the panelled door. Dan himself opened the door, lifting the plastic card from inside and hanging it outside with the words *Do Not Disturb* plainly in view. Then he closed the door and attached the safety chain before reaching for her.

'Julie,' he groaned, pressing her body closely against him. 'Oh, Julie, don't ever do anything like that to me again!'

'I won't,' she whispered huskily, then wound her arms around his neck as his mouth searched for hers.

There was a hungry eagerness in his kiss, a kind of feverish desperation, born of the agonies of anxiety he had suffered in those hours before he knew where she had gone. It was as if he couldn't get enough of her, and her lips parted beneath his.

After the emotional torment she had gone through, it was infinitely satisfying having him holding her again, and she arched closer, uncaring in those moments that there were still so many things to be said between them, so many things to explain. She wanted him and she knew he wanted her, and no other assuagement would ease the aching hunger inside her.

Yet she found she was still nervous when he drew her to the bed, and touching the fine mohair of his jacket, she murmured: 'Your—your suit—you'll ruin it!'

His reaction was immediate. 'If you're worried, I'll take it off,' he said softly, unfastening his waistcoat, and suddenly her fears deserted her.

'Let me,' she breathed, brushing his fingers aside, and he offered no resistance as she unbuttoned his shirt and loosened his tie.

'Do you know what kind of a night I had last night?' he demanded at last, pressing her down on to the bed and covering her trembling body with his own. 'I was desperate, not knowing where you'd gone or what might have happened to you. And if I'd known you were here—in New York—'

'Don't talk,' said Julie huskily, winding her arms around his neck and pulling his mouth down to hers. 'Not now. . .'

Their lovemaking was as ardent and tumultuous as Julie remembered. Dan brought her every nerve and sinew alive, so that she wanted to join herself to him and never let him go. Looking up into his taut features as he brought her to the heights, sharing his release when it came, sliding down through the aeons of pleasure and ecstasy, she felt an enormous over-flowing of love inside her, a deep sense of belonging, of involvement, of feeling herself a part of this man just as he was a part of her.

'No one—but no one—has ever made me feel as you do,' he groaned at last, lifting his face from the moist hollow of her nape. 'Oh, Julie, I love you so much. How could you believe I'd walk out on you?'

'You told me your father was sick,' she reminded him huskily, sliding possessive fingers along his thigh, and he sought her mouth once more before answering her.

'Didn't he explain that?' he asked, against her lips, and she moved her head in silent acknowledgement. 'He wanted to tell me about Price.'

'I know.' Julie shifted sensuously beneath him. 'But that wasn't all.'

'What else could there be?' Dan protested, imprisoning her teasing fingers. 'Julie, be still. What do you mean—that isn't all?'

Julie sighed. 'Let me get up and I'll show you.'

Dan pulled a wry face. 'Is that absolutely necessary?'

'Only if you want to know.'

Dan drew an unsteady breath. 'I don't want to let you go.'

'Then don't,' she whispered, her tongue appearing in silent provocation, and for a while there was only the sound of their tormented breathing in the room.

It was much later when Dan eventually rolled on to his back, letting her get off the bed. His eyes followed her, however, and half provocatively she put on his shirt, rolling up the sleeves and wrapping its folds closely about her. Then she picked up her handbag and took out the letter she had shown Lionel Prescott earlier.

'Here,' she said huskily. 'Now perhaps you'll understand.'

Dan sat up, pushing back his hair with a lazy hand. He frowned as he unfolded the letter, but the frown had deepened into a scowl when he had read it.

'The swine!' he muttered, crumpling it into a ball. 'The swine! So that was what he meant!'

Julie came to perch on the end of the bed, long legs curled under her. 'What who meant? Adam?'

'Yes, *Adam*!' said Dan savagely. 'The creep! I'd like to twist his guts!'

Julie shook her head. 'You've spoken to him?'

'Of course. Didn't my father tell you?'

'No. He—he only said what—what he had told you.'

Dan nodded, massaging the back of his neck with both hands. 'I guess he thought it would be easier if I told you. But—*hell*, it's not.' He looked at her compassionately. 'Honey, can't we just forget it?'

'Forget what?'

'Price! And his involvement with us! I doubt you'll ever see him again.'

'You mean—he's gone?'

Dan nodded. 'He took off right after our little—altercation. Don't ask me where. I don't want to know.'

Julie stretched out a hand and touched his knee, her fingers warm and gentle. 'Dan. . .' She gazed at him adoringly. 'If it's to do with my father, can't you tell me? Let's start as we mean to go on. Don't let's have any secrets from one another.'

'It's not my secret!' he muttered harshly, capturing her hand and carrying it to his lips. 'But maybe you're right. Maybe Price will always stand between us if you don't know the truth.'

Julie nodded, and with a sigh he went on: 'Exactly what did Dad tell you? I guess you don't know about—about your father's debts, do you?'

'Yes,' Julie reassured him. 'Your father didn't want to tell me, but I persuaded him.'

'Ah!' Dan breathed a sigh of relief, pressing his lips to her palm before continuing. 'Okay, so you know that Price had been running the business for a number of years.'

'I suppose he had.' This was something Julie had not thought of.

Dan nodded. 'What I guess you don't know is why—why your father killed himself.'

'Because of the debts!'

Dan shook his head. 'I thought that at first. But it didn't altogether make sense. I mean, he'd been in debt for years. Why should it suddenly become too much for him?'

Julie frowned. 'And you know why?'

'I didn't. I was still puzzling that one out when Price himself supplied the answer.'

'Adam?'

Dan sighed. 'Julie, I was desperate. You'd disappeared, and no one knew where you'd gone. I didn't even know why you'd taken off like that, and nor did the Galloways. They knew nothing about this letter, did they? Only two people knew about it. You—and the person who wrote it.'

'Everything comes down to him, doesn't it?' Dan pressed her cool fingers against his hot forehead. 'Okay—so I went to find Price. He was in your cabin. He seemed to be looking for something. I guess now it was the letter. He looked pretty sick when he saw me.'

'You told him you knew about—'

'Sure. I guess I said some pretty disgusting things, but whatever, it got him riled, the way I wanted him to be riled. A man can make mistakes when he's angry he'd never make when he's not. I told him that whatever happened, I intended *you* should know the truth before you entered into any further contract with him, and I think it dawned on him you weren't about to come back. Not to him, anyway.'

Julie stared at him. 'He didn't mention the letter?'

'Not in so many words. He only said that after what had happened, you'd never want to see me again, but I didn't know what he meant by that. And in any case, I was too hell-bent to care too much over the subtleties. I just wanted him to know that the English press were getting mightily interested in his affairs, and a police investigation was on the cards. I guess that threw him. Anyway, he went on about you—how he'd done it all for you—'

'For me!'

'—and how your father had defrauded him.'

'Daddy?'

Dan nodded, holding her startled eyes with his own. 'Yes. Apparently Price lent your father the money as a kind of—down-payment. For you!'

'Oh, Dan!'

He shook his head. 'I'm sorry, honey, but it's true. Your father was never for the deal, and I guess he tried every way to get out of it.'

'And when he couldn't. . .'

Dan pressed her fingers to his lips. 'Don't blame yourself, sweetheart. You couldn't help it. Price was relentless. I guess he knew you'd be finished school in a couple of months. Maybe he gave your father an ultimatum. Whatever, he couldn't take it.'

'If only he'd told me!'

'I guess he knew that if he did—'

'—I'd insist on marrying Adam?' Julie bent her head. 'He knew I would.'

Dan tugged her gently towards him. 'So Price lost his gamble. He saved your father's name at the expense of his own.'

'Oh, Dan!'

He sighed, pulling her close against him. 'Listen: your father could have gone to prison—'

'He knew I'd never allow that.'

'—so he did the only thing possible.'

'But I could still have married Adam,' she

exclaimed, half tearfully, and he cradled her head against his shoulder.

'There is one more thing,' he told her gently. 'He did confide in someone.'

'Who?' Julie lifted her head to stare at him.

'A—Mrs Collins?'

'Our housekeeper?'

Dan nodded. 'I don't know how much he told her. Maybe just that he was worried about your relationship with Price.'

'But she never said a word to me!'

'Perhaps when you went away she didn't realise how serious it was.' He paused. 'But from what my father learned from London, I would say that Price has been making a nuisance of himself, going to the house, acting like he owned it already. It got her thinking—and talking.'

'And that's how the story came out?'

'Honey, where suicide is concerned, particularly in the case of someone like your father, the press are always interested.'

'I can't believe it!'

'What? about Price?'

'No. That—that Daddy would agree to such a thing.'

'He was desperate, too, remember? And your mother was very ill, wasn't she?'

Julie nodded. 'She fell, quite by accident, and injured her spine. The condition developed complications, a spinal infection that affected her brain—'

'Don't go on,' said Dan huskily. 'I know all about it. Do you remember when you told me your father had committed suicide?'

'On the wharf? I remember.'

'Yes. Well, I had Uncle Maxwell find out all the facts for me then. I wanted to know everything about you.'

'And—and it didn't—deter you?'

'Does it look like it?' he murmured dryly, his lips against her temple. 'Price knew that, too. I guess he decided to get out while he could.'

'Where has he gone?'

'I don't know. Maybe the police will catch up with him. Whatever happens, nothing can bring your father back.'

'No.'

Julie nodded, and with an effort Dan said: 'How would you like to get dressed now and go out for dinner?'

'Is that what you want?'

'Me?' Dan's grin was rueful. 'No. But it's what you want to do that matters. Tomorrow you'll be meeting my mother. That's my decision. Tonight is yours.'

'Then let's eat up here,' said Julie throatily. 'We can ring room service, and—'

'You're delicious, do you know that?' he exclaimed, pulling her down on top of him. 'You can read my mind. Going out and sharing you with a hundred other guys is not my favourite occupation.'

'No.' Julie forced the lingering regrets about her father's death to the back of her mind, and smiled. 'I think I know what that is.'

'Why not?' he demanded irrepressibly. 'You know everything else about me.'

Julie rested her head in the hollow of his shoulder. 'Your mother? Is she very formidable?'

Dan's chest heaved beneath her as he laughed. 'Not very,' he said reassuringly. 'Not where I'm concerned.'

'You are her only son.'

'And you're going to be her only daughter-in-law.'

'Am I?' Julie lifted her head and looked into his eyes. 'Am I really?'

'You'd better believe it,' he told her fiercely, and there was no better conviction than the urgency of his kiss.

Eight weeks later, Julie walked out of the limpid blue-green waters of the Caribbean, up the honey-pale sand to where her husband was reclining beneath a date palm. Dan had propped himself against the bole of the tree to pluck the strings of his guitar, but he put it aside as Julie approached him, stretching out his hand towards her and pulling her down beside him.

'Mmm, you taste salty,' he murmured, nuzzling her nape. 'But I must admit I like the flavour.'

Julie returned his kiss with feeling and then pressed him away from her. 'You'll get wet,' she teased, indicating his sweatshirt, but he only flopped back on to the sand, pulling her on top of him.

'I guess I can stand it,' he remarked lazily. 'Did you enjoy your swim?'

'Very much,' she agreed, and then pleased him by turning pink. 'Were you watching me?'

'All the time,' he told her huskily. 'I told you it was good. Perhaps I'll join you tomorrow.'

'Dan, if this wasn't a private beach—'

'—I wouldn't suggest it,' he grinned, and she hid her face in the hollow of his throat.

Later, after she had towelled herself dry and resumed the bikini she had shed before bathing, Dan stroked a rueful finger down her spine.

'Only four more days,' he said, with a sigh. 'I don't want to leave. I don't want to take you back and share you with the rest of my family.'

Julie smiled. 'Darling, we'll have our own home, our own house. We needn't go out a lot, if you don't want to.'

Dan pulled her close to him. 'At least Dad's promised me that job in Toronto in the spring. You'll like Toronto. It's not so abrasive as New York. And we'll have more time to ourselves.'

Julie shook her head. 'You may get tired of that. . .'

'Never,' he said vehemently. 'I can never get enough of you. You're under my skin, and in my blood. You're a delight and a temptation, and I can't believe you're my wife.'

'You'd better believe it,' said Julie humorously, glancing down at her still flat stomach. 'Remember, there'll be three of us moving to Toronto in the spring.'

'I know.' Dan's eyes were gentle, and his hands slid possessively over her stomach. 'Don't you really mind?'

'Do you?'

'Oh, honey. . .' His lips stroked her ear with warm insistence. 'I can think of nothing more desirable than knowing my child is growing inside you.' His eyes darkened into passion. 'You don't know how good that makes me feel.'

'I do,' she breathed unevenly. 'The child—he's ours. He's part of you, in me. . .'

Dan was not proof against such emotive talk, and

for a while only the seabirds disturbed the deepening shadows of late afternoon. But at last he let her go, and Julie sat up, looping her arms around her drawn-up knees.

'Can we go and see Pam and David when we get back to New York?' she asked, gazing out towards the shadowy outline of Martinique, only twenty miles distant, and Dan stretched lazily.

'If you like,' he said drowsily. 'But be prepared for my mother to want to take care of you. You're going to have her first grandchild. She can be very possessive.'

'Like her son,' declared Julie provokingly, and then added: 'Do you think we could take Brad out in the yacht one evening? I once promised I would ask you, but I never did.'

'I guess so.' Dan grinned up at her. 'You know, perhaps we ought to stay with Anthea and Max. I got the feeling at the wedding that she admired you for what you did. And now that Corinne's decided to go to England. . .'

Julie shrugged. 'If you like. So long as we're together.' She glanced down at him. 'I never knew one person could be so happy!'

Dan sat up, and draped a lazy arm about her shoulders. 'We're very lucky,' he agreed, kissing her shoulder. 'Now, shall we go back to the villa? Clothilde will be preparing dinner, and I want to take a shower first.' He paused before adding wickedly: 'With you.'

Later that evening they sat on the verandah of the villa, at peace with the muted sounds of the island. The Prescotts owned this villa at Cap d'Emeraude in St Lucia, and these past four weeks of their honeymoon had been a heavenly time of sun and sand and water, and warm, intoxicating nights of love. Already Julie had a kind of glow about her, that wasn't just the result of the golden tan she had acquired, and Dan's possessive gaze rested often on her lissom form. They loved, and they were in love, and they needed no one else.

Now, however, Julie sighed, and Dan, attuned to her every mood, leaned towards her perceptively.

'I know,' he said. 'You're feeling sorry for Price. I'm sorry you had to find out.'

'Your father knew I would want to know,' she said, touching his cheek with tender fingers. 'You were right to show me his letter. Things have been kept from me for too long.'

Dan nodded. 'He had it coming.'

'What will they do to him?'

'What can they do? He didn't actually cause your father to take his own life. The business over the debts may warrant investigation, but I doubt there's enough evidence to convict him.'

Julie shook her head. 'Would you think I was silly if I said I'm glad?'

'No.' Dan covered her fingers with his, and squeezed, and she went on:

'I—I have so much, somehow. I can't begrude him his freedom.'

'I wouldn't have you any other way,' said Dan huskily. 'Come on, let's go for a walk. We still have four more days—ninety-six more hours! And I intend to make the most of them. . .'

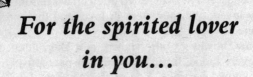

MILLS & BOON®

Anne Mather

COLLECTOR'S EDITION

If you have missed any of the previously published titles in the Anne Mather Collector's Edition, you may order them by sending a cheque or postal order (please do not send cash) made payable to Harlequin Mills & Boon Ltd. for £2.99 per book plus 50p per book postage and packing. Please send your order to: Anne Mather Collector's Edition, P.O. Box 236, Croydon, Surrey, CR9 3RU (EIRE: Anne Mather Collector's Edition, P.O. Box 4546, Dublin 24).

NEW YORK TIMES
BESTSELING AUTHOR

Anne Mather

Dangerous Temptation

He was desperate to remember... Jake wasn't sure
why he'd agreed to take his twin brother's place on
the flight to London. But when he awakens in hospital
after the crash, he can't even remember his own
name or the beautiful woman who watches him so
guardedly. Caitlin. His wife.

She was desperate to forget... Her husband seems
like a stranger to Caitlin—a man who assumes there
is love when none exists. He is totally different—like
the man she'd thought she had married. Until his
memory returns.
And with it, a danger that threatens them all.

"Ms. Mather has penned a wonderful romance."
—Romantic Times

MIRA®   **AVAILABLE NOW IN PAPERBACK**

Lynne Shelby writes contemporary wo[...]
and romance. Her debut novel, *French K*[...]
Accent Press and *Woman Magazine* Writing[...]
When not writing or reading, Lynne can usually be found
at the theatre or exploring a foreign city with her writer's
notebook, camera and sketchbook in hand. She lives in
London with her husband and has three adult children
who live nearby.

Connect with Lynne Shelby on Twitter **@LynneB1**,
Facebook **/LynneShelbyWriter**, or visit her website at
www.lynneshelby.com.

Praise for Lynne Shelby:

'A wonderful fresh new talent' Katie Fforde

'A genuinely witty and original romance, I loved it!'
Woman Magazine

'Delightful!' Jane Wenham-Jones, author of *Perfect Alibis*

'Warm-hearted, romantic, and beautifully written' Kate Field,
author of *The Winter That Made Us*

'Fun and dazzling – a wonderfully glittering romance'
Chicks, Rogues and Scandals

'A classic' *The Writing Garnet*

By Lynne Shelby

Standalone
French Kissing

The Theatreland series
The One That I Want
There She Goes
The Summer of Taking Chances

LYNNE SHELBY

the *Summer of Taking Chances*

ACCENT

First published in Great Britain in 2020
by HEADLINE ACCENT
An imprint of HEADLINE PUBLISHING GROUP

1

Cataloguing in Publication Data is available from the British Library

ISBN 978 1 7861 5734 8

Typeset in 10.5/13pt Bembo Std by Jouve (UK), Milton Keynes

Printed and bound in Great Britain by Clays Ltd, Elcograf S.p.A.

HEADLINE PUBLISHING GROUP
An Hachette UK Company
Carmelite House
50 Victoria Embankment
London EC4Y 0DZ

www.headline.co.uk
www.hachette.co.uk

the Summer of Taking Chances

Chapter One

'Such a glamorous life we actors lead,' I said.

Richard stacked the last of the chairs against the wall. 'I think we're done,' he said.

I took one final look around the hall. Satisfied that we'd removed all evidence of the South Quay Players' rehearsal, and the Mother and Toddlers' Group would have no cause for complaint when they arrived at the community centre the following morning – an unwashed coffee mug lurking in the kitchen sink had caused uproar only last week – I returned the brush and dustpan I'd used to sweep the floor to the broom cupboard.

'Emma, before we go and join the rest of the cast,' Richard said, 'can I ask you something?'

'Sure,' I said. 'What is it?'

Richard hesitated, and then he said, 'Just between ourselves, what's your honest opinion of the committee's choice of play for the summer show?'

'I think it's great.'

'You don't think we're being too ambitious?'

'Not at all,' I said. 'Of course, as I'm playing the female lead, I may be biased.' The Players might be a small amateur dramatics society who shared their rehearsal space with the Brownies, a Pilates class and the WI, but the thought that in just a few months' time I'd be performing as Juliet, my favourite Shakespeare heroine, in front of a live audience made me smile – just as much, I felt sure, as if I was acting in a West End theatre.

'You were good tonight,' Richard said, 'but you're a naturally talented actress.'

'Thanks. You weren't too shabby yourself.' Richard gave an exaggerated bow, reminding me of the time he'd played Dandini in *Cinderella*.

'I think I did OK,' he said, 'but some of the cast are mangling every line. I can see us being called in for a lot of extra rehearsals this summer.'

'I'm not saying it won't be a challenge to get it right,' I said, 'but surely it's good to stretch ourselves as actors?'

'I think that rather depends on why you took up amateur dramatics,' Richard said. 'Why did you join the Players, Emma?'

I stared at him. Where is he going with this? I thought. 'I love acting,' I said. 'I always have. When I was a teenager, the school play was the highlight of my year.'

'I enjoy acting,' Richard said, 'but I can't help thinking that it stops being enjoyable when the show is a disaster because half the cast aren't up to it.'

'It'll all come together,' I said, uncomfortable with the direction the conversation appeared to be heading. These were our friends Richard was talking about. 'It always does.'

'Well, we'll see. At least I get to wave a sword about.'

'I'm sure you'll make a brilliant Tybalt.'

'Not that it's the role I wanted,' Richard said.

So that's what this is about, I thought.

'Henry can't have done a better audition than me,' Richard went on, 'but once again he gets the lead. Obviously his being the son of two committee members had nothing to do with it.'

'That's not fair to Henry,' I said.

'He was appalling tonight.'

'He was a bit wooden,' I said, 'but he'll be fine once he's learnt his lines.'

'*If* he learns his lines,' Richard said. 'Given his track record, I'm not holding my breath.' He took the keys to the hall out of his jeans pocket. 'Let's lock up and get to the pub. I could do with a pint.'

Having no desire to continue the discussion – it wasn't the first time Richard had criticised Henry's acting, and I didn't want to encourage the habit – I picked up my coat, followed him out of the hall, through the bar area, and out of the main entrance, then waited while he locked the door. When all was secure, we walked across the dark, empty car park, and along the high street to the Armada Inn.

'I'll get the drinks,' Richard said, opening the door to the pub and gesturing for me to go in first. 'Your usual?'

'Please,' I said. While he headed over to the bar to fetch my white wine and his lager, I looked around for the rest of the cast of *Romeo and Juliet*. Even this early in the season, the dearth of places to drink or eat out in South Quay ensured that that the Armada Inn, on this Wednesday night, was crowded with holidaymakers, who stared quizzically at the horse brasses on the walls or listened to the landlord's much-repeated story of how the pub got its name, as well as the locals who drank there all year. Among the throng, I spotted the Players' chairwoman, Pamela, and her husband Maurice – Henry's parents – sitting at a large table along with other august members of the committee and George, our director. The older Players, those the committee cast in character parts, were as always gathered together in the snug, drinking gin and tonic and reminiscing about the shows they'd performed when they were young. Two forty-something couples who had young children were draining their wine glasses – one quick drink after rehearsal and then they had to hurry home to relieve the babysitter. And at the far end of the room, sitting in a booth, were Lizzie, my best friend since primary school, her boyfriend Noah (who was playing Mercutio), Henry, and Sofia, a newcomer to South Quay and the Players' newest recruit.

Edging past the tightly packed tables, I slid into the booth next to Lizzie. A moment later, we were joined by Richard, who placed my white wine in front of me and sat down next to Sofia.

'Did you see who just walked in?' he said. Without waiting for an answer, he added, 'Jake.'

3

'Not Jake Murray?' Lizzie said.

Henry raised his eyebrows. 'Jake Murray's back in South Quay?'

'Do you know anyone else named Jake?' Richard said.

To my disquiet, my stomach twisted into a knot. I picked up my glass, and gulped down a mouthful of wine.

Sofia looked from one of us to the other. 'Are you talking about Jake Murray the actor?'

'The very same,' Richard said.

Sofia gasped. 'Do you know him?'

'He and I were in the same class in high school,' Noah said. 'Lizzie, Emma and Henry were in the year below. We all got to know each other through the school drama club.'

'I can't believe you know Jake Murray,' Sofia said, half rising from her seat, her gaze travelling rapidly round the pub.

'I was in the year above him,' Richard said. 'I never knew him that well.'

Sofia was no longer listening. 'I see him,' she said. 'He's buying a drink.'

As one, the others turned their heads towards the bar, and I found myself doing the same. I saw him immediately, a tall dark-haired man dressed in a leather jacket and black jeans, holding a bottle of beer, chatting easily with the barman, apparently oblivious to the sidelong glances he was attracting from most of the clientele in the pub. His shoulders were broader and his hair shorter than the last time I'd seen him in the Armada, but he was still extraordinarily good-looking – that much hadn't changed. At that moment, he noticed me staring at him, and his mouth lifted in an achingly familiar smile. I managed to smile back, but my heart was thudding in my chest. I drank some more wine, replacing my glass on the table with a shaking hand. This is absurd, I thought. Jake Murray is nothing to me, and I'm certainly nothing to him. I clasped my hands together in my lap and told myself to get a grip.

'Oh my goodness, he's coming over,' Sofia said.

4

I watched as Jake threaded his way across the room, stopping to exchange a few words with other people he'd have known when he lived in South Quay – the girl who was now the manager of the supermarket on the high street, the boy who'd become a garage mechanic, Sofia's boss from the hairdressers – before coming to a halt by our table. Fighting a sudden impulse to leap out of my seat and flee, avoiding this encounter altogether, I forced myself to look directly into his grey-blue eyes.

He said, '*Ill-met by moonlight, proud Titania.*'

As if from a distance, I heard myself reply, '*What, jealous Oberon! I have forsworn his company.*' My voice sounded more high-pitched than usual. I cleared my throat.

'I think you missed out a line,' Jake said.

'I was fifteen when we did that play,' I said.

'I'm amazed you remember any of it,' Henry said. 'Hey, Jake.'

'Hello, Jake,' Lizzie said. 'It's been a while.'

'It's been ten years, Lizzie,' Jake said. 'It's good to see you all.'

'Good to see you too, mate,' Noah said, his face breaking into a broad grin. He raised his pint glass, Jake clinked it with his bottled beer, and they both drank. Richard held out his hand, and Jake grasped it, before transferring the focus of his attention to Sofia.

'Hi,' he said. 'I'm Jake Murray.'

Sofia gaped at him. 'Oh – I know who you are. I— I'm Sofia. I'm so pleased to meet you. I love all your films. I've watched every series of *Sherwood* on TV.'

'Thank you, Sofia,' Jake said. 'Good to hear.' Sofia's face flushed red.

'So what brings you back to South Quay, Jake?' Richard said. 'How long are you here for?'

'I'm not sure how long I'm staying—' Jake broke off to take a vibrating phone out of the inside pocket of his jacket. He studied the screen. 'Sorry, I need to take this. I'll have to catch up with you guys another time.' Bestowing a smile on everyone at the table, he retraced his route through the crowded pub, holding the phone to his ear – his progress again marked by the turning of heads and surreptitious glances – and went out into the night. I reached for my glass, but saw that it was empty. I didn't recall finishing my wine.

'That was unreal,' Sofia said. 'I knew Jake Murray was born in South Quay, but I never thought I'd get to meet him. I wish I'd asked him for his autograph.' Sitting next to her, out of her line of sight, Richard rolled his eyes.

'In a place the size of South Quay, you're bound to run into him again,' Henry said. 'Ask him next time you see him.'

'Do you think he'd mind?' Sofia said.

'What do you think, Emma?' Henry said.

'I've no idea,' I said.

'You know him better than the rest of us,' Henry said.

'Maybe I did once, but that was a long time ago.'

Sofia's eyes widened, and she leant across the table towards me. 'Emma, did you date Jake Murray when you were younger?' she said, breathlessly. 'Were you and he a couple?'

'No,' I said. 'I was never his girlfriend. We were friends up until he went off to London to train as an actor, and then we lost touch.'

'I have a vague memory of him coming home one Christmas,' Noah said.

'You're right, he did,' Lizzie said. 'It was the Christmas break after his first term at drama school.' To Sofia, she added, 'The following year, Jake's parents moved abroad, so he had no reason to visit South Quay. The only place any of us have seen him in the last ten years is on a laptop, a TV screen, or in the newspapers.'

'I'd like to know what's brought him back here now,' Noah said.

'Do you think he could be on location for his next movie?' Sofia said.

'I doubt it,' Henry said. 'If a film were being shot in South Quay, everyone would be talking about it.'

Further speculation about Jake Murray's reappearance was interrupted by Richard asking if anyone wanted another drink.

'Not for me,' Lizzie said. 'I can't teach my class of six year olds tomorrow if I have a hangover. Ready to go, Noah?'

'Your place or mine?' Noah said.

'Mine,' Lizzie said. 'Coming with us, Emma?'

I nodded, and got to my feet. ''Night all,' I said. Accompanied by a chorus of 'goodnights' and assurances that we'd see the others at *Romeo and Juliet*'s next rehearsal if not before, the three of us donned our coats and trooped out of the pub.

It was cold outside after the heat and alcoholic fug of the Armada's interior, cold enough that I was glad it took us only five minutes to walk from the high street to Lizzie's cottage. To my surprise, as I hadn't known that he had a key, it was Noah who unlocked the front door. Stooping in order to step over the threshold without bashing his forehead on the lintel, he went inside. Lizzie and I followed, ridding ourselves of our coats with some difficulty now that we were all standing together in the minuscule hallway.

'Is it OK if I watch the footy highlights?' Noah said.

'Go right ahead,' Lizzie said. 'I'll make us coffee.' Noah vanished into the sitting room, and a moment later I heard the blare of televised football.

'I won't have a drink,' I said to Lizzie, setting my foot on the stair. 'I'll go straight up.'

Lizzie put her hand on my arm. 'Do you have a moment to talk?'

'Of course,' I said, following her into the kitchen and sitting at the table. Lizzie shut the door, filled the kettle, and took two mugs from the dresser, but instead of making coffee she sat down opposite me.

'I have to ask,' she said, 'are you all right?'

'Why wouldn't I be?' I said.

'In a word – Jake.'

'I'm all right,' I said. I considered this statement, and decided it was true. It had thrown me, seeing Jake, even after all this time, but the moment had passed. 'I admit it was a shock seeing him tonight, but only because I didn't expect it.'

'So you're not going to be crying yourself to sleep?'

'Not a chance.' I've shed far too many tears over him already, I thought.

For a long moment, Lizzie regarded me in silence. Then she said, 'Emma, I know how much he hurt you.'

I thought, You don't know the half of it. Aloud, I said, 'I had a crush on a boy, and he wasn't interested. It's hardly a Shake-spearean tragedy.'

'It was more than a crush,' Lizzie said. 'At least, as far as I remember.'

'Whatever it was I felt for Jake Murray when we were teen-agers,' I said, 'I was over him a very long time ago.'

'You're sure you're OK?'

'I'm fine,' I said. 'Really I am. The kettle's boiled, by the way.'

Lizzie jumped up out of her seat, located the coffee jar, and reached into the fridge for milk.

'See you tomorrow,' I said. 'Goodnight, Lizzie.' I left her spooning sugar into Noah's mug – after dating him for four months, she had a pretty good idea of how he liked his late-night beverages – and went upstairs.

Considering it was almost midnight, my bedroom was sur-prisingly light. I went to the window, rested my hands on the sill, and looked out. The sky was clear and the moon was full. *Ill-met by moonlight.* A memory surfaced, the first time Jake had said those words to me …

I am fifteen, and I'm to play the role of Titania in my school's production of A Midsummer Night's Dream. *Jake is playing Oberon. He and I are rehearsing our scenes on the beach, proclaiming our lines to an audi-ence of indifferent seagulls.*

'Try it again,' I say. 'From the top.' I like using theatrical language. Even when I'm not talking about the theatre.

'Ill-met by moonlight, proud Titania.'

'What, jealous Oberon!' I say. 'Fairies skip hence; I have forsworn his bed and his company.'

'Tarry, rash wanton; am I not thy lord?' he says. The surf is pounding against the shore, and our words are snatched away by the wind. Grey clouds are scudding across the sky.

'Jake,' I say, 'there's something I've been meaning to tell you.' I take a deep breath. I haven't revealed this to anyone else yet, not even my parents or Lizzie. 'I've decided I want to go on with my acting after I leave school. I want to be a professional actress.' I study his face for his reaction, half expecting him to laugh – he laughs at a lot of the things I say to him. Instead, his expression is solemn.

He says, 'I'm glad you told me that, because I feel the same. Next year, I'm going to apply to drama school.'

'Oh, Jake,' I say, 'that's so great. Just think – we could end up training at the same place.'

Jake smiles. 'Some day, both of us could be performing in the West End or on TV.' He does laugh then, and so do I for the sheer excitement of all that lies ahead of us. He catches hold of my hands and spins me around, and we run down the beach to the edge of the sea. Both of us breathless, we stand looking out over the white breakers to the horizon.

Jake's attention is caught by something lying on the sand. He reaches for it and holds it up to the light, and I see it is a piece of sea glass, blue and worn smooth by the waves.

'It's beautiful,' I say.

'If you like it, you can have it,' he says, handing it to me. I bend my head to look at the glass more closely, and when I look up again, Jake's eyes meet mine. In that instant, it comes to me that this good-looking boy, my friend who shares my love of the theatre, is about to kiss me. A shiver runs through me that has nothing to do with the cold wind blowing in from the sea.

He says, 'It's time I went. I'm going out tonight.'

'Hot date?' I say, keeping my tone light.

'I may get lucky,' he says with a wolfish grin. He turns and starts walking back up the beach. Still holding the glass, I walk beside him. I

9

remind myself that we are friends. I wonder if whichever girl he's seeing tonight would be jealous if she knew he'd spent the afternoon on the beach with me. Probably not, I think, as all we did was recite Shakespeare.

I ask myself what I'd have done if Jake had tried to kiss me, and realise I wouldn't have pushed him away …

I gazed out of my bedroom window at the night sky. We were so young, I thought. Reminding myself that I was no longer the naïve teenage girl with stars in her eyes who'd fallen for Jake Murray, I drew the curtains, shutting out the moonlight.

Chapter Two

I surveyed my reflection in the full-length mirror on my wardrobe door. My new charcoal grey shift dress was a little severe – not the sort of dress I'd wear any place except work – but with a pair of high-heeled court shoes it did make me look thoroughly professional, I thought. I pinned on the badge that identified me as *Emma Stevens, Events Assistant*, and went downstairs.

In the kitchen, I found Noah, wearing the suit and tie demanded by his job at the bank in Teymouth, sitting at the table demolishing a bacon sandwich. Lizzie, also dressed for work in a blouse and skirt, her honey-blonde hair tied back in a ponytail, was stashing a pile of school exercise books in her bag.

'Morning, Emma,' Noah said. 'I was just saying to Lizzie that we should invite Jake over here one night for a meal.'

My heart sank. I might no longer have any *feelings* for Jake – I'd be a very sad case if I was still carrying a torch for him after so many years – but that didn't mean I was entirely comfortable with the prospect of spending an evening with him in Lizzie's cottage, talking over old times. Then it occurred to me that if my friends wanted to welcome Jake back into the fold, there wasn't much I could do about it. They'd also been his friends once.

'Oh, why not?' I said. Realising I was sounding distinctly unenthusiastic, I added, 'Good idea. Maybe we could invite some other people as well. We could have a party.' Less chance of my having to talk to Jake if there's a crowd, I thought.

'This cottage is too small for that,' Lizzie said. 'If we're going

11

to extend the invitation beyond the four of us, the only other person I'd want to invite is Henry. Unless there's someone else you'd particularly like to invite, Emma?'

'She's means a guy,' Noah said, with a grin. 'Anyone you've got your eye on?'

'None that I can think of right now,' I said. A thought struck me. 'Jake might want to bring someone. He might have someone staying with him.'

'You mean a girlfriend?' Lizzie said.

'If he has one,' I said.

'He's dating – what's her name?' Lizzie said. 'She had a guest role in *Sherwood* playing Jake's cousin.'

'Leonie Fox,' Noah said.

'That's her,' Lizzie said. 'I've seen photos of them on the internet.'

'So it'll either be supper for five,' Noah said, 'or six if Jake wants to bring his girl. I'll cook, if you like.'

'Now that's a splendid idea,' Lizzie said. 'The evening's looking up.' She frowned. 'Small problem. Jake's back in South Quay, but we've no idea where he's staying.'

'Oh, one of us will come across him soon enough,' Noah said. He checked his watch. 'Shite – I'm running late.' Pushing back his chair, he got to his feet. 'See you, Emma.'

'Bye, Noah,' I said.

Lizzie followed Noah into the hall. I heard the murmur of their voices, a long silence, and then the opening and shutting of the front door. She came back into the kitchen.

'I can't understand why I never fancied Noah when we were younger,' Lizzie said. 'I always liked him, but only as a friend. Whereas now ...'

'Now, you can't keep your hands off him?' I said.

A smile flickered across Lizzie's face. I thought of the number of Noah's belongings that had made their way to the cottage from his parents' house, where he still lived, and the amount of time he and Lizzie were spending together.

'Lizzie, are you and Noah getting *serious*?' I said.

Lizzie hesitated, and then she said, 'I think – I think we could be heading that way, but it's still early days. We've not been together as a couple very long.'

'I noticed that he has a key to the cottage,' I said.

'Oh – I hope you don't mind,' Lizzie said. 'I should have asked you before I gave it to him.'

'If you want to give your boyfriend his own front door key, you don't have to ask my permission,' I said. 'It's your cottage.'

'But it's your home,' Lizzie said.

'I honestly don't mind. It'd be different if you'd hooked up with a man who left wet towels on the bathroom floor or drank all the wine in the fridge, but Noah seems fairly well house-trained.'

'He's lovely,' Lizzie said. She put on her raincoat, which had been hanging on the back of a chair, and picked up her bag. 'About this invitation to Jake. Are you going to be OK with him coming here?'

'Didn't we talk about this last night?'

'Yes,' said Lizzie. 'Yes, we did. Sorry. I should probably stop talking now and go to work.'

'See you later, hun,' I said.

Hoisting her bag onto her shoulder, Lizzie headed off to the red-brick primary school that she and I'd attended ourselves. Still having a few minutes before I needed to leave to catch my bus, I sat and drank my morning tea, my gaze travelling round the kitchen, taking in the old wooden dresser that Lizzie had so lovingly repaired and decorated with painted flowers, the earthenware jug she'd placed on the windowsill, filled with daffodils from her garden, and the blue and white curtains she'd made on the sewing machine her parents had given her for her seventeenth birthday.

When I was seventeen, I thought, I'd never have imagined that ten years later I'd still be living in South Quay, renting a room in Lizzie Flowerdew's cottage. I drained my tea and sprang to my feet. I was *not* going to start raking over the past. I might not have the brilliant theatrical career I thought I was going to have when I was a teenager, but I had a good job, and amazing friends. My life, I thought, has turned out pretty well.

I found my bag, located my jacket in the hall, and went to work.

14

Chapter Three

'So we'll look forward to seeing you on Saturday,' I said to the woman on the other end of the line.

'It can't come soon enough for me,' the woman said. 'It's meant to be one of the best days of my life, but I can't help thinking of all the things that could go wrong.'

'It's our job to make sure that everything happens exactly as you want it,' I said. 'All you need to do is enjoy a wonderful day that you and your guests will remember for ever.'

'I just hope my cousin Harriet doesn't get drunk,' said the woman.

Me too, I thought. I could remember very few weddings at the Downland Hotel and Conference Centre where all of the guests had stayed stone-cold sober until the end of the evening reception.

'The day will be perfect,' I said.

'That's what I'll keep telling myself! Anyway, I'll see you Saturday morning at nine o'clock sharp. Goodbye until then.'

'Goodbye,' I said, as the woman ended the call.

Eve looked up from her computer. 'Bride or groom?'

'The bride's mother,' I said, 'although the way she carries on, you'd think it was her wedding, not her daughter's.'

Eve laughed. 'When – if – my daughter gets married, I'm sure I'll be the same.' She turned back to her computer screen.

I looked through the emails in my inbox. None of them were so urgent that they couldn't wait until tomorrow. I glanced at the clock on the wall. Already 5.25. It was hardly worth my starting on anything else now, but while Eve might be an amiable boss, she was a stickler for timekeeping. While the clock hands crept slowly round to 5.30, I kept my eyes on my screen.

'I'm off home now,' I said, finally. Eve nodded, distracted by whatever she was typing. I grabbed my coat and bag, and made my escape.

Taking a short cut out of the hotel through the bar, I found it full of men and women in suits, all talking loudly, and all necking their pre-dinner drinks as if alcohol was going out of fashion. If I'd had a working day like theirs, sitting through innumerable presentations and seminars, I suspected I'd be doing the same. Keeping my head down – I was off duty now – I skirted around them, and left the building. Walking as fast as I could in my high heels, I hurried along the long drive that led through the Downland's grounds to the coast road, my bus stop, and freedom from demanding guests – at least until tomorrow.

Half an hour later, I'd arrived back in South Quay, and was queuing up in the supermarket, while the woman in front of me brought Carol, who was working on the till, up to date on the doings of her extended family. Eventually, she ran out of relatives to gossip about, paid for her shopping, and left.

'Evening, Emma,' Carol said, as she swiped my pint of milk. 'You won't believe who came in here earlier.'

'Who?'

'Jake Murray,' Carol said. 'He's back in South Quay for the summer, so he told me. He bought a pizza.'

'He has to eat something,' I said, amused at the tone of awe in Carol's voice – she'd seen Jake in the supermarket often enough when he was a boy.

'Well, yes,' Carol said, 'but I wouldn't have expected him to be doing his own shopping. Not now that he's famous. Celebrities have people who do that sort of thing for them.'

The idea that Jake would employ someone to buy his groceries was, to me, unlikely, but not impossible. For all I knew of the

16

way he lived now, he could have any number of PAs and domestic staff.

'He's done so well,' Carol continued. 'I never thought he'd amount to very much. He was such a tearaway when he was younger.'

Before he discovered acting, I thought. I handed over the money for my milk, and Carol gave me my change.

'Thanks,' I said. 'Bye, now.'

'See you, love.'

Outside, it was still light, and in contrast to the previous night, unusually warm for May. I strolled the rest of the way home and let myself in, discovering Lizzie sitting on the floor in the front room, surrounded by lengths of different-coloured fabric that she was cutting into long thin strips.

'It's for a weaving activity for my class,' she said, seeing my questioning look.

'Sounds fun.' More fun than most of what I do at work, I thought.

'I haven't got any further with our invite to Jake, by the way. The return of our local-boy-made-good was the top goss in the staffroom, but no one I spoke to had any idea where he's staying.'

'I should've asked Carol if she knew when I called in at the supermarket,' I said. 'She was very excited to tell me he'd stopped by her till.'

'Well, it's not every day that you get to meet a *star*,' Lizzie said. We both laughed.

Leaving Lizzie among the piles of wool and silk, I deposited my milk in the fridge, went up to my room, and changed out of my work dress into a shirt and jeans. My over-flowing laundry basket was glowering at me, but it seemed wrong to waste such an unseasonably warm evening indoors doing household chores, especially as I was fairly sure that the tide would be out far enough for a walk along the sand. Calling out to let Lizzie know where I was going, I left the cottage, turning out of Saltwater Lane onto

17

the appropriately named Shore Road. Heading past the shops selling beach balls, sunblock, postcards and flip-flops, and through the car park – empty now of day-trippers' cars – at the end of the road, I came to the stones at the top of the beach.

The expanse of sea in front of me was as still as a mill-pond, and the sun was sinking towards the horizon, streaking the sky with red and gold. Two teenage girls were sitting on the stones sharing a portion of chips, while a family, mother, father and two boys, were playing cricket on the strip of sand between the stones and the incoming tide, which had yet to reach the end of the breakwaters. I went down onto the sand and started walking westwards towards the headland, glancing up occasionally at the large houses, built in a variety of styles, which lined this part of the shore. Gradually, the houses became fewer and further between. I passed a woman walking a dog, and a fisherman in waders casting a line, and then, as I rounded a particularly high breakwater, I saw Jake Murray, standing on the water's edge, with his back to me, throwing stones into the sea.

Meeting Jake alone like this, with no one else around to deflect any possible awkwardness between us, was not what I'd have chosen, but it seemed to me that darting back around the breakwater before he saw me was not a rational option. I started walking towards him.

'Hey, Jake,' I said. He spun around.

'Emma,' he said, his face breaking into a smile. 'I was trying to skim stones, but I seem to have lost the knack.' If he felt any disquiet at my accosting him on the beach, he gave no sign of it.

'Want me to show you?' I said. He passed me a flat round stone. I weighed it in my hand, turned sideways to the sea, and flicked my wrist to send the stone skimming across the glass-smooth surface. 'You taught me how to do that.'

'I remember.' Jake copied my stance, but the stone he threw immediately sank. He sighed and turned his face towards the sea, and it felt natural for me to stand beside him, while the sun vanished below the horizon, and the daylight started to fade. The tide rose higher, reaching the end of the breakwaters. 'It's so good to see you again, Emma,' he said.

I looked up at him, this attractive man in his late twenties, and despite the changes in him, the fine lines at the corners of his eyes, the dark shadow on his chin, I could still see the features of the boy I'd known. Suddenly, it seemed to me that standing here with him now, I was being offered a chance to renew a friendship that had been important to me, and I wanted to take it.

'It's good to see you again, too,' I said.

We both fell silent, but after a moment, Jake said, 'Have you eaten tonight?'

'Not yet,' I said.

'Would you like to come back to my place and share a pizza? If there's nowhere else you have to be.'

This was so unexpected that all I did was stare at him.

'If you need to get home,' Jake said, 'if someone's expecting you, maybe we can meet up some other time?'

Recovering myself, I said 'No, I don't have to hurry home. Yes, I'd like to come back to yours. Where are you staying?'

'I'm renting the old Victorian pile just up there,' Jake said, gesturing landwards.

Together we walked up the beach, our feet leaving a double set of footprints on the wet sand, and clambered up a steep slope of stones. Crossing over a narrow earth track – the only route along the shore when the tide was high – we came to a thick hedge that shielded Jake's rented house from both the salt-laden wind off the sea and the curious gazes of passers-by. We went through a wooden gate that opened on to a stretch of lawn, and the house itself – one of several ornate holiday villas with balconies and verandas built in South Quay by well-to-do Victorians, and the last building before the village gave way to open farmland – came into view. Jake led me across the grass to the back door, which he unlocked, and we went inside.

'Have a seat,' he said, switching on a light to reveal a fitted kitchen – spacious, but, with its hideously patterned wall tiles, in dire need of renovation. In the centre of the room was a wooden refectory table, with benches either side. I sat, while Jake took a pizza out of the fridge, and put it in the oven.

'I can only offer you red wine,' he said, 'but would you like a drink?'

'Isn't red wine compulsory with pizza?'

'If only I could remember where my landlady keeps the glasses …' After opening and shutting several cupboards, Jake found two tumblers, which he half-filled with wine. Sitting opposite me, he said, 'I've not had time to find out where everything is yet. I only arrived yesterday.'

Recalling the proposed supper invitation, and Lizzie's concern about numbers, I said, 'Will Leonie Fox be joining you?'

Jake raised one eyebrow. 'I'm guessing you haven't read the tabloids this week, or you'd know that Leonie and I broke up.'

'Oh, I'm so sorry,' I said, making a mental note to tell Lizzie that her information regarding Jake's love life was out of date.

'Yeah, me too.' His mouth tightened. 'It's meant I've had the press doorstepping me all week. I decided to get away until they lost interest, and by chance, I saw this house up for rent on the internet and had a sudden impulse to take it for the summer. I don't start shooting the next series of *Sherwood* until September, and I've told my agent I'm not accepting any other work for the next few months. I've some scripts to read through, but other than that, I'm on vacation.'

I get four weeks' holiday a year, I thought, and he doesn't need to work for *months*?

'What about you?' Jake said. 'Are you seeing anyone? You're not wearing a ring, so I assume you're not married or engaged?' Evidently the subject of his break-up with Leonie was now closed.

'Never got close,' I said. 'I've been in a relationship a few times in the last ten years, but right now I'm single.'

'Still living in the parental abode?' he said.

'I have a room in Lizzie Flowerdew's cottage,' I said. 'My rent helps her pay her mortgage.'

'Lizzie owns a cottage?'

'Her parents lent her money for a deposit when she moved back home after university. She'd trained as a teacher, there was a vacancy at South Quay Primary—' I broke off as Jake got to his feet, found two plates and cutlery, took the pizza out of the oven, and served it. 'Time hasn't stood still in South Quay while you've been living in London, you know.' It just seems that way, I thought.

Jake laughed. 'Maybe not,' he said, 'but when I saw you, Lizzie, Noah, and Henry in the Armada last night, I felt like I'd stepped back into the past.'

'Lizzie and Noah are a couple now,' I said.

'I'd never have seen that coming,' said Jake.

'I don't think they did either,' I said. 'They hooked up after the pantomime, at the cast party.'

'Whoa,' Jake said. 'Rewind. What pantomime?'

'These days, we're all members of the South Quay Players.' I took a bite of pizza. 'We do two plays a year, and a panto at Christmas. We're in the middle of rehearsals for our summer production, *Romeo and Juliet*. I'm playing Juliet.'

'Of course you are,' Jake said. 'You always had talent. I was surprised when you didn't go to drama school.'

'I wanted to,' I said, 'if you remember.'

'Yeah, I know you didn't get a place the first time you auditioned,' Jake said. 'I assumed you'd apply again the next year. A lot of people audition more than once.'

'I did want to become an actress,' I said, 'but when I wasn't able to go to the Royal College of Drama, I decided it wasn't going to happen.'

'You thought you weren't good enough to be successful?'

'I realised that I didn't want an acting career badly enough to find out.' I'm not lying to him, I thought. Not exactly.

21

'So what did you do instead?' Jake said. 'Did you go to university like Lizzie?'

I shook my head. 'The summer I left school, I saw an advert for an Events Assistant at the Downland Hotel. I applied, and got the job. I've been there ever since. Nearly ten years.'

Jake raised his eyebrows. 'You must *really* like your work.'

'I do enjoy some of it,' I said. 'When I see a newly wed couple take to the floor for their first dance and I know that I've helped to make their wedding day special, that's wonderful. But there's a lot of admin I'm not so keen on.' I shrugged. 'It's OK. Not everyone gets to earn their living doing something they're passionate about like you do.'

'I wouldn't act if I didn't get well paid for it,' Jake said. 'I'd turn down a part if the money wasn't right. That's why I've stopped doing live theatre. I can earn so much more in TV or film.'

'It's not only about the money though, is it?' I said. 'The high you get from acting – there's nothing like it.'

'Acting's just a job, Emma,' Jake said. 'I'll admit it has its moments – when I know I've nailed a difficult piece of dialogue or when there's really great chemistry between me and another actor – but they're fewer than you might think. When I'm filming, my working day consists of long hours of tedium waiting to be called to set, interspersed with bursts of frantic activity. On my last feature, I had to do twenty-five takes of one scene because another actor kept forgetting his lines. I was on set until ten o'clock at night, and I had to be in make-up by six the next morning.' He drained his wine, re-filled his glass, and topped up mine. 'I'm successful, I make good money from acting, but it's bloody hard work.'

I stared at him, remembering the boy who'd told me that he didn't care about money or material possessions, that he knew acting was a precarious profession, but it was all he wanted to do.

'I'm sure a lot of people would be glad to swap places with you,' I said.

'Yeah, what other job would give me the money and the life-style I have now?' Jake said. 'If I hadn't gone to drama school, if I'd stayed living in South Quay, I'd most likely be working nine to five in an office in Teymouth, staring at a computer screen all day, and drinking my meagre wages every night in the Armada. Not that there's anything wrong in living your whole life in a seaside village on the Sussex coast, but it was never going to be enough for me.'

There was a time, I thought, when I felt the same.

'Can I offer you a coffee?' Jake said.

I glanced at my watch. 'Not for me, thanks. I should make a move. I have to be up early tomorrow.' To catch the bus that will get me to my computer screen on time, I thought. 'Before I go – Lizzie, Noah and I were wondering if you'd like to come to the cottage for a meal. We thought we'd invite Henry as well.'

'Sounds good to me,' Jake said.

I fished my phone out of my jeans. 'Give me your mobile number, and I'll call you to sort out a night when we're all free.'

Jake hesitated. 'I will give it to you,' he said, eventually, 'but can I ask you not to give it to anyone else without checking with me first? There are people who'd pay good money for my private phone number.'

'OK.' This was a part of his success as an actor that had never occurred to me.

He told me the number and I keyed it into my phone.

'May I have yours?' He got to his feet and retrieved his phone from a work counter. Once I'd rattled off the number for him to add to his contacts, he said, 'If I really can't tempt you to a coffee, I'll walk you home.'

'Thanks for the offer,' I said, 'but there's no need.'

'I can't let you walk home alone late at night.'

'I'll be perfectly safe. We're in South Quay, not the mean streets of the metropolis.'

'Maybe so,' Jake said, 'but I wouldn't feel right, so you're going to have to put up with my company a little longer.'

23

Before I could make any further protest, he was opening the back door and stepping into the garden. I followed him outside, and we retraced our footsteps across the lawn and through the gate. The sea was high now, but still calm, and silvered with moonlight, and the night sky was scattered with stars.

'I'd forgotten how beautiful the sea can be at night,' Jake said.

'I don't think you took much notice of it when you lived here.'

'You're right about that,' Jake said. 'Back then, if I came down to the beach at night, it was to drink cider with my mates, not to admire the landscape.' He smiled, and then he offered me his arm – not a gesture he'd ever have made when he was a teenager. I slid my arm through his. We walked to Lizzie's cottage in a companionable silence.

'This is where I live now,' I said, as we arrived at the front gate.

'I'll say goodnight then,' Jake said. I went through the gate into the tiny patch of garden that separated the cottage from the street. The gate swung shut, leaving Jake standing on the other side.

'Goodnight,' I said.

'*Parting is such sweet sorrow,*' Jake said, '*that I shall say good night till it be morrow.*'

'Those are Juliet's lines,' I said.

'I know,' Jake said. 'I played Romeo in my third year at drama school.' Resting his hands on the gate, he added, '*If we do meet again, why, we shall smile.*'

'*If not,*' I said, '*then this parting was well-made. I did Julius Caesar for English A level.*'

Jake laughed. 'I'm all out of quotes,' he said. 'Goodnight, Emma.'

He turned away, and headed off along Saltwater Lane. I watched him until he turned the corner into Shore Road and vanished from my sight, and then I let myself into the cottage.

Creeping up the stairs so as not to wake Lizzie – or Noah, if he was there – and after a quick detour to the bathroom, I went to my bedroom, changed into an oversized T-shirt, and sat on the side of my bed. How different Jake's life was from mine, I thought. How different my life might have been, if I'd gone to drama school …

My parents are both at work. My sister, Scarlet, has gone down to the beach with Nathan, her boyfriend. I am alone in the house, sitting at the dining table surrounded by books, trying to revise for my next A level exam, when I see the postman walk up the drive and put something through the letter-box. I stand up and go out into the hall. On the front mat, along with the usual junk mail, is a large white envelope. My stomach lurches. Somehow, I know this is the letter I've been waiting for, even before I read my name on the address label. I pick the envelope up, open it, and take out the sheet of paper inside. I read the letter twice. Then I go back into the dining room, and call Lizzie on my mobile.

'I got my letter from the Royal College of Drama,' I say, when she answers. 'I didn't get in.'

'I don't believe it,' Lizzie says. 'There must be some mistake.'

'There's no mistake,' I say.

'But – you said the audition went well.'

'I was wrong,' I say.

'Oh, Emma,' Lizzie says, 'I'm so sorry.' After a moment, she adds, 'At least you can try again next year.'

'Yes, there's always next year, but I'm not even going to think about that 'til after the exams.' I know that I can't re-apply to RoCoDa. Not next year. Not ever. I say, 'How's your revision going?'

Lizzie groans. 'I've still loads to get through.'

'Me too,' I say. 'I wanted to tell you about the letter, but I really should get back to Julius Caesar.'

'I haven't even started on English yet,' Lizzie says. 'Listen, how about we meet up in the Armada on Friday night? There's going to be a live band.'

'I – I don't know if I can,' I say. 'It depends how much revision I

have left to do. I'll text you.' We end the call. I read the letter one more time. Then I rip it into shreds.

Tears sting my eyes. I'm seventeen, and my life is in ruins …

I sat on my bed and thought, I could have tried again, I could have auditioned for other drama schools. Except once I knew I wouldn't be going to RoCoDa, I no longer wanted to become a professional actress.

At seventeen, all I'd wanted was Jake.

Chapter Four

I let myself into the cottage and kicked off the high heels I'd worn to the Downland. Lizzie had already left for school before I'd come downstairs that morning, but now, going into the living room, I found her sitting cross-legged on the two-seater sofa, her laptop open on her knees.

'Are you working?' I said, knowing that parents often contacted her by email in the evenings if they worked during school hours and couldn't get to see her during the day.

'Either that or posting a photo of me in a bikini on Henry's boat,' Lizzie said.

I sat down in the rocking chair. 'I met Jake Murray on the beach yesterday,' I said. 'He's renting that gothic Victorian edifice on the seafront. I rather put my foot in it, by asking him if his girlfriend would be joining him. He and Leonie Fox are no longer an item.'

'Oh, no,' Lizzie said. 'Poor Jake. Is he very upset?'

'I couldn't really tell. He didn't go into any detail about what happened.' I pictured Jake as he'd been yesterday, saying very little about Leonie, which was entirely understandable, but relaxed and talking easily with me while we ate and drank wine. 'He seemed OK,' I said, 'but I got the impression that he didn't want to talk about her. I invited him to supper, by the way, and he said he'd come.'

'Oh, that's great,' Lizzie said. 'Did you arrange a date?'

'What? With Jake? No, why would you think—' Belatedly, I

27

realised that Lizzie was still talking about the supper party. 'No, we didn't get that far,' I said. 'How about we make it Saturday week? My Saturday nights are pretty much taken up with wedding receptions after that for the rest of the summer, apart from the weekend of the summer show.'

'That would suit me and Noah,' Lizzie said.

'Right, I'll let Jake know,' I said, starting at the sound of the front door opening. I reminded myself that Noah now had a key to the cottage. A moment later he appeared in the doorway to the living room.

'Evening,' he said, planting a kiss on the top of Lizzie's head, and lowering his lean frame down onto the sofa.

'Emma saw Jake yesterday,' Lizzie said, 'and he's accepted our invitation to supper. We just need to confirm the date with him.'

'Ah,' Noah said. 'About that supper. I sort of invited Richard to join us ...'

'What does *sort of invited* mean?' Lizzie said.

'I went for a quick half with Henry on my way back from work,' Noah said. 'I'd just invited *him*, and we were still talking about it, when Richard walked in. He assumed he was included in the invitation. I could hardly tell him he wasn't.'

'No, I suppose not,' Lizzie said. 'But do try not to accidentally invite anyone else or we won't fit around the kitchen table.'

'So what are we doing about eating tonight?' Noah said.

'Fish and chips?' Lizzie said. 'It's warm enough to eat them on the beach.'

'Sure,' Noah said. 'Coming with us, Emma?'

'Not tonight, thanks,' I said, mindful that even with friends I'd known as long as Lizzie and Noah, three people eating fish and chips out of newspaper on the beach while watching the sunset would likely be a crowd. 'See you later.'

The two of them left the living room, and again I heard the front door open and close. I took my phone out of my bag and texted Jake the proposed time and date of the supper party, and got a smiley face in reply, which I took as a confirmation he'd be there. I wondered what he was doing this Friday night, if he was having a quiet night in, or if he was planning on making a sortie to the pub. My gaze fell on Lizzie's laptop. On impulse, I picked it up and googled 'Jake Murray'.

Although I'd never felt the need to watch him on screen, Jake's name had cropped up both in the media and in the Armada Inn enough times over the years for me to be aware of the minor roles on TV he'd done when he'd first left drama school – back then, my family had never failed to inform me when they'd spotted 'Jake Murray' in the credits – the roles in theatre and film that followed, and his lead role in *Sherwood,* the TV series that had made him famous. Until tonight, I'd never come across anything in the media about his personal life – unlike some actors, he'd never courted that sort of publicity – but now my internet search flooded Lizzie's laptop with photos of him and Leonie Fox. Evidently, their being an item had made them a magnet for the paparazzi. Clicking on a gossip site, I found a recent picture of the pair of them leaving a cinema after a premiere, with a foot of space between them. The photo was captioned, 'Is this The End for Leonie and Jake?' The accompanying column inches informed readers that 'the on—off relationship between Jake Murray and Leonie Fox is once again in trouble.' On another site, Jake was photographed alone, walking past a London underground station – presumably the shot had been taken with a long lens, because he appeared unaware of the camera. The caption read: 'The final credits roll for the star of *Sherwood* and his Foxy Lady,' which made me cringe. Clicking on a video link, I found myself watching Jake being interviewed on a late-night arts programme, talking about his training and his career, mentioning that he'd first got into acting while he was at school. I watched the interview right through, but it didn't tell me anything about him that I didn't already know. I closed the laptop.

I thought, if I hadn't given him that flyer …

I am thirteen, and I'm standing with Lizzie, handing out flyers for the after-school drama club to the motley crowd of teenagers pouring in through

29

the school gates at the start of the day. Miss Sheridan, our new, young, and boundlessly enthusiastic drama teacher, has told the club that if we're to put on a play this year, we need to recruit new members.

Some students, mainly girls, take the flyers and stash them in their bags. Others, mainly boys, drop them on the playground. Jake Murray saunters past, hands in his pockets, shirt untucked, minus his tie, ignoring us. He is fourteen, tall for his age and very good-looking – too cool for school is how the girls in my class describe him – and I know he'd be perfect to play the lead in The Scarlet Pimpernel. If he can act.

'We need more boys,' I say to Lizzie. 'I'm going to give a flyer to Jake Murray.'

'He won't take it,' Lizzie says, but I'm already trotting after Jake. I call out his name and he turns and stares at me.

'What?' he says.

There are girls in my class who can't speak to Jake without giggling and tossing their hair, but I have a higher purpose. 'Drama Club,' I say. 'Auditions for The Scarlet Pimpernel. Today after school.' I offer him the flyer.

'I can't,' he says, 'even if I wanted to. I have detention after school.'

'That's a shame,' I say. 'Why don't you ask Miss Sheridan if she can get you out of it? Tell her how much you love acting.'

I smile as he takes the flyer …

I thought, it's because of me that Jake became an actor. Well, at least partly because of me. And because of him, I … Pushing *that* thought away, I switched on the TV, and found the first series of *Sherwood* on catch-up. Jake's performance as Robert Sherwood was every bit as good as I'd have expected of the boy I'd once known.

30

Chapter Five

What with my overseeing the smooth running of the wedding that Saturday – cousin Harriet managed not to disgrace herself, although by the time the bride's mother waved her daughter and new son-in-law off on their honeymoon, *she* was distinctly squiffy – and my going to my parents' for Sunday lunch, I didn't see much of Lizzie and Noah over the weekend, but on Monday night, the three of us walked to rehearsal together.

Arriving at the community centre, we went into the main hall, where we discovered Sofia and another *Romeo and Juliet* cast member, Zoe (like Lizzie, both of them had walk-on roles as citizens of Verona), setting out the chairs. Zoe, who taught a Zumba class in the community centre, had volunteered to choreograph the dance for the Capulets' ball scene. Which, I was fairly certain, was the reason why Phyllis, who taught a children's ballet class, and had choreographed the Players' shows for the last fifteen years, hadn't spoken to her since the first day of rehearsal. I made a mental note to praise Phyllis's acting the next time I spoke to her. She was excellent as Juliet's Nurse, and I didn't want her dropping out of the production in a huff when I had so many scenes with her.

As soon as she saw us, Sofia put down the chair she was carrying and bounded across the hall.

'Richard told me about the house party,' she said. 'I'm so looking forward to it. Such a great idea to welcome Jake Murray back to South Quay.'

The smile that appeared on Lizzie's face was a testament to her talents as an actress. 'I wouldn't describe it as a house party,' she said. 'It's just a quiet supper with friends.'

'I'm sure it'll be lovely,' Sofia said. 'Is there anything you'd like me to bring, apart from wine?'

'No,' Lizzie said, 'but thanks for offering.'

Zoe, who'd wandered over to join us, and was listening to the conversation with undisguised interest, said, 'I'd love to meet Jake Murray. I don't suppose you've room for one more at your party?'

'It's not a party,' Lizzie said. 'But I'm sure we can squeeze you in.' Her smile became a rictus grin.

'Oh, thank you so much,' Zoe said. 'My sisters are going to be so jealous.' Having chorused their thanks once again, the citizens of Verona returned to the task of readying the hall for the evening's rehearsal.

'That makes eight of us,' Lizzie said to me and Noah. 'I don't have enough chairs. Or matching plates.'

'It'll be fine, Lizzie,' I said. 'I'll borrow a couple of folding chairs from my parents.'

'What does Richard think he's doing, inviting Sofia to my cottage?' Lizzie said.

'Well, if he's got it into his head that we're holding a house party,' Noah said, 'he most likely assumed she was already on the guest list.'

'As for Zoe,' Lizzie said, 'I should've told her I'd introduce her to Jake some other time, but I simply couldn't do it. It'd be like telling a six year old they couldn't come to a birthday party.'

'Aw, Lizzie, you are such a sweet girl,' Noah said.

'I just hope Jake doesn't think we've invited him over to show him off to a roomful of starstruck fans,' Lizzie said.

'It's only two starstruck fans,' I said. 'I'm sure he'll cope. I'll text him and warn him he'll be eating off mismatched crockery.' Seeing Lizzie's frown, I added, 'Sorry. Bad joke.'

'I'm being ridiculous, aren't I?' Lizzie said. 'Ignore me. Oh, there's George – I need to ask him if he's happy with my design for the programmes.'

While we'd been talking to Sofia and Zoe, the rest of *Romeo and Juliet*'s cast had been drifting into the hall. Raising her arm to attract the attention of our director, Lizzie hurried off to speak to him.

'I'd better go and give Maurice a hand,' Noah said. 'If he puts his back out again, we won't have a Lord Capulet.' He walked over to our Chairwoman's portly husband, who was crawling round the hall floor, marking the positions of scenery in our performance area with masking tape, loudly supervised by his wife. I looked longingly towards the stage at the far end of the hall which except for the actual week of the show, was used by the various groups who frequented the community centre as a storage space. Did the RSC have to share their stage with badminton nets, yoga mats, and Wendy houses? It seemed unlikely.

Henry broke off a conversation with Eddie (landscape gardener, part-time lifeguard, and playing Servant to the Capulets) to approach me, brandishing his script.

'Before rehearsal starts, would you read through the balcony scene with me, Emma?' he said. 'I can't quite get my head around it.'

'My pleasure,' I said. Given Henry's relaxed attitude to learning his lines, an extra opportunity to rehearse any of our scenes together was not to be missed.

'I'm looking forward to your party, by the way,' Henry said.

'It's not a party,' I said.

My burnt-orange top and black jeans were definitely the right clothes for an evening entertaining at home, I thought, as I studied my reflection in the wardrobe mirror – with my dark brown hair and amber eyes, I suited strong colours rather than the pastels that Lizzie usually wore. I added a pair of dangly earrings and re-touched my lipstick, and I was good to go.

I went downstairs – admiring the garland of flowers and leaves that Lizzie had woven through the banisters — and into the kitchen, where I found my best friend stirring the large saucepan of curry that was simmering on the hob, still in the old clothes she'd been wearing all day to clean the cottage in preparation for our guests. I'd offered to help, but I'd been relegated to shifting furniture and setting out bowls of crisps. Lizzie having come to the conclusion that there was no way she could fit eight people around her kitchen table, we would be eating off our knees while sitting in a circle of chairs in the living room.

'Lizzie, it's almost half past seven,' I said. 'Don't you think you should go and change into your glad rags? I'll do that.'

'Would you mind?' Lizzie said. 'Noah will be back in a minute. He said his curry would be fine left to its own devices, but I'm worried it'll burn.'

'Where is Noah?'

'I sent him to the offie,' Lizzie said. 'We don't have enough beer.'

My gaze went to the array of beer, wine, and soft drinks lined up on the kitchen table. In my job, I'd learnt that it was almost impossible to overestimate the amount of alcohol that a small group of people could get through in an evening, but I felt sure that we had enough for eight, even if none of the guests thought to bring a bottle.

'I'll take over here,' I said, and held out my hand for the spoon. Lizzie made to pass it to me, but instead she let it fall to the floor, splattering sauce over the flagstones. To my alarm, she staggered forward, clutching at the table.

'Lizzie! What's wrong?' I hurried to her side.

'I felt faint,' Lizzie said. 'Just for a second. I'm OK now.' She let go of the table and stood up straight. 'I've been on my feet all day, and I skipped lunch. Stupid of me.' I saw that her face was unusually pale.

'Stupid if you're too exhausted to enjoy the evening,' I said. I poured her a glass of water, which she drank while I cleaned up the spilt sauce. 'You should eat something now, even if it's only crisps.'

'I will,' Lizzie said, 'as soon as I've changed my clothes and put

34

on some make-up.' She turned and walked slowly out of the kitchen. Still concerned at her pallor, I followed her, and watched her climb the stairs.

'Are you sure you're all right, hun?'

'I'm fine,' Lizzie said. 'Totally recovered.' When she reached the landing, she added, 'I feel such an idiot, fainting like some fragile Victorian maiden. Please don't tell Noah—' She broke off as the doorbell rang. 'Oh, no – I'm not ready.' She vanished inside her bedroom.

I went to the door and opened it to find Henry standing outside, carrying a six-pack of beer – along with Eddie, who was holding a bottle of wine. I thought, what is Eddie doing here? My smile of welcome faltered.

'Hope we're not too early,' Eddie said. 'Henry couldn't remember what time Noah said to get here.'

At work, I had no trouble in turning away uninvited interlopers from a private function, but informing a fellow *Romeo and Juliet* cast member who'd arrived on my doorstep clutching a bottle of Sauvignon that he wasn't on my guest list was not, I decided, the act of a friend. I pictured the curry simmering away on the hob. It would stretch to feeding nine, even if the portions would be slightly smaller than Noah had planned.

'No, you're not too early,' I said. 'Come on in.' I led the two men the short distance along the hall to the kitchen.

'I can offer you grape or grain,' I said. 'What would you like?' Eddie and Henry immediately began examining the various types of beer on offer, and were still discussing the merits of each when Noah returned bearing a further crate.

'Our first guests have arrived,' I said.

Noah set the crate down on the floor. 'Henry,' he said. 'And Eddie.'

'They came together,' I said. The evening performance had barely started and already we were wandering off the script.

'Glad you could make it,' Noah said, showing an admirable ability to ad lib. The doorbell rang again.

'I'll get it,' I said. Leaving Noah to sort out the drinks, I went and answered the door. On the doorstep were Zoe and Sofia, who greeted me with hugs and an enveloping cloud of perfume. They were both wearing strappy sequinned dresses and heels, which made me suspect they hadn't totally got their heads around the concept of 'a quiet supper with friends'.

'I'm super-excited,' Sofia said. 'It's ages since I've been to a house party. Or any party. Do you like my dress? I bought it off the internet a few weeks ago, but I've not had an opportunity to wear it.'

'It's lovely,' I said. 'Come on in – drinks in the kitchen, straight along the hall.' I waved the girls past me and into the cottage, just as Richard walked through the garden gate.

'Evening, Emma,' he said. 'Has the guest of honour arrived?' It took me a moment to realise he was referring to Jake.

'Not yet,' I said.

'He hasn't changed, then. He always did like to make a dramatic entrance.'

I laughed. 'We've all changed in the last ten years. You only have to look at us.'

'You've hardly changed at all since you left school.'

'I'm not sure that's a compliment,' I said.

'It was meant to be,' Richard said, going inside. I followed him into the hall, where we were met by Noah.

'Hey, Richard,' Noah said. To me he added, 'I seem to have mislaid my girlfriend. Any idea where she is?'

'In her bedroom making herself beautiful,' I said. 'I'll go and hurry her up.'

'She's already beautiful,' Noah said. 'And please feel free to tell her I said that.' With a grin, he beckoned Richard into the kitchen. I ran upstairs to Lizzie's room and knocked on her door. There was no reply, but I opened the door regardless and went in. Lizzie, her make-up now immaculate, but still in her old clothes, was lying on her bed asleep – her obsessive scrubbing of floors and polishing of windows had evidently tired her out. There is such a thing as being too house-proud, I thought. Deciding that she wouldn't want to doze through her own supper party, I reached out and touched her gently on her shoulder. She stirred, her eyes flickered open, and she sat up.

'W-what time is it?' she said.

'Nearly eight o'clock,' I said.

'*Eight?*' Swinging her legs over the side of the bed, Lizzie stood up, peeled off her jeans and T-shirt, and reached for the denim shirt-dress hanging on her wardrobe door. 'I only meant to lie down for a few minutes. Has anyone arrived yet?'

'Everyone except Jake,' I said. 'I should probably warn you that we are now a company of nine. Eddie turned up with Henry.'

'You let him in?' Lizzie said.

'I didn't feel I could tell him he wasn't welcome,' I said. 'He brought wine.'

'Oh, well, that's all right then,' Lizzie said, the tone of her voice uncharacteristically sarcastic. 'Sorry. It's Eddie and Henry I'm annoyed with, not you. If I'm honest, I'd have let Eddie in too. It wouldn't make for a good atmosphere at rehearsal if we banned him from our party – his role is small enough as it is.' She inspected herself in her dressing-table mirror, then picked up a comb and ran it through her hair.

'We have clearance,' I said. 'Dim the house lights. Let's get this show started.'

We went downstairs to find the entire company was now ensconced in the candlelit living room. The conversation, briefly interrupted by our entrance, was already flowing, as was the beer and wine. Noah, a bottle of red in one hand and a bottle of white in the other, was making his way around the room re-filling empty glasses. Lizzie put on some background music – a female voice I didn't recognise singing to the accompaniment of an acoustic guitar – and having secured myself a glass of wine, I went and perched on a dining chair next to Henry. Only to spring up again at the sound of the doorbell.

'That'll be Jake,' I said. Pausing to deposit my wine glass on one of Lizzie's hand-painted coasters, I hurried out into the hall, and flung open the front door. Jake, carrying a bottle of white wine and two bunches of roses, yellow and pink, was standing outside.

'*But soft! What light through yonder window breaks?*' he said, proclaiming Romeo's most often-quoted line in a sonorous tone that he must have learnt in drama school. '*It is the east and Emma is the sun.*' In his normal speaking voice, he added, 'These are for you,' and handed me the yellow roses.

'Oh, Jake, they're lovely.' I breathed in the delicious scent. 'Thank you so much.' My favourite flowers, I thought. He'd remembered.

'You're welcome.' He smiled, and I smiled back, before I realised that it wasn't me he was smiling at. I glanced back over my shoulder, and saw Noah and Lizzie standing right behind me.

'Flowers for Miss Flowerdew,' Jake said, reaching past me to give Lizzie the pink roses. 'And you'd better have this, Noah, as I didn't bring you any flowers.' He handed Noah the wine bottle. Not that I'm an expert, but I recognised the name on the label from the Downland's pricey wine list, and knew it must have cost him almost as much as my weekly supermarket shop.

'Thanks, mate,' Noah said. 'Would you like a glass now?'

'That wine's better chilled,' Jake said, 'but I wouldn't mind a glass of something else.'

'I'll put this in the fridge then,' Noah said, heading off towards the kitchen.

'And I'll put these gorgeous flowers in water,' Lizzie said. 'Yours too, Emma. You and Jake go through to the living room. Make the introductions.' I handed her my roses, and she followed her boyfriend.

'Come on in,' I said to Jake. 'Come and meet everyone.'

He raised one eyebrow. 'I thought it was going to be just the five of us tonight.'

'It was,' I said, 'but a couple of other people heard we were having friends round and invited themselves.'

Jake regarded me thoughtfully. 'I can't say this without sounding up myself, but am I the main attraction in this evening's line-up? I don't mind – it wouldn't be the first time I've gone to a social event and found myself posing for photos and signing autographs all night – but I'd rather know beforehand.'

What do I tell him? I thought, remembering Sofia's expressed desire for his autograph. 'Tonight is definitely an ensemble piece,' I said, 'but you might just possibly be top of the cast list.' I pointed to the living room. 'After you.'

He pushed the living-room door so that it slowly swung open, leaving him framed in the doorway, an actor standing in the wings, about to walk out into the spotlight. Inside the auditorium, the audience's chatter ceased – I half-expected to hear the sound of applause. Well, he certainly knows how to make an entrance, I thought, Richard was right about that.

Jake stepped forward into the room. 'Evening all,' he said, receiving a chorus of enthusiastic greetings in reply. I went and stood beside him.

'You know Eddie from school, of course,' I said, 'and you met Sofia the other night in the Armada, but I don't think you know Zoe?'

'Oh, no, you won't remember me,' Zoe said. 'I was twelve when you left South Quay. My sister, Flora, was in the same year as you at school.'

'You're Zoe Walters?' Jake said, raising his eyebrows. 'I do remember Flora had a younger sister, but I have to admit I wouldn't haven't recognised you.'

'Thank goodness,' Zoe said, 'as I had buck teeth and was a very plump child.'

Jake laughed, and went and sat on the empty chair beside her. 'What a difference ten years makes,' he said.

Which was when the doorbell rang again.

Chapter Six

I'd no idea what Richard was saying, even though he was sitting right next to me.

'What?' I said. 'I can't hear you.' It was hard to hear what anyone was saying above the heavy rock music pounding out of Lizzie's speakers – amplified by Noah and Eddie, among others, belting out the lyrics while playing air-guitar.

Raising his voice, Richard said, 'Best party I've been to in years.'

I glanced round the crowded living room. Over by the window, Henry was having a shouted conversation with Colin (South Quay's postman, playing Benvolio in *Romeo and Juliet*) and the couple who ran the refreshment kiosk in the seafront car park. Zoe and Tessa, Carol-from-the-supermarket's daughter, were dancing together with much tossing of hair and Zumba-influenced gyrating of hips. Jake was lounging on the sofa between Sofia and Gail (playing a citizen of Verona, former editor of our school magazine, and now a reporter on the *Teymouth Chronicle*).

The ringing of the front door-bell shortly after Jake's dramatic entrance had heralded the unexpected arrival at the cottage of Shane (Paris in *Romeo and Juliet* and maker of scenery on account of his owning a small construction company) and his girlfriend. Lizzie had come out of the kitchen and opened the door before I'd got there, and faced with the two of them blithely unaware that they were gate-crashing ('Everyone in the Armada's talking about your party, Lizzie. Where do you want the lager?'), she'd resignedly welcomed them in ('I couldn't turn away the guy who's building Juliet's balcony, Emma, I just couldn't'), and instructed Noah to cook extra rice. We'd just about eaten our curry when another couple turned up, and more people had followed, until the cottage was heaving with virtually all the members of the Players aged under thirty-five, and a fair number of their friends. The music had grown ever louder, the talk and the laughter more raucous, and the party had spilled out into the garden, where at one point a ragged conga could be seen lurching drunkenly around the apple tree. By then, I'd decided that since all these people were here, I might as well enjoy their company, and I'd joined the end of the conga line.

Now, at two in the morning, many of the uninvited guests had left, slurring their farewells and staggering off into the night. Those that remained seemed determined to party 'til dawn.

On the other side of the room, Jake said something that made Sofia and Gail laugh uncontrollably. Surrounded as he'd been by people who either wanted to introduce themselves as a fan of his films and TV series or remind him of the times they'd played football together on the beach, I'd not had a chance to talk to him all evening, and it seemed unlikely that we'd be having a meaningful conversation any time soon. I drained my wine glass and stood up to go and fetch myself another.

'Would you like to dance?' Richard said, also getting to his feet, his gangly body swaying alarmingly. I realised he was more than a little drunk.

'No,' I said, quickly. 'No, thank you. I'm going to get a drink.'

Richard subsided onto his chair. 'Would you get me one?'

'Yes, of course,' I said. Absolutely not, I thought, unless it's strong black coffee. Edging my way between the dancers and the air-guitarists, I made my escape.

In the kitchen, I found Lizzie, alone, broom in hand, sweeping up broken glass from the flagstone floor, which was sticky underfoot from spilt alcohol.

'This evening has *not* turned out the way we planned,' she said.

'I'm not arguing with you,' I said. 'But it's been a good party.'

'In what way exactly has this been a *good party*?' Lizzie said.

'I've had a good time,' I said. 'Everyone seemed to have enjoyed—'

'Look at this place – just look at it,' Lizzie said, gesticulating wildly around the kitchen.

'It's a bit of a mess,' I said, my gaze taking in the empty bottles and cans that covered every surface, the used glasses, paper cups, and half-eaten packets of crisps. There were empty pizza boxes – I'd no idea who'd brought the pizza – on the dresser, and the sink was piled precariously high with curry-ingrained saucepans and plates. Jake's roses were incongruous splashes of colour in vases on the windowsill. I wished I'd thought to hide the expensive wine he'd brought. Someone had liberated it from the fridge before I'd had a chance to try it, and the empty bottle was on the windowsill next to the roses.

'It's going to take for ever to sort it out,' Lizzie said, sounding as if she might be about to cry. 'It's a disaster.'

'It won't seem so bad in the morning,' I said. 'Leave it for now. Have another glass of wine.'

'I don't want wine,' Lizzie said. 'Noah's had more than enough alcohol for both of us. He's completely wasted.' To my consternation – I wouldn't have expected her to find either a trashed kitchen or Noah's having one or two drinks too many quite so distressing – her eyes filled with tears. She brushed them away with the heel of her hand. 'Sorry. I'm so tired, my head is spinning. It would be better to leave the clearing-up 'til tomorrow. I think I'll go to bed. If you don't mind my deserting you.'

'No, that's fine.' Looking at her more closely, I could see that she was practically asleep on her feet. 'I'll see you tomorrow. Not too early.'

She nodded, and went off upstairs. I finished sweeping up the broken glass – I'd been on too many Health and Safety in the

42

Workplace courses to leave it where someone might step on it – and searched through the wine bottles until I found one with enough wine left to half-fill a paper cup. Suddenly feeling tired myself, I went out into the garden for a breath of air, taking a seat on the ancient wooden bench that Lizzie had bought at a garage sale and renovated. There was just enough light coming from the kitchen for me to see that several of her carefully tended flower-pots had been overturned. She is *not* going to be pleased, I thought.

From behind me, I heard Richard say, 'There you are, Emma. I was lookin' for you. Couldn't find you.' I turned my head to see him stumble out of the kitchen. Walking unsteadily over to the bench, he sat down next to me, close enough that I could smell the alcohol on his breath. I shifted away from him, putting several inches between us. Time for him to exit the stage, I thought.

'Would you like a coffee before you go home, Richard?' I said.

'Nah, don't wan' coffee,' Richard said. 'Lookin' for you.'

'Well, you found me,' I said.

'I foun' you,' Richard said, sliding along the bench, so that his thigh pressed against mine. To my astonishment, he put his hand on my knee. Then he lunged towards me and kissed me on the mouth, tasting strongly of beer. I jerked back my head and pushed him away. He slumped against the back of the bench.

'What the hell do you think you're doing?' I said.

'Emma,' he slurred. 'I wan' kiss you, Emma.'

Oh, for goodness' sake, I thought. 'Stop it, Richard. You're completely pissed. You need to go home.'

Another male voice said, 'Emma, is that you out there? Ah – it is you.' Removing Richard's hand from my leg, I sprang to my feet, spun around, and saw Jake standing by the open kitchen door. Beside him, staring at me and Richard with unabashed interest, were Henry, Zoe, and Sofia.

'Yes, it's me,' I said. Jake walked over to the bench.

'You and a friend,' he said.

'A friend who's very drunk and is going home right now,' I

43

said. 'Goodnight, Richard.' For a moment, to my intense annoyance, Richard remained sitting on the bench, blinking owlishly at me, but eventually he rose ponderously to his feet. Drawing himself up to his full height, he walked – not in a straight line – past Henry and the girls, and into the cottage.

There was a long silence, before Zoe said, 'We're off home too. 'Night, Emma.'

'Fabulous party, Emma,' Sofia said. 'Thank you so much for inviting me.

Henry said, 'Yeah, great party. See you at rehearsal.'

They all saw Richard kiss me, I thought, my face growing hot. It'll be all round the Players, if not the entire village. Aloud, I said, ''Night. See you on Monday.' Henry and the girls went off, no doubt discussing the love scene they'd just witnessed in the garden, leaving me and Jake alone.

'So,' he said. 'You and Richard?'

'There's no me and Richard,' I said, 'I don't know what you think you saw, but—'

'I know exactly what I saw,' Jake said, with a grin. 'I hope I didn't scare him away.'

'Oh, whatever.' I'd forgotten how infuriating he could be, but I wasn't going to let him rile me. 'Shall we see if there's any wine left?'

'Not for me,' Jake said. 'It's too late for wine or conversation. Or do I mean too early? I only came out here to let you know I'm heading home.'

Disappointment washed over me. There was a time, I thought, when we'd have talked all night. I led the way into the cottage, through the kitchen and along the hall. Music was still pulsating from the living room, but for me the curtain had come down.

'Thanks for tonight,' Jake said, opening the front door. 'I'll see you, Emma.'

'See you soon,' I said, but he was already walking away, raising a hand in farewell, not looking back.

44

Chapter Seven

The ringing of my phone wrenched me out of a deep sleep. I groped around on my bedside table, before I realised I'd left it on my chest of drawers. By the time I'd dragged myself out of bed, it had gone through to voicemail, but whoever'd rung hadn't left a message before ringing off. I checked my missed calls, and groaned when I saw that the caller had been Richard. Whatever it was he wanted to say to me, it seemed likely to be an awkward conversation, and I had no intention of calling him back before I'd had a cup of coffee. It had turned colder in the night, and I opened my curtains to see a grey sky and the branches of the apple tree tossing in the wind. Shivering in my thin pyjamas, I put on a bathrobe and went downstairs, gathering up the wilting remains of Lizzie's garland as I went.

There was no sign as yet of Lizzie, but Noah was standing by the kitchen sink, drinking a glass of fizzing white liquid – I saw an open packet of soluble aspirin amid the empty bottles and cans on the kitchen table. His sports bag was by his feet.

'You're up earlier than I thought you'd be,' I said. 'Playing cricket today?'

Noah nodded, but without enthusiasm. 'I'd rather have had a lie-in, but I can't let the team down. Not that I'm going to be much use to them. I've the worst hangover.' He added his glass to the washing-up in the sink. 'Lizzie's feeling rough too. She must have had way too much to drink last night.'

'Did she?' I said. 'I thought she was just tired.'

45

'I don't think I've ever seen her so ill the morning after a party,' Noah said. 'As soon as she woke up, she rushed out to the bathroom to throw up. She's going to stay in bed and try to sleep it off.' He checked his watch. 'I need to get going.' Shouldering his sports bag, he left the kitchen, and a few seconds later, I heard the slam of the front door.

I looked at the detritus of the party strewn around the kitchen and sighed. On this dismal grey morning, it did not look any less awful than it had the previous night. Lacking the domestic staff who cleaned the ballroom and conference rooms after an event at the Downland, I resigned myself to reprising my role of Cinderella from the Players' Christmas pantomime, but this time without Lizzie and Noah – Fairy Godmother and Buttons respectively – in the cast.

The doorbell rang. Seriously? I thought. Who turns up on someone's doorstep at 10.30 on a Sunday morning? I was tempted to keep out of sight until whoever it was went away, but just in case it was one of our uninvited guests who'd left some vital possession behind when they'd staggered home in the early hours, I went and opened the front door just a crack. I peered out to see Richard, pallid and unshaven, peering back at me.

'Emma,' he said, 'I need to talk to you. We need to talk. About last night.'

My heart sank. Did we really need to talk? He'd behaved like an idiot, but as far as I was concerned, the sooner we and everyone else forgot the whole embarrassing incident the better.

Richard raked his hand through his hair. 'Can I come in?' he said, somewhat desperately.

I felt I'd done more than enough entertaining for one weekend, but taking pity on him I let the front door swing wide and ushered him inside the cottage and into the living room, wincing when I saw the number of beer cans left lying around on the floor and the crisps ground into the rug. I took possession of the sofa, while he perched on the edge of a dining chair that needed to be returned to the kitchen.

I said, 'How are you this morning?'

'Not good. Entirely my own fault.' He cleared his throat. 'Emma, I'm here because I owe you an apology. Last night – in the garden – I was completely out of line.'

'Forget it,' I said, eager for this conversation to be over. 'It's not a big deal.'

'When I woke up this morning, I couldn't remember anything about last night,' Richard said. 'Then it all started flooding back to me. What I did – it won't happen again. I'm so sorry.'

'You were drunk,' I said. 'You made a pass. I turned you down. Let's move on.'

'I'm mortified. I'd never want to – er – intimidate a woman.'

'I know you're not like that, Richard.'

'You're not mad at me?'

'No, I'm not mad at you,' I said.

'So we're still friends?' Richard said. 'After last night.'

'We've been friends far too long to fall out over one drunken kiss.'

Richard let out a long breath. 'Thank you, Emma,' he said, his body visibly relaxing. 'Can we not talk about this ever again?'

'Suits me,' I said. 'Although we may have to put up with other people talking about it until the next village scandal gives them something else to talk about. That's not a joke, by the way.'

'I know,' Richard said. 'Remind me again why I like living in South Quay?'

'Because you're a member of the South Quay Players?' I said.

'That must be the reason,' Richard said. 'Talking of which, I should get home and learn my lines for tomorrow's rehearsal. Can't have Henry off book before me.'

'I don't think there's much chance of that,' I said. We both got to our feet, and trooped into the hall.

'Thanks again, Emma,' Richard said. 'For – well, you know.'

'No worries,' I said, opening the front door. 'See you at rehearsal.' He went out, almost colliding with Jake, who was coming up the path.

'Hey, Rich,' Jake said, as Richard side-stepped awkwardly around him. 'You always seem to be leaving just as I'm arriving.'

Richard, who now that he was in the fresh air was again looking rather pale, paused only long enough to say, 'See you, Jake,' before walking off.

When he was out of earshot, Jake said, 'He must be keen if he's visiting you this early in the morning.' I rolled my eyes and he laughed.

'Come inside, Jake,' I said, glancing up and down the lane to check no other early risers were about to make an unscheduled appearance on the doorstep. 'I need a coffee.'

We went into the kitchen, and I located the coffee among the debris, while Jake retrieved the kettle which someone, for unfathomable reasons of their own, had put out of my reach on top of the dresser. If he was feeling any the worse for wear, Jake gave no sign. The Sunday-morning stubble on his chin suited him, I thought.

'So has Richard declared his intentions?' he said. 'Are they honourable? I mean, after that kiss—'

'Richard was very drunk last night,' I said. 'He came here this morning to apologise.'

'He doesn't want to kiss you now that he's sober?'

'You crack me up,' I said. 'Really you do.' The kettle had boiled, so I finished making our drinks and handed him a mug. 'What brings you here this morning?'

He swallowed a mouthful of coffee. 'When I left last night, I could see that the cottage was in a state. I thought you might welcome some help with the clearing-up.'

This was so unexpected that I almost choked on my drink – when he was a teenager, the only way his mother could get him to tidy his room was to bribe him.

'Thanks,' I said. 'I really could do with a hand. Lizzie and I would have done it together, obviously, but she's in bed with a hangover.' Recalling that I was still in my pyjamas, I added, 'I'll go and get dressed. I won't be long.'

48

'I'll make a start in here,' Jake said. His gaze travelled round the kitchen. 'I may be some time.'

Leaving him throwing bottles and cans into the recycling bin, I took my coffee upstairs to my room, groaning when I caught sight of my reflection in my mirror and realised I'd answered the front door with bed hair, and that my old, worn bathrobe wasn't fit for public consumption. Jake might be an old friend who'd seen me looking less than prepossessing more than once, but I didn't want him thinking I'd turned into a slattern in the last ten years. I jumped in the shower, dressed, added a dash of mascara, and ran back downstairs.

Four hours later – four hours of scrubbing saucepans, hoovering, collecting up glasses, and shifting furniture – the cottage was restored to its former pristine glory. Almost. If you ignored the wine stain on the arm of the sofa. The garden still needed attention, but having ventured briefly outside into the wind, I took the executive decision to leave the broken flowerpots for a less blustery day. Having looked in on Lizzie and found her still sleeping, I made me and Jake a batch of well-earned sandwiches, and we sat down at the kitchen table to eat them.

'We make a good team,' he said to me, through a mouthful of ham and pickle.

'Yes, we do,' I said, smiling at him across the table, thinking how good it felt to be sitting here with him in the warmth of Lizzie's kitchen. It was, I thought, as his grey-blue eyes met mine, as though he'd never left South Quay.

He said, 'You, Lizzie, and Noah certainly know how to throw a party.'

'We can't take all the credit for it,' I said. 'It was you who drew in the crowds.'

'Yeah, I got that impression ...'

'We honestly didn't plan to put you in the spotlight,' I said, 'but someone in the Armada heard you were here, and word spread. I hope it wasn't too awful for you.'

'I had a good time,' Jake said. 'Although if I'd known I have quite so many fans living in South Quay, I'd have brought my bodyguards down with me from London. They take out anyone who comes within ten feet of me.'

'You don't have bodyguards,' I said, not entirely sure that he was joking.

'No, I don't,' Jake said, with a grin. 'I don't need them – it's not like I'm in a boy band. Seriously, Emma, I enjoyed meeting up again with so many old acquaintances last night. It was fascinating to see how much some people have changed and how others are just the same.'

'Who do you think's changed the most?' I said.

'Gail Preston,' Jake said, without hesitation. 'Who'd have imagined that studious, high-minded girl would have grown up into *Sherwood*'s greatest fan. She knows more about the show than I do.'

'Did Gail tell you that she writes for the *Teymouth Chronicle* now?' I said.

'No, she didn't.' He frowned. 'I don't remember what I said to her last night.'

'Does it matter?' I said.

'She's a journalist,' Jake said. 'I'm a well-known actor. Go figure why she was so keen to talk to me.'

'She wasn't interviewing TV star Jake Murray last night,' I said, 'she was chatting to a former classmate at a party. Anyway, I can't see her writing a showbiz gossip piece in the *Chronicle*. School fetes, gymkhanas, and the lack of parking spaces in Shore Road are more her line.'

'We'll see when the paper comes out,' Jake said. 'But I fully expect to be misquoted all over the front page.'

'Anyone would think you were famous,' I said.

He grinned. 'I'm not going to pretend that my return to South Quay isn't the most newsworthy event in this village in more than a decade.'

He's right, I thought, but I'm not going to admit it. 'You haven't changed,' I said. 'You were always up yourself.'

50

'As you so often used to tell me,' he said. 'I feel as though we've picked up where we left off, you and I.'

'I was thinking the same,' I said. *Almost*, but not *quite* where we left off, I thought.

He gestured towards the window. 'Looks like it's going to rain,' he said. 'Time I made a move.' I realised that while we'd been talking, the sky had grown ominously dark.

'Not that I want you to go,' I said, 'but you probably should, if you don't want to get caught in a squall.'

'I'd forgotten how quickly the weather can change on the coast,' Jake said, getting to his feet. I followed him out of the kitchen.

'Thanks so much for your help with the flotsam and jetsam,' I said. A gust of wind blew through the cottage as I opened the front door. 'I really appreciate it.'

'You're welcome,' Jake said. 'When do you next have a day off work?'

'Not until next Sunday,' I said.

'Shall we do something together then? Weather permitting, we could spend the whole day on the beach. Like we did when we were teenagers.'

'Skimming stones, eating chips, and drinking cider?'

'Why not?' he said. 'Let's recapture our wild youth.'

'Your youth might have been wild,' I said. 'Mine was tame.'

'You had your moments.'

'Only when you led me astray.'

Jake laughed. Then he leant forward, and I felt the brush of his lips soft against my face. Deep inside me, I felt the faintest quiver of desire. Instinctively, I stepped away from him. I was so not going there.

'See you next Sunday, Jake,' I said.

'Come to my place for brunch,' he said. 'As early as you like. And, Emma …'

'Yes?'

'Best you don't mention this production to anyone in the

Armada. It's a two-hander play – we don't need a chorus.' With that, he walked off, leaning forward into the wind.

I shut the front door and went back into the kitchen. My heart was beating uncomfortably fast. I reminded myself that all I wanted from Jake was friendship. The easy, uncomplicated friendship we'd shared before I'd gone to stay with him in London, when I was seventeen ...

Chapter Eight

Waterloo Station on this cold autumn evening is more crowded than Shore Road at the height of summer, but once I've dragged my suitcase through the ticket barrier, I spot Jake straight away. He sees me at the same time, and strides up to me, enveloping me in a bear-like hug.

'Great to see you, Emma,' *he says.*

'You too,' *I say. It's so good to see him. I've missed him these past six weeks.*

'Let me take your case,' *he says.* 'The underground's this way ...'

He leads me confidently through the jostling crowds and the noise, railway announcements, people talking loudly on their phones, snatches of conversation in many different languages, to the escalator that takes us from the overground station to the tube. Our train, when it emerges from the tunnel, is so rammed with standing passengers that I don't see how we can possibly get on, but somehow we squeeze inside a carriage.

'Is the tube always this crowded?' *I say, clutching the overhead handrail, someone's briefcase digging into my back, as the train, rattling and juddering, gathers speed.*

'In the rush hour it is,' *Jake says. With a grin, he adds,* 'You're not in South Quay any more.'

Fifteen minutes later, we emerge from the underground into Marylebone, and walk the short distance from the station along a quiet street of elegant Georgian townhouses, skirting around a leafy garden square, to the modern purpose-built block of student accommodation where Jake now lives, sharing a flat with three other boys, all first-year drama students like him.

We arrive to find that two of Jake's flatmates, Andile and Justin, are on their way out to a nearby bar. The third boy, Benedict, is obligingly staying over at his girlfriend's place, so that Jake can sleep in his room for the next couple of nights, and I can have Jake's. Andile and Justin invite us to join them for a drink, but Jake declines, reminding them that I have an important day ahead of me tomorrow – he knows without asking me that I'd prefer to stay in tonight and go over my audition pieces. Once they've left, he shows me over the flat, apologising for the none-too-clean state of the bathroom and the galley kitchen.

'And this is my room.' He flings open a door to reveal what I imagine is a typical student bedroom, just wide enough to accommodate a wardrobe, a small desk, and a single bed. 'I'll leave you to unpack.'

Left alone, I take a look around Jake's room, running a finger along the spines of the slim paperbacks on the shelves above the desk – they are all plays – and smiling when I see that the heavy hardback is the Complete Works of Shakespeare *that I gave him when he turned eighteen. The scrawled notes in Jake's handwriting pinned to the corkboard on the wall read: 'Iago workshop – Mon 5.30,' and more cryptically: 'Tickets?' There is a flyer for a third-year student show, a timetable for classes in improvisation, singing, text … I think, this will be me next year. Excitement bubbles up inside me. I am in London. I am staying with Jake in his flat. And tomorrow I have my audition for the Royal College of Drama.*

The Head of Acting says, 'Thank you, Emma, that's all we need for today … You'll be informed by letter if your application to RoCoDa has been successful by the end of the summer term.' He half-rises from his chair and holds out his hand for me to shake.

I make myself walk slowly out of the rehearsal studio. Outside in the corridor, I take several deep breaths, smile at the girl and the boy – fellow auditionees – waiting their turn to be summoned inside, and head off down the broad staircase to RoCoDa's entrance hall, where I meet up with Jake.

'How did it go?' he says to me.

'I think it went OK,' I say.

'Don't be modest,' Jake says. 'I'm sure you did brilliantly. Are you tired after a long day of auditioning?'

It has been a long day, I think, but a thrilling day as well, performing my classical and modern monologues and my song to the audition panel in the morning, taking part in acting and movement workshops in the afternoon, and finally having a one-on-one interview with a senior tutor. I've done all I can to get into RoCoDa. Now I just have to wait for that letter.

'I'm shattered,' I say, 'but on a high at the same time. Does that make sense?'

'Totally,' Jake says. 'I felt exactly the same when I auditioned last year.' He adds, 'So you're not too exhausted to go to the theatre tonight? I ask because while you were impressing the audition panel, I went and got us tickets for Coriolanus.'

'Oh, that's amazing,' I say.

'One of the advantages of being a drama student,' Jake says, 'is that we get discounted tickets at West End theatres.'

'Are there any disadvantages to being a drama student?'

'None that I can think of,' Jake says. 'So far, I've found that training to be an actor is everything you and I always dreamed it would be.'

'That was incredible,' I say to Jake, as we come out of the theatre into the crisp night air. 'The actor playing Coriolanus – he's so talented.'

'He was excellent,' Jake says. 'Although, if I was the director, I'd be giving some other members of the cast more than a few notes.'

'For a first-year drama student,' I say, 'you are so up yourself.'

Jake laughs. Still discussing the play, we stroll along brightly lit streets teeming with assorted Saturday night revellers, theatre-goers, and tourists, to Leicester Square. Jake points out the cinema that holds red-carpet film premieres, and the white statue of Shakespeare surrounded by fountains and trees. We buy chips from a fast-food restaurant, and eat them while listening to a busker singing and playing guitar. I think, I've just seen a West End play, and now I'm in Leicester Square, in the heart of London's theatreland, with Jake. This is what my life will be like when I'm at drama school. I wish I didn't have to go home tomorrow.

★

Jake's flat is in darkness when he lets us in the front door – his flatmates are out at a party. He makes us coffee and we go into his room, sitting next to each other on his bed. I talk about school and the drama club. He talks about the street theatre project he'll be working on next week. We fall silent. Suddenly, I am acutely aware of him, this good-looking boy, his dark, tousled hair, his beautiful grey-blue eyes that change colour like the sea, and that he is looking at me in a way that he never has before. My heart is thudding in my chest.

Jake leans towards me, and kisses me. It only lasts a few seconds, but when he raises his head, I smile at him encouragingly, and he leans in again. I feel the pressure of his cool lips on mine, and then his tongue is in my mouth, and we're falling back onto the duvet, lying close together, kissing for a long time, and I'm breathless when we stop. He sits up, and I do the same.

'It's late,' he says. 'I should go.'

I think, I don't want him to go. I don't want to sleep alone tonight. My stomach tightens into a knot.

'Y-you d-don't have to go,' I say.

His eyes look deep into mine. 'I'd very much like to stay. If you want me to.'

'As long as you've got a—If you use a—If we're, you know, safe—'

'Yeah, I have condoms,' Jake says. He puts his arms around me, and kisses me, and then I feel his hand slide under my top, slowly easing it up my body and, finally, over my head. Kissing me all the while, he unbuttons his shirt and shrugs it off, reaching behind my back to unhook my bra, trailing a hand down my spine, his fingers scorching my skin, and then he stands up and takes off his jeans. Lizzie and I have had many discussions about boys and sex, and I've watched a lot of rom-coms, but I am unprepared for the fierce heat that lances through me when he takes off his boxers, and I see a naked and aroused male body for the first time. Jake's mouth curves into a lazy smile. He flicks off the harsh overhead light, and by the softer glow of the desk lamp, gets into bed. His gaze travels from my face to my breasts, and suddenly feeling almost shy, I quickly strip off my jeans and knickers at the same time, and lie down next to him. He pulls the duvet over both of us.

'Oh, Emma,' he whispers, 'why have we never done this before?'
Then he reaches for me …

I remembered the way I'd felt that night, Jake's touch awakening new delicious sensations in my body, the scent of him as we lay together naked in his bed, the thrilling shock of desire, the taste of him as we shared that star-crossed kiss … I pictured Jake as he was now, a man not a boy, but with the same dark tousled hair and beautiful eyes, the same way of making me laugh.

I told myself very firmly that nothing was going to happen between us. Yes, I was physically attracted to him – he was an undeniably attractive man – but sleeping with him had been the worst mistake of my life.

I was *not* going to let myself fall for him again.

Chapter Nine

'Why are you sitting in the dark?' Lizzie switched on the electric light, her voice summoning me back to the present – lost in thought, I hadn't heard her come into the kitchen. I noticed that rain was lashing against the windows, and hoped that Jake had made it back to the villa before the cloudburst.

'How are you?' I said, ignoring her question. 'Noah told me you weren't feeling too well.' She looked fine now, I thought.

'I'm OK,' Lizzie said, distractedly, staring round the kitchen. 'You've worked wonders in here. I'm so sorry you had to do all the clearing-up on your own.'

'It wasn't just me,' I said. 'Jake did as much as I did.'

'Jake?' Lizzie pulled out the chair opposite mine, and sat. 'Did he stay the night?'

'No,' I said. 'No he did *not* stay the night. He came round this morning especially to help.'

'That was kind of him,' Lizzie said. She added, 'I wasn't suggesting that you and he hooked up, Emma, we do have an airbed he could have crashed on.'

'Ah.' I felt my face flush. 'Anyway, moving on, Jake and I put the cottage to rights, but the garden could still do with some TLC. We'll need to fix the lights – maybe you can ask Noah to give us a hand – and you might want to replace a couple of pots—'

To my dismay, Lizzie burst into tears.

'Oh, it's really not that bad,' I said. 'It's mainly sweeping up cigarette butts and picking up bottles and cans.' When she continued to sob, I fetched her a box of tissues from the dresser, and waited quietly for her to get herself under control.

'Sorry,' she said, eventually, wiping her eyes and blowing her nose.

'That's all right, hun,' I said. 'I know how much you love your garden.'

'I'm pregnant,' Lizzie said, 'so I'm really not that concerned about a few trampled flowers right now.'

'*What?*' I said. 'Are you sure?'

'I did a test – several tests – a couple of days ago, but I knew what the results were going to be. I've been displaying enough of the symptoms.'

'I thought you were hung-over.' Suspecting that this was not the most appropriate response to my best friend's telling me she was expecting a baby, I added, 'Congratulations.'

'Let's not pretend this is good news,' Lizzie said, leaning forward, resting her arms on the table. 'It's as much of a shock to me as it must be to you. It's not something I planned or wanted. I love children, I always hoped I'd be a mother some day, but not now, not like this.'

'Oh, Lizzie …'

'I don't know what to do. I'm all over the place. I'm so tired all the time—' Her voice caught in her throat, and she reached for another tissue. 'I haven't told Noah yet. When I do, he'll probably be straight out the door.'

'Surely not,' I said. 'You two are so good together.'

'But we've only been dating a few months,' Lizzie said. 'It's not like we're living together. We haven't even talked about that sort of commitment. Neither of us is ready to become a parent. Noah certainly isn't. He's too fond of partying on a Saturday night.' She sounded as though she was about to cry again. 'It's all such a *mess*. I don't know what I'm going to do. I can't decide what would be best.'

'Before you make any decisions, you should talk to Noah.'

'I don't see why,' Lizzie said. 'I'm the one who's pregnant. What I do about it is my choice.'

'Of course it is,' I said, gently, 'but talking it through with your boyfriend, knowing how he feels, might help you to know what it is *you* want.' I put my hand over hers. 'Whatever you decide, I'm here for you in any way I can be.'

'Thank you, that means a lot to me.' She sighed. 'You're right. I should talk to Noah.'

'I really think you should,' I said. 'Are you seeing him tonight?'

'No, he's going to the Armada with the cricket team,' Lizzie said. 'He's coming round tomorrow after work to eat, but then we'll be rushing off to rehearsal, and he's bound to want to go to the pub afterwards, even if it's just for one drink. I'll talk to him once we're back at the cottage.'

'You could skip rehearsal,' I said. 'Just this once, you understand.'

'Miss a Players' rehearsal? Emma Stevens! I can't believe you said that.'

'Me neither,' I said. 'Don't tell Pamela or she'll be washing my mouth out with soap.'

A smile appeared briefly on Lizzie's face. 'You're a good friend, Emma,' she said. 'I feel a lot better now we've had this conversation. Oh, that's your phone.'

I twisted round in my chair and picked up my phone from the dresser. 'It's my sister,' I said. 'Hey, Scarlet.'

Scarlet shouted something down the phone, her words impossible for me to hear over the chatter and music in the background.

'I can't hear you,' I shouted back. The music faded slightly.

'I'm in the Armada,' Scarlet said. 'Can you hear me now?'

'I can,' I said.

'I've just been talking about you,' Scarlet said. 'Emma and Richard, sitting in a tree. K.I.S.S.I.N.G. You might have told me that you were dating Richard Parker. I'm your *sister*. I shouldn't have to hear that you've got a new boyfriend from someone in the pub.'

Oh, for goodness' sake, I thought. 'I'm not dating Richard or anyone else right now,' I said. 'Who told you that I was?'

'I heard it from Flora Walters,' Scarlet said, 'and she heard it from her sister, Zoe.'

'Well, you heard wrong.'

'That's such a shame,' Scarlet said. 'I've always liked Richard. And you've been single for such a long time. Not that there's anything bad about that. It's not like you're on the shelf.'

'Thanks for that, Scarlet. Good to know.'

'I'll go and report back to Flora,' Scarlet said. 'Talk soon.'

'Bye, *sis*,' I said, and ended the call.

'You and Richard?' Lizzie said.

Chapter Ten

'... *So you shall share all that he doth possess, by having him making yourself no less.*' Having informed Juliet that she was to be married, Pamela folded her arms and stuck out her chin, as though defying her daughter to argue with her. It struck me that our Chairwoman's performance as an imperious Lady Capulet wasn't much of a stretch for her as an actress.

Phyllis, as Juliet's Nurse, laughed raucously and said, '*No less! Nay, bigger; women grow by men,*' rolling her eyes and using her hands to mime the growth of her waistline, which got a laugh from the other Players who were watching the three of us rehearse. I glanced at Lizzie, who was sitting in the front row of chairs, next to Noah. Not surprisingly, she didn't appear to be particularly amused by a joke about pregnancy.

Focus, Emma, I thought. Realising that I'd almost missed my cue, I said my next line, and waited expectantly for the entrance of the Servant who would summon Lady C, the Nurse, and Juliet to the Capulets' ballroom to greet their guests.

'Enter a Servant,' George, the director, bellowed. 'Where's the Servant?'

'Eddie, that's you,' Pamela said.

'Sorry,' Eddie said, sprinting into position as speedily as he'd run into the sea to assist a swimmer in difficulty. He gabbled his short speech, and we all exited the performance space.

'Well done, everybody,' George said. 'Eddie, I know the Servant is in a hurry to get back to his duties, but try not to rush your lines, yeah?' He consulted his notebook. 'That's all for tonight, folks. On Wednesday, I'll need Romeo, Mercutio, and Benvolio here at seven to go over Act I, scene iv – off book if you can, gents. Everyone else to be here by eight o'clock sharp, for Zoe to teach you the dance for the ball scene.'

The Players began to disperse. Henry and Maurice started stacking the chairs – Pamela might see nepotism as the way forward when it came to casting, but to be fair, she didn't hesitate to put her own family on the cleaning rota. I joined Lizzie and Noah, and we went out of the community centre and across the car park.

'Are you going to the Armada, Emma?' Lizzie said, her voice unnaturally bright.

'Don't I always after rehearsal?' I said.

'Noah and I are going to give it a miss tonight,' Lizzie said. 'I've still got a few books to mark for school tomorrow.'

'We'll see you later back at the cottage.' Noah draped an arm around Lizzie's shoulders, and the two of them walked off down the high street. Deciding that I'd stay in the pub until it closed to give them some space, I hurried after the rest of the Players.

I didn't find it a hardship to stay in the Armada Inn drinking with my fellow cast members until the landlord called time – Sofia and Zoe exchanging knowing looks when Richard bought me a glass of wine had been only a mild irritation in the grand scheme of things – but once I'd left the pub, I was eager to get home. Not that I was going to barge in on any conversation Lizzie might be having with Noah, but I did want to assure myself that she was all right, whatever *all right* might mean for her.

I'd walked as far as the corner of Saltwater Lane, when I heard running footsteps behind me and a female voice calling my name. I turned around to see Gail skid to a halt in front of me.

'I've been trying to get a chance to talk to you all evening,' she said.

'It's late, Gail—' I began.

'Oh, this won't take long,' Gail said. 'I just wanted to ask you for Jake Murray's phone number.'

'I don't have it,' I said. Easier to lie, I thought, than admit I had the number but refuse to give it to her.

Gail gave me a long look. 'Do you know where he's staying?'

'No, I don't,' I said. 'Sorry.'

'I see,' Gail said. 'Well, perhaps you'd give him my phone number and ask him to call me.'

'I will,' I said. 'If I happen to see him.'

'Thanks.' Gail made to go, but then she said, 'If I could land an interview with Jake Murray, it'd make my editor very happy.'

'I'll tell him,' I said. 'Goodnight, Gail.' I moved away from her, walking swiftly around the corner. She was, I supposed, only doing her job, but to me it still felt wrong – grubby – that she'd presume on our friendship to try to obtain Jake's phone number. Reminding myself that I had other more immediate concerns than Gail's professional ethics, I walked up the path to the cottage and opened the front door.

The cottage was in darkness. Taking off my shoes, I walked upstairs to the landing, and saw a faint light shining from under Lizzie's bedroom door. From behind the door, I heard the murmur of voices, hers and Noah's. I couldn't make out what they were saying – nor did I want to – but both of them sounded calm. Relieved that I hadn't come home to find Lizzie once again crying a river, I decided that my presence was not required, and went to bed.

I awoke with a start. It was daylight, and Lizzie, wrapped in an embroidered shawl over a white nightdress, was standing in my open doorway.

She whispered, 'Emma? Are you awake?'

'Ye-es,' I said. Smothering a yawn, I sat up. 'What time is it?'

'About 6.30.' She came into my room, pushing the door shut behind her with her foot. 'Noah's still asleep,' she said. 'I wanted to talk to you before he wakes up.' She folded her hands protectively over her stomach. 'I'm having this baby. I think I'd already decided that before I stayed up half the night talking to Noah.'

'I'm guessing he's being supportive,' I said, 'as he's sleeping in your bed.'

'I wouldn't say he took the news that he's going to become a father in his stride,' Lizzie said. 'When I first told him, he totally freaked out.'

'Understandably,' I said.

Lizzie nodded. 'But then, when he'd got his head together, he was just so lovely to me. He said – he said we should get married.'

'Oh, Lizzie, that's great …' Seeing Lizzie frown, I let my voice trail off. 'It's not great?'

'We're not living in the 1950s,' Lizzie said. 'These days, I think you'll find that men don't have to *do the right thing* because they've got a girl up the duff. We're not getting married, but we do want to be together – to raise our child together – and we're thinking that Noah is going to move into the cottage.'

'But of course he must move in with you,' I said. Time I started searching for another room to rent, I thought. 'When do you need me to move out?'

Lizzie hesitated, and then she said, 'We don't have to discuss that now.'

'Every couple needs their own space,' I said, 'and you and Noah should have some time to get used to living together before the baby arrives.'

'Which won't be until the new year, so there's no rush for you to leave. Stay for the summer at least. You're not likely to find anywhere to rent in South Quay during the holiday season, in any case.'

'Then I'll plan on staying on here with you and Noah until the holidaymakers have gone,' I said, 'and when the season's over, I'll easily find myself a new place.' I smiled. 'This room will be perfect for a nursery. I'll help you and Noah decorate it, if you like.'

'You, Emma Stevens,' Lizzie said, 'are the best friend ever.'

'I'm happy for you, that's all,' I said, 'and for Noah.'

Lizzie looked down at her hands, still clasped over her stomach. Her smile lit up her whole face. 'It wasn't supposed to happen this way,' she said, 'and the timing's all wrong, but I'm happy too, so very happy.'

Chapter Eleven

On Sunday morning, my bag packed with all the paraphernalia needed for a day at the beach – sunglasses, towel, sunscreen, paperback – and wearing a bikini under my T-shirt and shorts, I came downstairs to find Noah crouched in front of the washing machine.

'Morning,' I said. 'Is the machine not working?'

'I think it's more that I can't get it to work,' Noah said, straightening up. 'I can cook, but I'm afraid I'm very ignorant when it comes to other household chores. My mother's always done my laundry and all that sort of thing.'

I showed him which buttons to press.

'Thanks, Emma,' he said. 'Now that I'm officially living here, I'm determined to do my bit on the home front. I know how house-proud Lizzie is, and I don't want her wearing herself out.'

'Well, let me know if you need assistance with any other white goods! How is Lizzie today?'

'She's still feeling tired,' Noah said, 'and she was sick again this morning, but that's normal in the first trimester. It's hard on her, but it's nothing to worry about health-wise.'

'That's good to hear,' I said.

'I've been doing some research online,' Noah said. 'How to support your partner during her pregnancy. This is a whole new area for me. I want to get it right.'

Touched by his concern for Lizzie's well-being, I said, 'You seem to be doing OK so far, Noah.'

'I'm getting there,' he said. Checking his mobile phone, he added, 'Right. Washing machine on. Next on my list is to see if Lizzie feels up to eating breakfast. We may go to the garden centre later to get some new flowerpots.'

'Aren't you going to cricket?' I said.

He shook his head. 'We couldn't get a team together this week – too many people away for the bank holiday. Not that I'm bothered. I'd rather spend the day with Lizzie.'

He's a keeper, this one, I thought. Aloud, I said, 'I'm out all day. Jake's invited me round for brunch, and then we're going to the beach.' I went to the fridge and retrieved the bottle of cider I'd bought the previous day, and stowed it in my beach bag.

'Say hi to him from me and Lizzie,' Noah said. 'You can tell him our news, by the way. We did think we might keep it to ourselves for a while, but now that we've told my mother and Lizzie's mother we're expecting their first grandchild, we may as well have announced it over loudspeakers in the high street.' With a grin, Noah went out of the kitchen, and I heard him run up the stairs. I let myself out of the cottage, and headed off to the seafront.

Although it was only mid-morning, it was already warm, and on this bank holiday weekend, the beach near the car park was crowded with families enjoying the traditional delights of the British seaside, toddlers solemnly filling buckets with shells and pebbles, older children digging sandcastles or racing their parents into the shallows. A short distance from the shore, a group of teenagers were pushing each other off a lilo with much shrieking and thrashing about in the water. I saw Eddie watching them through binoculars from his vantage point at the lifeguard station. Further out, a speedboat sliced across the bay, a water-skier bouncing like a skimmed stone in its wake. A young couple walked past me, the woman carrying a baby in a sling. That'll be Lizzie and Noah next year, I thought. It occurred to me that it could be me too some day. Not that I was looking to settle down to a life of maternal bliss quite yet. Which was just as well, for none of the single men of my acquaintance, lovely guys though they were, struck me as someone I'd want to audition as father of my future offspring. The casting of that role would have to wait until I met a guy as nice as Noah.

Going down onto the sand, I kicked off my sandals and walked barefoot along the beach in the direction of the headland. After I'd passed a couple of breakwaters, the crowds began to thin – day-trippers tended not to stray too far from the car park and the kiosk with its ice cream and candy floss – and by the time I'd reached Jake's breakwater, I had the beach to myself. Sliding my feet back into my sandals, I climbed up the stones, and went through the gate into Jake's garden.

He was lounging in one of two deckchairs on the lawn, dressed in swim shorts and a sleeveless T-shirt that revealed strong muscular arms – he hadn't had those muscles when he was eighteen – but when he saw me he stood up and air-kissed me on each side of my face, which I imagined was how he greeted actresses and other women who worked in showbusiness.

'Are you hungry?' he said.

'Ravenous.'

'Good,' he said, 'because I may have overdone the catering. Take a seat, and I'll fetch the food out here. It's too fine a day to eat inside.'

'Hold on one sec,' I said, producing the cider from my bag. 'Take this with you and put it in the fridge. Unless you'd like some now.'

He laughed. 'Even when I was fourteen, I knew better than to drink cider before I'd had something to eat.'

While I took a seat in a deckchair, he vanished inside the house, coming back after a few minutes with a tray piled high with cold meats, cheeses, rolls, fruit, pastries, and two mugs of coffee. Putting the tray down on the grass between us, he passed me a plate and told me to help myself.

'I have some news for you,' I said, through a mouthful of bread, mozzarella, and tomato. 'Lizzie and Noah are going to be parents.'

'I know,' Jake said, with a smile. 'I met Noah's mother in the supermarket yesterday. Everyone else in South Quay wants to talk to me about *me*, but strangely, Mrs Jameson's conversation never strayed from the topic of her grandchild.'

I laughed. 'Some people have very odd priorities.'

'I congratulated her, of course,' Jake said, 'when I could get a word in, but I have to say I'm surprised that Lizzie and Noah have decided to start playing happy families when they've only been dating a few months.'

'It was a shock to them too, at first,' I said, 'but now they're both ecstatic.'

'They weren't actually planning on procreating?'

'Maybe not quite so soon,' I said, 'but whose life turns out the way they plan?'

'My life has,' Jake said. 'I wanted to become an actor and I am.'

'Was becoming famous part of your Five-Year Plan?' I said.

'*Some are born great, some achieve greatness,*' Jake said, '*and others have greatness thrust upon them* by the tabloids.'

'It must take some getting used to,' I said. 'So many people knowing who you're dating or how much you drank last night.'

'Pretty much the same as living in South Quay,' Jake said. 'Any actor who needs practice in dealing with the media should spend a few months in this village.'

'Talking of the media,' I said, 'Gail Preston wants you to phone her. She's after an interview.'

'Well, she isn't going to get one,' Jake said. 'I'm taking the summer off work.' He surveyed the few pieces of fruit that were all that remained of our brunch. 'Would you like any more to eat? Or shall we hit the beach?'

'I couldn't eat another thing,' I said. Jake took the tray back into the villa, returning with a rolled-up beach towel under his arm and two bottles of water.

We went out of the garden and down onto the beach, setting our towels out next to each other on the stones. The mid day sun was fierce, the tide was still far out and the horizon between sea and sky was lost in a heat-haze. Jake stood a while gazing out over the bay. Then he reached back over his shoulders, and in one sinuous movement pulled his T-shirt over his head and threw it aside. He stretched out on his back on his beach towel, resting on his elbows, turning his face up to the sun. I took in the sculpted planes of his chest, and the taut ridges of muscle on his stomach, and I thought, has he been working out since the last time I saw him without his shirt or what? Feeling slightly self-conscious – and very glad that I regularly took advantage of the Downland's gym – I took off my T-shirt and shorts and sat down next to him. Burrowing in my bag, I found my sunblock and began covering myself in Factor 15.

Jake sat up. 'Would you like me to do your back?' he said.

'Oh – I – yes. Thanks.' I handed him the tube of cream.

'Lie on your front then,' Jake said.

Obediently, I lay down on my front, lifted my hair away from my neck, and rested my head on my bent arms. He leant over me, and I felt his hands smoothing sunblock over my shoulders and the tops of my arms, his touch gentle on my bare skin. I shut my eyes, breathing in the scent of sun cream and brine. I heard a sea-bird cry out overhead, and the whine of a motorboat. The sun beat down, a heat that was almost tangible. A languor stole over me, as Jake's hands continued to stroke my back, his fingers trailing down my spine to my waist and hips, and the bottom half of my bikini. My stomach tightened, and I became aware of a luscious tingling spreading throughout my entire body.

'There, you're done,' Jake said. 'You can do my back now.'

I opened my eyes and slowly sat up. My limbs felt limp, and my head was as muzzy as if I had actually been drinking cider in the heat of the noon sun. Wordlessly, I took the tube of sunblock from Jake, and he lay prone on his stomach. Get a grip, Emma, I told myself, and squeezed sun cream into the palms of my hands. Kneeling next to Jake, I put my hands on his broad shoulders and began to rub the cream into his skin, working my way over his shoulder blades and down his body, my fingers kneading the hard contours of his back, coming to a halt at the waistband of his swim shorts, which I couldn't but help notice he was wearing low on his hips, showing a tantalising glimpse of the curve of his rear. I reminded myself that I was applying sunblock – not giving him a sensual massage.

'Your back is now fully protected from the sun,' I said.

Jake turned his head and smiled. 'Thanks, Emma,' he said. Then he closed his eyes, and gave every appearance of drifting off to sleep. I retreated to my own towel and found my paperback. Sitting cross-legged, I bent my head over my book, a romantic Regency novel, but my attention kept drifting away from the devastatingly handsome highwayman hero on the page and back to the magnificent male lying next to me, the broad shoulders tapering to a narrow waist, the long muscular legs … That's quite enough, Emma, I told myself firmly. I drank some water, lay down on my side, head on my hand, and returned to my book with renewed concentration.

The sun climbed higher in the sky. A breeze sprang up, and the sea grew less calm, with small, white-crested waves rolling onto the shore.

'Fancy a swim?' Jake said. 'I'll race you in.'

I smiled, and without answering him, laid my book aside, sprang to my feet and ran down the beach into the surf. Jake caught up with me in the shallows, striding ahead of me and diving under a wave, surfacing laughing and shaking salt water out of his hair. I waded out to join him, gasping at the shock of the cold sea on my sun-warmed skin.

We swam, and body-surfed, just as we'd done as teenagers, and when we tired of swimming we went back to our towels and dried off in the sun, talking about other days we'd spent on the beach, with Lizzie, Noah, and Henry, long, hot days that we'd wanted never to end. I told Jake about the summer Lizzie and I'd had a week's holiday in Kos. He told me about the summer he'd spent months shooting a film in Croatia. He made me laugh with his anecdotes about the filming of *Sherwood*. I didn't tell him that I'd watched it for the first time only a couple of weeks ago.

The sun was hanging low in the sky when, despite the huge amount of food we'd eaten earlier, renewed hunger made us walk along the beach to the chippie on Shore Road. We'd just come out of the shop with our portions of chips liberally doused in salt, vinegar, and tomato ketchup, when a family of holidaymakers, mother, father, and teenage son skulking behind them, phone in hand, planted themselves in our path.

'Are you – are you Jake Murray?' the mother said.

'Yes, I am,' Jake said, favouring the woman with his most charming smile.

'Ooh, I knew I recognised you,' the mother said. 'We all love your films.'

'Thank you so much,' Jake said. 'You're very kind.'

'*Sherwood* is our favourite TV show,' the father said. 'Could we get a selfie with you?'

'It'd be my pleasure,' Jake said. The son having been prevailed upon to take the photo, the adults arranged themselves on either side of Jake, the father seizing his hand and shaking it, and the selfie was duly taken. With many thanks and smiles, the mother and father walked off jauntily in the direction of the car park, the son slouching behind them.

'Does that happen a lot?' I said. 'It must get irritating after a while.'

Jake shrugged. 'It's just another part of my job. I could have done without being accosted by a fan one time when I was on my way to the dentist with a raging toothache, but most of the time I honestly don't mind. That said, let's get away from the crowds before anyone else recognises me. I'd like to eat my chips while they're still hot.'

We went back down to the beach, eating our chips as we strolled back to Jake's breakwater. He fetched the cider from the villa and we drank it sitting on the stones, passing the bottle between us, watching the sun sink into the sea. It grew colder on the beach once the sun had set, cold enough that Jake made another sortie into the villa and brought out jumpers for both of us to put on over our shorts and T-shirts, but still we lingered on the shore, moving further up the stones out of reach of the returning tide.

It was getting on for midnight, and we were both yawning, when I told Jake it was time I made a move.

'I'll see you home,' he said, and happy to have a little more time with him, I made no objection. As we'd done before, we walked along the path at the top of the beach, and he came with me as far as Lizzie's gate.

'I've missed times like these,' he said. 'You and me. On the beach.'

I thought, did he really miss me while he was filming his TV show or rocking up at some red-carpet event? I doubt it.

'It was a good day,' I said.

'Are you working tomorrow?'

'No,' I said. 'The hotel's full for the bank holiday, but we don't have any events planned.' On a sudden impulse, I added, 'I'm going round to my parents' for a family lunch. Scarlet and her brood will be there. Would you like to join us?'

'I'm tempted,' Jake said. 'I have very fond memories of your mother's cooking. But I don't want to intrude.'

'You wouldn't be intruding,' I said. 'We were in and out of each other's houses practically every day at one time.'

'I remember,' Jake said. 'My parents thought you were a good influence on me – you got me involved in the drama club. At least when I was at rehearsals, they knew where I was and what I was doing.'

'I've no idea why my parents let me hang out with a bad boy like you,' I said, 'but my friends were, and still are, always welcome in their house.'

Jake smiled. 'I would like to come and have lunch with your family,' he said, 'as long as you check that it's OK with your parents first. I can't just turn up on their doorstep unannounced and expect them to feed me.'

Which was exactly what we did do as teenagers, I thought. 'I'll call them in the morning and text you.'

'I'll say goodnight, then.' He turned to go, but then swung around to face me again. 'I'm sorry we lost touch after I went to London,' he said. 'I don't know how it happened.'

I do, I thought. You stopped answering my emails and texts. You met another girl and forgot about me. Not that any of that matters to me now.

'I'm glad you're back in my life,' he said.

'Me too, Jake,' I said. 'I'm glad we're friends.'

Chapter Twelve

Having overseen a wedding reception for four hundred guests the night before, I felt I deserved a lie-in, and it was mid-morning when, carrying my script of *Romeo and Juliet*, I started to make my way downstairs. I was halfway down when Lizzie and Noah's voices came to me from the kitchen.

'Are you sure you don't mind my going to cricket?' Noah said.

'I honestly don't mind,' Lizzie said.

'Well, if you're sure. No, don't get up – I'll see myself out. I'll be back around six.'

'Aren't you going to the pub?'

'No, I'll come straight home after the match.'

'I've a better idea,' Lizzie said. 'You go to the Armada with the team, and I'll come and join you. We don't have to stay late.'

'Suits me,' Noah said. 'But text me if you're feeling tired and want to change your mind. I love you, Lizzie.'

'I love you, Noah.'

As I could make an educated guess as to what was happening in the kitchen during the minute or so of silence that followed this overheard conversation, I crept back up the stairs, and stayed on the landing until I heard Noah leave the cottage. I so need to move out after the summer, I thought. If not sooner.

I went downstairs and into the kitchen, to see Lizzie about to climb onto a chair.

'Lizzie – stop!' I said. 'What do you think you're doing?'

'I need to get a tray down from the top of the dresser,' Lizzie said.

'I'll get it,' I said, tossing my script onto the table. 'A pregnant woman shouldn't be clambering around on the furniture. What if you fell?' I stood on the chair and handed the tray down to her.

'Thanks,' she said. 'Now I have to find some household objects to put on it.'

'What does *finding some objects* involve?' I said.

'No climbing or heavy lifting, I promise you,' Lizzie said. 'Just collecting together a few things from around the house – cotton wool, a mirror, a rubber band – for my class to compare in their science properties activity tomorrow. Nothing too strenuous for my delicate condition.'

'Seriously, Lizzie,' I said, 'I know pregnancy isn't an illness, but you do have to take care of yourself.'

'I am,' Lizzie said. 'My boyfriend is making sure of it.'

'Well, if you need anything else retrieved from a great height and he's not here, ask me.'

'Actually, there is something you could do for me,' Lizzie said, sitting down at the table.

'Sure, what is it?'

'The pregnant lady would like a cup of tea before she starts work. Maybe you'd make it for her?'

'Don't push your luck,' I said, filling the kettle.

Lizzie laughed. 'What are you up to today, Emma? When you're not waiting on me hand and foot.'

'This morning, not a lot,' I said. 'I thought I'd read through Act III to make sure I'm word-perfect at tomorrow's rehearsal. In the afternoon I'm going over to Jake's.'

'Again?' Lizzie said. 'You've been round his place or drinking with him in the Armada every day for the past two weeks.'

'I don't think I have …'

I cast my mind back over the fortnight since the bank holiday when Jake and I'd had lunch at my parents' house. He'd slotted back into my family immediately, allowing himself to be

77

inveigled into a game of football in the back garden with my father, Scarlet's husband Nathan, and two of Scarlet and Nathan's sons, six-year-old Albie and five-year-old Kyle. He'd listened to my sister's inexhaustible supply of South Quay gossip with commendable patience, and had even managed to coax a few words out of three-year-old Harrison, who, unlike his boisterous brothers, was a very shy child. It had been a lovely, relaxed day, and before we'd parted at the cottage gate – he'd walked me home again – we'd arranged to meet up for a drink the following evening.

The night after that, he'd been propping up the bar in the Armada when I'd wandered in with the other Players after rehearsal, and he and I'd sat chatting over a bottle of wine long after everyone else had gone home. Then there had been the day when he'd invited me over for a barbecue, and the times we'd gone for an evening stroll along the beach ...

My thoughts interrupted by the boiling of the kettle, I made two mugs of tea and set one down in front of Lizzie.

'I guess I have seen quite a bit of Jake lately,' I said. 'Why wouldn't I? I like him. He's good company.'

Lizzie gave me a long look. 'Are you sleeping with him?' she said.

'I am *not*,' I said. 'I'm very glad to have him back in my life, but only as a *friend*.'

'You're not attracted to the ridiculously handsome, straight, single man you spend all your spare time with?'

'I can't deny that he's a good-looking guy,' I said, forcing an image of a shirtless Jake out of my mind, 'but I value our friendship too much to risk losing it again. And even if I were interested in him, he certainly doesn't think of me that way.'

'So if there happens to be an eligible guy in South Quay who *does* think of you that way,' Lizzie said, 'you might just possibly agree to go out with him on a date?'

'There aren't any guys in South Quay interested in dating me,' I said, 'eligible or otherwise.'

'There's Richard.'

'*Richard?*'

'He kissed you ...'

'That kiss meant nothing. He was drunk, and he apologised. End of story.'

'Richard told Henry that before the party, he was planning to ask you out on a date,' Lizzie said, 'but now he doesn't think he stands a chance with you. Not after pouncing on you the way he did.'

'He said all this to Henry?'

'Who told Noah,' Lizzie said. 'Who told me, obviously.'

'Those boys are worse gossips than my sister!'

'Richard's a nice guy,' Lizzie said. 'All he needs is a little encouragement from you.'

'Never going to happen,' I said. 'Richard isn't my type.' I drained my tea, and picked up my script. 'Do you have time to test me on my lines, hun?'

Lizzie opened her mouth as though to speak, but then closed it again and reached for the script. 'Enter Juliet ...'

Half an hour later, I was confident that I wouldn't need any prompts at tomorrow's rehearsal. Lizzie went off in search of objects to fill her tray, while I headed off to Jake's via the supermarket to buy the white wine that would be my contribution to our Sunday lunch on the beach. Our regression to drinking cider hadn't lasted beyond one bottle.

Queuing up to pay Carol for my bottle of Chenin blanc, I found myself standing by a rack of magazines and newspapers, and my eye was drawn to a photo of a man and a woman on the front page of one of the tabloids. I immediately recognised the man as Daniel Miller – Lizzie and I must have watched *Fallen Angel*, the film that made him an A-list celebrity, at least five times – and it took me only a little longer to recognise the woman as Leonie Fox. The two of them were strolling along a street, presumably in London from the look of the houses, and he had his arm around her waist. The caption under the photo read:

'The Angel falls for the Foxy Lady. More pictures and full story inside.' I don't need to read the gossip in a Sunday newspaper, I thought, I get enough of it in South Quay. But as the queue shuffled forward, I found myself lifting the paper from the rack and placing it on the conveyor belt.

'She's doing all right for herself, that Leonie Fox,' Carol said, as she scanned my shopping. 'Brought up on a rough housing estate, she was. Now she's bagged herself a Hollywood star.'

'Mmm.'

'It must be hard on Jake Murray. Seeing his girlfriend with her new man.'

'His ex-girlfriend,' I said. 'She's his ex-girlfriend.' I held out a ten-pound note.

'Mind you,' said Carol, ignoring my proffered money, 'our Jake seemed cheerful enough when he bought a copy of that newspaper this morning.'

'Did he?' I said.

'Maybe he's already found Leonie's replacement,' Carol said, her eyes suddenly boring into mine. 'What do you think, Emma?'

'Me?' I said, holding her gaze. 'I've no idea.'

With a knowing smile, Carol took my money and handed me my change. 'Have a good day, Emma, love,' she said. 'Enjoy your wine. Whoever you're drinking it with.'

'Thanks,' I said, smiling back. 'I'm sure I will.' Stowing my wine and newspaper in my beach bag, I walked out of the supermarket, resisting the urge to look back at Carol, who I felt sure was discussing Jake Murray's possible replacement for his foxy girlfriend with the woman who'd been standing behind me in the queue.

It was another fine day, with a light breeze, and Shore Road was crowded with holidaymakers dawdling on their way to the beach to examine the souvenirs on the stands outside the shops, ships in bottles vying for attention with shell-shaped chocolates and tea towels printed with a map of the village. I edged through them as quickly as I could, made my way onto the beach, sat on the stones, and retrieved the paper from my bag. Turning to the entertainment section, I found myself looking at one large photo of Jake's ex and her new man, and two smaller ones. The larger one showed Leonie and Daniel Miller standing together on a red carpet. Her blond hair was arranged in an up-do, but with escaping tendrils curling artfully past her bare shoulders, and her strapless evening gown had a thigh-high split on one side displaying an enviably long and slender leg. He looked handsome and stylish in a dark suit. The smaller photos were of the pair of them still looking extraordinarily beautiful, but more casually dressed, gazing into each other's eyes over a table for two at a pavement café, and lying on the grass in what was either a large garden or a park. The 'full story' consisted of a couple of gushing paragraphs informing the paper's readers that Leonie and Daniel (the lovely Leonie Fox, 27, and Daniel Miller, 28, seen here at the London premiere of Daniel's fab new movie *Summer Loving* – we can't wait to see it) were now an item (A close friend of the couple tells us that Leonie, the former girlfriend of actor Jake Murray, and Daniel, whose name has been linked with a string of Hollywood actresses, are inseparable. Leonie has never been happier, the friend confided to our reporter).

Apart from his reluctance to talk about her the first time I'd met him, Jake had given me no indication that he was suffering any heartache over the demise of his relationship with Leonie, but I doubted that he'd be exactly thrilled to see her and her new boyfriend smiling up at him from the pages of a Sunday tabloid. It occurred to me to wonder if she'd got together with Daniel before or after she and Jake had split up. Closing the offending newspaper, I got to my feet and resumed my walk along the beach. I wouldn't be the first to mention Leonie, I thought, but if Jake needed a friend's shoulder right now, I was there for him.

Arriving at Jake's breakwater, I clambered up the stones and went into the villa's garden. There was no sign of him there or on the veranda. I knocked on the back door, and when he failed to open it, tried the handle but found it locked, so went around the side of the house and rang the front doorbell. After a minute or so, I rang it again, and this time Jake answered the door, his mobile phone clamped against his ear.

'Hey, Emma, I won't be a sec. No, I wasn't talking to you, Stephanie, I had to let someone in … No, she's not a journalist, she's a friend …' Still listening to whoever was speaking to him on the phone, he gestured for me to go through to the kitchen, while he went into the living room. I did as he wanted, and was somewhat taken aback to see a copy of the same newspaper I'd been reading earlier, open at the photographs of Leonie and Daniel Miller, in the middle of the refectory table. I put the wine I'd brought in the fridge, and occupied myself by scrolling through the messages on my own phone. An instant later, Jake came into the room.

'That was my agent,' he said, leaning against a worktop, folding his arms and crossing one ankle over the other. 'She called to warn me that there are pictures of my ex and the Fallen Angel all over the media. And to ask me what I wanted her to say to the press if they asked for my reaction. We're going with something along the lines of 'Leonie and I may no longer be together, but I wish her every happiness.'

My gaze strayed to the photographs. 'I'm so sorry, Jake. Are you all right?'

Jake gave me a quizzical look. 'Yeah, I'm good. Why wouldn't I be?'

'Seeing those photos can't have been easy,' I said.

'You think I care that Leonie's jumped into bed with Daniel Miller?' He raised his eyebrows.

'You left London because you broke up with her,' I said. 'I thought – maybe – he'd come between you.'

'I left London,' Jake said, 'because I was pissed off with the press camping on my doorstep, and after working on two films back-to-back, I felt I deserved a holiday. As to why Leonie and I broke up, it was a mutual decision, made with a great deal of shouting, after we'd both had sex with other people. Our relationship may have lasted for almost a year, on and off, but both of us slept around—' He broke off to study my face. 'I've shocked you, haven't I?'

'You have,' I said, this unexpected glimpse into the world that Jake now inhabited making me feel distinctly uncomfortable. 'If I'm honest.'

'What you have to realise, Emma,' Jake said, 'is that it's virtually impossible to have an exclusive relationship when you work in showbusiness. You're living away from home as often as not, you're surrounded by attractive women …'

'So you risk losing your steady girlfriend for the sake of – what?' I said. 'A one-night stand?'

'Fame is a powerful aphrodisiac,' Jake said, 'and there are times when it's hard not to give in to temptation.'

There is such a thing as self-control, I thought. Then I recalled the night I'd given in to temptation with Jake, and told myself not to be judgemental.

'Maybe it's easier to stay faithful if you're in love,' Jake said. 'I wouldn't know.'

'You didn't love Leonie?'

'We had some good times together, when we weren't fighting, and I'm sorry we finally ended the way we did, but no, I wasn't in love with her.' He added, 'I've never been in love. Have you?'

'No,' I said. And that, I thought, is the first lie I've ever told you, in all the time I've known you. My face grew hot, and I felt sure that Jake would notice, but the sudden ringing of my mobile meant I could look away from him. I fished the phone out of my pocket and checked the caller ID. 'It's Gail Preston.'

'Unless she's in the habit of phoning you on a Sunday,' Jake said, 'don't answer it.'

I let the phone ring off, and then went into my voicemail and pressed the speaker key.

Gail's disembodied voice said, 'Emma, it's Gail. Carol-in-the-supermarket mentioned that you bought a paper this morning, so I'm assuming you've seen the photos of Leonie Fox and Daniel

Miller. If you happen to meet your good friend Jake Murray, would you tell him that I'm very keen to interview him, and hear his side of the story? Why should his ex-girlfriend get all the publicity?' There was a pause, and then she added, 'See you at rehearsal.'

'Text her that all requests for interviews have to go through my agent,' Jake said.

I did as he said, and switched off my phone. 'Perhaps we should get over to the beach before Gail comes knocking at your door?' I said. 'If we walk up to the headland, we can hide out in the dunes. The most hard-bitten newshound couldn't track us there.'

Jake laughed. 'I think walking a few breakwaters along from here will be enough to put our intrepid reporter off the scent,' he said. 'I'll go and change into my shorts.' He went out of the kitchen.

I drew the newspaper towards me across the table and took another look at the photographs of Jake's ex-girlfriend. Does she know that he never loved her? I thought. Did his infidelities hurt, or didn't she care about him any more than he cared about her?

A line from *Romeo and Juliet* drifted into my head: *'Love is a smoke and is raised with the fume of sighs.'* I realised I'd said it aloud.

When I was seventeen, I'd thought that Jake Murray loved me. What an idiot I was, when I was seventeen.

Chapter Thirteen

The two young men, one mopping his forehead, complaining about the heat, and trying to persuade the other to return home, strolled aimlessly along the street, coming to a standstill in a sun-lit piazza. Two more men appeared and swaggered up to the first pair, circling around them, jeering, trading insults, working themselves up into a rage, and finally drawing blades. A fifth young man ran between them, too late to break up the fight that left his friend wounded and dying, while his assailants fled.

'*A plague on both your houses,*' the wounded man gasped, clutching at his side. '*They have made worms' meat of me.*' He took a few tottering steps. '*Your houses—*' His friends stared at him in horrified silence.

George said, 'And Mercutio leaves the stage.'

Noah staggered out of the performance space, coming to sit with Lizzie and me at the side of the hall. There was another long silence.

'Henry, it's your line next,' said George.

'Sorry,' Henry said, hastily thumbing through his script. 'I've lost my place.'

'Go from Tybalt's entrance,' George said.

Colin, as Benvolio, said, '*Here comes the furious Tybalt.*'

Richard strode forward, brandishing the length of dowelling that was serving as Tybalt's rapier until the hired prop-swords arrived. It occurred to me that his convincing portrayal of the furious scion of the house of Capulet had less to do with his talent as an actor than his annoyance at Henry's inability to get through a scene without a prompt.

'*Fire-eyed fury be my conduct now*,' Henry said in a monotone.

'Henry, could we have a bit more *rage* here,' George said. 'The Montagues and the Capulets are sworn enemies. Tybalt of the house of Capulet has just slain Romeo *Montague*'s great friend, Mercutio. You need to let the audience know that you'll either revenge his death by killing Tybalt or die yourself in the attempt.'

Henry repeated Romeo's challenge to Tybalt, and did actually manage to inject some emotion into his speech. Romeo and Tybalt fought their carefully choreographed swordfight, Henry dropping his script in the process, and Tybalt fell dead.

'*O, I am fortune's fool*,' Henry said, striking his forehead with his hand, and exiting the stage.

He's definitely improving, I thought.

'That was much better, Henry.' George glanced at his watch, got to his feet, and walked to the centre of the performance space. 'Well done, everybody. We'll end there tonight, but before you go, I've an important announcement to make. If I could have everyone's attention—'

Several of the Players were already edging towards the door of the hall, no doubt thinking of the pint awaiting them in the Armada, but they turned back. A few people got out phones and rapidly keyed in messages, presumably alerting whoever was awaiting them at home that the rehearsal was overrunning.

'Quiet, please, everybody,' George said.

Lizzie yawned and Noah shot her an anxious glance. 'I hope this doesn't take long,' he muttered.

Pamela said, 'Can your notes wait until next time, George? We only booked the hall until ten, and it's already ten fifteen.'

'I'm not giving you any more notes tonight,' George said. He cleared his throat. 'Or ever. I have to tell you all that I'm resigning from *Romeo and Juliet*, and from the South Quay Players. This rehearsal was the last with me as your director.'

There was a collective intake of breath before everyone in the hall started talking at once. Now that, I thought, is a masterclass in how to create a dramatic climax. Pamela strode out of the ensemble and joined George centre stage. Here comes the furious Chairwoman, I thought, as the two of them began an intense conversation.

'I'm guessing your mother didn't know about this,' I said to Henry.

'If she did, she didn't tell me,' Henry said.

George held up his hands for silence and the uproar ceased. 'I'm so sorry to let you all down,' he said, 'but I've been offered a job in Bristol, which as many of you know is where I went to university and where I met my wife, Debbie, whose family still live there. It's a big promotion for me, an opportunity I couldn't refuse, and Debbie and I are both thrilled, but the downside is that I have to start work two weeks from today. Organising a relocation to another part of the country at such short notice is going to take all my time – I'm travelling to Bristol tomorrow to sort out accommodation – and I've no choice but to hand *Romeo and Juliet* to another director.'

And where will we find one of those? I thought. George must know that this could mean disaster for the summer show. Couldn't he have negotiated a later start date with his new employers? Almost immediately, I realised the selfishness of such a thought, but I couldn't help thinking it. Looking round the hall, I failed to see anyone who shared either George's directing experience or, more importantly, his ability to keep the peace between the various factions of Players – like Phyllis's cronies, who drank G&Ts with her in the snug and thought Zoe a subversive upstart, versus Zoe's Zumba students, who regarded her as South Quay's very own Bob Fosse.

Pamela, her lips pursed, her eyes like flint, took a step forward. 'I'm sure everyone will join me in congratulating George on his new position,' she said, silencing the brief burst of applause from her audience with one icy glance. 'There will be a full committee meeting at my house tomorrow evening, seven o'clock sharp, to

87

appoint a replacement director. Rehearsal as usual on Wednesday for the entire cast.' With a brusque nod to George, she swept off-stage and out of the hall, Maurice almost knocking over a chair in his haste to follow her. The Players began to disperse, most – but not all, I noticed – going up to our erstwhile director, shaking his hand and exchanging a few words, before heading off home or to the Armada. By the time I'd helped Noah stack the chairs, agreeing with him that Lizzie's name needed to be taken off the rota, nearly everyone had gone, leaving Richard, Zoe, and Sofia still chatting with George. I went and joined them, as did Noah and Lizzie.

'Many congrats, George,' I said. 'Well done, you.' Now I'd got over my immediate reaction to his news, which, to my shame, I recognised as little different from Pamela's, I could appreciate what this opportunity must mean for him. 'And thank you for all the work you've put in on the show so far.'

'Thanks, Emma,' George said. 'I do feel bad leaving you all in the lurch, but I have to put my family and my career first.'

'Of course you do,' I said. There was no denying his exit was hideously badly timed, but I couldn't blame him for taking it. 'Although, obviously, I'm gutted you're leaving, because I'm reliably informed that you're the best director the Players have ever had.'

'Aw. Now you're embarrassing me.'

'It's true,' I said.

'Thanks,' George said again. 'It all happened so fast – interview and job offer all on the same day – I'm still a bit shell-shocked. Debbie and I've often talked about going back to Bristol, but we never thought we'd be able to make it happen. Until now.' He smiled. 'Much as I'm excited about this new chapter in our lives, I'll miss directing you lot. So if I could give you one final note – learn your flippin' lines.' Everyone laughed, except Richard, who rolled his eyes.

Sofia said, 'Are you coming for one last post-rehearsal drink, George?'

'No, I don't think so,' George said. 'I may have got through my resignation speech without being lynched by the committee, but I don't want to push my luck.'

We all left the community centre together, and George locked up, posting his set of keys to the hall back through the letterbox for the caretaker to find in the morning, this mundane action acquiring a symbolic quality in the circumstances. He turned right out of the car park and, raising a hand in farewell, strode off. The rest of us turned left, Lizzie, Noah, Zoe, and Sofia strung across the pavement, Richard and I following behind them. We reached the Armada. Lizzie and Noah continued on their way to the cottage, the girls vanished inside the pub.

'Hold on a sec, Emma,' Richard said. 'Before we go in, I've something I want to say to you.'

Until then, I'd forgotten what Lizzie had told me about his plans to ask me out, but now I was alone with him, her words came flooding back. Oh, no, I thought, knowing that my refusal would hurt him, or at least his male pride, however tactfully I phrased it.

'Did you see Pamela's face?' Richard said. 'If looks could kill ...' If he was planning to invite me on a date, this seemed an unlikely opening gambit. I allowed myself to relax.

'I think everyone was shocked and angry at first,' I said.

'With good reason,' Richard said. 'The wretched man has left us without a director eight, no, seven weeks before opening night.'

'It's unfortunate,' I said, 'but I don't see that he had any choice. He could hardly turn down a job because it doesn't suit the Players' rehearsal schedule.'

'You're remarkably forgiving, Emma. You do realise the whole production could fold if we can't find a new director?'

'There'll be someone among the Players willing and able to take over,' I said, with more confidence than I felt. 'Or someone Pamela can coerce into taking over.'

'Actually, Emma, I'm thinking of putting myself forward as director.'

'Really?' I blurted. 'You've never mentioned that you wanted to direct.'

'You don't think I could do it?'

'It's a lot for anyone to take on,' I said. Recalling his stated aversion to extra rehearsals, I added, 'Do you have the time?'

'I realise it'd mean a lot of work,' Richard said, 'but just this once I'd be willing to put in the extra hours if the alternative was the show being cancelled. I'm sure I have the necessary skill set. I'm used to telling other people what to do. I supervise a team of six in my office.'

A vision of Richard directing Henry – still not off book – floated into my mind. I doubted their friendship would survive the experience.

'It'd be a huge disappointment for everyone involved if *Romeo and Juliet* doesn't go ahead,' Richard went on, 'particularly for a certain someone in the cast who I'd like to impress.' He hesitated, and then he added, 'I'm hoping that my stepping up and rescuing the production might make her see me in a more favourable light, as it were.'

I thought, is he talking about me? I need to get away from him before he embarrasses both of us.

'If I do manage to persuade the committee that I'm the man of the hour,' Richard continued, 'I hope I can count on your support, Emma.'

'I'll always support whoever takes on the task,' I said, carefully. 'Shall we go and find the rest of the cast?' Without waiting for an answer, I darted into the pub.

Once inside, I wasted no time in losing Richard among a gaggle of chattering holidaymakers, and after some difficulty in attracting the attention of the barman, I bought myself a glass of white wine. Elbowing a passage away from the bar, I spotted the G&T crowd ensconced in the snug, with Phyllis holding court. I was too far away to hear what she was saying, but if, as I strongly suspected, she was voicing an opinion about George, the expression on her face told me that it wasn't flattering. At a nearby table,

Henry, Eddie, and a couple more Players were muttering over their pints – no doubt they, too, were discussing our director's defection. Turning my head, I saw Sofia and Zoe settling into a booth, Richard, holding a pint, sliding in next to Zoe – and Jake sitting on a stool at the end of the bar. Gail was standing next to him, emphasising whatever she was saying to him with her hands. As I watched, he shook his head. Barely concealing her irritation, Gail went over to Henry's table and took a seat in the last empty chair. Taking a gulp of my wine, I went and sat on the barstool next to Jake's, relieved that his presence in the pub meant that I could avoid joining Richard in the booth.

'I see our intrepid local reporter is still after you for an interview,' I said.

'She's trying to wear me down,' Jake said, 'but she won't succeed.'

'She's already got her headline story this week,' I said. 'George has resigned from the Players.'

Jake raised his eyebrows. 'Are your fellow actors so bad that they've driven away their director?'

'No, not at all,' I said. 'The only reason George is leaving is because he's got a new job in Bristol and has an immediate start date. Which is great for him, but it does mean that *Romeo and Juliet* needs to find a new director. We open in seven weeks and we're nowhere near ready.'

'How long have you been rehearsing?'

'Since April,' I said. 'I know it sounds a long time, but we only have our rehearsal space two evenings a week.' I turned my head to look at the Players seated at the table behind us. Gail was now talking with Henry – or rather she was talking and he was giving every appearance of listening – but the others were either on their phones or staring morosely into their drinks. Jake's gaze followed mine.

'Amateurs,' he said. 'I don't know why you bother, Emma. I really don't. Why would you want to perform in an amateur show, which by its very nature can't be any good?'

91

I gaped at him, taken aback by the contempt in his voice, glad that the level of noise in the pub was such that none of my fellow cast members could have heard him.

'That's a horrible thing to say,' I said.

Jake shrugged. 'I'm only being honest. Why do most people join an amateur dramatics society? Because they want to improve their social life and they're not into sport.'

'That's so not true,' I said.

'Then there are the people who'd have loved to have acted professionally, but know they're not good enough to make it in such a demanding, overcrowded profession,' Jake said. 'At least they're realistic. It's the ones who think they're as good as professionals that I can't stand. The ones who don't realise that a professional actor trains at drama school for three years for a reason.'

I thought, you are so up yourself, Jake Murray. 'Not everyone who wants to be an actor gets the chance to go to drama school,' I said. 'I didn't.'

'Ah, yeah, well, I'm sure you've enough raw talent to carry you through,' Jake said, unabashed, 'but without training most people simply don't know how to act. They have no stagecraft. And that's before we get started on costumes, scenery, lighting – I could go on. Face it, Emma, an amateur show is never going to match a professional show for acting or production values.'

I took a deep breath. 'I'll admit that there are amateur actors who don't reach your exacting standards of performance,' I said, 'but there are many who do. And while the South Quay Community Centre may not have the resources of a West End theatre, the Players still manage to put on shows that are enjoyed by everyone in our audience. An audience who, I might add, come to all of our productions, so we must be doing something right.' I tilted up my chin, daring him to contradict me.

To my intense irritation, Jake laughed. '*She was a vixen when she went to school,*' he said. '*And though she be but little, she is fierce.*'

'*Oh, when she's angry, she is keen and shrewd,*' I retorted. I might not have had three years' drama training like him, but I still knew *A Midsummer Night's Dream* just as well as he did. 'Did you know that the word amateur comes from *amator* – Latin for lover?'

'No, I didn't.'

'The only real difference between me as an amateur and you as a professional actor,' I said, 'is that you act because you get paid for it, while I do it for love.' I picked up my wine and drained the glass.

For a long moment, Jake regarded me in silence. Eventually, he said, 'I'm sorry, Emma. What I said about amateur dramatics was thoughtless. I didn't mean to hurt you.'

You never meant to hurt me when I was seventeen, I thought, but you did all the same ...

It's Christmas Eve and a bitterly cold night, but the windows of the Armada are steamed up with the heat of many bodies crowded into one place. Lizzie and I, along with Henry, and Noah, who is back from university for the holidays, are standing near the main entrance, where I have a good view of everyone who comes in. Every time the door opens, letting in a flurry of snow with a rush of cold air, my heart beats faster. Lizzie, noticing my agitation, leans towards me so that I can hear her above the roar of shouted conversations that surrounds us.

'Has he texted you what time he's getting here?' she asks.

'Not yet.' I check my phone, re-reading the text Jake sent me yesterday: Home tomorrow night. See you in the Armada xx *I haven't seen him in eight weeks, not since I stayed with him in London, but soon he will be here.*

More people come into the Armada, and my stomach flips as I recognise Jake's tall figure among them, even before I make out his face. He brushes snow out of his hair, and gazes round the pub. I raise my hand and wave wildly to catch his attention.

'Jake,' I call. 'Over here.'

He sees me and his face breaks into a broad grin. I watch him edge his way towards me through the heaving throng, my knees distinctly weak. Then he is there in front of me, smiling down at me – and stepping to one side to usher forward the girl following him, draping an arm around her shoulders, drawing her close. She is very beautiful. Stunning, in fact. Tall and slender, with long red hair.

'Emma – good to see you,' Jake says. 'This is Chiara, my girlfriend …'

'Am I forgiven?' Jake said.

For an instant, the past still vivid in my mind, I thought he was talking about that awful Christmas. Then I remembered that he'd no idea of what he'd done to me all those years ago. Don't go there, Emma, I told myself firmly. He and I were friends again. I was not going to think about the time I'd believed myself more than a friend, and discovered I was wrong.

'You are,' I said, 'on one condition. You have to come to *Romeo and Juliet*. If it goes ahead.'

Jake risked a smile. He was, I thought, ridiculously good-looking when he smiled.

'You want me to come and watch a bunch of *amateurs* murder Shakespeare's poetry?'

'We may surprise you.' I was smiling now myself. 'We may even remember our lines and not bump into the furniture. Well, maybe not Henry—' I broke off as the bell rang for last orders.

'Would you like another drink?' Jake said.

I shook my head. 'I should head off home. I've an early meeting with a florist in the morning.' We left the Armada together, and strolled back to Lizzie's cottage arm in arm.

At the gate, Jake said, 'How about I pick you up from work tomorrow and we drive over to Teymouth for a meal?'

'I'd like that very much,' I said.

'Goodnight, then, Emma,' he said, *'To sleep perchance to dream.'*

'We are such stuff/As dreams are made on,' I said.

He touched me fleetingly on my arm, before turning away and walking off into the night.

Chapter Fourteen

'With me being Irish and Gustavo's family coming from Brazil,' Mairead O'Brien said, 'we want our wedding to reflect both our cultural heritages. So for the evening entertainment we're thinking Irish dancers and a Samba troupe.'

'What a lovely idea,' I said, cradling my desk phone between my ear and my shoulder so I could add this request to my notes. 'We'd be able to source commercial dance companies for you, or liaise with any particular performers you'd like to hire.'

Mairead spoke rapidly in Portuguese to her fiancé. His voice came to me faintly over the phone line speaking in the same language.

'Gustavo and I would like to come and take a look at the venue,' she said to me, 'tomorrow, if possible.'

'Absolutely,' I said. I checked tomorrow's diary, we arranged a time, and having assured my potential new client that I was looking forward to meeting her and Gustavo, I ended the call.

Mairead O'Brien and Gustavo Fernandes, I thought, I wonder how they met. Hopefully, if they decided to hold their wedding at the Downland and I got to know them a little better, I'd find out. An aspect of my job that I really enjoyed was hearing other people's love stories. Compiling invoices, on the other hand, was a part of the job that I could very easily do without, but it had to be done and Mairead's call had interrupted the task. With a sigh, I focused my attention on my screen. Which was just as well, as Eve, who'd been showing a couple planning their golden wedding anniversary celebrations around the hotel, chose that moment to burst into the office. She wouldn't have appreciated finding her assistant gazing into space.

'You'll never guess who's just walked into reception,' Eve said to me, collapsing onto her chair, and fanning her face with her hands. 'Jake Murray. The actor.'

'Jake's here already?' I said.

'You knew he was coming?' Eve said, sitting bolt upright.

'He's an old friend of mine,' I said, recalling that Eve, who lived in Teymouth, wasn't part of my village's news network. 'We're going out for a meal.'

Eve's eyes widened. 'You and Jake Murray are *friends*? Oh, my goodness, I'm Jake Murray's greatest fan. I watch every episode of *Sherwood* as soon as it's shown on TV, and I buy the box sets.'

I smothered a smile. This seemed to be pretty much the default reaction of anyone not native to South Quay who discovered I knew Jake.

'I saw him in a play up in London once,' Eve said. 'It was years ago, back before he was famous, but I remember thinking what a good actor he was even then. I'd love to meet him.'

'Would you like me to introduce you?' I said.

'Oh, could you?' Eve said, as if the thought had never crossed her mind. She stood up, patting down her hair and smoothing her skirt. 'Lead me to him.'

'What, now?' I said. 'It's only just gone five.'

'Ah, well, you'd better close down your computer so you can go straight off,' Eve said.

I thought, who are you and what have you done with my boss? Switching off my computer, I picked up my bag, and preceded Eve out of our office and along the corridors that brought us to reception. Jake, tanned from the days he'd spent on the beach over the last few weeks, was sitting in one of several leather chairs that were provided for guests, leafing through a Downland brochure. I walked towards him, Eve at my side. He looked up, and when he saw me, sprang lithely to his feet. Behind their desk, the man and woman on reception that evening peered at the three of us over their computer screens.

'Jake,' I said. 'Here's someone I'd very much like you to meet – Eve Lambert, my boss.'

'Delighted,' Jake said, holding out his hand to Eve, who shook it.

'Eve is a great fan of *Sherwood*,' I said.

'I think it's the best thing on TV,' Eve said, breathlessly, 'and Robert Sherwood is my all-time favourite character.' A flush stole over her face. The thirty-nine-year-old woman with whom I shared an office seemed to have regressed into a starstruck teenager.

'Thank you so much,' Jake said, sounding both surprised and grateful, as though no one had ever told him they liked his TV show before. 'You're very kind.'

'I have to ask,' Eve said, 'do Robert and Marion finally get together in the next series?'

'I'd tell you if I could,' Jake said, 'but I'm afraid I'm sworn to secrecy.' Before Eve could press him for further details of his on-screen love life, he added, 'I was reading the hotel's brochure while I was waiting for Emma. I'm very impressed with the range of facilities on offer, particularly the gym.'

'Perhaps you'd like a tour?' Eve said.

'I would,' Jake said, 'but I'm afraid it'll have to be another time.' He took his car keys out of his pocket. 'Good to have met you at last, Eve. Emma often talks about you.'

'I won't ask you what she says,' Eve laughed. 'You two have a good evening. I'll see you tomorrow, Emma.' She fairly skipped off down the corridor towards the Events office.

'Sorry to spring my boss on you,' I said, 'She was *very* keen to meet you. You may have just got me a pay rise.'

'You're welcome. You look great, by the way. I like your dress.'

'Thanks, Jake,' I said. It had been a while since I'd been wined and dined, and it had felt good that morning to put on my sleeveless floral-print dress rather than my usual sober office gear, and to know that an attractive man was picking me up from work and taking me out. Even if he wasn't a boyfriend, and our outing wasn't a date. I need to remember that, I thought. This is *not* a date.

'Are you ready to go?'

'Yes—' I was interrupted by the buzzing of my phone. With an apologetic glance at Jake, I rummaged for it in my bag, but by the time I'd fished it out, it had stopped. While I was holding it in my hand, it pinged with the arrival of a text: *Our new director is Pamela! I'm to take over her role as Lady Capulet so I'll be playing your mother lol! ☺ Lizzie xx.* I gasped. Pamela's credits for directing consisted of telling members of the WI where to stand on their float in the parade that wound its way through South Quay as part of the annual village fete. I thought, Richard is *not* going to be happy.

'Everything OK?' Jake said.

I nodded. 'I suspect there'll be some members of the cast who won't be overjoyed to hear it, but it's good news. A text from Lizzie to tell me that Pamela Wyndham is the Players' new director. The summer production is saved, and you'll get to see my Juliet.'

Romeo and Juliet now had a director who'd never directed a play before, and a Lady Capulet who was a month younger than her daughter, but at least the show was going ahead.

'I get to see a Shakespeare play directed by Henry's scary mother,' Jake said. 'I can't wait.'

We drove along the coast road to Teymouth, and Jake parked near the waterfront. He'd booked a table at the Wharf, a restaurant with a roof terrace overlooking the harbour, with its sailing dinghies, motor boats, and catamarans riding at anchor, and seabirds wheeling and swooping overhead. There were only four other diners: an older couple and a couple in their mid-twenties – if they recognised Jake, they didn't feel the need to ask for his autograph – and after they'd left, we had the rooftop to ourselves.

We ate lobster caught that day by local fishermen, new potatoes and salad, all locally grown, and shared a carafe of white wine. I talked about the Downland, admitting that I'd never had any particular ambition to work there, but when I was looking for employment after leaving school, it had been the only available job that wasn't just for the holiday season. Jake told me that after he'd left drama school, before he'd started making what he described as *real* money from acting, he'd taken any job offered, including the part of a corpse in a murder mystery. He talked about the actors he knew from back then who were still his friends, and the bar in Drury Lane that they frequented, which had framed photos of well-known performers on its walls ('That's when I knew I was successful, Emma. When I saw my photo on the wall of the Troubadour.'), and how on a Sunday morning, he liked to run along the canal towpath from his house in Islington to Regent's Park. I sat across the table from him, in the warm golden glow of a summer evening, and I thought how much I liked being with him, just the two of us. Not that I was going to let myself get too used to having him around. When the summer was over and the holidaymakers left South Quay, he would be among them.

'It sounds like you've made a good life for yourself in London,' I said to him, after we'd finished eating and were drinking one final cup of coffee.

'I've worked extremely hard to get where I am today,' Jake said, 'but now I'm earning enough money to live the way I want. There are times when I wonder what the hell I'm doing in such a tough profession, but going to drama school was the best decision I ever made.' Briefly, he rested his hand on mine. 'I haven't forgotten that it was you who got me into acting in the first place, Emma. If you hadn't persuaded me to join the drama club, I wouldn't have applied to RoCoDa to train as an actor, and I wouldn't have the life I have now.'

I felt an overwhelming fondness for him, a delight that he remembered the small part I'd played in his success. 'Just make sure you thank me in your Oscar acceptance speech.'

'If I'm ever nominated for an Oscar,' Jake said, 'I'll fly you out to LA and you can be my plus-one for the ceremony.'

'I'm holding you to that,' I said. 'Given your talent, I'd say it was *when* not *if*. I'll start thinking about what I'm going to wear.'

He laughed. 'Shall we have coffee back at your place?' he said. I nodded and he signalled to the waiter to bring the bill.

Having left Jake's car parked on Shore Road, we walked through the twilight along the lane to Lizzie's cottage. Jake held open the gate and I went ahead of him up the path. Standing on the front step, I took a moment to breathe in the scent of the delphiniums and summer phlox that Lizzie had planted when we'd first moved in, the honeysuckle that almost covered the garden wall, and the rose that had rambled its way around the front door. Jake came and stood beside me.

I said, '*I know a bank where the wild thyme blows/Where oxslips and the nodding violet grows.*'

'*There sleeps Titania,*' Jake said, '*Lull'd in these flowers ...* Did you know tonight is Midsummer's Eve?'

'So it is,' I said. He moved closer to me, so that our bodies were almost touching.

'*In such a night as this/When the sweet wind did gently kiss the trees and they did make no noise ...*' Jake's voice trailed off. He looked down at me with hooded eyes.

I thought, this isn't a date, but if it was, he would lean in and kiss me now. My senses flooded with the heady night fragrance of summer roses and my heart started beating hard and fast.

'Emma? Are we going inside?'

'Ye-es,' I said. '*Good friend come in and taste the wine with me –* the coffee, that is.' Pull yourself together, Emma, I thought. No more alcohol for you tonight. I fumbled in my bag for my key, and let us into the cottage.

As soon as we stepped into the hall, Noah and Lizzie's voices came to us quite clearly:

'There's no point in us arguing about it, Noah,' Lizzie said, 'I've already told Pamela I'll do it.'

'Then you need to call her back and tell her you've changed your mind,' Noah said. After a pause, he added, 'I can't believe you'd agree to something like this without speaking to me first.'

'I have to ask your permission before I do anything now?' Lizzie said.

'No,' Noah said, 'no, of course not. That came out all wrong.' There was a pause, and then he added, 'I'm only thinking of you, Lizzie. And our child.'

'Oh, for goodness' sake,' Lizzie said, 'it's not going to hurt me or the baby if I play Lady Capulet. It's not as though I'm going to be leaping around the stage waving a sword.'

Jake and I exchanged glances. Putting his hand on the front door, he slammed it shut so that the noise echoed round the cottage. Lizzie and Noah fell silent.

'Hello?' I called out. 'I'm back and Jake's with me. Anyone home?'

From inside the front room, Lizzie said, 'Noah and I are in here.' I put my head round the door. They were sitting on the sofa, as far apart as was possible on a two-seater.

'I'm making coffee,' I said. 'Would either of you like one?'

'Not for me,' Noah said.

'I'll have a coffee,' Lizzie said. 'Jake – come and talk to us. Did you have a nice meal? What was the restaurant like?'

Leaving Jake describing the Wharf to Lizzie and Noah, I went to the kitchen, made three cups of coffee, and carried them back to the living room on a tray.

'Did you get my text about *Romeo and Juliet*?' Lizzie said.

'I did,' I said. 'It should be *interesting* having Pamela as a director.'

'I just hope none of the cast drop out,' Lizzie said. 'Richard called round earlier ranting about how he'd have been a better choice.'

'He told me last night that he wanted to direct,' I said.

'Apparently he gatecrashed the committee meeting and volunteered to step in,' Lizzie went on, 'but Pamela wouldn't even consider it, and as always the other members of the committee agreed with her. She told Richard that she needs him to play Tybalt, and she doesn't believe anyone can direct a play and act in it. Which is why she's resigned her part and promoted me from the ensemble.'

Noah had been silent up until then, but now he said, 'Lizzie is very keen to play Lady Capulet, but I'm worried it'll be too much for her.'

'It'll be fine,' Lizzie said. Noah sighed, but he moved closer to her, and put his arm around her. She leant against his shoulder, and he kissed the top of her head. I looked down at my lap so that they didn't see my smile.

Jake said, 'Time I went home. I've got a long day at the beach tomorrow.' He stood up and put his empty coffee mug back on the tray.

'It's all right for some,' Noah said.

'See you, Jake,' Lizzie said.

I followed him out into the hall. He reached around me and closed the sitting-room door.

'Are Noah and Lizzie OK?' he said in a low voice.

'They're solid,' I said. 'Lizzie would tell me if they weren't.'

'Amateurs,' Jake said, with a grin. 'Always more drama off-stage than on.' He opened the front door, gave me a quick hug, and stepped out into the night. I stood and watched him walk away. Again, I breathed in the scent of the garden flowers.

I thought, I have a few glasses of wine, Jake recites a bit of Shakespeare and I'm feeling like I'm seventeen again, and longing for his kiss. It was, I decided, a moment of midsummer madness, and it was not going to happen again.

Chapter Fifteen

Shane (playing Juliet's would-be suitor, Paris) took my hand and led me out onto the dance floor, where other couples were already swaying in time to the music. I smiled at him encouragingly, while hoping fervently that he wouldn't tread on my toes like he'd done the last time we'd danced together. The music swelled, we stepped towards one another, he stepped away from me – and there was a yelp from Sofia as he collided with her, almost knocking her off her feet. Half the dancers came to a halt, the others kept moving, and chaos ensued.

Zoe switched off the music.

'Sorry, Sofia,' Shane said.

'No worries,' Sofia said.

'You went too soon again, Shane,' Zoe said.

Phyllis, who as Juliet's aged Nurse was not required to dance at the Capulets' ball, and was watching from the edge of the dance floor, said, 'Maybe you need to simplify the choreography, Zoe.'

Zoe shot her a look, but made no reply.

'I'll allocate more practice time for the dance another night,' Pamela said. She wrote something in her notebook. 'For now, I want to move forward to Act V, scene iii, so everyone please clear the stage. Maurice, would you set up Juliet's tomb?'

The cast scattered about the hall, talking among themselves. Maurice carried a camp bed into the middle of the performance space.

'If I could have some quiet, please,' Pamela snapped. The cast fell silent. 'Emma, take up your opening position on Juliet's bier.' I lay down on my back on the camp bed, folded my arms across my chest, closed my eyes, and waited for my cue.

If Pamela had any qualms about her lack of experience as a director in the fortnight since she'd taken over from George, she'd managed to keep them well hidden. At the first rehearsal after his departure, she'd given a rousing speech, informing the Players that she'd cleared her diary of everything except her essential work for the WI, the South Quay Village Fete Committee, and the Parish Council, so she could devote herself to the summer production, and she was certain that her cast would be equally committed to ensuring that *Romeo and Juliet* was a success. Commitment turned out to mean longer and more rehearsals, accepting the questionable changes she made to the scenes that George had set months ago without protest, and worst of all, the reduction of the tea break from fifteen minutes to ten. Several citizens of Verona, used to George's laid-back approach and gentle encouragement, decided that Pamela's more strident style of direction ('No, *no*, that's wrong, all wrong. Please *try* to concentrate') wasn't for them, and left the production. As Henry's friend, I'd kept out of any post-rehearsal conversations over drinks in the Armada complaining about his mother, but I was aware that such conversations were taking place.

We'd now reached the play's final scenes, where Juliet is faking her death with a drug-induced sleep, Romeo, believing her truly dead, poisons himself, and Juliet, awakening to find his dead body lying beside her on her bier, stabs herself with his dagger. After tonight, I thought, we've little more than a month left to polish the entire play, get the dancers up to speed – literally – and get everyone off book ...

Henry said, '*Here's to my love.*'

Concentrate, Emma, I thought, or you'll miss your cue and Pamela will implode. I opened my eyes just wide enough to see Henry raise the bottle of poison to his mouth, and shut them again as he knelt beside me and planted a perfunctory kiss on my lips.

'*Thus with a kiss, I die.*' He fell forward onto the camp bed, which promptly collapsed and deposited the pair of us onto the hard wooden floor. With gasps and shrieks of dismay, the rest of the cast leapt from their seats and crowded around us, asking if we were all right. Noah took my hand and hauled me to my feet.

Henry, I saw, was still lying on the ground. 'Are you OK?' I said.

'No,' Henry said. 'My arm——' With a groan, he sat up, cradling his left arm with his right hand. Eddie (Servant to the Capulets, landscape gardener, part-time life guard and, now I came to think of it, trained first-aider), crouched down next to him.

'Let's have a look, mate,' he said. Henry held out his arm, still supporting it with his other hand. His face was very pale.

'I can't straighten it,' he said.

'That arm's broken, mate,' Eddie said. 'I'll put a sling on it, and then you need to get to A&E. Anyone got a car?'

'We do,' Pamela said. 'Maurice, you drive Henry to Teymouth General.'

My leading man had just broken his arm. This rehearsal had to be the worst in the entire ninety-year history of the Players.

Chapter Sixteen

'I still don't see how he broke it,' I said, as Jake drove me, Lizzie, and Noah along the coast road, turning off into the lane lined with large, detached houses with acres of garden – the most des res in South Quay – one of which, the Moat House, was the Wyndham family home. 'It wasn't much of a fall. I don't even have any bruises.'

After Henry's accident – I wouldn't be lying down on that camp bed again, for sure – and his departure for A&E in his father's car, Pamela had wasted no time in resuming the rehearsal, with me sitting on a chair. It was probably a little unkind of me to suspect that her tetchiness ('*Louder*, Prince of Verona, I can't hear you. Gail, *stand still*, you're drawing the eye') during the time it took to get through the rest of the scene was due less to her concern for her son than her worry that his injury would upset her rehearsal schedule.

'Does he know how long he's going to be in plaster?' Jake said.

'Unfortunately,' I said, 'it's broken in three places. They told him last night at the hospital that it'll take at least eight weeks to heal, possibly longer.'

'Which means he's going to have to drop out of the play,' Noah said. 'He can't be climbing up Juliet's balcony with his arm in a sling.'

'He must be so disappointed,' Lizzie said.

'You'd think so,' I said, 'but he seems to be bearing up.' When

I'd spoken to Henry on the phone earlier that day to find out if he was up to receiving visitors, he'd been remarkably upbeat, reminding me that there would be other shows, and that it was only a few months before the auditions for the Players' annual pantomime. I put it down to the painkillers he was taking.

'Who's Henry's understudy?' Jake said.

'There isn't one,' I said. 'We're an *amateur* company, remember. We don't have the luxury of understudies. No one's going to give up two evenings a week to attend rehearsals when they're unlikely to ever go on stage.'

'However much they *love* acting,' Jake said, a remark I decided to ignore.

I sighed. 'First we lose our director. Now we don't have a male lead.'

'*For never was a story of more woe,*' Jake said.

'*Than this of Juliet and her Romeo,*' I said, automatically.

From the back seat, Lizzie said, 'I just hope Pamela can persuade someone to take on a lead role so close to opening night.'

'From what I remember of Pamela Wyndham,' Jake said, 'her powers of persuasion are formidable. My mother used to refer to her as "that terrifying woman who always talks me into baking cakes for the WI."'

'It's not only finding someone willing to play Romeo,' Lizzie said, 'it's finding someone suitable. All the younger men in the society are already cast in other roles.'

'It's a problem, Lizzie,' Noah said. 'I can't think where the Players are going to get hold of a twenty-something guy with enough acting experience to give a decent performance after only a month of rehearsal.'

'It would help if he already had a good knowledge of the play, wouldn't it, Noah?' Lizzie said.

'Can you think of anyone we know who is familiar with the works of Shakespeare, Lizzie?' Noah said.

'Someone who's living in South Quay, Noah?' Lizzie said.

Sitting next to Jake in the front passenger seat, I could see his hands tighten on the steering wheel. I thought, I'm not getting involved in this conversation.

'Enough,' Jake said. 'Did you put them up to this, Emma?'

'No,' I said, 'they thought it up all on their own.'

'Never going to happen, guys,' Jake said.

'I don't see why not,' Lizzie said. 'You and Emma were always terrific when you acted opposite each other.'

'That was years ago,' Jake said, turning into the Wyndhams' horseshoe-shaped driveway and bringing his car to a halt. 'These days, I don't perform in amateur shows in a school hall. Or a community centre.'

'Think yourself too good for us now, I suppose?' Noah laughed.

'Frankly, yes,' Jake said. He switched off the engine and twisted round in his seat to face Lizzie and Noah. 'Acting is my job, and I expect to get paid for it.'

Both Lizzie and Noah appeared taken aback by this remark, but after a moment, Noah said, 'Fair enough, mate,' and the conversation was at an end. The four of us got out of the car, and crunched over the gravel to the Wyndhams' front door. I rang the bell.

'I'd forgotten how massive this place is,' Jake said, looking up at the Grade II listed Tudor mansion.

'It's a lovely house,' Lizzie said, 'and it has a fascinating history. Did you know that there's a beam in one of the upstairs bedrooms taken from the same shipwrecked Spanish galleon whose timbers built the Armada Inn?'

'If you believe local legend,' Jake said. 'Which I never have.'

The door opened then, to reveal Pamela, formally dressed in a skirt suit and pearls. 'Good evening, Emma,' she said. 'Lizzie. Noah. Jake. Please, do come in.' She stood aside, and we trooped past her into the oak-panelled hallway, which was larger than the whole of the ground floor of Lizzie's cottage, and dominated by a mahogany table on which there was an elaborate floral arrangement in a blue and white china vase. I recalled how anxious I'd been as a teenager, whenever the five of us had hung out at

Henry's, that I'd accidentally knock over one of his mother's priceless antiques.

'Henry told me you were coming,' Pamela continued. 'So kind of you to visit him. Maurice is out, and I, myself, am just about to leave the house – things to do, people to see – but I have some good news to impart before I go.' She favoured us with a satisfied smile. 'It's taken me most of the day, and I had to make a great many phone calls, but I have found us a new Romeo. Eddie Taylor. One of the ensemble can take over his former role as the Servant.'

Eddie, I thought. An enthusiastic member of the Players, but not much of an actor.

'That is good news,' I said, trying hard to sound as though I meant it. You can do better than that, Emma, I thought, you're a star of the amateur stage. 'That's wonderful. I'm so relieved. I did worry that without Henry, *Romeo and Juliet* might have to be cancelled.'

'I can assure you, Emma,' Pamela said, 'that will never happen. Ever since my great-grandfather founded the society, the Players have performed three productions every year, even during the darkest days of World War II, and while I'm Chairwoman they will continue to do so. The show must always go on. As I'm sure you all agree.'

'I'm a great believer in the show going on,' Jake said, 'but only as long as the actors are getting paid.'

Pamela laughed, evidently not taking Jake's remark seriously. 'Well, I must be off,' she said, 'the village fete isn't going to organise itself. Henry's in the garden. Do go on through.' She breezed out of the house, got into her Mercedes, and drove off.

'So,' Noah said, 'Eddie as Romeo. I have to say I'm surprised. He's only ever done small roles. I hope he's up to taking on a lead.'

'He's going to find it a challenge to learn so many lines in such a short time,' Lizzie said. I was inclined to agree with her, but knowing Jake's opinion of amateur actors, I wasn't going to admit it in front of him.

'I guess he can't be any worse at learning lines than Henry,' Noah said.

'Speaking of Henry,' Lizzie said, 'we should go and join him, don't you think?' She and Noah hurried across the hall and into the large reception room at the back of the house, which opened out onto the garden. I followed after them, with Jake walking close behind me. I told myself not to react when I heard him mutter 'amateurs' under his breath.

Chapter Seventeen

Jake brought his car to a stop on the corner of Shore Road and Saltwater Lane.

'Door-to-door service,' he said. 'Well, almost. As close as I can get the car.'

'Thanks, Jake,' Lizzie said, opening the car door. Noah leapt out of his seat and rushed around to her side of the vehicle, hovering protectively over her as she got out.

We'd had a good evening, the five of us talking in Henry's garden, retreating into the pool house when it grew dark, just as we had when we were teenagers. Henry was still remarkably sanguine about having to pull out of *Romeo and Juliet,* and not particularly bothered that he'd had to give up his job crewing for an entrepreneurial friend who ran fishing trips for affluent holidaymakers out of Teymouth harbour. His only complaint was that a broken limb meant he wouldn't be able to surf or take his own boat out for the rest of the summer.

Jake leant towards me. 'Emma, can I have a quick word?' he said quietly.

'Yes, of course,' I said, still watching Noah and Lizzie as he took her hand in his. They turned to face the car, obviously waiting for me. I pressed the button that opened the window. 'You guys go on ahead. I'll catch you up.'

'OK, see you in a bit,' Lizzie said. She and Noah started walking towards the cottage. I twisted around in my seat to face Jake.

111

'What's up?' I said.

'Would you be able to take a couple of days off work next week? Thursday, Friday, and possibly Saturday?'

I ran through my diary in my head. 'Thursday and Friday shouldn't be a problem. On Saturday, we have an evening event, but I don't have to be at the hotel until mid-afternoon. Why d'you ask?'

'You remember that conversation we had about you coming to LA if I was ever nominated for an Oscar?'

'You've been nominated for an Oscar!'

'I wish,' Jake laughed. 'No, I've not been nominated for an Oscar, a Bafta, an Emmy, or any other award. But I do have an invitation for me and a guest to the *Muse* press night at the Aphra Behn Theatre, and the after-show party, on the Thursday. I was hoping you'd like to come with me.'

I gasped. 'You want me to be your plus-one at an event in a West End theatre?'

'I think you'd enjoy it,' Jake said.

'I'm sure I would,' I said. 'Yes, Jake, I would very much like to come with you to the theatre next week. What exactly is a press night?'

'Just another name for a first night,' Jake said. 'There'll be a lot of theatre critics there, and a lot of people in the audience you'll probably recognise.' He added, 'The show is a new musical. A friend of mine from drama school, Zac Diaz, is the male lead, and the female lead is his wife, Julie Farrell Diaz.'

'Those names sound familiar,' I said.

'They've both starred in other West End musicals, although not always together,' Jake said. 'I expect you've seen their photos in the media at some point.'

I thought, this is the world Jake lives in now, and I'm going to be a part of it, if only for a short while.

'I have to see my agent on the Thursday morning,' Jake said. 'She's arranged a meeting with a director who's keen for me to do his next play. I've no intention of accepting the role, but I've told

Stephanie I'll at least discuss it, so it'd suit me to drive up to London the night before. I'll pick you up from work and—'

'You're talking about the *Wednesday* of next week?' I interrupted. My heart sank. The Players met on Wednesday.

'Problem?' Jake asked.

'I have rehearsal Wednesday evening.'

'Yeah, I know,' Jake said. 'Why don't you miss it for once?'

I thought about missing rehearsal. For about two seconds. 'I'm really sorry, Jake,' I said, 'but I can't. Not when we've a new Romeo, a new director, and the show's only a few weeks away from opening. I'd be letting down the rest of the cast.' I hesitated, and then I added, 'I really do want to come with you to the press night. If you have to go to London on Wednesday, maybe I could travel up by train on Thursday?'

'Or I could pick you up after your rehearsal's over,' Jake said.

'Could you?' I said. 'The thing is, Jake, I may be an *amateur* actress, but I like to think I know how to behave like a *professional*.'

'Relax, Emma,' Jake said. 'I get that. Skipping the rehearsal was only a suggestion. If we leave a few hours later, it's no big deal.'

'Oh. Right. Thanks, Jake.'

He smiled. 'We'll have a couple of days in London – my flat has a guest room you can stay in, by the way – and I'll drive you back to South Quay in plenty of time for you to get to work on Saturday.'

'Sounds good to me,' I said, smiling back at him.

'Have a think if there's anything else you'd like to do while we're in London.'

'I will,' I said. 'Goodnight, Jake.' I planted a kiss on the side of his face, got out of the car, and headed off. Knowing that he would watch me from the corner until I reached the cottage, I raised a hand and waved before I went through the garden gate. Jake flashed his car's headlights, and pulled away from the kerb.

I let myself in the front door to find the hall light still on, but

113

no sign of Lizzie and Noah, who must have gone straight to bed. My head whirling with thoughts about my imminent visit to London: What does a girl wear to a press night? Would I get to meet the cast of the play? I floated upstairs to my bedroom.

I'd just changed into my pyjamas, when there was a faint tap on my bedroom door.

'Emma?' Lizzie said softly. 'Are you still awake?'

'I am,' I said, sitting down cross-legged on my bed. 'Come in, Lizzie.' She came in, closed the door, and sat down next to me. Her still-slender figure was swamped by one of Noah's shirts.

'So,' she said. 'You and Jake.'

Not this again, I thought. 'What about me and *our friend* Jake?' I said.

'You can't fool me, Emma,' Lizzie said. 'I've known you too long.'

I rolled my eyes.

'The two of you were doing that Shakespeare thing again this evening,' Lizzie continued.

'What Shakespeare thing?' I asked.

'One of you says a line from a Shakespeare play, and the other comes straight back with the next line. You used to have whole conversations like that when we were in school – it used to drive me insane – but I'm pretty sure it wasn't England's greatest playwright you and Jake were talking about when you had your private moment in his car tonight.'

'You're right,' I said. 'Actually, we didn't talk at all. We just snogged in the back seat.'

Lizzie's eyes widened.

'You are so gullible!' I said.

'I am not,' Lizzie said. 'What really happened?'

'Nothing much,' I said. 'Jake invited me to the opening of a West End musical next week.'

'You're going to the opening night of a West End show!' Lizzie said. 'Oh. My. Goodness. I'm not at all jealous. I want you to know that.'

I laughed. 'We're going to drive up to town after Wednesday's rehearsal, and stay at his place until Saturday. I'm so looking forward to having a couple of days in London.'

Lizzie gave me a long look. 'You're staying *at Jake's place* for a couple of days?'

I sighed. 'He has a guest room, Lizzie.'

There was another light knock on the door, and Noah's voice came to us, saying, 'Lizzie? Are you going to be long?'

Lizzie frowned. 'I thought he was asleep,' she muttered.

'Come in, Noah,' I said. He put his head around the door.

'Just checking you're all right, Lizzie,' he said.

'I'm good, Noah,' Lizzie said. 'As you can see. I'm having a chat with Emma.'

'Don't forget you have to be up at seven,' Noah said.

'I won't,' Lizzie said.

Noah nodded and retreated onto the landing, closing the door behind him.

'It's lovely the way Noah looks after you,' I said. 'He is *so* nice.'

'Yes, he is,' Lizzie said. 'Now, back to you and Jake—'

'Enough, Lizzie.'

'You told me that you were over him,' Lizzie went on, 'and I believed you. But seeing you two together tonight, it's obvious that there's still *something* there.'

'There is,' I said. 'It's called friendship.'

Lizzie gave me a long look. 'If you say so.' She stood up. 'I'd better go before Noah comes back and drags me off to bed.'

I raised my eyebrows.

'To sleep, Emma,' Lizzie said. 'Women need more rest when they're pregnant. As my boyfriend keeps reminding me.'

115

Chapter Eighteen

'I didn't think there could be a worse Romeo than Henry,' Richard said, 'but that was until Pamela decided to give the part to Eddie.'

A wave of irritation surged through me. I'd been less than thrilled to see my name once again next to Richard's on the clearing-up rota – if he still harboured thoughts of asking me out, I'd prefer to avoid situations that might give him the opportunity. And I'd certainly no desire to listen to his litany of complaints about Eddie's acting. My new leading man was doing his best.

'Tonight was only his third rehearsal,' I said. 'And keep your voice down. They'll hear you.' I glanced towards the other side of the hall where Pamela, having dismissed the rest of the cast, was still giving Eddie his notes, which he was scribbling frantically on his script.

'You do realise there are only five weeks until we open?' Richard said.

'Yes, Richard,' I said, through gritted teeth. 'I'm aware of that.' We may need extra rehearsals, I thought, but we can still make *Romeo and Juliet* a success. I surveyed the hall. The chairs were stacked, the floor was swept. I was free to go and meet Jake.

'Coming to the Armada?' Richard said.

'I can't tonight,' I said. 'Jake's waiting for me outside with his car. We're driving up to London.'

'You're going to London with Jake Murray?' Richard said.

'Yes, I am,' I said, smiling at the thought. 'Just for a few days.'

Calling out goodnight to Pamela and Eddie, and with Richard following me, I went out of the hall, retrieved my suitcase from the bar area where I'd left it earlier, and wheeled it out into the car park. Jake was leaning against the bonnet of his car, chatting with Zoe and Sofia.

'Hey, Emma,' he said, when he saw me. 'Let me get your case.' He opened the car boot, and lifted my suitcase inside.

'Jake's been telling us about this press night you're going to,' Sofia said. 'Make sure you take lots of photos.'

'I'll try,' I said, doubting that the opening night of a West End show was the sort of event that encouraged the taking of selfies.

'Have fun,' Zoe said.

'That I will do,' I said, with much more confidence.

'We need to get on the road, Emma,' Jake said.

Sofia, Zoe, and Richard chorused their goodbyes. The three of them stood and watched as Jake and I got into his car and drove out of the car park. It occurred to me that they would be going straight to the Armada, where they would be regaling the Players with the news that Emma Stevens was off to London with Jake Murray and everything that implied.

I glanced at Jake. His attention, as we left South Quay behind us, was all on the winding road that would take us over the South Downs to the motorway and on to the city. I turned my head and stared out of the window, although there was nothing to see other than the two beams of light from the car's headlamps and the dark shape of trees against the starry night sky. My mind drifted back to the last time I'd visited London …

I wake up in a strange room, in a bed that isn't mine. At first, still drowsy, I can't think where I am. Or why there is someone lying next to me, their breath warm on the back of my neck. Then I remember. For the first time in my life, I didn't sleep alone. Slowly, I roll over so that I am facing him, the boy whose head is next to mine on the pillow, and find myself looking directly into his grey-blue eyes. There is a faint shadow on his chin that wasn't there last night. He smiles, and I smile back at him.

'Morning,' he says. 'I was wondering when you were going to wake up.'

'Morning, Jake.'

'Are you hungry?' he says. 'D'you want some breakfast?'

To my surprise, I realise that I am hungry. Ravenous, in fact. 'I'm starving.'

'Me too.' He sits up and pushes back the duvet. 'I'll go and see if I can find anything edible in the kitchen.' I gaze at his naked body as he stands and stretches, drinking him in. I have never before understood how a male body could be described as beautiful, but I do now.

Jake retrieves his clothes from the floor, and pulls on his boxers and jeans. We exchange another smile. He turns to leave the bedroom.

'Jake,' I say. 'Last night ... I didn't know ... I didn't realise it would feel so good.'

'It was good for me too,' Jake says, reaching for the door handle. Then he lets his hand fall to his side, and turns back to face me. 'Have you never ....? Was last night the first time you've been with a guy?'

'Yes,' I say.

'But you went out with Callum for months.'

'I didn't sleep with him.'

Jake sits back down on the bed. He touches my face, brushing a strand of hair out of my eyes. Then he leans in and kisses me very tenderly.

'I'm glad your first time was good for you,' he says, 'and I'm glad it was with me ...'

'That isn't my phone,' Jake said, 'so it must be yours.'

Jolted out of my reverie, I scrabbled in my bag, found my ringing mobile and pressed answer.

'Emma? It's Eddie. I hope this isn't too late for me to call you?'

'No, it's fine,' I said.

'I was hoping to catch you in the Armada, but Richard said you'd left for London.'

'That's right,' I said. Well, that didn't take long, I thought. 'What's up?'

118

There was a long silence, long enough for me to check that my phone still had a signal, and then Eddie said, 'The thing is, Emma, playing Romeo just isn't working for me. I'm hoping that you might be able to think of someone who could take over the part. Someone I could suggest to Pamela when I tell her I'm pulling out of the show.'

Nooo! Telling myself to keep calm, I said, 'But why would you want to leave, Eddie? You're doing so well.'

'We both know that's not true,' Eddie said. 'I enjoy doing a bit of acting, maybe having a few lines, but I've never wanted to take on a lead. I only agreed to do it to help out, but after tonight's rehearsal, I've realised I'm not up to it. I can't learn all those speeches, Pamela criticises everything I do, and I know that I'm going to make a complete fool of myself in front of the whole village.'

'There's still time for you to learn—'

'I can't do it, Emma,' Eddie said, cutting across me. 'The thought of standing on the community centre stage and forgetting my lines terrifies me, if I'm honest.'

This, from a man who more than once has dashed into the sea to rescue a holidaymaker from the waves, I thought.

'If you're that worried,' I said, 'we can always make an announcement before the show starts to let the audience know that you've taken on the role at short notice. We need you, Eddie, we're never going to find another actor to play Romeo, not now.'

'There has to be someone.'

'There really isn't,' I said. Desperately, I added, 'I don't see how the summer production can go ahead without you.'

After another silence, Eddie said, 'I don't want to be the reason the show's cancelled.'

'Then stay on as Romeo,' I said. 'I'm sure Pamela will be happy to arrange some extra rehearsals, if you feel you need them.'

'Or you and I could go over my scenes on our own,' Eddie said. 'If you wouldn't mind. If you have the time.'

119

'Of course,' I said, quite understanding why he might not want to spend any more time with our director than was strictly necessary. 'We'll sort something out on Monday.'

'Yeah, OK, I'll see you Monday,' Eddie said. 'Thanks, Emma.'

'You're welcome. Goodnight, Eddie.' I ended the call, weak with relief that another calamity had been averted.

'Everything all right?' Jake said.

'I think so. Eddie's nervous about playing Romeo, but he'll be fine after a few more rehearsals.' Suddenly, for the first time since I joined the Players, I was less than certain that our show was going to be a success. 'It'll be all right on the night.'

'I hope so,' Jake said, 'because I've bought my ticket. I was hoping for a seat at the back so that I could slip out to the bar if the show's really bad, but I'm right in the middle of the front row. I'm going to have to sit through all five acts.'

I laughed at that. He switched on the radio, which was tuned to a late-night music station, and returned his attention to the road. I settled back in my seat. My eyes grew heavy, and I let them close. When I opened them, Jake was reversing into a parking place between two other cars. The light from the street lamps showed me that we were outside a Victorian terraced house separated from the pavement by a low brick wall.

'Oh – we're here,' I said, somewhat needlessly. Ten years since I was last in London, I thought.

'That's my place,' Jake said, pointing to one of the houses. 'I have the flat on the ground floor.'

We got out of the car. Jake retrieved our cases and a box of groceries from the boot, and I followed him to his front door. While he unlocked it, I checked my phone and saw that I had one unread text: *London! My sister! With Jake Murray!! Why am I the last to know? xx*

Chapter Nineteen

Despite having slept in the car, I didn't wake up the following morning until gone nine o'clock. Knowing that Jake was planning to leave for his meeting with his agent and the director around that time, I leapt straight out of bed, concealed my pyjamas under a silk kimono that Lizzie had given me for my birthday, and hurried out of the guest room.

The scent of coffee drew me across the hallway and into the long open-plan room that I'd only glimpsed when Jake had given me a brief tour the previous night. The room, which ran the length of one side of the flat, with glass doors at the far end opening onto a courtyard garden, was high-ceilinged, light-filled, and airy, and the walls were painted a pale dove grey. There was just one picture, a large black and white photo of Piccadilly Circus, the statue of Eros in the centre. The furniture in the room was contemporary, a dark wooden dining table and chairs, a couple of grey armchairs, and a grey L-shaped sofa that separated the living area from the kitchen area, where Jake was now standing by a worktop, pouring freshly made coffee into a mug. When he saw me, his face lit up with a smile.

'Morning, Emma,' he said, 'I was just about to bring this in to you.'

'Thanks,' I said, taking the mug from his outstretched hand. 'I didn't mean to sleep so late. I should have set my alarm.'

'You can sleep as late as you like,' Jake said. 'You're on holiday.'

'So I am,' I said, delightedly.

'I have to go out now,' Jake went on, 'but I reckon I'll be back by twelve.'

'I'll see you later then,' I said. 'I hope your meeting goes well.'

Jake grimaced. 'I only agreed to it to keep my agent happy. Help yourself to breakfast. I've left my spare keys in that drawer, if you want to explore the neighbourhood. Turn right outside the flat, and my road comes out on Upper Street where the shops are. See you later.' He headed off.

My gaze travelled over the living area, with its minimalist furnishings and cool, clean colours. I thought of Lizzie's cottage, with its bookcases, paintings, and embroidered cushions filling every room with a riot of hues and textures. It was hard to imagine two more different living spaces. Knowing that Lizzie would be interested to see Jake's flat, even if she didn't share his taste in domestic décor, I fetched my phone and took a photo of the living/kitchen area, the room I was staying in, and the dark grey-tiled bathroom. He hadn't included it in the previous night's guided tour, but I was unable to resist putting my head round Jake's bedroom door, and saw that his room was decorated in the same monochrome colours as the rest of the flat, with sleek black fitted wardrobes taking up one wall, and none of the CDs, DVDs, and piles of clothes that had cluttered his teenage bedroom. Taking a picture of this room, his private space, seemed wrong, however good friends we were, so I decided Lizzie would have to make do with a verbal description. I was about to close the door, when my attention was caught by another framed photo on a shelf by the window. I hesitated, but then I went into the room and picked it up.

It was a picture of a group of men and women, some of whom I recognised as actors from the cast of *Sherwood*, sitting around the table in Jake's courtyard garden, smiling at the camera and each other, laughing, raising glasses of wine. Jake was at the head of the table. Next to him was Leonie Fox.

A stab of jealously went through me. Why would Jake still

122

have a photo of *her* by his bedside? Almost immediately, I realised that my reaction was both irrational and ridiculous. If Jake chose to keep pictures that included his ex on view, it was no concern of mine. I returned the photo to the shelf, careful to place it in exactly the same position as I'd picked it up from, and left the room.

Having breakfasted, showered, and dressed, I decided to venture outside, and whiled away the rest of the morning wandering along Upper Street, Islington's busy main thoroughfare, gawping at the sheer number and variety of restaurants, cafés, bars, and shops that were within a few minutes' walking distance of Jake's home, along with a cinema and a pub-theatre. I got back to the flat only a few minutes before Jake, who came home with the news that he'd managed to sound enthusiastic about the play without giving a direct answer as to whether or not he'd do it, and the suggestion that we spend the afternoon walking along the Regent's Canal, adding that it was a place he thought I'd like.

We left the flat, heading in the opposite direction to the one I'd taken earlier. Cutting through the Chapel Street Market, a road lined with stalls selling fruit, vegetables, and household goods, and a housing estate, we came to a flight of steps that brought us down to the Regent's Canal. Behind us, the canal was lost to sight in a dark, round tunnel; in front of us, its surface smooth and green with duck-weed, it headed westwards into central London, between high, ivy-clad brick walls, the towpath vanishing tantalisingly around a bend. A brightly painted houseboat was moored to the opposite bank, under a willow tree. After my morning on Upper Street, I was struck by how quiet it was.

'It's so peaceful down here,' I said. 'I didn't know places like this existed in London.'

Jake smiled. 'It's one of the capital's best-kept secrets,' he said.

We strolled along the sunlit towpath, chatting easily about everything and nothing, passing more colourful houseboats – stopping so that I could take photos on my phone – low-rise, canal-side apartments, and office blocks. A cyclist and a couple of joggers overtook us, and I remembered Jake telling me that he liked to run beside the canal on a Sunday morning.

Walking around another curve in the canal and under a bridge, we saw a houseboat that was, amazingly, a floating bookshop, and another that was a café, and a little further along what looked oddly like green-carpeted giant steps, where a number of people, young and old, students, and a party of schoolchildren, were sunbathing or eating their picnic lunch. Taking a detour up a short flight of stone stairs, we came to Granary Square, a paved piazza, where a fountain sent hundreds of jets of water spurting out of the ground and up into the air, to the unbridled delight of the toddlers darting in and out of them and their watching parents. I took a photo of me and Jake in the square and on the grassy steps.

Back on the towpath, we passed a group of boys fishing, and on the opposite bank, surrounded by trees and plants, a pyramid-shaped structure that Jake informed me was a viewing platform from which visitors to the Camley Street Natural Park, a nature reserve in the heart of the city, could observe the canal's wildlife.

'Is there much wildlife alongside an urban canal?' I asked him.

'You'd be surprised. I've seen herons and kingfishers many times.'

We walked on, coming to our first lock – St Pancras Lock, according to a helpful sign – and another photo opportunity for me, which Jake was happy to indulge. Beyond the lock, for a short distance, the canal ran through a less attractive landscape, where towering cranes scraped the sky, and former warehouses were being transformed into new housing developments, and we walked under several graffiti-spattered bridges before reaching a pleasant residential area of apartments and trees.

At Camden, we were drawn into bustling Camden Lock Market by the mouth-watering aromas of cooking and exotic spices, buying ourselves a delicious street-food lunch of burritos, and browsing for a while among stalls selling silver jewellery, hand-stitched leather bags, shoes, and vintage clothes – I resisted temptation, but Jake bought a leather belt – before returning to the calm of the canal.

We walked on through the hot afternoon, passing several young couples sitting on the edge of the towpath, their feet dangling over the water. I took photos of a turreted red-brick building with the words 'pirate castle' painted on the side, and a flotilla of kayaks. After a sharp turn to the right by a floating restaurant, the towpath became wider, with tall leafy trees on both banks, and overhanging willows trailing their branches in the water. We saw swans, moorhens, and a flock of Canada geese. A punt glided past us, heading towards Camden, its occupants drinking wine, singing and playing guitar. We waved and they waved back.

'The Regent's Canal is one of my favourite London walks,' Jake said.

'It's beautiful,' I said, with feeling. 'Thank you for sharing it with me.'

'My pleasure, Emma,' he said with a smile.

We continued walking, our shadows lengthening as the sun sank lower in the sky, the canal taking us through the middle of London Zoo – above the trees I glimpsed the famous aviary – and then on through Regents Park, where I found myself staring in awe at the palatial white mansions surrounded by trim green lawns that stood on the opposite bank. The towpath narrowed, leading us through a metal gateway to a stretch of the canal that Jake told me was called Lisson Grove. Here, the owners of the houseboats moored alongside each other had turned the towpath into gardens, with flowers and plants in hand-decorated pots, mirrors and mosaics on the canal wall, leaf-covered arbours, and lanterns and wind chimes strung among the trees. Lizzie would love this part of the canal, I thought.

'This is as far as we go,' Jake said. 'We need to give ourselves enough time to get home to my flat and then travel back into town.'

'I'll just take one more photo,' I said, and took a shot of Jake, standing on the towpath, the canal glinting in the sunlight behind him.

We went through another metal gate, along a narrow alley, and up a flight of steps that returned us to street level and the roar of passing traffic. A short walk past Lord's Cricket Ground brought us to the underground, and we caught a train back to Islington, Jake drawing my attention to the rather fetching angel statue formed out of twisted metal at the top of Angel station's escalators.

'I hope I haven't tired you out,' he said, as we reached his flat, and went inside.

'Not at all,' I said. 'Thank you for today, Jake. It was lovely.'

'It isn't over yet,' he reminded me. 'Not that I'm suggesting it'll take you more than an hour to get ready, but I'd like to leave for the theatre at six.' I took the hint, and went off to get changed.

As he was the only one of my acquaintance who'd ever attended the opening of a West End play, I'd asked Jake if there was any sort of dress code. His reply, that he'd be wearing a suit and that the last time he'd been to such an event, as far as he could remember, the women were wearing dresses, had left me still with little idea of what I should wear myself. Googling 'what to wear for a West End press night' had fortunately proved more informative, bringing up a number of images of actresses wearing outfits ranging from ankle-length designer gowns to little black dresses that barely reached mid-thigh. The photos having convinced me that there was nothing in my wardrobe that I could possibly wear as Jake's plus-one, I'd trawled both the internet and Teymouth for a suitably glam frock, finally discovering not one but two dresses that I thought would do, in one of the quirky little shops down on the waterfront. One was reasonably priced, the other was eye-wateringly expensive, but when I tried them on there was no contest as to which I wanted. I'd told myself that this might be the only time in my life that I went to a press night at a London theatre, and got out my credit card.

Now, standing in front of the mirrored wardrobe in Jake's guest bedroom, I was glad I'd gone for the more expensive dress, even if it left a gaping hole in my bank balance. Deep coral in colour, with a low, scooped neck and a *very* low back, caught in at the waist, and falling softly to an inch or so below my knees, it could have been made for me. I slid my feet into my metallic bronze high-heeled ankle-strap sandals – also newly purchased, because I wasn't about to ruin the glamorous impression created by the dress by teaming it with old shoes – and picked up my matching bag and coral pashmina. Tossing my hair, which I'd decided at the last minute to curl rather than straighten, over my shoulders, I went in search of Jake.

The living room was empty, but through the open glass doors at the far end, I saw him standing by the iron-work table in the courtyard garden, in the golden evening light. Absorbed as he was in opening a bottle of prosecco, he didn't notice me. I stood silent and still, watching him pour the fizzing liquid into a glass, thinking how good he looked in his formal black suit and collarless white shirt, urbane, sophisticated, and *hot*. I stepped out into the garden. Jake raised his head, and looked straight at me. His gaze travelled from my face down over my entire body, sending a shiver along my spine. Suddenly, for the first time since he'd come back into my life, I knew that he was seeing me as a woman, not simply as a friend.

He said, 'O, *she doth teach the torches to burn bright.*'

I was quite unable to think of a single line of Shakespeare's that would make a suitable reply.

Jake was still staring at me. He cleared his throat. 'Would you like a glass of prosecco before we go out?'

'Please.' I tried to ignore the fluttering in my stomach. He poured another glass and handed it to me. I gulped half of it down in one. Get a grip, Emma, I told myself. Guys look at girls that way all the time. It doesn't mean a thing, other than he's male and straight. 'Do you know anything about the show we're going to see?'

'Only that it's about an artist in nineteenth-century Paris who falls in love with his model – his muse,' Jake said. 'According to

Zac, the previews have gone very well.' He refilled my glass, and I made myself sip it more slowly, while he wrote 'break a leg' in the good luck cards he'd bought for Zac, Zac's wife and co-star Julie, and a couple of other actors in the cast of *Muse* that he knew. He glanced at his watch. 'We should get going. We have to be in our seats by seven, before the VIPs arrive.'

'Isn't the star of *Sherwood* a VIP?' I said.

Jake laughed. 'Not as much of a VIP as some of the other people who are going to be in the audience tonight, apparently.'

We took the tube from Angel, standing crushed together in the train carriage among office workers and tourists, some weighed down with monstrous backpacks, queuing to get on the escalators that brought us up out of the underground. Emerging into an only slightly less crowded Leicester Square, I saw that since I'd last been there with Jake and he'd pointed out the statue of Shakespeare, it had been extensively refurbished. The cinemas were the same, but there were different restaurants around the edge of the square, now divided from the park area in the middle by concrete seating and a new metal fence. For a moment, I couldn't see Shakespeare among the summer foliage of the trees, but then I spotted him through the leaves, still looking out over Theatreland, which made me smile.

'Emma?' Jake, who hadn't stopped to commune with the bard of Avon, was standing a few yards away, turning his head from side to side, scanning the crowd flowing around him. Catching sight of me, he raised a hand. 'Over here, Emma.' I hurried to his side and linked my arm through his.

We headed out of Leicester Square and along Charing Cross Road, skirting around a gaggle of students poring over a street map, by-passing the book-lovers examining the window displays of the numerous second-hand bookshops. Turning into Shaftes-bury Avenue, we'd not gone far when we came in sight of the Aphra Behn Theatre, and a small crowd milling around out-side, behind a metal security barrier. As we walked closer, I saw a limo pull up at the kerb, and a man and a woman got out, both middle-aged and very smartly dressed. As one, the on-lookers held up their phones to record the moment for posterity. I felt a *frisson* of fannish excitement as I recognised the couple as actors from *Family Matters*, my sister's favourite soap. One of several large men in evening dress standing by the security barrier gave the soap stars' tickets a cursory glance, and waved them past onto a red carpet that had been rolled out across the pavement. As they reached the steps that led into the theatre, there was a sudden burst of flashing lights as a small coterie of press photographers by the entrance took their photo.

'I'll drop the cards off at the stage door,' Jake said, 'and then we'll go in.'

I gasped. 'We go in the main entrance? We walk along the red carpet?'

'It's no big deal,' Jake said. 'Just another part of an actor's job.'

While he went off to deliver the good luck cards to the stage door, which was in an alleyway at the side of the theatre, I stood and watched as other members of the invited audience arrived at the Aphra Behn, some stepping out of taxis, others rocking up on foot like me and Jake. After a couple of minutes or so, he returned, and we went over to one of the security guys and showed him our tickets.

'Thank you, Mr Murray,' the security man said. 'Enjoy the show.'

Jake put his head close to my ear. 'Walk slowly,' he said. 'Smile. And when I squeeze your arm, turn your head towards the press photographers so they can get a good shot of us.' He grinned. 'It's show time.'

Arm in arm with Jake, my pulse racing, I stepped out onto the red carpet. Telling myself firmly that I was *not* going to fall over my feet, I walked beside him, dimly aware of the crowd on the other side of the barrier, remembering to smile in the direction of the flashes of light from the cameras when I felt the pressure of Jake's hand on my arm. Suddenly, I realised I was enjoying this fleeting moment of borrowed fame. Perhaps if I'd strolled along a red carpet as often as Jake had, I, too, would be blasé about the whole experience, but somehow I doubted it.

Once inside the theatre, we were welcomed by the front of house staff who directed us across the foyer to the staircase that led up to the royal circle. We climbed the stairs, stopping off in the bar so Jake could order drinks for the interval – he refused my offer to pay – and then made our way into the auditorium. Pausing at the top of the steps that led from the back of the circle to the front, I stared down at the stage. The open curtains revealed a set dressed as an attic bedroom, with an iron bedstead, an artist's easel, and a small table on which stood a candle and bottle of wine. Windows in the middle of the backdrop revealed grey rooftops stretching into the distance, with the Eiffel Tower a silhouette on the horizon against a cloudless blue sky.

In just over half an hour, I thought, Jake's friends will be walking out onto that stage. I wondered how they were feeling while they waited backstage for the show to start, if they were nervous or high with adrenaline, or if to them starring in a West End musical was *just another part of an actor's job*. Noticing that Jake, less enthralled by an empty stage than me, was making his way along a row of seats, I hurried after him, scrambling apologetically past those people who'd already taken their places. I reached my seat, picked up the complimentary programme that had been left there – and on every seat in the auditorium – and sat down next to him. A moment later, a woman of about my age, whose face was vaguely familiar to me, sat in the empty seat on his other side.

'Hey, Jake,' the woman said, leaning towards him and air-kissing each side of his face. 'I didn't expect to see you here tonight. I'd heard you'd deserted us for the summer.'

'You heard right, Alexa,' Jake said. 'I'm only up in town for a few days. Officially, I'm on holiday by the sea.' Turning to me, he added, 'Emma, this is Alexa Hamilton-Jones, who plays my troubled sister in *Sherwood*. Alexa – Emma Stevens.'

'Good to meet you,' I said, smiling at the actress. With her long blonde hair, and in her off-the-shoulder, pale pink dress, she was stunning, I thought, and barely recognisable as the leather mini-skirted, wild-child Katherine Sherwood, she of the kohl-ringed eyes and black lipstick, in Jake's TV series.

'Good to meet you, too, Emma,' Alexa said, her cut-glass accent very different from Katherine's permanently petulant whine. She indicated the man a few years older than herself who was seated on her left. 'This is my boyfriend, Tim Devereaux. Jake, you've met Tim before, I think.'

'Yeah, at the *Sherwood* wrap party,' Jake said, shaking Tim's outstretched hand. 'Good to see you again.' While he, Alexa, and Tim launched into a discussion about the *Sherwood* cast, whose contract had been renewed for the next series and whose had not, I looked round at the tiered seats of the circle, starting as I recognised a white-haired theatrical knight and two theatrical dames sitting in the very next row. Further back, I spotted the presenter of a late-night arts programme, a much-loved comedienne, well on her way to becoming a National Treasure, and a celebrated documentary maker. There were also a number of younger actors I recognised from TV, even if I didn't know their names. South Quay suddenly seemed very far away. I opened my programme and started to read the cast's bios, marvelling at the number of credits that Jake's friends, Zac and Julie, had managed to accumulate between them.

Jake nudged my arm to get my attention. 'Looks like the VIPs have arrived,' he said. Suddenly aware of a decrease in the level of conversation in the theatre as the audience turned their heads towards the royal box, I also looked in that direction, just in time to see the box's previously empty seats fill with men in dinner jackets, and a young woman in a satin gown.

'Is that who I think it is?' I said.

'If you think she's one of our most popular royals,' Jake said, 'you'd be right.'

'Oh, my goodness,' I said. 'Will she be at the after-party, do you think? Should I have practised my curtsey?'

'I doubt very much that we'll get to meet her,' Jake said, 'although Zac and Julie might.'

The royal party having settled in their seats, the house lights dimmed until the audience was sitting in complete darkness. A flute began to play a haunting melody. The stage lights came up to reveal a tall, dark-haired man holding a paintbrush and an artist's palette, and a petite, dark-haired girl dressed in a ragged, patched dress standing by the window, staring out over Paris …

As soon as Zac and Julie, the artist and his model, had sung their first duet, his voice a rich tenor, hers a pure soprano, I knew I was watching two exceptional musical theatre actors. By the end of Act I, with the artist's model now an *etoile*, a ballet dancer at the Paris Opera, being pursued by *le duc*, a villainous aristocrat, while the poverty-stricken artist worked on her portrait in his garret, I was so caught up in their story that it was a shock when the house lights came up for the interval. Along with Alexa and Tim, Jake and I headed out to the bar, as did the majority of the audience, most of whom, from the comments I overheard as I drank my pre-ordered interval wine, were just as stunned by Zac and Julie's performances as I was.

'Your friends are incredibly talented,' I said to Jake.

'The whole cast are good,' Jake said, 'but you're right, Zac and Julie are outstanding.'

'Julie and I have been best friends since we were at drama school,' Alexa said, 'but when she's on stage, I forget it's her I'm watching, and only see the character she's playing.'

'I've never understood how you actors do that,' Tim said.

'Become someone else?' Jake said. 'Three years of training.'

'You're not an actor?' I asked Tim.

He shook his head. 'I'm a lawyer. I do have to put on a show in court at times, but I'm still *me* when I do it. What about you, Emma? Are you an actress?'

I glanced at Jake. 'Sort of,' I said.

'Resting?' Alexa said, with a sympathetic smile. 'We all know what that's like.'

132

I felt my face flush. Fortunately, before I had to explain to this successful professional actress, whose opinion of am dram was probably the same as Jake's, that I wasn't out of work, but an amateur, the ringing of the second bell alerted the audience that the interval was over. The four of us quickly drained our glasses and returned to our seats.

Throughout Act II, I was once again spellbound by the story in front of me, so much so that when the show came to its bittersweet final scene, my eyes brimmed with tears. I wasn't the only one. As the cast vanished into the wings, there was a moment when the only sounds that could be heard were the soft sighs of the audience, followed by thunderous applause. The applause grew louder as each member of the company took their bow, and when Zac and Julie came running downstage, the cheers were ear-splitting. At the second curtain call, I stood up, as did Jake, and soon the entire audience was on its feet, staying there while the cast sang one of the songs another time, and for the half dozen or so curtain calls that followed, until the actors, Julie holding a large bouquet of flowers presented to her by Zac, were finally allowed to exit the stage. Glancing across at the box, I saw that the royal guest and the other VIPs had already slipped away, presumably to get out of the theatre ahead of everyone else.

'What happens now?' I said to Jake.

He smiled. 'Now we get to party,' he said.

The venue for the *Muse* after-show party was Paradise, a club in Seven Dials that Jake, Alexa, and Tim had all been to before. After a brief debate outside the theatre as to whether it was worth trying to find a taxi, it was decided we might as well walk, and by cutting through the backstreets, it really wasn't very far. Arriving at the club's imposing double doors, we were greeted by more security guards, who examined our invitations before allowing us to cross the threshold.

Inside, we found ourselves on a wide mezzanine, from which a grand staircase swept down to a lower floor furnished with high, circular tables where people could put their drinks while they stood and talked, and bar stools for those who didn't care to stand. We went down the stairs and were met at ground level by smiling young men and women in crisp white shirts and black trousers – Jake whispered to me that they were most likely resting actors – who offered us champagne from silver trays. Having accepted a glass of fizz, we staked a claim at one of the tables, where we had a good view of the whole room.

The club was already half-full, and it rapidly became crowded as more people arrived and descended the staircase. Among them I spotted most of the well-known performers I'd seen in the audience at the Aphra Behn. Jake identified a dignified elderly man as a writer whose avant-garde, sexually explicit and violent plays had shocked the nation back in the day, and another man dressed in a very shabby jacket as a fabulously wealthy TV producer. Alexa pointed out the editor of showbiz magazine *Goss*.

I'd just returned my empty glass to the tray of one of the circling waiters, and helped myself to another full one, when *Muse*'s cast appeared at the top of the staircase. Mimicking the curtain call, the ensemble were the first to walk down, followed by the actors with named parts, and finally the leads, Zac and Julie – she was now wearing a fabulous red floor-length dress and her dark hair was piled in curls on top of her head – together with an older man, who Jake told me was *Muse*'s director. Conversation among the guests was replaced by clapping, growing ever louder. I clapped so hard that my palms actually stung. The director held up his hands for quiet, made a short speech thanking all those who'd worked so hard to bring *Muse* to the stage, and then with a broad smile exhorted everyone to enjoy the rest of the evening.

Conversations sprang up again all around the club. The *Muse* cast and their director were surrounded by their families, friends, and other admirers, and there was a *lot* of air-kissing and hugging. The waiters brought round trays of miniature fish and chips in white paper cones, bite-sized burgers in rolls, and more drinks. People started to drift from table to table, groups forming and re-forming, talking, laughing, drinking champagne.

'Come and meet my agent,' Jake said, and swept me into the throng, introducing me to his agent as his oldest friend, agreeing that *Muse* was an extraordinary piece of theatre, moving on, the light touch of his hand on the small of my back steering me among the famous and not-so-famous. I followed his lead, juggling my glass of champagne and my programme, exchanging air-kisses and a few words with the actress who played Marion in *Sherwood*, falling into conversation with other performers Jake knew, far too many for me to remember all their names.

'Jake!' A male voice cut through the chatter and the clinking of glasses. Jake and I spun around to find ourselves face to face with Zac Diaz. Now that I was standing close to him, I saw that he was an extraordinarily handsome man, like a lot of actors, including Jake.

'You made it back to London, then,' Zac said.

'I wouldn't miss a night like this.' Jake shook his friend's hand. 'Well done, Zac. Many congrats. You and Julie were superb tonight. As always.' He smiled down at me. 'This is Emma Stevens.'

Zac leant towards me, and we air-kissed. By this stage of the evening Jake had introduced me to enough of his friends that I'd accepted that being kissed and even hugged by total strangers was just another part of being an actor's plus-one.

'I'm so pleased to meet you and have the chance to tell you how much I enjoyed *Muse*,' I said. 'It's such a wonderful show. And you and your wife were amazing.' Realising I was gushing, I decided not to mention that the artist and his model's final scene had made me cry.

'Thank you so much, Emma,' Zac said. 'Julie and I have certainly enjoyed working together again – it's been a while.'

At that moment, Julie Farrell Diaz, as exquisitely beautiful off-stage as on, materialised at Zac's side, along with Alexa and Tim. There was more air-kissing and embracing, and what with Jake introducing me to Julie, and me enthusing over her awesome performance, I became included in the general melee.

'Our car's outside,' Julie said to Zac. 'I've invited Alexa and

135

Tim back for an after-after-party. Or at least a coffee.' To me and Jake, she added, 'I hope you'll come too?' Much to my delight, because I really wasn't ready for the night to end, Jake was of the opinion that it would be great to go back to his friends' place.

By now the party was beginning to wind down. The six of us made our way towards the stairs, our progress necessarily slow due to the number of people who wanted to have one last word with *Muse*'s leading actors, but eventually we made it out of the club. It did occur to me to wonder if there would be room for us all in Zac and Julie's car. Then I saw the dark, sleek limousine waiting by the kerb.

'That's us' Julie said.

The driver got out and opened the passenger door. I felt like royalty myself as I climbed inside.

Chapter Twenty

'So is it going to be coffee or more champagne?' Zac said, as he opened the door to his and Julie's apartment on the top floor of a high-rise building in Docklands, and ushered us into a long narrow hall. Theatre posters hung on both walls, and I read the words 'starring Zac Diaz and Julie Farrell Diaz' above the title of every show.

'Let me think about that,' Julie said. 'I guess I could force myself to have one more glass of fizz.'

'Well, it's not *every* night that you get to open a new musical in front of royalty,' Zac said.

'Absolutely.' Julie's smile lit up her whole face. 'Tonight was so *wonderful*. Walking out onto the stage, the lights coming up, singing the opening notes of my first song …'

'And there was I thinking you'd be over the whole starring in a West End show thing by now,' Alexa said.

'Never going to happen, hun,' Julie said.

'Champagne it is, then,' Zac said. 'I'll fetch it. You all go on through.'

I followed the others along the hall and through a doorway, and almost gasped aloud at the sheer size of the white-painted, high-ceilinged room that lay beyond, which was spacious enough for the grand piano situated in one corner next to an acoustic guitar on a stand, as well as several armchairs, two leather sofas, and a long dining table. On one wall there was a photograph of Zac and Julie in a dance pose, spot-lit on an empty stage, Zac supporting Julie as she bent so far backwards that her head almost touched the floor, and on the wall opposite was a photograph of the Aphra Behn Theatre. The far wall of the room was made up of floor-to-ceiling windows and glass doors opening onto a wide balcony that appeared to run the entire length of the flat. Realising that while I was gawping at my surroundings, the others had settled themselves on the sofas, I hastened to take a seat next to Jake.

Zac came in carrying six glasses of champagne on a tray, and we all drank a toast to *Muse*, wishing it a long run, and talked over the evening. Julie kicked off her high-heeled shoes, and took the pins out of her hair so that it tumbled loose down her back. Zac fetched the guitar from its stand and strummed it softly while we talked. Alexa rested her head on Tim's shoulder. Julie mentioned how much she was enjoying being back at the Aphra Behn, adding for my benefit that it was the theatre where she'd made her professional debut, playing opposite Zac, before they were married.

'Is that how you two met?' I asked.

'No, the first time we met was at an audition,' Julie said. 'Neither of us got the job.'

'We overheard the casting director say that we had no chemistry,' Zac said. 'I'm pretty sure he was wrong.' He and Julie exchanged affectionate smiles. 'When we work together, we generally get good reviews.'

Alexa raised her head. 'Have you and Jake ever worked together?' she said to me.

'Er, no, we haven't,' I said, suddenly feeling like an impostor among these actor friends of Jake's. 'I'm not an actress. Not really. That is, I'm an amateur.' I glanced from Alexa to Julie to Zac, fully expecting their eyes to have glazed over at the mention of amateur dramatics, but they were all regarding me with apparent interest. 'I act with my local am dram society.'

'So how did you and Jake meet if it wasn't through work?' Julie said.

'We were brought up in the same small seaside village,' I said. 'We went to the same school.'

'We performed in the same school plays,' Jake said. 'It was Emma who got me into acting, dragging me along to the drama club.'

'We lost touch when Jake went to RoCoDa,' I said. 'Then after ten years, he walks into the village pub. He caused quite a stir.'

'That night I did,' Jake laughed. 'Now, it's as though I'd never been away.'

The conversation moved on, the others talking about their mutual acquaintances who all seemed to be actors, singers, dancers, or choreographers, and it was gone three in the morning when Alexa and Tim decided they really should be getting home and called a cab, which came within five minutes. A short while later, Jake phoned to order a cab for me and him and was told there would be a half-hour wait. Zac made the four of us a coffee, and offered scotch to go with it, which Jake accepted and I declined.

'I hope we're not keeping you up,' I said to Julie.

'You're not,' she said. 'I couldn't sleep now if I tried. I feel as though I could dance all night.' Suddenly she sprang up from the sofa. 'Come and see the view, Emma.' Beckoning me toward the far end of the room, she slid open a glass door and stepped out onto the balcony.

Leaving Jake and Zac lounging on the sofas, I joined her outside, gasping when I saw the glorious panoramic view of London at night spread out in front of me, the lights of the buildings reflected in the dark waters of the Thames.

'It's spectacular, isn't it?' Julie said. 'I never tire of looking at it.'

'Have you always lived in London?' I said.

'No, like you and Jake, I grew up in a small village,' Julie said, 'but I trained at a London drama school.' She rested her elbows on the balcony wall and gazed dreamily out over the city. 'I was out of work for a year after I graduated. I kept going to auditions, but I began to think that I'd never get cast in *anything*, that I'd never achieve my dream of becoming an actress. Then I landed my first West End role ... Sometimes I can hardly believe all that's happened to me since then. I've had the chance to perform in so many fabulous shows, and to work with such amazing actors, directors, and choreographers.'

I thought, she's a successful actress, a star of the West End stage, and unlike Jake, she is *passionate* about acting. It came to me that the girl standing next to me had the theatrical career that I might have had. If I'd gone to drama school. If I'd followed *my* dream ...

'How long are you and Jake going to be in London?' Julie said.

'We're driving back to South Quay on Saturday morning,' I said. Only one more complete day, I thought.

'Zac and I'd rather got the impression that Jake had cut all ties with his home village,' Julie said. 'We were really surprised when he texted that he'd rented a house down there.'

Not as surprised as I was, I thought. 'It was more by chance than design,' I said. 'He told me he was fed up with the attention he was getting from the paparazzi over his break-up with Leonie Fox, and wanted some time out.' Jake's relationship with his ex was so well documented that I didn't feel I was saying anything that he wouldn't want his friends to know. 'He just happened to see the house he's renting online.'

'The paps certainly gave him a hard time when he and Leonie split,' Julie said, 'but that was weeks ago. I'd have expected him to be back in town by now.' She hesitated, and then, with a smile, she added, 'I hope you don't mind my asking, Emma, but are *you* the reason he's stayed in South Quay?'

'Oh, no,' I said. 'No way. Jake and I aren't—We're not together. We're old friends.'

'Really?' Julie said. 'Zac and I were convinced Jake must have met someone new. Why else would he leave London for so long? I mean, I'm sure South Quay's a perfectly nice place, but Jake's friends are here. Sorry, *most* of his friends are here. His life is here.'

'He'll be back after the summer,' I said. 'Right now, he's simply taking a holiday.'

140

Julie's eyes widened. 'Well, that's a first. I don't think he's taken a vacation in all the time I've known him.'

'Yes, he's told me how hard he works,' I said, dryly.

'Acting is a demanding profession,' Julie said, 'but when I'm performing on stage like I was tonight, I know all the work that goes into putting on a show is worth it.' As she talked, her eyes shone. 'Alexa tells me she feels exactly the same when she's on a film set.'

From inside the flat, Jake called, 'Emma, our cab's here.'

'I'll be right with you,' I said. To Julie, I added, 'It's been so great to meet you and Zac.'

'It's been lovely to meet you, Emma,' Julie said.

We joined the men inside the flat. I collected up my bag and pashmina, and my programme. Briefly, I considered asking Julie and Zac to sign it, but decided against it. I didn't want to embarrass Jake by appearing starstruck in front of his friends.

'We should get a photo,' Julie said suddenly. 'Where's my phone?' She retrieved her mobile from her sequined clutch. 'Zac, you take it, your arms are longer than mine.'

She handed Zac her phone, and he took a photo of the four of us. It came out rather well, I thought, when she showed it to me. Jake asked her to text it to him, and after a short hiatus while we repeated once again how much we'd enjoyed the show, he and I made our exit. Zac and Julie stood in their doorway, arms around each other's waists, watching us as we walked across the landing and stepped into the waiting lift, calling goodnight as the lift doors closed.

'Now *that* was a good night out,' Jake said, as the lift glided smoothly down to the ground floor.

'It was,' I said. 'I didn't realise your life in London was so glamorous.'

He laughed. 'My life isn't always like this. I do have to work for a living.'

'So you keep telling me,' I said.

The lift doors opened. We stepped out into the atrium, headed

141

through the revolving doors that led onto the street, and got into the back of the cab drawn up by the kerb. Jake gave the driver his address and the cab pulled away.

'I like your friends,' I said.

'Oh, Zac and Julie are great,' Jake said, 'and seriously talented.' The cab sped on through the empty streets. Glancing out of the window I saw that the sky was streaked with grey.

Julie Farrell Diaz and her handsome husband, I thought, both successful actors, a couple working together in the theatre, living the life that Jake and I might have had …

Jake's voice came to me from a distance, 'Emma, time to wake up, lovely.'

I opened my eyes to find myself half-lying on the back seat of the cab, slumped against Jake's shoulder. It was now fully light.

'You slept the whole way home,' Jake said.

'I may have drunk more champagne than is wise,' I said. I sat up, undid my seat belt, gathered my belongings, and climbed stiffly out of the cab. I stood yawning by Jake's front door while he paid the cab driver.

'No need to set your alarm,' Jake said, as he unlocked the front door to his flat and we went inside. 'You know your way around my kitchen if you wake up before I do?'

I nodded. 'Thank you so much for tonight, Jake, it was *fabulous*. I'll see you tomorrow.'

'Yeah, see you tomorrow,' he said. 'Julie sent me that photo, by the way, I'll text it to you.' He smiled and kissed me on each side of my face. Then he put his arms around me, and gently drew me towards him until my head was resting on his chest. I felt the hardness of his muscular body pressing against mine, and the strength in his arms.

'Thanks for being my plus-one,' he said. 'I'm glad you had a good time.' Slowly, he released me from his embrace. 'Goodnight, Emma.'

'Goodnight,' I whispered.

He went straight into his bedroom, so I dived into the bathroom, and quickly washed off my make-up and cleaned my teeth before going into the guest room. I touched my face where he'd kissed it. Deep within me, I felt the delectably insistent ache of desire.

'*Jake.*' I said his name aloud. My stomach clenched. I wanted him. I wanted to kiss him on the mouth, to lie beneath him on a bed, and feel him thrust inside me.

I slid my feet out of my shoes, took off my dress, hung it over the back of a chair, and sprayed myself with perfume. Then I took off my underwear, put on my silk kimono, and went out of the guest room. Walking quickly across the hall, I went to Jake's bedroom door and, my heart racing, reached for the handle.

I thought, am I about to do something really stupid? What if he doesn't want me? I'll have wrecked our friendship for ever. There'll be no coming back from this a second time.

For what seemed like ages, I stood outside Jake's bedroom, desire coursing through my body, before letting my hand drop to my side. I backed a few steps away from his door, and then I bolted across the hall and into the guest room, closing my door as quietly as I could. My heart pounding, my legs shaking, I took off my kimono, pulled on my pyjamas, climbed into bed, and switched off the light.

What was I *thinking*, creeping about Jake's flat half naked? In all the weeks he'd been back in South Quay, in all the days we'd spent lazing on the beach, and the evenings we'd sat on his veranda and shared a bottle of wine, he'd never given me any indication that he had any feelings for me other than those of an old friend. Champagne-fuelled lust was not a reason to risk his rejection, and the humiliation that would follow.

I was attracted to Jake, but I was *not* going to throw myself at him. I did have some sense of self-preservation. Unlike when I was seventeen.

Chapter Twenty-one

I woke up to find that it was almost midday. My head still full of the show and the after-party, relieved that I hadn't ended such a magical night by making a total fool of myself, I showered, put on jeans and a T-shirt, and went into the kitchen – living room. There was no sign of Jake, so I helped myself to orange juice and went out into the garden.

I was still sitting in the sun, imagining what Lizzie would want to do to the paved courtyard, with its white-painted walls and single Japanese maple tree – certainly she'd want to train a rambling rose over those plain white bricks – when Jake wandered into the living room, wearing just a pair of jeans, his hair still wet from the shower. I saw him through the glass doors before he saw me, and without conscious thought, my gaze went straight to his washboard stomach. Quickly, I looked away.

'Morning, Emma,' he said, coming out into the garden and standing right in front of me, so I'd no choice but to look at his toned body. My face grew warm. This is ridiculous, I thought. I've seen him in swim shorts often enough.

Pulling myself together, I said, 'Hey, Jake. Can I make you some tea? Coffee?'

'Not for me,' Jake said. 'I thought we'd have brunch at the café on the corner, and then – if you're up for another walk – we'll head into town and I'll show you a bit more of London.'

'Great,' I said. 'Where exactly are we going?'

'The Queen's Walk, which runs along the South Bank of the

Thames,' Jake said. 'I thought you might like to start at Shake-speare's Globe.'

'You know me so well,' I said.

We took the tube from Angel to London Bridge station, a short walk past Borough Market bringing us to the Thames and the replica of the original Globe theatre. I suspected that my excite-ment at seeing Shakespeare's 'wooden O' was somewhat greater than Jake's – he told me that when he was a student, he'd taken part in a stage combat workshop on the Globe's stage – but he made no objection to my taking photos of the two of us with the theatre in the background. Only when he noticed a woman star-ing at him, and pointing him out to her companions, did he suggest that it was time we walked on.

From the Globe, we strolled along the wide paved path by the river, past the Millennium Bridge, and the Tate Modern, stop-ping for me to take panoramic shots of the London skyline, the City skyscrapers and the dome of St Paul's Cathedral, on the other side of the river.

'I've spent many an afternoon in the Tate,' Jake remarked.

'Really?' I said. 'It would never occur to me to visit an art gallery – not that we have any galleries in South Quay.'

'There's so much to do and see in London,' Jake said. 'I've loved the energy of the West End, the theatres and the nightlife, since I was a student, but over the last ten years I've made a point of exploring different parts of the city, doing things I'd never have done if I didn't live here.'

'*O brave new world*,' I said, reminded once again of how far his life had diverged from mine.

He smiled. '*To unpathed waters, undreamed shores*.'

Linking arms, we strolled on, among meandering tourists and energetic joggers, under Blackfriars Bridge, and past the landmark Oxo Tower, home to design studios and exclusive apartments, leaving the riverbank to take a look at Gabriel's Wharf, a pretty enclave of cafés and shops selling clothes, paintings, ceramics, and prints. Returning to the path, we stopped to take a photo outside the National Theatre, browsed the second-hand bookstalls under Waterloo Bridge, and marvelled at the leaps and turns of the skate-boarders in a graffiti-adorned skatepark. A little further along, where leafy trees lined the path, the South Bank grew more crowded, with pop-up food stalls attracting long queues. I saw a red double-decker bus that was also a café, street entertainers – musicians, pavement artists, a man blowing giant bubbles – a carousel, and to my surprise an artificial beach complete with deckchairs, where a number of people were soaking up the last rays of the late-afternoon sun. Finally, we came to the London Eye.

'What would you like to eat tonight?' Jake said, as I stood mesmerised, staring up at the slowly turning white Ferris wheel. 'Brazilian? Italian? Japanese? My treat, by the way.'

'Oh my gosh, so much choice,' I said, tearing my attention away from the iconic landmark, realising that he'd had enough of sight-seeing – and that I was hungry. 'I know, take me somewhere you go with your London friends.'

'It's not that far to walk to Drury Lane from here,' Jake said. 'Shall we eat at the Troubadour?'

'Is that the bar you told me about?' I said. 'The one where your headshot's on the wall?'

'Yeah, I'm up there.' He smiled disarmingly. 'I'm in very good company. I expect you to be suitably impressed.'

I laughed. 'I'll do my best,' I said.

Drury Lane was crowded with theatre-goers queuing for evening performances, and workers having a Friday-night drink with their colleagues or striding purposefully towards home – walking along the pavement arm in arm with Jake, I saw a number of women wearing trainers with their smart office dresses, presumably having changed their footwear to make their commute a little easier.

We came to the Troubadour, edged through the people congregated on the pavement by the entrance, and went inside. The place was crammed, its clientele loud and animated as they shed the tensions of the working week, but Jake said there was more seating downstairs that was reserved for diners. Once we'd made our choices from the day's menu, which was chalked up on a board by the bar, Jake joined those vying for the bartenders' attention, to place our order. I craned my neck above the crowd to study the black and white signed headshots of famous actors displayed on every wall. Some of these men and women had been household names for decades, some were the stars of TV shows that I'd watched as a teenager, while others were of much more recent vintage. Manoeuvring myself further into the bar, I spotted Jake's photo among them. He was looking straight at the camera, his mouth half-raised in a lazy smile, his hair tousled and falling over his forehead just the way it had when he was younger.

'Ah, you found my picture,' Jake said.

I spun around to find him standing directly behind me, the same half-smile on his face as in the photo. His gaze caught mine, and held it.

'I hope you like what you see,' he said. The tone of his voice could only be described as flirtatious. I became aware of a fluttering in my stomach.

Before I had time to think of all the reasons why flirting with Jake was a *really* bad idea, I said, 'Yes, I do like what I see.'

After a long moment, during which my pulse rate increased considerably, he put his mouth close to my ear and said, 'So do I.' Then he held up a bottle of white wine and two glasses. 'We have a table downstairs.' Again he smiled, and then he turned away from me and headed for a wooden staircase at the far end of the bar. On shaking legs, I followed him down to the Troubadour's dimly-lit basement, where only a few tables were taken, and sat down opposite him at a table for two. My thoughts skittered around my head. Was he coming on to me just then? Had I misread the signs? No, the way he'd looked at me was a definite come-on. What if I was wrong?

Jake poured the wine, and leant back in his chair.

'What I said just now. I meant it,' he said. '*For I ne'er saw true beauty till this night.*'

I raised my eyebrows. '*She is beautiful, and therefore to be wooed?*'

'*She is woman and therefore to be won,*' Jake said.

My heart soared. He put his hand over mine – and then removed it as a waitress arrived at our table. She set our plates down in front of us, instructed us to enjoy our meal, and left. Jake picked up his venison burger and bit into it with evident relish. I ate my Greek salad more slowly, savouring the pungent taste of the feta cheese and the sweetness of the tomatoes. We didn't talk while we ate, but whenever our eyes met across the table, which was often, we exchanged smiles. I couldn't remember ever before eating a meal that tasted so good.

Jake re-filled our glasses. 'Emma,' he said, 'I think we ...' He trailed off mid-sentence as his attention was caught by something over my shoulder. I twisted around in my chair to see two women descending the stairs into the basement, their heels clattering on the wooden steps. One woman, small and curvy, with a halo of dark curls, looked vaguely familiar. I thought she might have been an actress I'd seen on TV, although I didn't recall her name. The other was taller, with long blonde hair. I recognised her immediately as Leonie Fox.

I turned back to Jake. His face was expressionless.

'Do you want to leave?' I said.

'What?' he said, incredulously. 'No, of course not.'

I looked again at Jake's ex and her companion. The dark-haired woman had sat down at a table, and was drinking a glass of wine, but Leonie was threading her way through the other diners towards me and Jake. I noticed several of the Troubadour's male customers watching her progress. Even if they hadn't recognised her, she was strikingly attractive, and her flimsy summer dress revealed a figure that must surely turn heads wherever she went. She reached our table and came to a halt.

'Hello, Jake,' she said.

'Leonie,' Jake said. There followed a long silence which

148

neither of them seemed inclined to break. Jake swallowed a mouthful of wine. I shifted uneasily in my chair.

'I didn't expect to find you in here tonight,' Leonie said, eventually. 'I heard you were sulking in some backwater by the sea.'

'Yet here I am,' Jake said.

Leonie's gaze travelled from him to me. 'Aren't you going to introduce me to your ... er ...?'

'We can do the introductions another time,' Jake said. 'Looks like your meal's just arrived. You should go and eat.'

'Perhaps you already know who I am?' Leonie said, her blue eyes locking on mine.

'Yes, I know who you are,' I said, looking levelly back at her.

'But who are you?' Leonie said. 'Who *are* you?'

'Don't do this, Leonie,' Jake said. 'Go back to your friend. She's looking lonely.'

Leonie ignored him. 'I have it,' she said, her voice pitched loud enough to carry across the entire basement. 'You're the scheming little slut who stole my boyfriend.'

Startled faces turned towards us. The murmur of the other diners' conversation abruptly ceased.

What the hell? I gaped at her, speechless. With difficulty, I suppressed a sudden urge to fling what was left of my wine in her face.

'Leonie, you're embarrassing yourself,' Jake said. 'You need to stop.'

She looked me up and down. 'Seriously, Jake? You left *me* for *her*?'

'Enough!' Jake's eyes blazed and he slammed a hand down on the table, making the cutlery rattle. 'You've had your fun — now go.'

Leonie's mouth curled into a venomous smile. Tossing her hair over her shoulder, she turned on her heel, walked over to her own table and spoke a few words to her friend, before the pair of them abandoned their meal, and clattered off up the stairs. The other diners resumed eating and talking. I was uncomfortably aware that they were in all probability discussing the scene they'd just witnessed. The waitress who'd served us earlier gave Jake and me a long look, but evidently decided that the show was over, and started to clear Leonie's table.

'Emma?' Jake leant towards me, his forehead creased with concern. 'You're very pale. Are you OK?'

Realising that I was sitting bolt upright, my hands clutching the seat of my chair, I relaxed my shoulders, and placed my hands in my lap.

'I'm fine,' I said. 'Although, I won't be asking your ex for her autograph any time soon.'

'Of all the actors I know who drink in the Troubadour,' Jake said, 'it would have to be *her* who was in here tonight.' He sighed. 'It seems she's still angry with me.'

'I kind of got that impression too,' I said. 'She doesn't seem to like me much either. Of course, she may have mistaken me for someone else.'

Jake smiled briefly at that. 'Emma,' he said, softly, 'today has been so good. Don't let Leonie ruin it.'

'I won't,' I said.

'Would you like another drink? Or shall we make a move?'

'I'm ready to go,' I said. 'We could have another drink back at your place.' For once, I'd had quite enough time centre stage in front of a live audience.

'I think we should definitely go back to my place now,' Jake said. His grey-blue eyes caught my gaze and held it.

'Me too,' I said.

150

Chapter Twenty-two

We came out of Angel station and walked the short distance to Jake's flat through the dusk. We'd not gone very far when he took hold of my hand, lacing his fingers through mine. It struck me that while we often walked arm in arm, he'd never before taken my hand. I thought, lovers hold hands, not friends. My stomach tangled itself into knots.

Arriving at his flat, he let us in, and I followed him into the living area. While he went to the fridge for a bottle of wine, I went and stood by the glass doors, looking out at the small court-yard garden, lit up now by solar lights, the branches of the tree casting dancing shadows on the white brick walls. Impulsively, I slid open the glass door, letting in a soft breeze.

'Emma, we appear to be out of wine,' Jake said. 'I can offer you a beer.'

I turned around to face him. 'Thanks, but not for me,' I said. 'You have one.'

He shook his head. 'I don't want another drink,' he said, his voice suddenly hoarse. He walked across the room until he was standing face to face with me, and put his hands on my waist. For a long moment, we just stood there. Then he bent his head and kissed me gently on my mouth. I melted into his arms, just as I had when I was seventeen, my heart beating against his, reaching up to put my arms around his neck, my body flooding with desire.

For an instant, we broke apart, breathless, gasping, and then he kissed me again, fiercely now, his tongue entwined with mine. Still kissing, we stumbled over to the nearest sofa, and he sat, drawing me down onto his lap. His hand slid under my T-shirt, and then he was pulling the T-shirt off over my head, and I was undoing the buttons on his shirt, he was kissing me, and I was taking off my bra. I sank back onto the sofa, lying half beneath him, as his hand cupped my breast and he kissed my throat, my whole body tingling at his touch. I hadn't wanted a man so badly, hadn't felt the way I was feeling now, since I was seventeen. When I'd slept with a man for the first time, when I'd thought he was mine ... and then he'd walked into the Armada Inn on Christmas Eve with another girl on his arm, trampling on all my dreams ...

'This is Chiara, my girlfriend.'

'Good to meet you,' she says to me. 'Jake's told me so much about you.'

I think, has he told you that when I came to London, he slept with me? I stare at the pair of them, this stunning girl and the boy I love, and tell myself this isn't happening – not to me. I look directly into Jake's beautiful eyes and he smiles at me. It occurs to me that he has no idea that he has done anything wrong. My head starts pounding, and my throat feels very tight. Dimly, I'm aware that I need to get out of the Armada before I make a show of myself by bursting into tears, but I can't seem to move.

Lizzie, who does know I slept with Jake, because I've told her, says, 'I'm Lizzie – lovely to meet you, too, Chiara.' To Jake she adds, 'Emma and I were just leaving.'

'Oh, that's a shame,' Jake says. 'Can't you stay for one more round?'

'No,' I say, forcing my face into a smile. I've told myself – and Lizzie – that the absence of texts, emails and calls from Jake since I visited him in London is because he's busy with drama school. Now, I know that the reason I haven't heard from him is because he's simply not interested. He's met another girl. I'm not going to cry, I thought, not here in the Armada, in front of half the village.

'Will you two still be around for a while after Christmas, Jake?' Lizzie says.

'Absolutely,' Jake says. 'We're staying on until the New Year.'

'Great,' Lizzie says. Gathering up our coats, she links her arm through mine, and practically force-marches me out of the pub. I manage to keep from crying until we're outside in the falling snow.

'I love him,' I wail through my sobs. 'I thought he loved me ...'

I felt Jake kiss my bare shoulder, and the touch of his tongue on my breast, his hand caressing my body. He started to unzip my jeans. I kissed him and held him tighter, but I couldn't get the memory of that long ago Christmas Eve out of my head.

'Jake – wait –' I said. For a moment I didn't think he'd heard me, but then his body froze completely still, his hand heavy on my stomach. He lifted his head.

'Is something wrong?' he said.

I thought, I don't want a night of casual sex with Jake Murray. I've been there, done that, and it really didn't end well for me. Much better that we don't go there, but remain good friends.

'I – I can't do this,' I said.

Jake's eyes widened in surprise, but then his face grew serious. He raised himself off me, and sat up.

'I want very much to make love to you tonight, Emma,' he said. 'You seemed to want it too.'

I sat up also. Suddenly acutely conscious that I was half-naked, I folded my arms over my breasts.

'I thought I did,' I said.

'So what's changed?' he said.

I've remembered how much you hurt me, I thought. 'This doesn't feel right,' I said. 'Sleeping with a friend – not a good idea.'

'I see.' Jake got to his feet, retrieved my T-shirt from the floor, and dropped it next to me on the sofa. Picking up his shirt, he turned his back to me, and put it on.

'I'm sorry,' I said.

'Just give me a minute, yeah?' he said, stepping out through the open door into the garden. Resting his hands on the back of a chair, he stood very still, looking up at the night sky.

153

My throat tightened. I thought, what have I done? With shaking hands, I pulled on my T-shirt. I got to my feet, and unable to stop myself, followed Jake outside.

'Jake …' I said.

He turned around, his face in shadow. 'Hey, Emma,' he said, quietly.

'I'm sorry,' I said, again.

'It's all right, lovely,' Jake said. 'We both got carried away, that's all. It happens.'

'You're not angry with me?' I said. A lot of guys would be, I thought.

'I'm not a jerk, Emma.'

'I know that,' I said.

'You can tell me you're not attracted to me physically,' he said, stepping towards me, into a pool of light. 'I can take it.'

'It's not that—'

'You are attracted to me?'

I sighed. 'I've had the best time with you this summer, but I'm not going to sleep with you.' I don't want to find myself falling for you again, I thought, not when I know that after the summer you'll be gone. 'You and I aren't going to have a summer fling.'

Infuriatingly, his mouth lifted in a knowing smile. 'I think we should stop talking now, and go to bed.'

'Jake – don't.'

'What? It's not late, but we've an early start in the morning. Ah, you thought I meant …'

'Jake!'

He laughed softly. 'Let's call it a night, Emma. I'd like to be on the road by nine tomorrow.'

I followed him inside to the living room – and immediately saw my black lace bra lying accusingly in the middle of the pale, wooden floor. Embarrassed, I leapt across the room and snatched it up. Jake made no comment, but his eyes definitely had an amused glint in them. He closed the door to the garden and locked it. We went into the hall.

'I'll say goodnight, then,' he said. '*For we have heard the chimes at midnight.*'

A rush of affection for him made me smile. '*Goodnight, sweet prince,*' I said. I went into the guest room and closed the door behind me.

Jake Murray had wanted to have sex with me, I'd turned him down, and he was fine with that.

Our friendship was intact.

155

Chapter Twenty-three

Jake drove slowly along Shore Road, weaving his way between the parked cars, his progress frequently brought to a halt by bucket-and-spade-laden families heedlessly wandering off the pavement as they headed for the beach.

'I'm not going to find a parking space,' he said, as we approached the corner of Saltwater Lane. 'I'll let you out here.' He pulled in next to another car.

'Thanks, Jake,' I said. 'And thank you so much for inviting me to London. The press night – meeting your friends – I had such a good time.'

'Me too,' Jake said. He grinned. 'We had our moments of drama, but it was a great couple of days.'

'I knew your life in London was rather more dramatic than mine in South Quay,' I laughed. 'Well, I guess I'd better go and get myself sorted and off to work.' We both got out of the car, and Jake retrieved my case from the boot.

'Shall we have a lunchtime drink in the Armada tomorrow?' he said.

'Sure,' I said. My few days in Jake's world were definitely over. No more press nights and walks by the Thames. It was back to working at the Downland and drinks in the Armada for me now.

'I'll pick you up from your place,' he said. 'I'll call you when I'm on my way over.'

Another car drew up behind his. The driver immediately sounded his horn.

Jake rolled his eyes theatrically. 'Doesn't he know who I am?'

I laughed. 'Apparently not.' The horn sounded again.

'All right, mate, I'm going,' Jake muttered. Then he leant forward and planted a kiss on my mouth. Desire lanced through me, a fierce, searing heat, and when he raised his head from mine, all I wanted was for him to kiss me again. My head reeled.

'I'm not giving up, Emma,' he said. 'The summer isn't over yet.'

Abruptly he stepped away from me, got into his car, and drove off. Stunned, I stood motionless on the pavement, staring after him until his car was lost to my sight behind the holidaymakers. In my mind, I ran over the earlier part of the morning, breakfast in Jake's garden, the car journey back to South Quay, both of us chatting casually as we'd always done. I'd thought nothing had changed between us, that Jake was content to be my friend. It seemed that I was wrong. Not only about his feelings, but also my own.

On shaking legs, trundling my suitcase behind me, I walked along Saltwater Lane to Lizzie's cottage, and went in the gate. Jake had kissed me. Despite everything I'd said the previous night, he'd kissed me, and my feelings for him had come flooding back. The feelings I'd buried for so long.

I love him, I thought. *I love him.* I stood in Lizzie's cottage garden, the summer sun high overhead in a cloudless sky, the roses around the door, the sunflowers and the hollyhocks unusually bright, and knew that I'd fallen in love with Jake Murray. Just as I had when I was seventeen. When my life had gone so terribly wrong.

The door of the cottage opened, and Noah came out, starting in surprise when he saw me standing on the path, gazing at the flowers.

'Hey, Emma,' he said. 'How was your city break?'

'What?' I said.

'Your visit to London,' Noah said. 'Did you and Jake have a good time?'

'I … We … It was good,' I said.

Noah gave me a quizzical look. 'Are you going inside?'

Realising that he was holding the front door open for me, I hastened to wheel my suitcase as far as the step.

'Let me,' Noah said, taking hold of the handle and hefting the case over the threshold. 'I'm on my way out to the supermarket. Can I get you anything?'

I was fairly sure that after two days away, I'd need to restock my half of the fridge, but at that particular moment I was quite unable to gather my thoughts and give him a shopping list.

'No, I don't think so,' I said. 'Thanks, Noah.' He headed off down the path. I went into the cottage and shut the door.

Lizzie's voice came to me from the back of the cottage. 'Emma? Is that you?'

Leaving my suitcase in the hall, I went into the kitchen, where I found Lizzie seated at the table, which was covered in squares of felt, balls of wool, buttons, sequins and embroidery silk.

'I'm making glove puppets,' she said, seeing the direction of my gaze. 'Very useful for story-telling to Year 2.' She put her elbows on the table and rested her chin on her hands. 'Well, come on, don't keep me in suspense. Tell me about your trip to London with the *famous actor*. Was the press night *fabulous*?'

'It was,' I said, sitting down opposite her. 'Even before we went into the Aphra Behn …' With Lizzie exclaiming in all the right places, I described my and Jake's night at the theatre, the show and the after-party, how much I'd liked his friends. I told her about our walks along the Regent's Canal and the Thames, and that Jake had taken me to the Troubadour, where his head-shot hung on the wall. Then I told her about our encounter with Leonie Fox. By the time I got to the part where Leonie stalked off, Lizzie's mouth was actually hanging open.

'But—But that's *outrageous*,' she said. 'Who makes a scene like that in public? Was she drunk?'

'Not that I noticed,' I said. 'Anyway, that's quite enough talk about Leonie, except to say that Jake and I agreed not to let her spoil our evening.'

'Good for you,' Lizzie said. 'Did you go on somewhere else?'

'No, we just went back to Jake's,' I said. 'I took some photos of his place, by the way.' I got out my mobile and Lizzie eagerly scrolled through the photos I'd taken of Jake's flat.

'A definite minimalist vibe going on there,' she said. 'It's very stylish, of course, but those sofas really could do with a few scatter cushions.' She handed me back my phone. 'Now tell me the rest of the story.'

'The rest of it?' I said.

'Emma! What happened between you and Jake while you were in London?'

I thought, where do I begin?

'Did you sleep with him?' Lizzie said. 'You did, didn't you?'

'He asked me to,' I said.

'Well, he was hardly going to invite you to be his plus-one at a red-carpet event, wine and dine you, and take you on romantic riverside walks because he wants you as a *friend*.'

'I didn't sleep with him,' I said.

'I knew it,' Lizzie went on. 'I knew you had the hots for him, you just wouldn't admit it—Emma, did you say you *didn't* sleep with Jake?'

'He made a move,' I said. 'I turned him down. He thinks I'll change my mind, but he's mistaken.'

'Are you telling me you don't *want* to sleep with him?' Lizzie said. 'Because I don't believe you.'

'I didn't say I wasn't tempted last night,' I said, 'but it's better that we just stay friends.'

'Why?'

'I'm not going to start a relationship with Jake. There's no future in it.'

'You can't know that,' Lizzie said. 'You like the guy, he likes you—'

159

'I love him.' My heart constricted. 'I loved him when I was seventeen. He didn't want to know, and I got hurt. I can't go through that pain again.'

Lizzie regarded me silently for a moment and then she said, 'But if you love him—'

'I'm not going to make the same mistake twice,' I said. 'As I'm no longer seventeen, I know that loving Jake doesn't mean that I get to be *with* him. Our lives have taken different paths. We're never going to be a couple.'

'No relationship is *guaranteed* to last for ever,' Lizzie said. 'Give Jake a chance and see what happens.'

'I'll tell you what'll happen,' I said. 'After the summer, he'll go back to his life in London. He'll be shooting the new series of *Sherwood*. I'll still be living here in South Quay, still catching the bus to work at the Downland and rehearsing with the Players—' I broke off at the sound of a key in the front door. 'Lizzie, please don't say any of this to Noah.'

'Of course not,' Lizzie said. 'I never tell him anything I don't want repeated in the bar of the Armada.'

'Hey, you two,' Noah said, coming into the kitchen. 'Emma, is it OK if I carry your bag up to your room? It's taking up a lot of floor space in the hall, and we don't want Lizzie tripping over it.' He put two carrier bags of shopping on a worktop.

'Oh, sorry, I didn't think,' I said. 'Thanks, Noah, it'd be great if you took it up for me. It is rather heavy.'

'No worries,' Noah said. 'Leave the shopping, Lizzie, I'll put it away as soon as I'm back.' He returned to the hall, and I heard his footsteps going up the stairs.

Lizzie groaned. 'That man is going to drive me crazy.'

'Aw, he's so sweet. So protective.' I glanced at the clock on the wall. 'I need to get my act together, or I'm going to miss my bus. I'll see you later.'

'Oh, I'm sure I'll be in bed by the time you get home,' Lizzie said. 'Noah is most insistent that pregnant women need their eight hours.'

160

'I'll see you tomorrow then.' I pushed back my chair and stood up.

'Emma – wait.'

'What is it?'

'London isn't that far away from South Quay,' Lizzie said. 'I'm just saying.'

'Maybe not in miles,' I said.

Chapter Twenty-four

I was woken by footsteps thudding down the stairs and the slamming of the front door. Noah going off to cricket, I thought, and running late by the sound of it. He was usually more considerate than to disturb those of us who preferred a lie-in on a Sunday morning. I rolled over, with every intention of going back to sleep, but instead I found myself thinking of Jake, the look in his eyes as he leant in to kiss me ... My mind drifted back over the weeks since the night he'd walked into the Armada and back into my life. How could I have believed I could spend a summer with him, my first love, whose smile set my heart soaring, whose touch set my body on fire, and all I was ever going to feel for him was friendship?

The previous evening's wedding reception at the Downland had been unusually fraught – a page boy had managed to knock over the five-tier wedding cake, the bride had torn her dress, three waiters had called in sick – and I'd had no leisure to think about my newly discovered feelings for Jake. By the time I got home in the early hours, I was beyond thought, too exhausted to do anything other than crawl under my duvet. This morning, lying alone in my bed, staring at the dust motes dancing in the beam of sunlight streaming through a crack in the curtains, all I could think about was the man I loved.

I sat up and stretched. Picking my phone up off my nightstand, I scrolled through the photos I'd taken in London, stopping at the pictures of Jake and me outside the Globe, his arm around me, both of us laughing, quoting Shakespeare. Anyone who'd seen us together would have assumed we were a couple. I dropped my phone on the bed.

Yesterday Jake had kissed me, and told me that he wasn't giving up. He wanted me. It wasn't complicated unless I made it so. I wanted him, come what may. And who was to say that a summer fling couldn't become something more.

I have to let him know how I feel, I thought, I have to tell him that I want us to be more than friends.

My alarm clock showed me that it was only 10.30, too early for Jake to be thinking about heading out for a lunchtime drink with me, but not too early for me to go to him. Throwing off the duvet, I got out of bed, and took a quick shower. Having blow-dried and straightened my hair, sprayed myself with my signature perfume, and put on rather more make-up than I normally wore on a day when I wasn't working, I took a while to rifle through the clothes in my wardrobe, rejecting my usual weekend wear of T-shirt, shorts, and trainers in favour of a strappy cotton sundress, sky-blue with flowers around the hem of the skirt, and sandals. Surveying myself in my full-length mirror, I couldn't help but smile. Looking good, girl, I thought. Grabbing my bag, I went out onto the landing. There was neither sight nor sound of Lizzie. I walked softly down the stairs and let myself out.

It was another glorious summer day, the sun already hot, the holidaymakers already out in force. On impulse, I turned towards the high street, went into the supermarket and picked up a bag of croissants and a jar of jam, picturing Jake and I eating breakfast together on his veranda, going for a walk along the beach, finding a quiet spot among the dunes, him leaning in for a kiss … Ignoring the fluttering in my stomach, I went over to Carol's till, where for once there was no queue.

'You look nice, Emma,' Carol said, as I transferred the contents of my wire basket to the conveyor belt. 'Is that a new dress?'

'It's fairly new,' I said.

'Going somewhere special?'

163

'I don't know yet,' I said. 'Maybe.' I paid her, and stashed my purchases in my bag.

'Well, you've got a lovely day for it,' Carol said, 'wherever it is you're going. And whoever you're going with.'

I smiled. 'Yes, I have.' Leaving Carol's implied question unanswered, I left the supermarket, and joined the holidaymakers ambling towards the shore.

Arriving at the beach, I discovered that it was low tide. In front of me, on the broad expanse of sand between the stones and the water, a group of lads were playing a rowdy game of Frisbee. Parents herded toddlers towards the pools left by the retreating sea at the end of breakwaters and encouraged them to dig for crabs. Older children raced each other into the shallows. Everywhere I looked, I saw the building of sandcastles, the throwing of beach balls and, even though there was only the gentlest of breezes blowing off the sea, the attempted flying of kites.

Smiling at the sight of so many families enjoying a day by the sea, I picked my way down the stones and, carrying my sandals, headed along the beach in the direction of the headland, and Jake. Soon the shouts and laughter that accompanied the traditional pursuits of a seaside vacation faded as I left the holidaymakers and day-trippers behind, and the only sound was the sigh of the wind, and the occasional cry of a gull.

I'm coming for you, Jake Murray, I thought. My heart leapt.

I passed one breakwater, another and another, and then I came to the breakwater where I'd met Jake skimming stones when he'd first arrived back in South Quay. I walked up the beach, putting on my sandals to clamber up the sloping stones, and crossed the footpath. Pushing open the gate, I stepped into Jake's garden.

It was Jake I saw first, wearing just a pair of cut-off jeans, sitting on the steps of the veranda, exactly as I'd pictured him earlier. I almost called out to him, but then I saw that he wasn't alone, that a woman was standing in the doorway, and she was dressed in one of Jake's T-shirts. I stared at her as she came further out onto the veranda, into the sunlight, her blonde hair shining like spun silk, and put her hand on his shoulder. *Leonie Fox*. She was *here*. In South Quay. With Jake.

Even as I stood there stupefied, unable to make sense of what I was seeing, Jake stood up, took his ex-girlfriend in his arms, and kissed her passionately on the mouth. When they broke apart, he took her hand and led her inside the house.

The world reeled around me, and I had to clutch at the gate-post to stop myself from falling to the ground. I took one step back and another, and then I turned and fled, plunging down the stones at the top of the beach, running blindly along the sand, my breath coming in gasps, until I could run no more.

I thought, how could I let him do this to me *again*? Jake had told me that he and Leonie were over, and I'd believed him, but less than twenty-four hours since he'd kissed me outside Lizzie's cottage, it seemed that they were back together. Tears stung my eyes, tears of misery and of anger, anger at myself for being such a fool as to fall in love with a man who'd never given me the slightest indication that he felt the same, but also anger at Jake who wasn't above using me as a temporary amusement until he got back with his girlfriend.

I'd loved Jake Murray when I was seventeen and I'd lost him. I loved him now, but once again, he and I weren't reading from the same script.

Chapter Twenty-five

A leaden weight in my chest, I forced my way through the holi-daymakers milling around the shops in Shore Road, trudged along Saltwater Lane, and, thankful to reach home without meeting anyone I knew, let myself into Lizzie's cottage. After the heat of the midday sun outside, it was a relief to step into the cottage's cool, dim interior, to slide off my sandals and walk bare-foot on the cold flagstones in the hallway. Going into the kitchen, I dumped my bag on the table, and poured myself a large glass of tap water. Through the window, I saw Lizzie, a wide-brimmed sunhat on her head, kneeling by a flower bed. I went out into the garden.

'Hey, Lizzie,' I said.

She started and dropped the trowel she was holding 'Oh – thank goodness it's you,' she said. 'I thought Noah had come back early from cricket. Don't tell him you caught me weeding a flower bed. He's decided that gardening is too strenuous for pregnant women. The most I'm allowed to do these days is deadhead roses.' She sighed and stood up, brushing earth from her jeans. 'It's getting too hot to work in the garden in any case.' She gave me a long look, and then she grinned. 'You've got a lot of make-up on for a Sunday morning. Are you seeing Jake?'

'I – I've already seen him,' I said. 'I walked along the beach to his place. He was outside on the veranda. Leonie Fox was with him.'

166

'*What?*' Lizzie said. 'She was at his house? But … Why? What's she doing there?'

'He – they –' My throat tightened. 'They're back together.'

Lizzie frowned. 'He told you that?'

'No, he didn't see me,' I said. 'They were on the veranda. I was at the other end of the garden. They didn't know I was there.'

'I don't understand,' Lizzie said.

'I walked up from the beach. I went into the garden. I saw – they – Jake and Leonie – he kissed her.'

'But isn't Leonie Fox supposed to be in a relationship with that Hollywood actor? What's-his-name – Daniel Miller?'

'Not any more, apparently,' I said. Suddenly, my body was trembling. I walked over to the wooden bench and sat down. Lizzie followed and sat next to me.

'I'm so sorry, Emma,' she said, quietly.

'This morning, I was going to tell Jake that I had feelings for him,' I said, 'but it's obvious that he doesn't want to be with me now any more than he did ten years ago. I'm such an idiot.'

'You're not,' Lizzie said. 'Or if you are, I am too, because I honestly thought that you and Jake were going to work out this summer. The way he looks at you … Sorry, that's not a very helpful thing to say right now.' She put her hand on my arm. 'Emma, I know you're hurting, but you will get through this.'

'I did before,' I said.

We both fell silent. I became aware of how hot it was in the garden, and that I was developing a headache. Suddenly, I felt unbearably tired. 'I think I might go inside and lie down for a bit.'

'You do whatever you need to do, hun,' Lizzie said. 'Can I get you anything? Tea? Gin?'

I managed a smile. 'No,' I said, 'but thanks, Lizzie.'

I got to my feet and went into the cottage. Collecting my bag and another glass of water from the kitchen, I went up to my bedroom, took an aspirin, and lay down on top of my bed. The scene I'd witnessed on the veranda replayed in my head. Jake was back with Leonie Fox. At what point after their confrontation in the Troubadour – after what she'd said to *me* – had Jake decided to get back with his ex? I was still having trouble getting my head around how Leonie came to be in South Quay at all. Now it occurred to me to wonder how long she would be staying, and if I was going to have to watch Jake parade her around the village.

I thought, the last ten years might never have happened …

'But you have to come,' Lizzie says. 'Henry's bought fireworks.' It is New Year's Eve. Henry's parents are going to a dinner dance at the posh Downland Hotel. They have treated themselves to a room for the night and will not be back until the following morning. Henry has invited everyone in his address book to a party in the Wyndhams' poolhouse.

'I can't,' I say, 'Jake'll be there – with that girl.' The thought of being at a party with all my friends, Henry switching on the TV so we can count down the seconds to midnight, along with the chimes of Big Ben, Jake kissing his girlfriend while fireworks light up the sky above their heads, turns my stomach.

'You'll have to face them sometime,' Lizzie says. 'You can't hide away in your bedroom for ever.'

I've not seen Jake since Christmas Eve – since then I've barely left the house – but Scarlet has seen him and his girlfriend in the Armada and has told me that he was 'snogging her face off,' her eyes lighting up as she reports this scandalous behaviour, oblivious to the pall of misery that settles about my shoulders as she speaks. My mother has met Jake's mother in the supermarket and is able to report that Mrs Murray thinks Chiara a very sweet girl. Lizzie let drop that when she and Henry went round to Noah's a couple of days ago, Jake and his girlfriend were there too – I have to remind myself very firmly that my friends are also Jake's friends, and I can't reasonably expect Lizzie to avoid him – but if she has formed an opinion of Chiara, she is tactful enough not to say. I have made her swear that she won't talk to Jake about me. For him to know how I feel about him when he's chosen another girl over me would be just too humiliating.

'I can't see in the New Year with them,' I say. 'I couldn't bear it.'

'If you don't go, neither will I,' Lizzie says. 'I'm not going out party-ing on New Year's Eve without my best friend.'

'Don't try to guilt trip me.' I already feel bad about letting Henry down, guilty that I've lied and told him I have to go to a family do. I'll feel worse if Lizzie's New Year's Eve is ruined because of me. I think, I can do emotional blackmail just as well as she can.

I say, 'Imagine how Henry will feel if neither of us comes to his party.' We toss the argument back and forth between us, but eventually I manage to persuade Lizzie that her going to Henry's party is the right thing for her to do, and she rings off.

My family are all out that night – my parents at Lizzie's house, cele-brating the New Year with her parents, Scarlet at a bar in Teymouth with her new boyfriend, Nathan. I spend the evening watching dire com-edy shows on TV and feeling thoroughly wretched.

It is fifteen minutes to midnight when there is a ring at the front door. I go to answer it and find Lizzie standing on the doorstep, clutching a bottle of cider and a packet of sparklers.

'Why are you here?' I say. 'You're supposed to be at Henry's party.'

'Henry won't know I've left,' Lizzie says. 'He's completely wasted. Everyone's drunk except me. Noah's already let off the fireworks – far too close to a house with a thatched roof, in my opinion – Gail threw up in a flower bed, and there's talk of skinny-dipping in the pool.'

'You didn't fancy skinny-dipping in the middle of winter?'

'Obviously I was tempted,' Lizzie says, 'especially as half the boys in our year were there, but then I had this amazing idea of celebrating the New Year on the beach. You need to get your coat, because you're coming too.'

'I've nothing to celebrate,' I say.

She holds up the cider. 'If you won't come to the beach and see in the New Year with me, you sulky mare, I'll just have to drink the whole bot-tle myself.'

'We're too old to drink cider on the beach,' I say.

'Suit yourself.' Lizzie turns to go. I think, I can't let her go off to the beach in the middle of the night on her own.

'Wait,' I say. 'I'm coming with you.'

169

It's freezing on the beach, and very dark, the only light coming from the houses along the seafront. The tide is out, the white crests of the waves phosphorescent against the night sky as they crash onto the shore. Despite the cold, we sit on the stones, passing the bottle of cider between us, talking about anything other than Jake. When the alcohol has gone, Lizzie jumps up and lights the sparklers one after another, waving them around, writing her name in the air in lines of fire. I suspect she'll be disappointed if I don't join in, so I do the same.

'It must have gone midnight by now,' Lizzie says, when the last of the sparklers has died away. 'Happy New Year, Emma.'

'Happy New Year, Lizzie,' I say, although I know that I'll never be happy again. Because she's my best friend, and because I realise that this nocturnal visit to the sea is meant to be for my benefit rather than hers, I add, 'Coming down here was a good idea.'

'Yeah, when we're old and grey we can look back and remember the time we drank cider on the beach on New Year's Eve,' Lizzie says.

We head home. At Lizzie's house the downstairs windows are open, electric light and rock music spilling out into the street. Lizzie's parents, my parents and their friends can be seen dancing – or rather lurching – around the living room. Lizzie rolls her eyes and goes inside. My house is dark and silent. I let myself in and go straight up to my room. I get ready for bed, and then I scroll through the messages on my phone. Among the many texts wishing me a Happy New Year, there is one from Jake: Sorry not to see you at Henry's party. I go back to London tomorrow. Catch up next time I'm home. Happy New Year xx

I think, that's it? That's all he has to say to me?

As I have done every night since he came home from London, I cry myself to sleep.

The new school term starts. I sit my mock A levels, and do badly. I go for long, solitary walks on the beach, as far as the headland, where I can cry an ocean of tears among the sand dunes without anyone hearing me. I leave the drama club and don't audition for that year's school play because acting only reminds me of Jake. I don't want to go out with my friends at weekends, to attend an endless round of birthday parties in the South

Quay Community Centre – there are so many eighteenths this year – but Lizzie is relentless, insisting that I have to go with her, telling me she hates going to parties on her own, that I'll enjoy myself once I'm there. I force myself to dance and smile, but I'm crying inside. I have no plans for an eighteenth party of my own.

Months pass. Winter becomes spring. The holidaymakers return to South Quay like migratory birds. I hear nothing from Jake, and neither do Lizzie or Henry, although Noah, away at uni, finds time to text all of us. I only go on Jake's Facebook page once – I can't bear to see the photos of him with Chiara, and then another girl who I assume has replaced her in his affections. My mother occasionally relays news from Mrs Murray – Jake is enjoying drama school, Jake is the lead in a student play – that she imagines I want to hear, what with Jake and I being friends. Then Jake's parents retire, sell their family home, and move to Spain, a long-term plan of theirs apparently. I am alone in my room, distracted from the essay I'm supposed to be writing by thoughts of Jake, when it occurs to me that I'll probably never see him again. I double up in pain, as though someone has punched me in the stomach.

Spring becomes summer. I go sailing with Lizzie and Henry in the boat his parents buy him for his eighteenth birthday. I revise for my impending A levels. I go shopping in Teymouth with Lizzie for the dresses we will wear to the Senior Prom. I try not to think about Jake, but something always reminds me: a piece of blue sea glass that I find at the back of a drawer, a pressed flower, a yellow rose from the bouquet he gave me when I played Titania to his Oberon, which falls out of my Complete Works of Shakespeare, the arrival of a letter from the Royal College of Drama … and all the colour drains out of the world. I know I will never get over him. I am broken.

I am wrong. I do get over him. As summer becomes autumn, he intrudes into my thoughts less and less. I take a job at the Downland Hotel. It's not the sort of job that I once hoped for, but somewhat to my surprise, I find that I am good at it, and there is satisfaction in that. When Henry,

who, unlike Lizzie, hasn't gone to uni, asks me if I want to tag along
to the auditions for the South Quay Players' Christmas panto, I think,
why not?

The pinging of my phone announcing the arrival of a text jolted me sharply back to the present. I sat up, drank some water, and fished my phone out of my bag which I'd left on the floor beside my bed. The text was from Jake: *I'm not going to make it to the Armada today. Sorry. See you later in the week. xx*

I thought, I've been here before. Steeling my heart, I texted back: *OK. See you.*

I was not going to let him derail my life again.

Chapter Twenty-six

'So once we pay the deposit, the booking is confirmed?' Polly said. Her gaze travelled around the ballroom, and I knew she was imagining herself as a bride, listening to the speeches, cutting her wedding cake, dancing with her new husband.

'Exactly,' I said.

She wandered over to the glass doors that led onto the terrace. 'Oh, Gareth, there's such a beautiful view. Think of the photos.'

Gareth, who appeared not to share his fiancée's enthusiasm for vistas of the South Downs, was looking at his phone. 'We need to get a move on, Polly,' he said. 'We're behind schedule.' To me, he added, 'We've another venue to check out this afternoon.'

'Planning a wedding is so time-consuming,' Polly said.

'It certainly is,' I said.

We left the ballroom, and I showed them back to reception.

'If you have any questions, please don't hesitate to give me a call,' I said.

'I've a question,' Gareth said. 'Any chance of mates' rates?'

Resisting the temptation to point out that he and Polly were Scarlet's friends, not mine, I flashed him my most professional smile. 'As I mentioned earlier, the Downland has various wedding packages. I'd be delighted to talk them through with you at any time.'

'We'll get back to you,' Gareth said.

'Bye, Emma,' Polly said. 'Remember us to Scarlet and Nathan.'

'I will,' I said. As I watched the pair of them leave the hotel,

I felt sure Gareth had already decided that holding their wedding at the Downland was beyond their budget. It would be interesting, I thought, to see if Polly managed to change his mind. I turned to go back to the Events office, and from the corner of my eye caught sight of a dark-haired man sitting in a leather chair, reading one of the Downland's brochures. *Jake.* In the next instant, I saw that it wasn't him, but a stranger, just some guy staying at the hotel who didn't even look like him. The image of Jake and Leonie on the veranda flashed into my head. *Don't, Emma,* I told myself. *Don't think about him.*

I returned to the Events office. Eve, who'd been in a managers' meeting since lunchtime, was now back at her desk, frowning in concentration at whatever was on her screen. I sat down at my desk and switched on my computer.

'Don't start work just yet,' Eve said. To my surprise, she stood up and closed the office door. 'I've something I need to talk to you about.'

'OK,' I said, hoping that whatever she wanted to say to me wouldn't take long. It was already twenty past five, and I didn't want to miss my bus.

'Tom is leaving the Downland,' Eve said. 'He's retiring at the end of the month.'

It took me a moment to realise who she was talking about. I was on first name terms with everyone else I worked with, but I'd never called the hotel's General Manager anything other than Mr Gates.

'That's a bit sudden,' I said.

'The management team have known for a while now,' Eve said, 'but it was decided that the news wouldn't be made public until after the appointment of Tom's successor, when we could assure the staff that the Downland Hotel remains in safe hands.'

'So who's got Mr Gates's job?' I said.

'Janine will be stepping up to become General Manager,' Eve continued, 'and Philip will take over from her as Assistant

Manager.' She paused. 'I am to take Philip's place as Deputy Assistant Manager.'

I gasped. 'Oh, but that's fantastic news,' I said. 'Congratulations, Eve, massive congratulations. Obviously, I'm sorry you're leaving Events, but I'm delighted for you.'

'Thanks, Emma.' Eve smiled. 'There'll be an official announcement to the rest of the staff tomorrow, but I wanted to give you a heads up, because this change is going to affect you directly.'

'I'll have a new boss,' I said. That'll be strange after all this time, I thought. 'Do you know who it's going to be yet?'

'Actually, Emma,' Eve said, 'I'm hoping it's *you* who'll be the new Events Manager.'

'Me?' In the ten years I'd worked at the Downland, the thought of applying for a management position had never entered my head.

'You'll have to fill in an application form, of course,' Eve continued, 'and attend an interview with HR, but all that's just a formality. You're more than ready to take on a managerial role, and it would, of course, mean a significant pay rise for you.'

I gaped at her. 'You're offering me the job?'

'It's yours. If you want it.'

A promotion, I thought, an increase in salary. But also longer hours and considerably more paperwork. I recalled the number of times I'd gone off to rehearse with the Players, leaving Eve still bashing away at her keyboard or talking to a client on the phone. And yet … I was perfectly capable of doing the job. I'd be a fool not to take it.

'So, Emma,' Eve said, 'are you interested in becoming Events Manager at the Downland Hotel?'

'I – I – Could I have some time to think it over?' I stuttered.

Eve looked startled – evidently this was not the response she'd been expecting – but quickly recovered herself. 'Of course,' she said. 'Shall we say that you'll let me know by the end of the week?'

I nodded. 'Thanks, Eve. I'm almost sure I do want the job. It's just that it's so unexpected.'

'No worries,' Eve said. She glanced at the clock. 'It's almost half past. You may as well get off early for once.'

Muttering my thanks, I switched off my computer, and made a hasty exit.

Back at the cottage, I swapped my office dress and heels for my rehearsal outfit of jeans and T-shirt, and joined Lizzie and Noah in the kitchen, where they were eating lasagne.

'I cooked far too much,' Noah said. 'There's loads left, if you'd like some.' I helped myself to a small portion, and joined them at the kitchen table.

'It was sports day at school today,' Lizzie said. 'It never ceases to amaze me how competitive the parents are.'

'I remember my parents cheering me on at sports day,' I said. 'They were so excited when I came second in the egg-and-spoon race. Much more than I was.'

'I'm talking about the mothers' and fathers' races,' Lizzie said. 'Several mums turned up in Lycra running gear. One father literally flung himself across the finishing line.'

I laughed. 'Were Scarlet and Nathan there? Did they win any races?'

'Scarlet came third,' Lizzie said, 'and is now the owner of a rather fabulous cardboard medal covered in tinfoil, as are your nephews. Nathan was way back in the field.'

'Oh dear, he won't be happy about that.' I ate some lasagne, and then laid down my knife and fork. 'I was offered a new job today,' I said. 'Taking over from my boss as Events Manager.'

Lizzie and Noah both paused with forkfuls of pasta halfway to their mouths.

'Well done, you,' Noah said.

'Emma! That's terrific. You should have told us straight away.' Lizzie jumped up, ran round the table and gave me a hug. 'I'm really pleased for you, hun. Congratulations!'

'Thanks,' I said, 'but I'm not sure if I'm going to accept it.'

'But why wouldn't you?' Lizzie said, resuming her seat. 'It's a *promotion.*'

'I'm not sure it's what I want,' I said. 'It's not like I've ever dreamed of a career in the hospitality industry.'

Noah smiled. 'I remember you telling me it was your dream to become an actress. Your brilliant theatrical careers were all you and Jake would talk about at one time. When you weren't reciting Shakespeare at each other.'

Ill-met by moonlight, proud Titania. A wave of sadness broke over me. *Love is a smoke and is made with the fumes of sighs.*

'Do you remember, Lizzie, how Emma and Jake used to do that Shakespeare thing?' Noah said.

'Vaguely,' Lizzie said. 'Noah, isn't it time you went and got changed for rehearsal?' She collected up her and Noah's empty plates and put them in the sink.

'I'd have done that,' Noah said.

'Go and get changed, Noah,' Lizzie said. 'I don't want to have to run all the way to the community centre.'

'No, you really don't,' Noah said. He shot out of the kitchen and leapt up the stairs.

'I'm sorry, Emma,' Lizzie said. 'Noah would never have talked like that about you and Jake if he knew how you felt.'

'I'm sure he wouldn't,' I said.

'I haven't told Noah about Jake being back with Leonie,' Lizzie said. 'I couldn't think how to tell him about *her* without telling him the rest of it. I thought it was best I didn't say anything at all.'

What a tangled web we weave when first we practise to deceive. 'He'll find out that Jake's back with his ex soon enough,' I said. 'Along with everyone else in the village, I'd imagine.' When she continued to regard me anxiously, I added, 'I'm OK, Lizzie. If you and Noah decide to invite Jake and Leonie over to dinner, I'll make sure I'm out that night, but I can cope with hearing people talk about him.'

'Oh, if Noah gets any bright ideas about welcoming Jake's

177

girlfriend to South Quay,' Lizzie said, 'I'll tell him I'm far too pregnant to host a dinner party.' She bit her lip. 'I like Jake – I'm sorry, Emma, I can't *not* like him – but I wish he'd never come back here.'

'You're not alone in that,' I said.

From the hall, Noah called, 'Ready to go, ladies?' Hurriedly, I swallowed my last mouthful of lasagne.

'We're just coming,' Lizzie said. Lowering her voice, she added, 'I know you're not in a good place right now, but a new challenge could be just what you need. Don't be too quick to turn that job down.'

'I won't,' I said. 'I've got 'til the end of the week before I have to make a decision.'

I followed Lizzie and Noah out of the cottage, and we made our way towards the community centre, carried along by the in-coming tide of holidaymakers returning to their B&Bs and holiday lets after a day on the beach – the queue outside the fish and chip shop stretched around the corner from Shore Road into the high street.

'There's Jake,' Noah said, suddenly. He raised his arm and waved.

Following the direction of Noah's gaze, I saw Jake *and* Leonie – with her sunglasses, cropped white trousers, crisp striped shirt and leather tote bag on one arm, she looked every inch the movie star – standing on the other side of the road by the entrance to the supermarket. I felt a tightening in my chest.

'Who's that with him?' Noah said. 'She looks ever so familiar.' Jake, who evidently hadn't seen Noah's waving hand, went into the supermarket, leaving Leonie outside on the pavement.

'I believe that's Leonie Fox,' I said.

Leonie took off the sunglasses she was wearing, and shook out her mane of blonde hair. She turned her head, and her gaze fell on the three of us standing there staring at her. I'd no idea whether or not she recognised me as the woman she'd insulted in the Troubadour, or if she thought us beneath her interest, but almost instantly she looked away.

'You're right,' Noah said. 'It is her. She and Jake must have hooked up again.'

'Presumably,' I said. 'Anyway, let's get on. We can't be late for rehearsal.' I might be able to hear people talk about Jake or see him and Leonie together without collapsing in a weeping heap on the pavement – I could even say her name aloud – but I'd no desire to stand in the high street gawping at her like a starstruck fan. We resumed walking.

'I'm guessing we won't be seeing so much of Jake in future if he's patched things up with the Foxy Lady,' Noah said, as we reached the community centre car park. 'You won't know what to do with yourself, Emma, the amount of time you've been spending at his place.'

'If I take this new job,' I said, 'filling my spare time is not something I'll need to worry about.'

He and Lizzie climbed the steps to the community centre and went inside. I followed rather more slowly.

I thought, Jake will be gone from South Quay by the end of the summer, maybe before then, now that he's back with his girl-friend. I wanted him to leave, the sooner the better. I wanted him to go back to his life in London, and let me move on with my life.

Chapter Twenty-seven

The bus drew up at my stop. I stepped down onto the pavement, said goodnight to a chambermaid from the Downland who'd caught the same bus home as me, and headed off along the high street. In my bag, was the application form for the position of Events Manager that I'd collected earlier that day from HR. I'd yet to decide whether or not to fill it in.

Three more sleeps, I thought, and I have to give Eve my answer. At work that day, in my lunch hour, in my tea break, in my every spare moment, I'd gone over all the reasons why I should accept the job – I'd even written a list – but the prospect of signing the contract left me feeling distinctly underwhelmed.

Arriving at the supermarket, I was temporarily relieved from dwelling on the decision I had to make about my future career by the more pressing question of what I was going to eat that night. Grabbing a ready-made salad, I went and queued up at Carol's till behind a harassed-looking holidaymaker who was struggling to prevent her toddler destroying the till display. In front of her, Zoe's older sister Flora was packing up her shopping while chatting to Carol. I couldn't hear all of what they were saying to one another, but the words 'our Jake' and 'that Leonie Fox' and 'I read that other actor Leonie was dating has gone back to Hollywood,' came to me quite clearly.

Jake. I reminded myself I was *not* going to think about him.

Suddenly, the toddler took off, running down the nearest aisle, with his mother in hot pursuit. Half a minute or so later,

I saw her carrying him, now red-faced and screaming, out of the shop. Stepping past the woman's abandoned wire basket, I took her place in the queue next to Flora.

'I heard she went to London with him,' Flora said to Carol. 'Zoe told me he picked her up from the Players' rehearsal in his car.'

'Hello, Emma,' Carol said loudly. Flora started and spun round to face me.

'Oh—Hi, Emma,' she said. 'I didn't see you there.'

Evidently not, I thought. 'Hi,' I said, through gritted teeth. Flora hastily stuffed the rest of her purchases in a canvas bag and scurried out of the supermarket. For once, Carol made no effort to engage me in conversation as she took my money and gave me my change, other than expressing the hope that I'd have a good evening. Forcing a smile, I picked up my salad, wished her the same, and left.

For most of the day, the sky had been overcast, but now, as so often happened when the tide was on the turn, the weather changed and the cloud lifted. As I walked along Shore Road, my high heels tapping on the pavement, I began to plan my evening. A walk on the beach. Eat in the garden. Take a look at that application form.

I turned into Saltwater Lane – and came to an abrupt halt when I saw the figure sitting on the stone wall outside Lizzie's cottage. Unaware of my presence, he was looking down at his phone, one strong hand resting on the wall, his long denim-clad legs stretched out in front of him, one ankle crossed over the other. Jake. My heart started thumping hard in my chest. I looked wildly up and down the lane, but thankfully there was no sign of Leonie. Reminding myself that he was blissfully ignorant of my feelings for him and knew nothing of the misery he'd caused me, I squared my shoulders and resumed walking. When my shadow fell across him, he looked up from his phone, and his face broke into his familiar smile.

'Hey, Emma,' he said. 'I rang the bell, but there was no answer.'

'I think Lizzie and Noah were going round to her parents' tonight,' I said.

'Ah, well, it was you I came to see,' Jake said, 'not them.'

I wanted to tell him to go away, that I had things to do, that I was tired after work, that I was going straight out again, but something, maybe the memory of the friendship we'd shared, made me say, 'I guess you'd better come in then.' I can do this, I thought, I can invite Jake into the cottage, I can offer him a beer, talk to him as though he's no more to me than an old acquaintance, a boy I grew up with, and send him back to his girlfriend. I will get through this. And if I see him again before he goes back to London, it won't be so hard.

I opened the front door, and the two of us went inside the cottage. In the hall, I toed off my heels, and headed into the kitchen, Jake following after me.

'Beer?' I said.

'Er, yeah,' Jake said. 'Thanks.' I put my salad away in the fridge, found him a bottle of beer, poured myself a glass of fruit juice and sat down on one of Lizzie's beautifully painted wooden chairs. Jake leant against a worktop.

'I'm sorry I haven't seen you for a few days,' he said. 'I had a visitor.'

'I know,' I said. OK, I thought, let's get the conversation about you being back with your ex out of the way. 'Leonie.' To me, my voice sounded unnaturally bright, but Jake didn't appear to notice.

'I suppose the whole village is talking about her coming down here,' he said.

'One or two people may have recognised her standing outside the supermarket yesterday,' I said. 'Have you left her all on her own this evening?'

'No,' Jake said. 'She's gone. She drove up to London late last night, and she won't be coming back.'

Leonie was *gone*. I would not be stumbling across her and Jake sunbathing on the beach if I walked up to the headland. He would not be introducing her to our mutual friends when we dropped into the Armada after rehearsal.

'Was South Quay not to her liking?' I said. 'I imagine she'd find

182

it a bit quiet.' Not enough wine bars for her to make a scene in, I thought. 'I suppose you'll be following her up to town fairly soon?'

'I'm not going anywhere right now,' Jake said. 'Leonie and I are over.'

I stared at him. Was I expected to sympathise because he'd had another fight with his on – off girlfriend? After the way she spoke to me? Was he that insensitive?

'You seem to make a habit of breaking up with Leonie,' I said, 'so forgive me if I don't offer you my shoulder to cry on.'

'That's not why I'm here,' Jake said. To my amazement, he reached out his hand and trailed a finger down the side of my face. 'Emma ... It's you I want, not her. And I know that you want me.' He stepped forward, put his hands on my arms, drew me to my feet, and bent his head towards mine. For an instant, stunned into silence, I just stood there looking up at his handsome, smiling face, but then anger speared through me.

'Let go of me,' I said. Shaking his hands off me, I backed away from him, until I felt the dresser digging into my rear.

'What's wrong?' he said.

'I'll tell you what's wrong,' I said. 'One day you're kissing me in the street, the next day you're back with your girlfriend. Now you come round here, tell me you and Leonie have broken up *again*, and expect me to fall into bed with you. *That's* what's *wrong*.'

'No, Emma, you don't understand,' Jake said. 'It's like I told you, Leonie and I split up before I came to South Quay.'

'And you invited her to stay with you because?'

'I didn't *invite* her,' Jake said. 'She got my address from my parents – they always liked her – and literally turned up at my door on Saturday night.'

'She drove eighty miles on the off-chance you'd be in?' I said. 'That seems very unlikely.'

'Well, she did,' Jake said. 'It was that important to her that she saw me. She had things she needed to say.'

I thought, hasn't the woman heard of mobile phones? 'She must have had plenty to say, if it took her three days,' I said.

Jake raised his eyebrows. 'Are you mad at me?'

'What do you think?' I snapped. 'You tell me you want me, but as soon as Leonie's back on the scene you forget about me. And you seem to think that's OK.'

'Listen, Emma,' Jake said, 'Leonie and I ended badly, but we were together – on and off – for more than a year. When I opened the door and saw her standing there, I wasn't going to tell her to get in her car and drive back to London in the middle of the night. We talked—'

'You slept with her.'

'No,' Jake said. 'All we did was talk.'

'Don't lie to me. I saw you kiss her.'

He frowned. 'When?'

'On Sunday. I walked along the beach to your house, and I saw you from the end of your garden. You and Leonie were on the veranda. She was wearing your T-shirt.'

For a long moment, Jake was silent, then he said, 'All right, I kissed her, but I didn't have sex with her. I could have done, if I'd wanted to – she offered – but I chose not to.'

'You chose not to for *three days*?' I said. 'I may live in a backwater, as your girlfriend so charmingly put it, but I'm not completely naïve.'

'If you'd let me explain—' Jake said.

'You do that.'

'First of all,' Jake said, 'you need to know that Leonie apologised for what happened in the Troubadour.'

Like that makes it all right, I thought.

'She was angry with me,' Jake went on, 'but she was still attracted to me. She came down here to see if there was any chance we could salvage our relationship.' His eyes fastened on mine. 'She came on hard to me, and I – my body – responded. You saw me kiss her, but that really is all that happened between us. I no longer felt *involved* with her emotionally. And she realised that she no longer has feelings for me either.'

'And yet she stayed on in your house?' I thought, he actually

184

expects me to believe he didn't sleep with her? He must think I'm a complete idiot.

Jake shrugged. 'She stayed. We talked. And then we parted. Amicably, this time.' He paused, and then he said, 'Before Leonie left, she asked me if I'd met someone else. I told her I had, but I hadn't realised until then how important she is to me.' His confident smile infuriated me.

'Get this into your head,' I said. 'I am *not* going to sleep with you.'

'Emma, you're not hearing me. I want to be *with* you.'

'You want a *relationship* with me?' I said. 'And what happens when you swan off back to town? Oh – I know. You forget me and hook up with Leonie again. Or someone else. Just like you did ten years ago.'

'Ten years ago? What are you talking about?'

'Do you even remember the night we spent together the first time I visited you in London? You made me think you cared for me, you got me into bed, and then you didn't want to know.' I broke off. It meant nothing to him. I meant nothing to him.

'I do remember,' Jake said. 'We were good together, but it was only the one time. It was just two teenagers messing around.'

'Not to me it wasn't,' I said. 'I fell for you that night, and you – you broke my heart.'

'Oh, come *on*, Emma,' Jake said.

'I didn't go to drama school because of you.'

Jake frowned. 'You didn't get into RoCoDa,' he said. 'That was nothing to do with me.'

'I did get in,' I said. 'I was offered a scholarship, but I turned it down.'

'*What?*' Jake's body went rigid. 'You texted me that you didn't get a place.'

On the front mat, along with the usual junk mail, is a large white envelope. My stomach lurches. Somehow, I know this is the letter I've been waiting for, even before I read my name on the address label. I pick the

185

envelope up, open it, and take out the folded sheet of paper inside. I read
the letter twice. I have a scholarship to the Royal College of Drama. Tears
sting my eyes. I already know that I'm going to turn it down. I can't go
to the same drama school as Jake, I just can't …

'I lied,' I said. 'To you, to Lizzie, and to my family. I couldn't face
going to the same drama school as the boy who'd had sex with
me, and then never called.' My pulse was racing. I'd never told
anyone – I knew they'd never understand – but now I'd told him.
There was no coming back from this. 'I was in love with you, and
when you didn't want me, I fell apart. It took me months to get
over you. I gave up acting—' My voice caught in my throat.

'I didn't know,' Jake said, quietly. 'How could I have known?
I only came back to South Quay that one Christmas.' He ran his
hand through his hair. 'It's all in the past. You need to let it go.'

'I can't,' I said, my voice rising. 'It was because of you that I
didn't become an actress. I'll never forgive you for that. *Never.*'

'It wasn't my fault—'

'Get out,' I was shouting now. 'I was doing fine until you
barged back into my life. Why don't you go back to London
before you do any more damage.'

Jake half-turned towards the kitchen door, but then he swung
around to face me. 'I'm sorry if ten years ago you imagined that
us having sex was going to lead to something more, but I'm certain I never said anything to make you think that way.'

Suddenly, I was incandescent with rage. My whole body was
shaking. 'You ruined my life!'

His eyes grew hard. 'It was *you* who turned down the opportunity to train as an actress, and if your life hasn't worked out the
way you hoped, you have only yourself to blame.' He turned on
his heel and strode out of the kitchen. His trained actor's voice
came to me from the hall, '*The fault, dear* Emma, *is not in our stars,*
but in ourselves.'

The entire cottage shook as he slammed the front door.

Chapter Twenty-eight

I tottered to the nearest chair and sank down. The scene had ended, Jake had stormed offstage, but his parting words still hung in the air, written in lines of fire. *The fault is not in our stars, but in ourselves.* You have only yourself to blame.

Images of the past flashed into my mind with unremitting clarity. Jake, an eighteen-year-old boy, in his first term of drama training, ambitious and talented, his thoughts all of acting, his new independent life as a student in London, and his new friends. Me still at school, living with my parents and sister, my head full of Shakespeare's poetry and Jake ...

The wind in my face, I walk down the beach, across the wet sand, down to the water's edge. Today, the sky is grey, and the sea is grey also, mottled with white foam, the waves rushing into the shore. I put my hand inside the pocket of my parka, and my fingers curl around the smooth, cold piece of sea glass.

I take the glass out of my pocket and hold it up to the light. It is beautiful, but it is Jake who on a day very much like this one, picked it up from the sand and gave it to me, and every time I see it now, it makes me sad. I know what I have to do. I have made my decision.

Tears blur my eyes, but I raise my hand and cast the glass as far out as I can. It is lost beneath the waves ...

We'd both been so young. Jake had been arrogant and thoughtless and he'd hurt me, but *I* had made the decision to reject my offer of a place at RoCoDa. He hadn't destroyed my dreams. I'd done that all on my own.

I sat very still, the daylight fading into dusk, my anger fading with it. Jake was as self-centred as he'd been at eighteen, his behaviour towards me – and Leonie Fox, now I came to think of it – appalling, and I wanted nothing more to do with him, but in accusing him of ruining my life, I'd gone too far. If *I* had made a different decision, if I hadn't torn up that letter …

Enough, Emma, I thought, you can't change the past. There was no point in my sitting in the dark in Lizzie's kitchen, indulging myself with maudlin regrets about what might have been. Jake's words had stirred up memories that had been better left buried, and what I needed to do was get them and him out of my head. And I'd begin by deleting the photos of us I'd taken on my phone.

I stood up, switched on the electric light, took my mobile out of my bag and scrolled through my photos until I came to the ones I'd taken that summer. Pictures of the two of us on the beach, one of Jake in Lizzie's garden, another of him and me with Lizzie, Noah and Henry with his arm in a sling, I trashed without a thought. The photos I'd taken of our time in London, Jake by the canal, me and him outside the Globe, caused me more of a pang, but I deleted them all the same. Then I came to the photo Jake had sent to me, the picture of us with his friends Zac and Julie, and I found my finger hesitating over the delete icon. That had been such a special night, probably the only time in my life I'd go to a West End press night and after-party and talk about acting with a West End leading lady. I stared at the image of Julie Farrell Diaz on my screen. She'd told me that there had been a time when she'd doubted she'd ever become an actress, but unlike me, she'd never given up her dream. Jake's words – Shakespeare's words – echoed around my mind. *The fault lies … in ourselves.*

My phone dropped from my hand onto the table. No one was forcing me to go on living in South Quay, working at the Downland, and rehearsing with the Players. Ten years ago, I'd turned down the offer of a place at drama school, but there was absolutely no reason why I couldn't re-apply. And if I didn't get into RoCoDa this time around, there were other drama schools I could apply to. Another line of Shakespeare's came into my head: *We know what we are, but not what we may be.*

I couldn't rewind the last ten years, and I couldn't change the decision I'd made when I was seventeen, but I didn't have to let it define the rest of my life.

Chapter Twenty-nine

I opened the door of the cottage to find Lizzie and Noah, who I hadn't seen since the previous morning, in the hall, already on their way out to the community centre.

'You're late home this evening,' Lizzie said.

'I missed my usual bus,' I said. 'Eve was out of the office most of the day, and I needed to speak to her.' I glanced at my watch. 'I can still make rehearsal on time.'

'Didn't you get our great leader's email?' Lizzie said. 'The costumes have arrived. We're not wearing them for tonight's rehearsal, but Pamela wants everyone there half an hour early to try them on.'

'No, I didn't get it,' I said. 'At least, I don't think I did.' I found my phone and scrolled through my emails. 'Oh, lord, there is one from Pamela.' I hadn't checked my phone messages all day. When I hadn't been making out invoices or talking to clients, I'd been busy researching drama schools on the internet, and drama courses at universities and colleges, not just in London, but all over the country.

'Honestly, Emma,' Lizzie said, 'you won't win Businesswoman of the Year if you ignore your emails.'

'I hope the Downland is planning to send you on a management training course,' Noah said, with a grin.

'They won't need to,' I said. 'I'm not going to take the job.' The moment I'd told Eve that I appreciated the offer, but I wouldn't be accepting the role of Events Manager, I'd felt a

190

weight lift from my shoulders. Eve had been disappointed, and, I suspected, shocked, but mollified when I'd assured her I was perfectly happy to go on working at the hotel with a new boss. I didn't feel the need to tell her that if my life went in the direction I hoped, I'd only be working there for one more year.

Lizzie and Noah exchanged startled glances.

'But why wouldn't you take it?' Lizzie said.

'It isn't what I want,' I said. I took a deep breath. 'I have other plans. I'm going to apply to drama school to train as an actress.' I looked from Lizzie to Noah, trying to gauge their reaction. Not that I was going to let them dissuade me, but I'd rather start this new venture with my friends' support.

'You're what?' Lizzie gasped. 'Seriously? You're going to try again? After all this time?'

I nodded. 'I know it's unexpected, and I may not get anywhere, but I don't want to spend the rest of my life wondering *what if?*'

Lizzie's mouth actually fell open. 'Oh my goodness, but that's—that's *brilliant*. You go, girl.'

'Yeah, good for you, Emma,' Noah said. 'Can we get comps for your West End debut?'

I laughed aloud. 'You're getting a bit ahead of yourself. The application process for RoCoDa doesn't open until the autumn, and *if* I get a place, I won't start training until the following year.' A thought struck me. 'I'd appreciate it if you'd keep all this to yourselves. I'd rather not have every member of the Players giving me advice on audition technique.'

'Hear that, Noah?' Lizzie said. 'Don't go discussing Emma's plans with Henry.'

'As if I'd do that,' Noah said, adding, 'I do know who you should ask for advice about auditions, though, Emma. You should talk to Jake.'

'I don't think that would be a great idea,' I said, awkwardly. 'Jake and I don't share the same views on acting.' I'd no intention of telling Noah or even Lizzie about the row Jake and I'd had the previous night. Or about the decision I'd made when I was seventeen to turn down a place at drama school, and the lie I'd told. It seemed foolish now but it had made sense to me at the time, and there was no point in discussing it with my friends ten years later. As it could only make him look bad, I was confident Jake wouldn't be discussing it with them either.

Lizzie gave me a long look. 'Noah, we really should get a move on,' she said. 'Pamela's going to go ballistic if we mess up her schedule.'

I shuddered at the thought. 'You two go on ahead,' I said. 'I'll catch you up as soon as I can.'

Lizzie and Noah left. I ran upstairs to my bedroom, exchanged the tight pencil skirt and blouse I'd worn to work for jeans and a T-shirt, and knowing that if we were trying on costumes Pamela would expect us to bring the right footwear, grabbed my character shoes from under my bed. Back downstairs, having raided the kitchen for food I could eat on the way to the community centre – all I came up with was a cereal bar, but it would have to do – I finally headed for the door.

My phone rang, and automatically I fished it out of my bag and checked the caller ID: *Jake*. My heart sank. It was too much to think that I'd be able to avoid him completely while he was in South Quay – we had too many mutual friends, we both frequented the Armada Inn – but I saw no reason why I should talk to him on the phone. I'd said all I ever wanted to say to him, and I certainly had no interest in hearing anything he might want to say to me. We were done. I pressed the reject key, and hurried out of the cottage.

I arrived at the community centre to find the cast of *Romeo and Juliet* standing in a ragged line in the main hall, everyone attired in motley-coloured costumes of approximately medieval design. The women were in voluminous, high-waisted gowns, some with sweeping trains and floor-length sleeves. Lizzie as Lady Capulet, and one or two others, were also provided with elaborate gravity-defying headwear draped with gauzy veils. The male characters' costumes, apart from Friar Lawrence's sombre, hooded habit, were just as colourful. The Lords Capulet and Montague, and the Prince of Verona, were resplendent in velvet robes, while the other male cast members were sporting either tabards or doublets and tights, along with a fair number of hats with feathers stuck jauntily through the brim. It struck me somewhat forcibly that tights were not necessarily a good look for men, especially if they were designed for a more muscular physique than their wearer possessed and wrinkled badly around the knee. There was a colour scheme for the younger guys, the Capulets sporting different shades of red, the Montagues in green. Unfortunately, what with the tights and the jaunty feathered hats, Romeo and his kinsmen looked as though they were performing in pantomime as Robin Hood and his Merry Men. I struggled to keep a straight face.

Pamela was stalking up and down in front of the cast, directing them to turn left or right or to face the other way, to throw back a cloak or smooth a skirt. Clearly any attempt that I might have made to join the company unobserved was doomed to failure, so I went over to her.

'Ah, here's our Juliet,' she said. 'At last.'

'So sorry I'm late,' I said. 'I was unavoidably delayed at work.'

Pamela gave an exasperated sigh. 'Well, now you're here, please go and change into your costume. It's over there on the clothes rail.' She returned to her inspection of the assembled cast. 'Gail, those shoes won't do at all. You'll need to obtain character shoes before the dress rehearsal.'

I walked quickly over to the clothes rail, and started looking through the various garments still hanging there for my own costume.

Pamela said, 'Romeo, where's your doublet?'

Eddie, dressed in pale green tights – in his case, they were stretched almost to transparency across his thighs – and a billowing white shirt, fortunately long enough to preserve his modesty, stepped forward and held up a dark green doublet.

'I can't get into it, Pamela,' he said. 'It's too small.'

'It can't be,' Pamela said. 'Unless you gave me the wrong measurements to send to the costumiers.' Her gimlet eye raked across the Players. 'Lizzie, you're good with a needle, could you sort out Romeo's doublet?'

'I'll see what I can do,' Lizzie said.

Richard said, 'I have an issue with my costume too, Pamela. In my opinion, Tybalt shouldn't be wearing tights.'

I'll second that, I thought. Still rifling through the costumes on the rail, I glanced towards Pamela. She did not look happy.

'I see,' Pamela said. 'And what, in your opinion, would be appropriate garb for a nobleman of Verona during the Middle Ages?'

'Tybalt's a swordsman,' Richard said. 'He needs to look tough. I'm thinking leather trousers.'

Pamela pursed her lips. 'When our audience are watching this year's summer production,' she said, 'I want the costumes to remind them of a medieval fresco, not a gang of bikers. So, no leather, if you please, Richard. Also, no jeans, and no tracksuits.'

Richard frowned. He opened his mouth, but evidently thought better of whatever he'd been about to say, and shut it again. Sofia put up her hand.

'Yes, Sofia,' Pamela said. 'What is it?'

'I'm a bit concerned about dancing on stage in this dress,' Sofia said. 'The skirt's too long, even when I'm holding up the train, and the sleeves are trailing on the floor.'

Zoe said, 'If we're tripping over our costumes, the ball scene will be a disaster. And someone could get hurt.'

'Lizzie?' Pamela said. 'Could you shorten Sofia and Zoe's skirts and sleeves?'

'Sure, no problem,' Lizzie said.

'Will you have time for all this sewing, Lizzie?' Noah said. 'Won't it be too much for one person?'

'It's fine, Noah,' Lizzie said. 'I'll see to it.'

'Thank you, Lizzie,' Pamela said. 'Now, unless anyone else has a query about their costume—' Immediately, the hall erupted with the clamour of the other cast members whose medieval garb was too long, too short or impossible to dance in. I found my own costume, and made a timely exit through the door that led to the female changing room at the back of the stage.

Designed as they were for the various groups – badminton, yoga – who used it every week, the changing rooms lacked a traditional theatrical dressing room's lightbulb-surrounded make-up mirrors, but they provided the Players with lockers to store their belongings, benches on which to sit when they weren't on stage, and plenty of hooks on which to hang up costumes. I quickly stripped off my jeans and T-shirt, and was stepping into Juliet's pale pink gown, when Lizzie appeared in the doorway.

'I've come to see if you need any help with your dress,' she said. 'Some of the other girls had problems with broken zips and missing hooks-and-eyes.'

'Thanks, Lizzie.' I turned around so that she could zip me up. 'These really aren't the best set of costumes the Players have ever worn.'

'Mine certainly isn't.' Pushing back her long, wide sleeves which had fallen over her hands, carefully holding her cumbersome train off the floor, Lizzie walked over to the full-length mirror on the far wall. 'Oh, my days,' she said. 'I'm not even showing yet, but this outfit makes me look nine months pregnant.'

I went and stood next to her and studied my reflection. My dress was not encumbered by a train, and the sleeves ended at my wrists, but its design, a high waist with acres of material gathered under my bust, was not at all flattering.

'It could be worse, I suppose,' I said. 'Tights. That's all I'm saying.'

'Don't mention the tights,' Lizzie said. 'With the doublets being so short, I didn't know where to look.'

Suddenly, I was no longer able to keep myself from laughing, and then Lizzie started laughing too, both of us doubling up with laughter, unable to stop.

'It's not funny,' I gasped.

195

'It's not remotely funny,' Lizzie said, collapsing onto a bench, causing her headdress to fall into her lap, which set us off again.

'But would leather trousers be an improvement?' I said, when we finally got ourselves under control.

'The thought of Richard in leather trousers ...' Lizzie said. 'I don't mean to be unkind, but *no*.'

'Do you think he owns a pair of leather trousers?' I said.

'I sincerely hope not,' Lizzie said. She stood up, grimacing as she caught sight of her reflection again in the mirror. 'Anyway, we'd better go back to the hall before my over-protective boy-friend sends out a search party.'

Clutching Eddie's hands, I said, '*Wilt thou be gone?/It is not yet near day./It was the nightingale, and not the lark./Believe me, love, it was the nightingale.*'

'*It was the nightingale, herald of the morn* ... No, that's not right,' Eddie said. '*It was the nightingale* ... I mean, *It was the lark* ... *It was the lark* ... Sorry. Can we start the scene again, Pamela?'

'No, just keep going,' Pamela said. 'And do try to imagine how Romeo and Juliet must feel at this point. It's the morning after their wedding night, and he must flee for his life. Show us *desperation*. Show us *agony*.'

We staggered on through the scene, with Eddie forgetting every other line – ironically, Henry had volunteered to be the prompt – until at last we reached the point where Romeo was about to climb down from Juliet's balcony and ride off into exile in Mantua.

'*Farewell, farewell!*' Eddie said. '*One kiss, and I'll descend.*' He gave me a perfunctory peck on the side of my face.

'Oh, for goodness' sake, Romeo,' Pamela said. 'You're a young man about to be torn apart from your wife. Neither of you knows when you'll see each other again. I think you'd bid her farewell with a little more *passion*.'

'I don't see why she doesn't just go with him,' Eddie muttered.

'It would hardly be a tragedy if they rode off *together*, now would it?' Pamela said. She sighed. 'I had hoped to go over the whole of Act III tonight, but we're out of time. Thank you, everyone, I'll see you all next week. Please check your emails for precise rehearsal times, and make sure you arrive promptly. Remember, we've only three more weeks of rehearsal before *Romeo and Juliet* opens.'

Apart from Sofia and Shane who were on chair-stacking duty, Maurice who was wheeling the costume rails into the caretaker's office, and Pamela who was ensuring that Maurice locked the office door, there was a mass exodus of Players. Eddie waited for me while I collected my bag, and we went out of the hall together.

'I'm really sorry about tonight, Emma,' he said to me, when we were outside in the car park. 'I've been going over and over my lines, but just when I think I know them, my mind goes blank.'

'I'm sure you'll be word-perfect by opening night,' I said, 'but we did talk about putting in some extra practice, so if you feel it'd help …'

'When?' Eddie said, immediately.

'How about Sunday afternoon?' I said. 'You could come round to the cottage. If you're not working?'

'I'll change my shift,' Eddie said.

'Shall we adjourn to the Armada?' I said. 'Are you *desperate* for a beer?'

'I'm in *agony*,' he said.

'Was I imagining it,' Lizzie asked, an hour or so later, when she, Noah and I were walking back to the cottage from the pub, 'or was Richard in a particularly foul mood tonight?'

'It's the tights issue,' I said. 'He's gone home to google medieval men's clothing in the hopes of discovering an historically authentic alternative.'

I'd been wary, earlier, when Richard had cornered me in the Armada's beer garden – after the falling-out I'd had with Jake, I'd no desire to have to deal with another unwelcome suitor – but to

197

my relief, all he'd wanted was to rant about his legwear. I'd allowed myself to hope that asking me out on a date was no longer on his agenda.

'Richard does have a point,' Noah said. 'I don't know how you women wear those things.'

Lizzie gasped. 'I've just realised what's wrong with Eddie's doublet,' she said. 'When Pamela hired the costumes, Henry was still playing Romeo, so the doublet was hired to fit his measurements, not Eddie's. Same with the tights. Henry, bless him, has very skinny legs.'

'Oh, my goodness,' I said, 'but that means you're wearing a gown hired for Pamela.'

'Which explains why it's so massive on me,' Lizzie said. 'But please don't tell anyone I said that.'

We'd reached the cottage gate. Lizzie opened it, and the three of us filed along the path. Noah reached past her and opened the front door, and then stood aside so she and I could precede him inside.

'Coffee?' Lizzie said. We trooped into the kitchen. Noah went straight to the kettle, so Lizzie and I sat at the table while he made the drinks.

'The costumes aren't great,' Noah said, once we were all holding steaming mugs, 'but they could be the least of our worries about this show. I was talking to Maurice in the pub, and he said that ticket sales are way down on last year's summer production.'

'That's strange,' I said. 'Romeo and Juliet is one of Shakespeare's most popular plays. Maybe we need more publicity. We could put up a few more posters round the village or hand out more flyers.'

'I don't think publicity's the problem,' Noah said. 'I hate to break it to you, Emma, but not everyone is as enamoured of England's greatest playwright as you are.'

Lizzie said, 'I was chatting to some of the mothers at the school gates today, and they were saying that they thought the Players should be performing something more family-friendly.'

'We can't always cater for children,' I said. 'They do get a panto at Christmas.'

'I agree,' Lizzie said, 'but a lot of adults are wary of Shakespeare. My headmistress told me that the one time she'd seen a Shakespeare play, she didn't understand a word of it.'

'I don't see why,' I said. 'The language is so beautiful.'

'It is,' Noah said, 'but the verse is difficult for an audience that isn't used to it. Especially if the actors don't understand it either. Which is true of some of our fellow cast members.'

I couldn't argue with that. All of *Romeo and Juliet*'s cast were off book, but not all of them were necessarily saying their lines in the right order.

'OK,' I said, 'the costumes are ridiculous, half the cast don't know their lines, and no one's buying tickets. The show is a mess right now, but there's still time for us to fix it.'

'I hope you're right and I'm wrong,' Noah said, 'but I've a horrible feeling that this year's summer production is going to be a complete disaster.'

'It'll be all right on the night,' I said, with more confidence than I felt. 'It always is.'

Chapter Thirty

'That was really good, Eddie,' I said.

'Well done, Eddie,' Lizzie said. 'No prompt needed in that scene.'

Eddie bowed. 'What's next?'

'Act III, scene v,' I said.

That morning, I'd come downstairs to find the living-room sofa piled high with mock-medieval dresses that Pamela had dropped off at the cottage the previous day. Lizzie had been pinning, tacking and sewing for hours, and when Eddie arrived after lunch to rehearse our scenes in *Romeo and Juliet*, she'd been happy to take a break and read in the other parts. She was also acting as prompt.

'Sorry, which scene is that?' Eddie said.

'Desperation, agony and passion,' I said. 'Let's go straight into it … *It is not yet near day/It was the nightingale, and not the lark/That pierced the fearful hollow of thine ear/Nightly she sings on yonder pomegranate tree/Believe me, love, it was the nightingale.*'

Eddie said, '*It was the nightingale* – No, it wasn't. These damn birds – sorry.'

And he'd been doing so well up to then, I thought. Two Romeos, first Henry and now Eddie, and neither of them able to remember their lines. What were the chances? 'No worries,' I said. 'Let's go again. *Believe me, love, it was the nightingale.*'

'*It was the ni—the lark, the herald of the morn—*' Eddie broke off as the living-room door opened and Noah walked in.

'South Quay won the cricket,' Noah said. 'We beat Milton-on-Sea by thirty-four runs.'

Lizzie and I chorused our congratulations.

'Well done, mate,' Eddie said. They exchanged high fives.

'Would you care to join me in a celebratory beer?' Noah said.

'I will do later, mate,' Eddie said, 'but we're still rehearsing *Romeo and Juliet*. That is, if Emma wants to keep going?'

'Absolutely,' I said.

Noah sat on the arm of Lizzie's chair. 'Carry on.'

Another male voice said, 'Yeah, don't let us interrupt you.' I spun around as Jake appeared in the doorway, carrying two beers. Handing one bottle to Noah, he moved aside the costumes, and sat down on the sofa. I gaped at him, not quite able to believe that he was there – that he had the effrontery to be there – in Lizzie's cottage, my home – after what had passed between us. Suddenly, I was finding it hard to get my breath, as though all the air had been sucked out of the room.

I blurted, 'What are you doing here, Jake?'

His steady gaze met mine. 'I was watching the cricket, and now I'm helping Noah celebrate our village team's victory.' He relaxed back in his seat, drew up one leg so that his ankle was on the other knee, and swallowed a mouthful of beer. 'Which scene are you guys working on?'

'Act III, scene v,' Lizzie said.

'*It was the nightingale not the lark*,' Jake said.

'That's the one,' Eddie said. 'How did you know?'

'I played Romeo when I was a drama student,' Jake said. '*It was the lark, the herald of the morn,/No nightingale/Look, love, what envious streaks/Do lace the severing clouds in yonder east/Night's candles are burnt out, and jocund day/Stands tiptoe on the misty mountain tops/I must be gone and live, or stay and die.*' His voice was low and sonorous, bringing out the beauty, meaning and emotion of the words in a way that I knew neither Henry nor Eddie ever could.

'Shite, Jake, how long ago did you learn those lines?' Noah said.

'It was eight years ago.'

'And you still know them?' Eddie said. 'I'm having trouble remembering them week to week.'

'I don't remember every speech in the play perfectly,' Jake said, 'but Romeo was one of my favourite roles. It wouldn't take me long to learn the part again.'

'For me, it's not only remembering the lines, though,' Eddie said. 'It's figuring out the right way to say them.'

'Shakespeare can be challenging for any actor,' Jake said. 'Especially one without three years of training to fall back on.'

That's right, Jake, I thought, don't miss a chance to remind everyone that you're a professional and we're not.

Eddie said, 'You wouldn't do me a favour, and act out that larks and nightingales scene with Emma, would you, Jake? I'm really struggling with it, and I'm sure it'd help if I saw how you'd do it.' He turned to me. 'Is that OK with you, Emma?'

No, I thought, my playing Juliet to Jake Murray's Romeo is *not* OK under *any* circumstances. Aloud, I said, 'Jake may not want to reprise his favourite role with an amateur actress like me.'

'Do it, Jake,' Noah said. 'Remind us why you and Emma were the stars of the school play every year. Give him the script, Lizzie.'

Jake said, 'I don't mind playing that scene with you, Emma.'

My eyes narrowed. 'I thought you never act unless you get paid for it.'

'I'll make an exception for my old school friends,' Jake said. 'I won't need the script, thanks.' He stood up and joined me in the centre of the room. Eddie took his place on the sofa.

A part of me wanted to refuse to act with him and storm out of the room, but public displays of temper were Leonie's style, not mine. Instead, I launched into Juliet's speech:

'*Wilt thou be gone? It is not yet near day;/It was the nightingale ...*' I wish you were gone, Jake Murray, I thought, I wish you were anywhere but here.

'*I must be gone and live, or stay and die,*' Jake responded as Romeo.

'*Yond light is not daylight,*' I said, trying to focus on Juliet's feelings towards her new husband, not mine towards Jake. '*... Therefore stay yet; thou need'st not be gone.*' The sooner you go back to London the better, and then I'll never have to see you again or find myself in hideously awkward situations like this.

'*... I have more care to stay than the will to go,*' Jake said.

'*O, now be gone!*' I said. '*More light and light it grows ...*' Why are you still here? Why don't you go back to your life in London with Leonie, and leave me alone?

'*Farewell, farewell! One kiss and I'll descend,*' Jake said. My body tensed as he put his arms around me, but I managed to stay in character and return his embrace. At least he hadn't attempted a stage kiss. If he had, I suspected I might not have been able to stop myself from slapping him.

'*O, think'st thou we shall ever meet again?*' I said. We won't if I have anything to do with it, I thought.

'*I doubt it not,*' Jake replied. '*... Adieu, adieu!*'

He exited the stage. I hung my head as if in sorrow, hiding my relief that the scene was over. There was a burst of clapping from our audience.

'That was so good,' Lizzie said. 'The chemistry's still there ...' Her voice trailed off and her face reddened.

'You two were great together,' Noah said. 'You always were.'

'I'm in awe of both of you,' Eddie said.

'Not bad, Emma,' Jake said, 'but you need to watch the way you pitch your voice, and trust the rhythm of the verse. At times you sounded as though you were angry with Romeo.'

'Did I?' I glared at him, irritated beyond measure by his patronising tone. 'Well, maybe I have good reason to be angry with Romeo.'

'Personally, I don't know what Juliet sees in him,' Eddie said. 'All that sighing and ranting.'

'He thinks only of himself,' I said.

'Maybe he does at the start of the play,' Jake said, 'but not once he falls for Juliet.'

203

'He's not the sort of guy you'd want to meet up with for a pint in the Armada, though, is he?' Eddie said.

'Speaking of which,' Noah said, 'anyone want another beer?'

'Not for me,' Jake said. 'Time I went home.' Too right it is, I thought.

'Me too,' Eddie said. 'Thanks for the rehearsal, guys, and the masterclass. Not that I'm ever going to be able to act like that.'

'You're doing great, Eddie,' I said. He could only do his best. 'See you tomorrow.'

Amid a general chorus of goodnights, the men, including Noah, went out into the hall. The front door opened and closed. Through the living-room window, I saw Jake and Eddie heading down the path. Noah called out that he was going to start on his and Lizzie's evening meal. I sank down on the sofa. For tonight, Jake was gone. I felt the tension drain out of my body.

'I'd forgotten just how good an actor Jake is,' Lizzie said. 'Sorry, Emma, I know playing that scene with him can't have been easy for you.'

'Jake is a good actor,' I said. 'It's the way he behaves offstage that I have a problem with. Oh – that's my ring tone.' A brief search around the living room located my phone on the mantel-piece, and identified the caller as my sister. I hit the answer icon. 'Hey, Scarlet.'

'Are you at home?' Scarlet said. 'Are you doing anything tonight?'

'Why?' I said.

'Did you know that Nathan and I got married eight years ago today?' Scarlet said.

'Did you?' I said. I was good at remembering my nephews' birthdays – the date of my sister's wedding, not so much. 'Of course you did. Happy anniversary.'

'We were going out to dinner, but our babysitter's let us down. I tried Mum and Dad, but they're at Lizzie's mum and dad's bar-beque, and Nathan's parents are off on a city break in Paris, so I was wondering ...'

204

'Would you like me to babysit?' I said.

'Oh, would you?' Scarlet said. 'Bring Jake with you, if you like, if you want some company after the kids are asleep. I'll leave a bottle of wine for you in the fridge. Can you get here by seven o'clock?'

'I'll be there,' I said. 'I won't be bringing Jake.'

I arrived at my sister's house to find Albie and Kyle in their pyjamas, and Harrison already in bed and asleep. Once Scarlet and Nathan had gone out, the older boys were eager to tell me about their day's adventures, but tired out as they were after an afternoon running around on the beach, when I announced it was time for them to go to bed, they went upstairs with only a token protest, listened quietly while I read them a bedtime story, and fell asleep before I'd switched off their bedroom light. When their parents returned, I was able to report that they'd been absolutely no trouble, that I'd had a relaxing evening reading a book.

I strolled back through the village, reaching Lizzie's cottage just after midnight, and was surprised to see light shining through a chink in the living-room curtains – it was late for Lizzie and Noah to still be up on a Sunday night. I let myself in and opened the living-room door, halting on the threshold when I saw Lizzie lying asleep on the sofa, partially covered by swathes of crimson velvet, which I recognised as Lady Capulet's dress. While I hesitated, trying to decide whether to wake her, she stirred and opened her eyes.

'Oh – Emma – you're back.' Yawning, she sat up. 'What time is it?'

'It's gone midnight,' I said.

'That late?' she said. She glanced down at the fabric draped over her knees. 'I wanted to finish taking this dress in tonight, but I guess I'd better leave it for now.' Her face, I noticed, was very pale.

'Definitely leave it,' I said. 'You look exhausted.'

'I am tired,' Lizzie said. She moved the dress aside, but made no move to get up off the sofa. 'Emma – I'm so glad you're here – I need to tell you – Noah – Noah and I have decided—Listen, why don't you sit down a moment?'

They want me to move out of the cottage, I thought. Well, I can't blame them for wanting their own space. I sat down on the nearest armchair.

'Noah and I,' Lizzie said, 'have decided that living together simply isn't working out. We're no longer a couple.'

'*What?*' I said. 'I don't understand.'

'We've both tried to make it work,' Lizzie said, 'but since Noah moved into the cottage, all we do is get on each other's nerves. You must have noticed.'

'I know you don't always agree on everything,' I said, recalling Lizzie's thinly veiled irritation at some of Noah's pronouncements on the subject of pregnancy, 'but I thought you were solid.'

'We were fine when we were dating,' Lizzie said, 'but we'd never talked about living together. Not until I found out I was pregnant. We were nowhere near that stage in our relationship. Thinking we could make a go of it was a huge mistake.'

I pictured Lizzie and Noah as I'd seen them so often, her smiling up at him, Noah bending over her to kiss the top of her head.

'I can't believe I'm hearing this,' I said. 'Did something happen tonight while I was out? Did you have a huge row?'

'No,' Lizzie said. 'Not a row. Noah mentioned that Shane had asked him to ask me if I'd help paint the scenery for *Romeo and Juliet*, but Noah had told him I was doing too much for the summer show already, what with all the sewing. I told Noah that he'd no right to say that, and what I did with my time was up to me. And then he was saying that he didn't think he could do this any more, that he couldn't go on living in my cottage pretending that everything was fine between us, and I was saying that I felt the same. We decided it was best if we called it a day.'

I stared at her in shock. 'But this makes no sense,' I said. 'I've seen the way you look at each other – the way you are together. You love him.'

'I – I do care about him,' Lizzie said, 'but if we carry on living under the same roof, we're going to end up hating each other.'

'He's your baby's father—'

'I am aware of that, Emma,' Lizzie said. 'He can still be involved in bringing up our child as much as he wants. Just because we're not together it doesn't mean that we can't be good parents.'

'Where is Noah anyway?' I said. 'Is he upstairs?'

'No,' Lizzie said. 'Once we'd decided it was over between us, he wanted to leave straight away. He packed a bag and went to Jake's place.'

Jake. He would have to interfere, I thought. Aloud, I said, 'OK, so he's staying at Jake's tonight—'

'I think he'll be there for a while. He's coming back for the rest of his stuff tomorrow.'

'Then tomorrow,' I said, 'when you've both calmed down, you need to talk to him and get this sorted out.'

'I'm perfectly calm,' Lizzie said, 'and there's nothing to *sort out*. It's not like we're married. Fortunately.'

I remembered coming across Noah gravely studying the workings of the washing machine on his first morning in the cottage, his determination to do all he could to support Lizzie through her pregnancy, the way his eyes lit up whenever he talked about her. I thought, he adores her.

'Don't do this, Lizzie,' I said. 'Noah's one of the good ones. Don't give up on him.'

'He's a kind man,' Lizzie said, 'and I'm sure he'll make a good father, but I can't be in a relationship with him.'

'*The course of true love never did run smooth.*'

Lizzie raised her eyebrows. 'That's from *A Midsummer Night's Dream*, isn't it?'

'Yes, it is,' I said.

'And you're quoting Shakespeare because?'

'What I'm saying is that you and Noah have hit a rough patch, but you can get through it. Shakespeare's saying the same thing, but in blank verse.'

207

Lizzie sighed. 'Noah and I aren't lovers in a Shakespeare comedy, Emma. We've not lost each other in the woods, and we're not going to be re united by Oberon, king of the fairies, for a wedding in the final scene.' Yawning, she got slowly to her feet. 'Anyway, I really need to get to bed.'

I decided there was no use in trying to talk some sense into her tonight. 'Me too,' I said, 'but the pregnant lady gets first turn in the bathroom.'

'You're a good friend, Emma,' Lizzie said, with the shadow of her usual smile. 'I'll see you tomorrow. At rehearsal, if not before.'

'Goodnight,' I said. This is just *wrong*, I thought. Lovers don't break up because of a disagreement about *sewing*.

Lizzie went out of the room, and I heard her footsteps going upstairs. I waited until I heard her come out of the bathroom and go into her bedroom, and then I fished my mobile out of my bag and called Noah's number. His phone rang and rang, but finally he answered.

'Noah,' I said, 'I'm sorry if I woke you up – I know it's late – but I had to call.'

'I wasn't asleep,' Noah said. 'I'm guessing you've spoken to Lizzie? You know we're no longer together?'

'Ye-es,' I said. 'I'm so sorry, Noah.'

'Don't be,' Noah said. 'I'm not, and neither is she.'

'I don't believe that,' I said. 'Whatever's gone wrong between you and her, you need to talk to her and put it right.'

There was a long silence on the other end of the line, and then Noah said, 'That isn't going to happen, Emma. I know you and Lizzie are best friends, and you've shared her cottage for years, but I find her impossible to live with. I've tried so hard, I really have, but nothing I do is right. Tonight, she told me that ever since I moved into the cottage she's felt *smothered*, when all I've done since she told me she was pregnant is try to take care of her. I've had enough.'

'Won't you at least *try* talking to her?' I said.

'There's no point,' Noah said.

208

I decided that I wasn't above guilt-tripping him, if it got him back with Lizzie. 'For goodness' sake, Noah, Lizzie isn't just some girl on a week's holiday in the caravan park who you've chatted up in the Armada. She's the *mother of your child.*'

'I'm not *abandoning* her, if that's what you're thinking,' Noah said. 'When the baby's born, I'll be as much of a hands-on father as I possibly can. And I've every intention of supporting my child financially.' He paused. 'Listen, Emma, I'm sure you mean well, and I appreciate your concern, but all this is really just between me and Lizzie. And I have to go to work tomorrow.'

'Yes, of course you do, but—'

'Goodnight, Emma,' Noah said, and rang off before I could reply.

Well, I tried, I thought. An image drifted into my mind, a scene from my school production of *A Midsummer Night's Dream.* Me as Titania, lying on a bank of fake grass under painted trees, Jake as my jealous lord, chanting a spell:

'What thou seest when thou dost wake/Do it for thy true love take.'

Sadly, unlike Oberon, I didn't have access to magic that would mend a lovers' quarrel.

Chapter Thirty-one

'I hope you've got your ticket for *Romeo and Juliet*,' I said to Carol, as she handed me my change.

'Not yet,' Carol said. 'I have to be honest with you, love, but I may give the Players' summer show a miss this year. I'm not that into Shakespeare. I did *Twelfth Night* for O level and I never understood it.'

'Watching a Shakespeare play performed on stage is very different to reading it in school,' I said, trying not to sound too desperate. The Downland's waitress I'd sat next to on the bus home after work had also told me she'd yet to buy a ticket. 'I'm sure you'll enjoy it if you come.'

'I'll think about it,' Carol said.

Aware that the queue at the till was stretching half way round the supermarket, rather than continuing the conversation, I contented myself with reminding Carol that tickets for the Thursday performance of *Romeo and Juliet*, and the Saturday matinee, were half the price of those for Friday and Saturday night, and went on my way.

It had been stiflingly hot all day, but now, as I left the supermarket's air-conditioned interior and started walking along the high street with a heavy bag of shopping in each hand, I became aware of just how humid it was, and that there was an eerie, almost green cast to the evening light. I glanced up at the sky. It was clear, no sign of cloud, but knowing how quickly that could change, I thought it likely that the exceptionally warm weather of the last few weeks was about to break.

By the time I turned into Saltwater Lane, I could feel sweat trickling down my back. Kicking off my shoes, I went into the kitchen. The back door was open, and I could see Lizzie sitting in the mottled light and shade under the apple tree, leaning against the trunk, her head bent over a length of red fabric, her hand rising and falling as she sewed. Calling out that I was home, I put away my shopping, and as it was too hot to even think about cooking, set about making myself a sandwich. Carrying my plate and an ice-cold can of cola from the fridge, I went out into the garden and sat down on the grass next to Lizzie.

'Another costume?' I said. 'I thought you'd done them all.'

'This is a banner for the Capulets' ballroom,' Lizzie said. 'Pamela brought the material round earlier when she collected the dresses I shortened, and Romeo's doublet. Don't tell—'

'Don't tell …?' I said.

'I was going to say "don't tell Noah", but it doesn't matter. Now that he no longer lives here at the cottage, I don't need to have his permission before I agree to do a bit of sewing for the Players.'

But he should be living here at the cottage, I thought, and all he was trying to do was look out for you, even if he got it wrong. I nearly said as much to Lizzie, but bit back the words for fear of making things worse between her and Noah than they already were.

It had been disquieting these last few days to get up and go off to the Downland without encountering Noah in the kitchen, mug of morning coffee in his hand, muttering that he was running behind schedule. The cottage seemed unnaturally silent now that I no longer heard his heavy tread on the stairs. At some point on Monday, while Lizzie and I were at work, he'd let himself in, collected his clothes and other belongings, and gone again, leaving his front door key on the kitchen table, a gesture that had made me sad, but had apparently left Lizzie unmoved. At rehearsal that evening, when they weren't acting in the same scene, they'd ignored one another. It had been the same at yesterday's rehearsal, and afterwards in the Armada, where they'd sat in the beer garden at opposite ends of a long table. I'd sat midway between them, assuring Eddie he didn't need to apologise because yet again he'd forgotten his lines in the scenes we'd worked on at the weekend, all the while wondering how I might make Lizzie and Noah see sense. When she and I were walking home along Shore Road, I'd spotted Noah walking a few yards ahead of us, and I'd increased my pace with the intention of inveigling him into the cottage. Unfortunately, my hopes that he and Lizzie, if forced into proximity, would make up over a coffee and her home-made biscuits, were dashed when he'd crossed over to the other side of the street. Lizzie and I'd turned down Saltwater Lane, and Noah had continued walking towards the beach and Jake's house …

'Don't you agree, Emma?'

'What?' I said. 'Sorry, Lizzie. I was miles away.'

'I was saying that it's been unbearably muggy today, and I've seen any number of seagulls flying inland. I think we're in for a storm.'

'It's certainly getting darker,' I said. Looking up at the sky I saw that it was beginning to cloud over. The branches of the apple tree stirred uneasily.

'That's the hem tacked up,' Lizzie said, breaking off her thread. 'I'm going inside before it rains.' Even as she spoke, I heard the rumble of distant thunder.

We both went inside the cottage. Lizzie set up her sewing machine on the kitchen table, and began hemming the Capulets' banner. I left her to it, and still feeling unpleasantly clammy, took myself off to have a shower.

By the time I came back downstairs again, refreshed, wearing my kimono over my thinnest pyjamas, and armed with my laptop, on which I was intending to google monologues suitable for drama school auditions, the wind was rising, and the sky was obscured by towering clouds the colour of graphite. Lizzie was still sitting at the table, now working her way through a pile of her Year 2s' exercise books. Again, I heard thunder.

'It's getting closer,' I said, sitting down opposite her.

She nodded distractedly, and wrote something in the book in front of her on the table. 'I've just marked your nephew Albie's maths,' she said. 'He's got every question right. I think he deserves a star for that.' Selecting an ink stamp from several on the table, she stamped Albie's book.

'Go, Albie,' I said. Lizzie picked another exercise book off the top of the pile, and continued with her marking. I switched on my laptop, typed 'female monologues auditions' into my browser, and began wading through the numerous websites that came up.

A sudden gust of wind caused the back door to slam shut, making both me and Lizzie jump. I glanced at the window. All light had faded from the sky, leaving it the colour of ink.

'It's not like you to work at home,' Lizzie said, nodding at my laptop.

'This isn't work,' I said. 'I'm researching audition pieces.'

'Ah,' Lizzie said. She picked up her pen and then put it down again. 'I have my first ultrasound scan next week.'

'Ooh – exciting.' I smiled.

'Do you think I should ask Noah to go with me?' Lizzie said.

'Of course,' I said. 'He'd want to be there – no question. I remember Scarlet saying that Nathan cried when he first saw the image of a baby on the screen, although he denies it.'

'I suppose it'd be wrong to deny Noah that special moment,' Lizzie said.

'Yes, it would,' I said.

'It's just that I don't want him fussing over me,' Lizzie said. 'Or thinking that I want him back.'

'As you threw him out of your cottage,' I said, 'I'm sure he's got the message.' I probably shouldn't have said that, I thought. 'Sorry, that came out wrong.'

'Noah's leaving was a mutual decision,' Lizzie said.

'That doesn't mean it was the right decision,' I said. 'I know you two have had your differences, but I honestly think that you can still make your relationship work. If you'd only try.' Outside, rain started to fall, huge droplets spattering against the window panes.

'Noah is impossible to live with,' Lizzie said.

'In his opinion, so are you,' I said, 'but as I've shared a cottage with both of you, I have to disagree.'

'You've spoken to Noah about me?' Lizzie said. 'I thought you'd be on my side.'

'There aren't any *sides.*' I shut my laptop. 'All I want is for the pair of you to get back together.'

'Don't you dare tell me that Noah and I should stay together for the sake of the baby,' Lizzie said.

'I'm not saying that.'

'What do you know about being a couple?' Lizzie said. 'You've never stayed with a guy longer than a few weeks.'

'We're not discussing my love life right now,' I said, 'we're talking about you and Noah.'

'In the last ten years, you've not had one long-term serious relationship,' Lizzie said. 'And I know why.'

'What are you getting at?'

'For you, no one can ever measure up to Jake,' Lizzie said, as the sky was split by lightning.

'That's ridiculous,' I said. The rain was coming down in cascades now, lashing against the windows, driven by the wind. There was a roar of thunder.

'It's true.' Lizzie's voice rose to a shriek. 'You can't keep away from him. You're still in love with him.' There was another flash of lightning.

'*No.*' I said, 'I did love him, but not any more.' My voice was shrill above the clash of thunder and the howling wind. 'Now I can't stand to be in the same room as him.'

A flash of lightning that briefly illuminated the kitchen as bright as day, was followed by a thunderclap directly overhead. A screeching and crashing came from the garden and a loud thud. Then the electric light went out, plunging us into darkness as black as pitch.

214

'W-what was that?' Lizzie said.

'I've no idea,' I said, shakily. I got to my feet and peered out of the window above the sink. 'It's too dark to see anything. There are no lights anywhere.' Feeling my way along the wall, I tried switching the kitchen light switch off and on again, and the switch just outside the kitchen in the hall. 'I think there's a power cut.' There was another flash of lightning and a crack of thunder.

'I'm going to take a look outside,' Lizzie said. I heard the sound of a chair scraping back, and then a beam of torchlight from her phone cut through the darkness.

'I'll get our coats,' I said. With Lizzie aiming her phone to light my way, I fetched our raincoats and our boots from the hall. Dressed to face the storm, I opened the back door. Lizzie, standing next to me, shone the phone out into the garden. All I could see was falling rain, sheets of it, as though we were shining the torchlight through a waterfall, and beyond the rain, leaves and branches. Then lightning lit up the garden just long enough to show us the apple tree, uprooted, fallen on the grass. The wind turned, driving rain into the cottage, its ferocity making us stagger back inside, clutching at each other for support. Lizzie tried to close the door but the wind tore it from her grasp. I seized the handle and wrestled it shut, as thunder shook the sky. For a moment, we stood in silence, both of us shivering and dripping rain onto the flagstones.

'The tree – did you see it?' Lizzie said. She sounded as though she was about to cry.

'I saw it,' I said.

'I loved reading a book under that tree,' Lizzie said.

'Me too,' I said.

'I can't remember a worse summer,' Lizzie said.

Realising that water was running down my neck inside my coat, I said, 'I'm freezing. I'm going to get a jumper.'

'Would you get my blue cardigan for me?' Lizzie said. 'It's on my bed. Take my phone.'

I returned our wet coats to the hooks in the hall, ran upstairs, retrieved a warm jumper and my phone from my room, and

Lizzie's cardigan from hers, and went back down to the kitchen. In my absence, Lizzie had lit a candle, and was sitting at the table in its soft glow. I sat down opposite her.

'I'm sorry I shouted at you,' Lizzie said. 'I don't know what came over me.'

'I'm sorry *I* shouted.' I ventured a smile. 'But I meant what I said about you and Noah.' To my consternation, Lizzie's eyes filled with tears.

'I miss him,' she said. 'I never thought I would, but I do.' She rubbed her eyes with the heel of her hand. 'It was all going so well before I got pregnant and he moved into the cottage. I thought we'd be fine, but it was too much, too soon.'

I thought, she loves him, I know she does. 'You and Noah can work things out,' I said. 'At least you can try.'

'It's too late,' Lizzie said. 'I've lost him.'

Lightning flickered across the night sky. After almost half a minute, we heard the thunder roll.

'The storm's moving away,' Lizzie said. 'I'm going to try and get some sleep.' She stood up and went to the door. Standing in the open doorway, she said, 'Emma, I meant what *I* said about you and Jake. For you, he's always been the one.'

'Maybe he was,' I said. 'But I feel nothing for him now. And he cares nothing for me.'

'Are you sure about that?' Lizzie said.

'He's back with his girlfriend,' I said. 'So, yes, I'm sure.'

'Then why is he still here in South Quay?' Lizzie said. Before I could frame an answer, she headed off upstairs. Outside, the rain continued to fall.

There was, I thought, still a chance for Lizzie and Noah, but not for Jake and me. He was no longer my friend, he was no longer a part of my life. What he did, who he was with, was no concern of mine.

Suddenly, I felt very tired. Switching on the torch on my phone, I picked up my laptop, blew out the candle, and took myself up to bed.

Chapter Thirty-two

I drew back my bedroom curtains, looked down into the garden, and gasped in dismay at the sight of the stricken apple tree, the smashed pots strewn on the grass, the broken panels in the wooden fence, and the flowers flattened by the wind and rain. The storm had blown itself out during the night, but grey clouds still scudded across the sky. Shivering in the cold air, I quickly washed and dressed, and went downstairs to the kitchen. To my relief the power had come back on, and I immediately switched on the kettle and put two pieces of bread in the toaster.

Lizzie hadn't appeared downstairs by the time I'd finished my breakfast, so I made her a mug of tea, and had just set foot on the stairs to take it up to her when the doorbell rang. Still holding the mug, I opened the front door. Noah, his shoulders hunched, his hands in the pockets of his jacket, was standing on the doorstep. Jake was standing behind him, halfway down the path.

'Er, morning, Emma,' Noah said.

'Hello, Noah.'

'I – we – came to see if Lizzie – and you – were OK,' Noah said. 'It was a rough night.'

'It was,' I said, 'but we survived. Lizzie's garden's a mess though.' From behind me, I heard footsteps. I turned to see Lizzie running down the stairs, her hair unbrushed, barefoot, and wearing only a thin cotton nightdress.

'Emma, have you looked outside?' she said. I stepped aside so

217

that she could see who I was talking to. 'Oh – Noah – it's you. You're here.'

'Lizzie,' he said. 'I came – I wanted – I want—'

'You came back.'

'Yes.'

Lizzie stared at him for a moment, and then she said, 'The storm brought down the apple tree.' She turned and headed off into the kitchen. Noah glanced at me.

'After you,' I said, gesturing towards the back of the cottage. With a grateful smile, he went after Lizzie, and I trailed after both of them.

Lizzie opened the kitchen door, and stepped out into the garden. Noah followed her, and they stood side by side surveying the destruction wrought by the storm. I hovered in the doorway.

'It's ruined,' Lizzie said. She turned to look at Noah, and I saw a tear running down her face. His eyes on hers, he took off his jacket and placed it around her shoulders.

'We can fix it,' he said.

'It'll never be the same,' Lizzie said. 'My beautiful garden is gone.'

'You and I can make it beautiful again,' Noah said.

'Can we?' Lizzie said.

'We can plant a tree and flowers,' Noah said, 'and together we can watch them grow.'

Lizzie burst out crying. Noah reached for her, and folded her in his arms. She buried her face in his chest and sobbed. He stroked her hair, holding her close.

'It'll be OK, Lizzie,' he murmured. 'We'll be OK.'

Time for me to exit the stage, I thought, backing into the kitchen, and quietly closing the door. The clock on the dresser informed me that it was also time for me to go and catch my bus. I suspected that Lizzie might be a little late for work, but as she'd never been late before or taken a day off in her entire teaching career to date, I reckoned her colleagues could cover for her for once. Realising I was still clutching her mug of tea, I drank it, retrieved my bag from the chair where I'd left it, collected my coat from the hall, and went out the front door. And to my irritation, saw Jake sitting on the garden wall. His back was towards me, but he must have heard me, because he swung around and watched me as I stalked down the path, trampling on broken sunflowers and delphiniums, and out onto the street.

'Hey, Emma,' Jake said. 'Are Lizzie and Noah all right in there?' He nodded towards the cottage. Much as I would have liked to walk straight past him, it seemed churlish not to reply. He was their friend, if not mine.

'They will be,' I said.

'That's good to hear,' he said, getting to his feet.

'I think they could do with some time on their own,' I said, quickly.

'Don't worry, I'm not about to interrupt whatever it is they're doing,' Jake said, with a grin that set my teeth on edge. 'I only tagged along with Noah on the off-chance that there actually was some storm damage to the cottage that he needed my help to repair. I was going to give him another ten minutes to come out and request my services as a handyman's apprentice, and then I was heading off.' He added, 'Are you on your way to the Downland?'

'Yes. And if I don't get a shift on, I'm going to miss my bus.' I turned away from him and started walking towards Shore Road. To my astonishment, he fell into step beside me. I stopped walking. 'Why are you still here, Jake?'

'I told you,' he said, 'I came with Noah.'

'Now. Why are you here with me *now*?' I said.

'We're both walking in the same direction,' he said. 'You're walking to the bus stop, I'm going to the supermarket.'

Oh, for goodness' sake, I thought, is the wretched man deliberately trying to annoy me? I continued walking, turning into Shore Road, my eyes widening when I saw the amount of storm debris – broken branches, roof tiles, sodden newspapers – that littered the pavement. With Jake still walking doggedly beside me, I rounded the corner into the high street – and froze on the spot. In front of us, one of the many parked cars had been crushed by a fallen tree, which a band of local council workmen in high-vis jackets were now attacking with chainsaws. On the other side of the road, the bus shelter was no longer standing, but as if thrown by a giant hand, had smashed through the window of the hairdressers, which was now a heap of shattered glass, wood and metal. Two more workmen were setting up a bright orange mesh security barrier to cordon off the pavement outside, while instructing passers-by to keep well back.

'Oh. My. God,' I said. 'I hope no one was hurt.'

Jake said, '*Things that love the night/Love not such nights as these/ Such sheets of fire, such bursts of horrid thunder.*'

'*King Lear*,' I said, automatically. '*Such groans of roaring wind and rain, I never—*' I broke off. The time when I'd have been happy to recite Shakespeare with Jake Murray had long passed. 'I have to get to work.' I marched along the pavement to my bus stop, which had fortunately survived the carnage. Gazing along the high street, hoping to see the bus approaching, I spotted Scarlet walking from the direction of the school, holding Harrison by the hand, Albie and Kyle trotting beside her, chatting with several other mothers also shepherding children of varying ages. When she saw me, she left the other women, and crossed over the road to join me.

'Hello, Emma,' she said. 'Oh, there's Jake.' She raised her voice. 'Hey, Jake.'

I turned my head to see Jake standing a few yards away, observing the activity outside the hairdressers. Hearing his name, he strolled over to me and my sister. I shifted my stance so I didn't have to look at him.

'Morning, Scarlet,' he said.

'Jake!' Kyle said.

'Hello, Jake,' Albie said. 'We're going to the beach.'

''Lo, Jake,' Harrison said.

'Hey, guys,' Jake said, giving each of the boys a high five. He was good with kids, I'd give him that, but I couldn't help wishing that my nephews had greeted him with a little less enthusiasm.

'No school today?' I said to Scarlet.

'The school's closed,' Scarlet said. 'The storm lifted half the slates off the roof last night, and the headmistress is worried that the other half could come down on a child's head. Fortunately, I've a day off today. Nathan's still trying to get to work.'

'Trying?' I said.

'The coast road's blocked by fallen trees,' Scarlet said.

'Whereabouts?' I said. 'I have to get to the Downland.'

'No chance,' Scarlet said. 'The word at the school gates is that there won't be any buses running until this afternoon at the earliest. Nathan went by car, but he had to turn off the main road. He's making his way inland, trying to find a way around. Last time he phoned, he'd only got as far as Upper Teyford.'

'Oh, Lord,' I said. 'I'd better let Eve know I'm going to be late.' I took my mobile out of my bag.

'I should crack on too,' Scarlet said. 'I thought I'd do something educational with the kids today – a bit of beachcombing maybe, to see what the storm's left behind – but we'll probably end up playing football. We usually do.' She smiled at Jake, and I winced as she added, 'You and Emma must come over to dinner one night. See you both soon.' She made as if to go, but then turned back. 'I guess you've not heard about the community centre?'

'What about it?' I said.

'It was struck by lightning last night. Everyone at the school was talking about it!'

I gaped at her. 'No!'

'I'm afraid so,' Scarlet said.

'Is there much damage?' Jake said.

She shrugged. 'Flora told me it's burnt to the ground, but I think that's highly unlikely with all that rain, don't you? Flora always exaggerates.' Ushering her sons before her, she continued on her way. I stared after her, unable to get my head around what she'd said. And what it could mean for *Romeo and Juliet*.

221

'Are you coming?' Jake said.

'Where?' I said.

'I'm going to the community centre,' Jake said. 'I want to see for myself what's happened. I assume you do too.'

Was there no getting rid of him this morning? 'Obviously I do,' I said. Not with you, though, I thought. 'But first I need to speak to my boss.' Turning my back on him, I rang Eve's number at the Downland, leaving a voice message when I got no answer. Ending the call, I spun around to see Jake still there, now talking to Zoe, who was dressed in a tracksuit and carrying a sports holdall.

'You know about the community centre, then, Emma?' Zoe said. 'Isn't it dreadful? I'm on my way there now, but from what I've heard, I won't be teaching Zumba this morning.'

She and Jake started walking, and it seemed to me that unless I wanted Zoe to think me extremely odd, I'd no option but to go with them.

Chapter Thirty-three

'The sirens woke me up late last night,' Sofia said. 'I looked out of my bedroom window, but I couldn't see a fire.'

'I saw the fire engines hurtling along the high street,' Eddie said, 'but it never occurred to me that they were going to the community centre.'

Richard drained his beer and set the glass down on the table. 'So this is how it ends,' he said. 'The final curtain comes down before the show even opens.'

I thought, *For never was a story of more woe/Than this of Juliet and her Romeo.*

My gaze travelled over the downcast faces of my friends – Zoe, sitting next to me, Richard on her other side, Sofia sitting across from me, next to Eddie and Henry, who were morosely sipping their pints, Gail squashed in beside them – and came to rest on Jake, sitting on a chair he'd dragged over to the booth, at the end of the table. His eyes met mine and I quickly looked away.

I'd arrived at the community centre with Jake and Zoe to find that many of my friends and neighbours, including a number of *Romeo and Juliet*'s cast, and members of other groups who used the main hall, alerted by rumour and Facebook posts, had got there before me, and were clustered on the pavement in front of a high metal security gate that had been erected across the entrance to the car park. Tied to the fence was a large notice emblazoned with the words 'Danger. Do Not Enter.' Gail, brandishing her press card, was talking to two men, one in overalls, the other in a suit, both wearing hard hats. A gaggle of teenagers, presumably unable to get to high school in Teymouth, were posing by the fence taking photos. I'd jostled my way to the front of the crowd and peered through the fence's metal bars, gasping with dismay when I saw the jagged hole where the roof had been over the community centre's main hall, and the charred pile of rubble which was all that remained of the office, the changing rooms, and the stage. Sick to my stomach, I'd turned away, and found myself face to face with Henry, who'd informed me that he and a few others were going to the Armada, and invited me to join them. It was, I'd thought, a little early in the day for a consoling glass of wine, but wanting to give Lizzie and Noah more time alone in the cottage, I'd accompanied my friends to the pub, and bought myself a coffee. If I'd known that Jake was included in Henry's invitation, I'd have gone home regardless.

The Armada was more than usually crowded for the time of day, with locals unable to get to work and holidaymakers reluctant to spend a morning on the beach under a lowering sky, their conversation all of the storm, the flooded caravan park, a garden shed flattened by the wind, heartfelt praise for the emergency services, relief that no one was injured, speculation as to when the hairdressers would reopen, and the loss of the community centre. It'd been Maurice, coming into the pub with Pamela, and having seen her seated at a table for two, who'd stopped by our booth on his way to the bar, and had confirmed what we'd already guessed: that for the first time in the Players' ninety-year history, there was no option but to cancel the summer show.

I glanced across the room to the table where Maurice and Pamela were still sitting. He was talking earnestly, and downing his fourth whisky, judging by the number of glasses lined up in front of him. She appeared to be listening to him without interruption, which also had to be a first.

Richard said, 'Months of rehearsal, and all for nothing.'

'And with only fourteen days before opening night,' Zoe said.

'It would have been my first time on stage,' Sofia said. 'I can't tell you how disappointed I am.'

You and me both, I thought. *A glooming peace this morning with it brings/The sun for sorrow will not show his head.*

'There'll be other Players' shows, Sofia,' Eddie said.

'Not for a very long time,' Richard said. 'The community centre isn't going to get rebuilt overnight.'

Until then Jake hadn't entered into the conversation, but now he said, 'Am I missing something here? I don't understand why you have to cancel *Romeo and Juliet.*'

I thought, what's it to him? 'We no longer have a theatre,' I said, 'that seems like a good enough reason to cancel a show to me.'

'You could consider performing at another venue,' Jake said. I rolled my eyes. Seriously? If there had been any other suitable building in South Quay in which to put on a play, did he imagine the Players wouldn't have thought of it? He was so up himself.

'Like where?' Sofia said, eagerly. Oh, please, I thought, don't encourage him.

'Our cast signed up for the *summer show,*' Zoe said. 'If we're going to keep everyone on board, we need to find an alternative venue fast. People do have other commitments.'

'Yeah,' Eddie said, 'and I can't face rehearsing that flippin' bird scene much longer.'

'Not that I've set foot in the place since I was eleven,' Henry said, 'but what about the school hall?'

'You obviously don't remember it,' Richard said. 'It's far too small.'

'I was thinking of the Downland Hotel,' Jake said. Everyone at the table looked at me.

'Oh, I don't think so,' I said. 'All the Downland function rooms are booked up months ahead—' I broke off as a thought struck me. 'That is, they're fully booked at weekends. But there are no events booked on weekdays for the next fortnight. As far as I know.' I pictured the ballroom, with its lighting and sound system, its numerous side-doors that we could use for our entrances and exits, and its space for five hundred guests. I imagined the red and gold chairs we used for weddings set out in rows ... 'I guess, if we performed during the week, we might be able to use the ballroom.'

Jake said, 'Hold that thought. There's someone else who needs to listen to this.' Pushing back his chair, he went over to Pamela and Maurice. After a brief conversation, they stood up and came back to our table with him, carrying their drinks. Pamela took Jake's chair, and he pulled up a couple of stools for him and Maurice.

'So, we were discussing the Players' summer show,' Jake said, 'and Emma's come up with something you'll want to hear.'

'There isn't going to be a summer show,' Pamela said, in a monotone.

Maurice put his hand on her arm. 'They're all aware of that,' he said. 'I told them.'

'That such a thing should happen on my watch,' Pamela said. 'The Players have never cancelled a show before. Never.'

'We may not have to cancel this one,' Henry said. 'Emma's suggested that we perform *Romeo and Juliet* in the ballroom at the Downland.'

'It's such a wonderful idea,' Sofia said, her eyes shining. 'I've never been inside the Downland Hotel, but I hear it's fabulous.'

'What do you think, Pamela?' I said.

'No – we c-can't do the play – n-not at the Downland,' Pamela said, visibly agitated. 'I'm sorry.'

I thought, when did Chairwoman Pamela ever apologise for anything? I remembered that she'd been performing in the community centre for the last forty years. It was, I supposed, no wonder if the shock of its destruction had hit her hard.

'I realise it wouldn't be the same as performing on our usual stage,' I said, 'but I'm sure we could make it work.'

Pamela slowly shook her head. 'It's not – it's not p-possible,' she stuttered. 'I wouldn't know where to begin.'

226

Maurice cleared his throat. 'I know you mean well, Emma,' he said, 'but the Players aren't in a financial position to pay for the use of the ballroom or any other room at the hotel. What with the hire of costumes, printing the tickets, the fee we pay to the community centre ... I could go on, but let's just say that the cost of putting on our productions is astronomical, and it rises every year. Even with a sell-out show like last year's pantomime, we barely break even. We don't have the funds to cover the Downland's charges for room hire.'

'Everything was in the community centre,' Pamela said, her voice now scarcely above a whisper. 'We've lost all of it. Even the programmes ...'

'We've spent a small fortune on *Romeo and Juliet*,' Maurice said, 'and given what's happened, we're unlikely to recoup any of it. We're going to have to refund the money already paid to us for tickets.' He hesitated, swallowed a mouthful of whisky, and ploughed on, 'I have to tell you that the future of the Players is in doubt. Our financial situation is such that we may have no choice but to disband the society.'

Gasps all round the table were followed by a stunned silence. I became aware that my mouth had fallen open, and shut it.

Gail leant forward. 'Let's get this perfectly clear, Maurice,' she said. 'Are you saying that the South Quay Players are going to declare themselves *bankrupt*?' I saw that she'd opened her bag and taken out her reporter's notebook.

'It may not come to that,' Maurice said. 'But we can't continue as we are, getting further into debt.'

'All the more reason for the society to perform *Romeo and Juliet* at the Downland,' Jake said, causing everyone to swivel round to look at him.

'Have you not been listening to Maurice?' Richard said. 'The Players can't hire a room at the Downland. *We have no money.*'

'What if the hotel let you perform there for free?' Jake said.

'Why would they do that?' Richard said.

'Good PR,' Jake said. 'For a high-profile business like the

Downland to help out a local group like the Players – to assist victims of the storm that's caused so much damage – can only be good for its relationship with its customers and its staff, most of whom are drawn from the local community. Isn't that right, Emma?'

'Ye-es,' I said. 'Actually, we do occasionally let people use the function rooms for free for charity events.'

'The South Quay Players aren't a charity,' Richard said.

'But we are an asset to the life of the village,' I said. 'Our shows bring the whole community together. And our future is under threat.' I thought rapidly. *Romeo and Juliet's* planned opening night was the last Thursday in July – and there were no events booked on that date. 'Even if the Downland's management will only give us the ballroom for one night, it would mean the show can go on. Let me call my boss and run it by her.' I reached for my mobile.

'Hang on a sec,' Richard said. 'We can't just walk into a ballroom and start spouting our lines in front of an audience. We'll need time to do a run-through at least.'

'Ask for two days, Emma,' Jake said. 'That'll give you time for one rehearsal and one performance.'

I shot him a look, irritated that I hadn't thought of this myself. 'Yes, I will,' I said.

'What'll we do for costumes?' Zoe said, suddenly. 'The ones we had are all buried under the ruins of the community centre. Along with the props and scenery.'

'Do the play in modern dress,' Jake said, 'and with minimalist scenery.'

I picked up my phone and brought up my contacts.

'Wait, Emma,' Richard said, 'there's no point in you asking the hotel for a performance space if the Players don't have an audience.'

'Why wouldn't we have an audience?' Sofia said.

'A lot of people in the village have told me that *Romeo and Juliet* isn't a play they particularly want to see,' Richard said.

'Ticket sales haven't been what we'd hoped,' Maurice said.

'We'll sell more tickets on the door,' I said. 'We always do.'

'I disagree,' Richard said. 'People aren't going to drag themselves out to the Downland on a weeknight to watch Shakespeare.'

'They will,' Jake said, 'if I play Romeo.'

The noise of the pub, the talk, the clink of glasses, receded to the edge of my consciousness. The blood started pounding in my head. *No*, I thought, we can save this show, and the Players, without involving Jake Murray.

'We already have a Romeo,' I said. Jake caught my gaze, his eyes boring into mine. Then he turned his head away from me and focused his attention on Eddie.

'I know that this is a huge ask,' he said, 'and in a way, I feel bad for suggesting it, but for the sake of the show, could you bring yourself to step aside and let me take over your role?'

Eddie's face lit up with a broad smile. 'Mate, if you want the part of Romeo, I'm not going to stand in your way. I never wanted it.'

Richard said, 'Now, hold on. No offence, Jake, but the South Quay Players do have rules as to who's eligible to perform in our shows.'

Thank you, Richard, I thought. 'You can't play Romeo, Jake,' I said. 'You're not a member of the society.'

'Oh, hang the rules,' Henry said. 'We're talking *survival* here.'

'I don't have a problem with Jake being in the cast,' Zoe said.

'Neither do I,' Gail said.

'Do you still want that exclusive interview, Gail?' Jake said. 'A mention in the *Chronicle* that the star of *Sherwood* has joined the cast of the South Quay Players' production of *Romeo and Juliet* for one night only would be great publicity for the show. And it wouldn't cost the society anything.'

Gail almost fell off the bench.

'At any other time, I'd say that we couldn't permit a non-member to perform,' Maurice said, 'but in present circumstances, we need to do anything that's going to bring in a paying audience.'

My heart sank. I can't fight this, I thought, I may not like it, but the Players need Jake Murray.

'But, of course,' Maurice went on, 'whether or not Jake takes over as our male lead, is a decision for our director.'

As one, the Players turned towards Pamela, who was sitting slumped in her chair, staring down at the table.

Henry leant forward. 'Mum, are you OK?' he said. At the sound of her son's anxious voice, Pamela looked up with a start, her hands fluttering about her face.

'I – I'm sorry, but I can't do this,' she said, her mouth quivering. 'Not any more. I tried, I really did, but I can't – I can't carry on as director – I don't know what I'm doing – I should never have taken it on. It's all too much for me … You'll have to find another director or the show remains cancelled.'

'You don't mean that,' Henry said.

'I c–can't carry on,' Pamela said. 'Find someone else.' I noticed a film of sweat on her forehead. She really didn't look well.

'There is no one else,' Henry said.

Maurice put his hand over Pamela's. 'Don't upset yourself,' he said. He looked at each of the Players in turn. 'The show's cancelled. I know you'll understand.'

Pamela said, 'I – I'm s–so s–sorry.'

Into the shocked silence that followed, Jake said, 'I'll do it. I'll direct *Romeo and Juliet*.'

Oh, for goodness' sake, I thought, can this day get any worse?

'You mean you'd act *and* direct?' Richard said.

Jake smiled. 'If the Players will have me.'

'Hell, yes,' Eddie said.

Richard frowned, but all he said was, 'I guess some rules are meant to be broken.'

'For Jake to direct would seem the only solution,' Maurice said. 'Don't you agree, Pamela?'

'I – I – yes – th–thank you, Jake,' Pamela said.

I thought, if *Romeo and Juliet* goes ahead – and I want it to go ahead very badly – it will only be because of Jake. *My only love sprung from my only hate.*

'I know how much you've done for this production, Pamela,' Jake said. 'And if we can get ourselves a stage, I'll do everything I can to make a summer show that the South Quay Players can be proud of. I won't let you down.'

I thought, why is he doing this? He despises amateur dramatics.

'Thank you, Jake,' Pamela said. 'I'll let the committee know what we've decided.' Sounding a little more like her old self, she added, 'I'm fairly certain there'll be no objections.'

'Oh, come *on*, Mum,' Henry said, 'the committee always do exactly what you tell them.' With a grin, he added, 'You're our director, Jake, and our male lead. No getting out of it now.' The table erupted, everyone cheering, laughing, all talking at once.

Jake's voice cut through the cacophony. 'So, Emma,' he said. 'We're still in need of a theatre. You'd better make that call to your boss.' He raised his glass, holding it towards me. *'The play's the thing.'*

I have to go along with this, I thought. If I'm to play Juliet, it will be with him as my director and him as my opposite. I don't have any choice. There's no other way to save the show.

The play's the thing.

Jake said, 'Now I come to think of it, as director, I should be making that call.'

Wordlessly, I passed him my phone.

Chapter Thirty-four

'*Draw, if you be men!*' The Capulets and Montagues sprang towards each other. Lacking weapons, they mimed a swordfight, with much waving of arms. Benvolio jumped between the combatants.

'*Part, fools,*' he said. '*Put up your swords; you know not what you do.*'

Richard, as Tybalt, ran into the somewhat cramped performance space – the long through-room in Jake's rented holiday villa – and planted himself firmly centre stage. '*Turn thee, Benvolio; look upon thy death … As I hate hell, all Montagues and thee/ Have at thee, coward.*' He mimed drawing his sword.

'Hold it there,' Jake said. 'We no longer have swords, so we'll need to re-choreograph the fight scenes. I'll schedule a rehearsal. Go from Lord and Lady Capulet's entrance.'

Lizzie, as Lady Capulet, with Maurice, as Lord Capulet, entered stage right. Lord and Lady Montague entered stage left, and *Romeo and Juliet*, Act I, scene i, continued.

My attention wandered from the performers to the other members of the cast – some seated on the benches and sofas that Jake had placed against one wall, some, like me, sat on the floor – to Jake himself. He was sitting astride a chair, arms resting on its back, his gaze fixed unswervingly on his actors.

I thought, what is he getting out of this?

I should not, I supposed, have been surprised that it had taken Jake just one short phone call to persuade Eve of the PR benefits to the Downland of supporting South Quay's local am dram soc. She was, after all, a self-confessed fan of *Sherwood* and Jake himself. An hour or so after he'd first phoned her, an hour during which Pamela had gone home 'to have a bit of a lie-down', and Jake had decided that the ground floor of his house would become our rehearsal studio, Eve had called back to inform him that his request had been approved by Mr Gates himself. The Downland's soon-to-be-retired general manager, a local man, was delighted that the hotel could do something to help the Players, Eve told Jake, having fond memories of their pantomimes, which he'd watched as a child. He'd readily agreed to our having the ballroom for *four* days, which gave us a day each for the get in, the tech, the dress, and our performance.

Our theatre secured, Jake suggested that he, Henry, and I relocate from the Armada to his house – as director, he could use our help with getting up to speed on *Romeo and Juliet*. And for the sake of the show, however much I resented the way he'd insinuated himself into the Players, I knew I had to put my feelings towards him aside and give him my support. At his request, we sent him the videos of rehearsals that we had on our mobiles, and while he watched them, Henry and I rang everyone in the cast to let them know that despite the loss of the community centre, which had put the future of the Players at risk, the show would still be going ahead, that they had a new leading man and a new director, and that he was calling a rehearsal that evening for anyone free to attend at such short notice. Without exception, all the cast had abandoned their planned Friday-night pursuits and turned up, Sofia being one among many citizens of Verona who'd confided to me that they were 'super-excited to be acting on the same stage as Jake Murray'. Pamela, much recovered if a little subdued, had arrived with Maurice, telling anyone available to listen about her executive decision to ask Jake to take over from her as director 'because having such a knowledgeable theatre practitioner in our midst, it seemed to me only sensible to make use of his talents,' which wasn't quite how I remembered the conversation we'd had in the Armada, but in the circumstances, I felt she should be allowed a certain amount of dramatic licence.

Lizzie and Noah had arrived at Jake's house hand in hand, which had made me smile.

'*Once more, on pain of death, depart.*'

At the command of the Prince of Verona, most of the actors exited the performance space, leaving Benvolio to announce the imminent arrival of Romeo. Jake stood up and went to the side of the room – where the wings would be if we were performing on an actual stage – ready to make his entrance.

Richard came and sat down on the floor next to me. 'I hope Jake can pull this off,' he said, pitching his voice so that only I could hear. 'It's a hell of a lot to take on with less than two weeks before the curtain goes up.'

Jake, as Romeo, said, '*Ay me, sad hours seem long.*'

Colin, as Benvolio, said, '*What sadness lengthens Romeo's hours?*'

'*Not having that which makes them short.*'

'*In love?*'

'*Out—*'

'*Of love?*'

'*Out of her favour where I am in love.*' Jake sighed, as if his heart was breaking. I glanced sideways at his audience. He'd only spoken Romeo's first few lines, but all of the Players appeared enraptured.

'I think he'll manage,' I whispered to Richard. The question is, I thought, why would he bother?

'I could've directed this show just as well as Jake,' Richard muttered. 'I should've spoken up when Pamela had her meltdown.' I pretended I hadn't heard him.

Scene i segued seamlessly into scene ii. While Romeo and his friend Benvolio made plans to gatecrash the Capulet's ball, Lizzie, Phyllis, and I went and stood in the wings, ready for the next scene. The Montagues left the stage. Jake returned to his director's chair.

'We won't have the tabs that you're used to at the community centre when we perform at the Downland,' he said. 'So after scene ii, we'll go to a blackout, during which Lady Capulet and the Nurse need to get to their places.' Lizzie and Phyllis went to their opening positions. 'Emma, keep in mind that this is the first time the audience sees Juliet. You need to have their attention the moment you walk on stage.'

As if I didn't know that, I thought.

'And lights up,' Jake said.

Swallowing my irritation, I made my entrance, and the three of us played the scene, Phyllis as always getting a laugh from her audience. Jake, I saw, was smiling.

'Good job, ladies,' he said. 'Emma, your entrance was perfect.' Ridiculously, I felt pleased that I'd managed to impress him.

The rehearsal continued. Romeo and Benvolio arrived at the Capulets' ball, along with Noah as Mercutio. I moved to my position on the opposite side of the stage to Jake who, as Romeo, was about to see Juliet across a crowded room. He would watch me dance, we'd talk, and then we'd kiss … A knot of tension twisted my stomach. With an effort, I made myself breath evenly. I reminded myself that it wasn't me who'd be kissing Jake, but Juliet who'd be kissing Romeo.

Music from Zoe's iPod flooded the room. The guests at the ball went straight into their dance, getting as far as the first turn before Shane stepped the wrong way, causing the front row of dancers to fall into one another like a line of dominos.

'OK, hold it,' Jake said. 'Zoe, could you start the music from the beginning again, please.'

Phyllis, on stage in the ball scene, but not one of the dancers, said, 'Jake, before they go again, I have a suggestion to make about the dancing. I feel we need to change the choreography.'

The room became very quiet. Richard rolled his eyes. Phyllis's friend, Marjorie, vigorously nodded her head. A lot of the cast became very interested in something they'd seen on the floor.

Oh, not this again, I thought, not now. Haven't the Players got enough problems?

Zoe said. 'You're not the choreographer, Phyllis. I am.'

'I know that, Zoe,' Phyllis said. 'I'm only trying to help.'

Jake looked from one of them to the other. 'From what I've seen on video, Zoe,' he said, 'your choreography is extremely good, but if a member of the cast has a suggestion that might make it even better, I need to hear it. What are your thoughts, Phyllis?'

'Zoe's choreography is good,' Phyllis said, causing Zoe to look at her askance, 'but some of our dancers are finding it a little hard to remember. I suggest that we keep the dance as it is for eight bars of music, but with only the older characters dancing. Then the music changes to another track, one of those up-tempo songs young people are so fond of – I believe they call them hip-hop? The older dancers stop dancing. Zoe runs to the centre of the stage and goes into one of her Zumba routines. She's joined by the younger characters, including Juliet, who stand behind her and copy her dance, as they would if they were in one of her classes, so they wouldn't have to learn new choreography. Juliet moves forward and performs a solo. At which point Romeo sees her for the first time.'

'I like it,' Jake said. 'Zoe, it's a huge ask for someone to create new choreography so late in the rehearsal process, but do you think you could make Phyllis's idea work? Now that we're doing the play in modern dress, a Zumba-inspired routine would be a good fit.'

'I could,' Zoe said, 'but I have a suggestion to make as well.'

'Go ahead,' Jake said.

'I want Phyllis in the Zumba routine,' Zoe said. 'She's a brilliant comic actress, and I'm sure that between us, we could come up with a short comedy solo for the Nurse.'

'Some light relief for the audience amongst the passion and the violence on the streets of Verona,' Jake said. 'I'm liking this more and more. Are you comfortable doing a solo, Phyllis?'

'I – Yes, I am,' Phyllis said. She regarded Zoe with an expression that might have been a smile. 'Nothing too lively, mind.'

'Great,' Jake said. 'I'll leave it with the two of you. OK, guys, let's go from the end of the dance.'

I wasn't the only member of the cast to sigh with relief. The

236

Capulets and their guests resumed their places. Tybalt, enraged by the presence of Romeo, stormed off into the wings. The rest of the cast moved upstage, leaving Romeo and Juliet alone in the spotlight, with eyes only for each other.

He held up his hand. '*If I profane with my unworthiest hand ... My lips, two blushing pilgrims, ready stand/To smooth that rough touch with a tender kiss.*'

My hand shook as I placed my palm against his. '*You do wrong your hand too much ...*'

'*Let lips do what hands do.*'

Somehow, I managed to say my next lines, and then he leant in for a kiss. I shut my eyes, trying not to flinch, as his lips lightly brushed mine, reminding myself that I was an actress, that this was acting. My heart was pounding so hard that I felt sure that the entire cast must be able to hear it. I opened my eyes. Jake's eyes gazed tenderly into mine. An image filled my mind, him and me standing on stage in our school hall, the two of us acting in a Shakespeare play for the first time ...

Henry, as prompt, said, '*Then have my lips ...*'

Oh, *no*, I thought, I've missed my line. '*Then have my lips the sin that they have took.*'

'*Sin from my lips? O trespass sweetly urg'd!/Give me my sin again.*' Again, I felt the gentle pressure of Jake's mouth. Breathe, I told myself, just breathe. It's only a stage kiss. Get a grip, Emma.

The ball was over, Romeo left the stage, along with the other actors, giving me time to get myself fully back into character before my next cue.

My bedroom door opened, just a crack, and from the landing, Lizzie said, 'Emma, I saw your light's still on. Can I come in?'

'Sure,' I said. I put aside the book I'd been reading while lying on my bed, and sat up. Lizzie, wearing a bathrobe, came into my bedroom, and perched on the chair by my dressing table.

'Just in case you're wondering,' she said, 'I thought I'd let you know that Noah's moving back into the cottage.'

'I kind of guessed that,' I said, 'what with seeing the two of you going up the stairs and into your room just now.' I smiled. 'I'm very glad you managed to work things out.'

She smiled back. 'He and I talked for *hours* today. Before this summer, we hadn't discussed living together, let alone if we might want children someday. We may have been heading that way, but it was still a huge shock when I found out I was pregnant, a massive change in our lives, and neither of us dealt with it very well, me especially. But now we've talked things through, we know that even if we don't get the whole live-in partner thing right straight away, we'll get there eventually. I love Noah, and he loves me, and when the baby comes, we'll be a family. It's happened sooner than we expected or planned, but that's OK, because we're doing it together.'

'I'm so happy for you, Lizzie,' I said.

'Thank you, Emma,' Lizzie said, smiling. She stood up, as if to go, but then sat down again. 'Noah and I could hardly believe it when we got your email this afternoon. Jake suddenly playing the male lead and directing the summer show? We never saw that coming.'

'No one did,' I said. Briefly, I described to Lizzie the events that had taken place in the Armada Inn.

'Poor Pamela,' Lizzie said. 'I do feel sorry for her. Although I have to say that tonight's rehearsal was the best we've had since George left.'

'Jake knows what he's doing,' I admitted. 'I can't say that I'm overjoyed that I'm forced to share a stage with him and take his direction, but if anyone can fix the show, he can. And as we're all aware, he's a brilliant actor.'

'As are you,' Lizzie said.

'I wasn't so great today,' I said. 'I forgot my lines.'

'Did you?' Lizzie said. 'I thought Henry jumped in too soon with the prompt.'

'No, I blanked,' I said. 'I'm finding it hard to play a love scene with Jake, however good an actor he is.'

'Ah, yes, awkward,' Lizzie said. 'Still, only two weeks 'til opening night, and then you never have to see him again, if you don't want to.' She hesitated, and then she said, 'This may be the Players' last show, so let's enjoy it as much as we can, yeah?'

'I'll do my best,' I said.

Lizzie went back to her room and Noah. I set about getting ready for bed.

All I had to do was get through the next two weeks, do the play, and then I could forget Jake Murray.

Chapter Thirty-five

I followed Lizzie and Noah up from the beach, across Jake's lawn, around his house, and to the front door, which in anticipation of the arrival of the Players for rehearsal, he'd left ajar. Lizzie and Noah went straight inside. I took a deep breath and went after them, and into the room that Jake had designated as our rehearsal space.

We'd left Lizzie's cottage in good time, but most of the cast seemed to have arrived before us. In one corner of the room, Zoe was demonstrating a dance move to Richard, in another corner, Colin and Eddie were circling around each other, both of them holding knives. I presumed that the weapons were fake and that they were practising the stage fight that Jake had choreographed with the male Capulets and Montagues at the weekend. Other Players, many of whom were not required at rehearsal for another hour at least, had already found somewhere to sit, and were chatting animatedly with their fellow cast members. Jake was talking to Shane, but when he saw me, he broke off what he was saying and beckoned me over.

'We're discussing scenery,' Jake said.

'And the fact that we won't have any,' Shane said.

'Actors don't need scenery to perform Shakespeare,' Jake said. 'The scene is described in the words they speak. But I think our audience would be disappointed if they don't see a balcony. It's so iconic.'

'I've suggested we use a scaffold tower,' Shane said, 'which I can provide.'

'Would you be comfortable standing on open scaffolding, Emma?' Jake said. 'It would look good for the street scenes.'

'I'm fine with that.' I pictured scaffolding on a bare stage, actors in the jeans, checked shirts (for the Capulets) and T-shirts (the Montagues) as specified in the costume list that Jake had emailed to the cast. I thought of the red silk banner – all that remained of Lizzie's hours of sewing for the show. 'Scaffolding would help create the right atmosphere for the street scenes,' I said, 'and we could drape it with silk for the ballroom scene.'

'Good idea,' Jake said. 'You get what I'm going for? Gritty and urban for the fight scenes—'

'And an implication of luxury for the Capulets' house,' I said. 'Maybe some branches at the side of the stage to suggest the Capulets' orchard?'

'And a bed that doubles as Juliet's bier,' Jake said. 'That's the set sorted.' He and Shane laughed and I found myself laughing as well. 'Time we got this rehearsal started.'

Raising his voice above the general chatter, Jake called for quiet, and we went straight into the rehearsal of Act II. Romeo concealed himself in the Capulets' orchard. Benvolio and Mercutio failed to find him, and exited stage left. I entered stage right, positioned myself behind the ladder-back chair that was tonight standing in for Shane's scaffolding and Juliet's balcony, and gazed out into the night.

Jake said, '*But, soft! What light through yonder window breaks?/It is the east, and Juliet is the sun …*'

A shiver ran through me. I'd heard Romeo's most famous lines often enough over the last few months, spoken ineptly by Henry and Eddie, but now, as Jake spoke them with all Romeo's love for Juliet, it was as though I was hearing them for the first time.

'*O Romeo, Romeo!*' I said, '*wherefore art thou, Romeo?/Deny thy father and refuse thy name … What's in a name? That which we call a rose/By any other name would smell as sweet …*' I felt all of Juliet's anguish as she talked of the man who should be her enemy, but was the man she loved.

From offstage, the Nurse was heard repeatedly calling for Juliet. The lovers vowed that they would wed. Juliet left the balcony, only to return twice more, unable to tear herself away from Romeo.

'*A thousand times goodnight,*' I said.

Jake said, 'It's not in the text, but I think Romeo and Juliet would kiss at this point.'

'Oh.' I'd been so immersed in Juliet's thoughts and feelings, that it took me a few seconds to come back to myself. I reminded myself that we were *acting*. 'Yes – you're right.'

'When we have our scenery, I'll swing myself over the scaffolding and onto your balcony,' Jake said. Putting one foot on the seat of the chair, he sprang over the back to land next to me on Juliet's balcony, eliciting an intake of breath from our audience. His eyes smouldered with Romeo's passion. Placing his hands on my waist, he briefly kissed my lips, and then he stepped away from me. I – as Juliet – wanted him to stay.

'*Good night, good night,*' I said. '*Parting is such sweet sorrow/That I shall say good night till it be morrow.*' With a lingering look at Romeo, Juliet exited the stage. There was a moment's silence, and then the watching Players gave us a round of applause. Jake and I exchanged smiles.

'Well done, Emma,' he said. Almost light-headed, I went and stood offstage at the side of the room, waiting for my next entrance. I'd forgotten what acting with him could be like, how well we worked together, how good it felt.

He said, 'Moving on to scene iii. Friar Lawrence on stage please …'

The rehearsal continued. Romeo arranged for him and Juliet to be married – without their warring families' knowledge – and was joined on stage by the Nurse in a scene that gave Phyllis another opportunity to show what a terrific comedienne she was. And as I watched Jake moving effortlessly between portraying Romeo and stepping out of character to give direction to the other actors, getting more out of them than they knew they had within them, it came to me that despite everything he'd done to me, everything that had gone wrong between us, I was no longer angry with him. He'd hurt me. I'd said some terrible things to him. That had happened. I might not be able to forget, but I could put it behind me. As Jake, given the way he'd behaved towards me at this rehearsal, was apparently also prepared to do.

'Scene v,' Jake said. 'The Capulets' orchard. Enter Juliet.'

I thought, it's time I let go of the past.

'Emma, I'd like you to get to centre stage quicker than that, please,' Jake said.

Focus, Emma, I thought, as I walked to the centre of the performance space, and into the heat and passion of an afternoon in Verona.

Chapter Thirty-six

'Rehearsals going well?' Carol said, as she swiped my shopping.

'Yes, they are,' I said. 'We're doing a complete run-through of the play today at Jake's house, and then tomorrow we have our get in at the Downland.'

'Get in?'

'It's a theatrical term,' I said. 'It means we're moving our set and props into our theatre.' I started to bag up my purchases.

'That was a lovely interview Jake gave to the *Chronicle*,' Carol went on. 'He said such nice things about South Quay.'

I smiled. In Jake's interview with Gail, which had been in this week's edition of our local paper, he'd spoken at length about how glad he was that *Sherwood*'s shooting schedule had allowed him to return to South Quay for the summer, and that he was pleased to be able to 'give something back' to the village where he was born by appearing with 'our talented local amateur theatre group, who are such a fabulous asset to the community'. Given his stated opinion of amateur dramatics, I'd read that part of the interview twice to make sure I hadn't misunderstood him, but whether or not he truly thought us talented or was good at telling journalists what they wanted to hear, I'd no idea. The paper had been published on Friday, and now, on Sunday morning, there were no copies left in the rack by Carol's till.

'I'd more or less decided I wasn't going to bother with the summer show this year,' Carol went on, 'but now that our Jake's playing Romeo, I thought I might as well put up with a bit of

Shakespeare to see him live on stage, so I've bought tickets for me and Tessa.'

'That's great, Carol,' I said.

The woman standing behind me in the queue, one of Lizzie's colleagues at the primary school, said, 'I'm not a great fan of Shakespeare either, but I'm looking forward to seeing the star of *Sherwood*. It's my favourite TV series.'

The man standing behind her, the owner of the caravan park, said, 'I do like Shakespeare, but seeing it performed by Jake Murray can only be a bonus.'

'Have you sold many tickets?' Carol said.

'We're sold out,' I said, smiling at everyone in the queue.

The Prince of Verona surveyed the scene before him. Romeo and Juliet lay dead, her head resting on his chest. The assembled Capulets, Montagues, and citizens of Verona bowed their heads in grief.

The Prince said, '*For never was a story of more woe/Than this of Juliet and her Romeo.*'

'And blackout,' Jake said. 'You can move now, Emma.' I sat up, and he did the same, swinging his legs over the side of the divan that was Juliet's bier, and springing to his feet. As one, the cast of *Romeo and Juliet* turned to look at him. 'It's been a long day, but we got through it, and through the play—'

Henry called out, 'And without one prompt.' A ripple of laughter spread through the room. The cast visibly relaxed.

Jake grinned, and went on, 'Those of you who are helping with the get in, I'll see you tomorrow night at the Downland. Everyone else, see you at the tech on Tuesday. Well done, everybody. Thank you all very much.'

With a ragged chorus of 'thank *you*,' and some discussion as to who was going to the Armada, the Players began gathering up their belongings, and drifting out of the rehearsal room. I stood up off the divan.

'You did well tonight, Emma,' Jake said.

245

I beamed at him. 'You're not doing too badly yourself,' I said. 'The way you've staged the fight between Tybalt and Mercutio – and your fight with Tybalt – it's terrifying to watch.'

'I told Noah to imagine that Tybalt was the captain of Milton-on-Sea's cricket team,' Jake said. 'It helped him discover Mercutio's motivation.'

I smiled. 'Where did you get the knives?'

'From a website that supplies theatrical weaponry,' Jake said. 'They complement the style of this production better than swords, I think.'

'They're scarily realistic,' I said. 'When Romeo stuck his knife into Tybalt and then twisted his neck to break it, I nearly screamed.'

Jake laughed. 'By the way, would you like a lift to the Downland for the rehearsals and the show? I was thinking it might be a bit crowded in Noah's car with Lizzie, you, and all your costumes.'

'Oh – yes,' I said. 'Thanks, Jake. If you don't mind.'

'Of course I don't mind giving lifts to my friends,' Jake said. He hesitated, and then he added, 'Emma ... I hate that we argued. Are we OK?'

I looked straight into his grey-blue eyes. 'We're good, Jake,' I said. His mouth lifted in a smile. It's as though we've never been anything but friends, I thought.

'In that case,' he said. 'Do you fancy staying for a coffee?'

'Yes, I'd like that,' I said. 'I'll let Lizzie know. Tonight, I was going to walk back to the cottage along the beach with her and Noah.' I looked round the rehearsal studio. Lizzie and Noah were still there, evidently waiting for me. Zoe and Richard were chatting by the door. Everyone else had left.

Raising his voice to carry across the room, Jake said, 'Would you guys like to stay for coffee?'

I told myself that I didn't mind in the slightest when all of them said that they would stay.

Chapter Thirty-seven

At last the hands on the clock reached 5.30. I logged out of my computer and stood up, hoisting the tote bag containing my make-up and my dance shoes onto my shoulder, and collecting my costume bag containing the clothes I'd selected to wear as Juliet from the coat rack where I'd hung it that morning. As I did every year, I'd taken some of my annual leave to coincide with the Players' summer show – and a few days afterwards – and I wouldn't be back in the Events office until the end of next week. And as it was now the school holidays, Lizzie would be around, and we'd already planned a picnic on the beach.

'I'm heading off to the theatre,' I said to Eve. 'The ballroom, that is.'

'I took a quick look in there earlier today,' Eve said. 'You must have worked so hard to get it all set up in just a few hours.'

'It was teamwork,' I said. 'Shane and his mates did most of it – with Jake telling them what he wanted – but almost the entire cast came along once they'd finished work and helped carry chairs and that sort of thing.'

I couldn't remember a Players' show where so many people had turned up unasked for the get in. Nor a show where a cast had remained so amiable throughout a technical rehearsal. At last night's tech, no one had moaned when they'd had to stand around on stage for hours while the crew, Marjorie's husband Peter (soundman for the Players, and B&B proprietor), and Colin's sister, Dee (lighting techie for the Players by night, doctor's

247

receptionist by day), went through the technical cues, an essential rehearsal for the smooth running of a show, but inevitably tedious for the actors. The arrival of a troupe of Downland waiters bearing trays of tea, coffee, and biscuits, courtesy of Mr Gates, was an unexpected bonus.

Eve said, 'I probably won't see you before tomorrow night, so I'll wish you good luck now. Break a leg, as you actors say.'

'Thanks, Eve,' I said. 'I hope you enjoy the play.'

Leaving my boss studying the spreadsheet on her computer screen, I went out of the office. I walked a short way along the corridor, and then, smiling broadly, I took off my name-badge and put it in my bag. I was no longer *Emma Stevens, Events Assistant.* For tonight's dress rehearsal and tomorrow's performance, I was an actor.

Jake, dressed only in a pair of jeans, sat on the edge of Juliet's bed, and slid his feet into his trainers. I lay stretched out beside him on the cool, white, cotton sheet, resting my head on my arm, gazing up at his tanned muscular body.

'*Wilt thou be gone,*' I said. '*It is not yet near day/It was the nightingale and not the lark…*'

'*It was the lark, the herald of the morn …*' Jake stood up, and went towards the balcony. I also got off the bed, and joined him. He had to leave, and soon.

'*O, now be gone!*' I said. '*More light and light it grows …*' I didn't want him to go.

He put his arms around me, holding me close so that I could feel the heat of his skin through the thin silk of the short, white slip that I was wearing as a nightdress. He reached up a hand and gently touched my face.

'*One kiss and I'll descend.*' He lowered his head, and kissed me, his lips warm and tender against mine. I felt empty when he broke away.

'*O think'st thou we shall ever meet again?*' I said. Suddenly, the thought that when he went back to London he would once again no longer be a part of my life, was unbearable.

'*I doubt it not ...*' Jake said. '*Adieu, adieu!*' He put on his shirt, and exited the stage, leaving Juliet alone.

I lay in my own bed in Lizzie's cottage staring up at the ceiling, reliving the rehearsal, my scenes with Jake, and the way I'd felt when he took me in his arms. I told myself I had to get him out of my head – I very much doubted that he was lying awake thinking about me – but when I shut my eyes, all I could see was him. I sat up, switched on my lamp, and picked up the novel that was on my bedside table, but the words danced before my eyes. Glancing at my alarm clock, I saw that it was nearly three a.m. With a sigh, I got out of bed, put on my kimono, went downstairs, and made myself a mug of tea. Going into the garden, I sat on the bench, relishing the coolness of the night air, inhaling the scent of the newly turned earth in the flower beds, where Lizzie was planning a display of autumn-flowering plants. The sky was clear, the stars bright. When Juliet was waiting for Romeo to come to her on their wedding night, she would look out of her window and see a garden and a night sky.

Come night; come Romeo, I thought. The touch of his hand, his mouth ... Aloud, I said, '*Come, gentle night, come, loving, black-brow'd night/Give me my Romeo*,' My body ached with longing.

A male voice said, 'Emma?' I turned my head to see Noah standing in the kitchen doorway, silhouetted against the light from the kitchen.

'Hey, Noah,' I said. He came out into the garden, and I saw that he was wearing just his boxers and a T-shirt, and in his raised hand, he was holding his cricket bat.

'We heard a noise,' Noah said, lowering the bat. 'Lizzie was worried it might be a burglar.'

'No – it's only me,' I said. 'I'm sorry if I disturbed you two.'

'Don't worry about it.' He glanced ruefully at his improvised weapon. 'I don't know why I brought this down with me. Stage combat I can do, but if it had been a stranger in our garden reciting Shakespeare, I'd have locked the kitchen door and dialled 999.' Turning back to the cottage, he called out, 'It's OK, Lizzie, it's just Emma practising her lines.'

Lizzie, wrapped in a bathrobe, appeared in the kitchen doorway. 'In the middle of the night?' she said.

'I couldn't sleep,' I said.

Lizzie came to stand beside her boyfriend. 'Why don't you go back to bed, Noah,' she said. 'You've got to be up for work in a few hours. I'll stay with Emma for a while, and hear her lines.'

'Oh, there's no need,' I said, but she'd already sat down on the bench. A look passed between her and Noah that I couldn't interpret. He smiled, nodded, and went back inside the cottage.

'So you can't sleep,' Lizzie said, 'and you're sitting alone in the dark, reciting lines of blank verse from a tragic love story. Does this have anything to do with Jake?'

'No – I – I don't know any more—' Lizzie is my best friend, I thought. I lied to her once, but I won't lie to her again. And I need to stop lying to myself. I said, 'I thought I was over him, but I'm not.'

'You're still in love with him,' Lizzie said. It wasn't a question.

'It doesn't make any difference how I feel,' I said. I do love him, I thought. I can't help myself. 'Once the play's done, he'll be off back to London and Leonie.'

We both fell silent. I noticed that it was less dark now in the garden. On the horizon, the sky was streaked with pale grey light.

Lizzie said, 'Tonight, after we got back from the dress, Noah asked me what was going on with you and Jake – why are you no longer spending your every free moment together? I told him that you and Jake had almost become more than friends, but you weren't prepared to let yourself get involved with a man who has a girlfriend. Noah insisted that Jake isn't with Leonie. They were definitely over before he came back to South Quay.'

250

I raised my eyebrows. 'And Noah knows this how?'

'Jake told him on the night of the thunderstorm,' Lizzie said. 'While you and I were sitting in the kitchen talking and listening to the thunder, they were at Jake's place doing the same. Although I guarantee more beer was consumed at Jake's place.'

'I saw Jake and Leonie together,' I said. 'I saw him kiss her.'

'Noah and I talked about that as well,' Lizzie said. 'Jake told Noah that he'd kissed Leonie – and that he regretted it, because he knew immediately that he felt nothing for her. But that was all that happened. He didn't sleep with her.'

'That's what Jake told Noah, is it?' I said.

'Noah believes him,' Lizzie said. She hesitated, and then she added, 'I know you need to focus on *Romeo and Juliet* right now – I wasn't going to tell you any of this until after the show – and I know things are complicated between you and Jake, but don't give up on him for the wrong reason.' She laid her hand briefly on my arm, and then stood up, and went inside the cottage.

Jake. I said his name, 'Jake,' and felt a delicious warmth in my stomach. I loved him. I wanted to be with him. I thought about what he'd said to Noah – he'd said the same to me, except I'd refused to listen to him. I asked myself if I trusted him, and knew that deep down inside me, in my heart, I did.

I stayed in the garden, and watched the sun come up, knowing that I wanted Jake and me to have another chance, willing him to want the same.

251

Chapter Thirty-eight

'When we were teenagers, I told you that we'd still be acting together when we were older,' Jake said. 'I was right.'

'But you didn't think it would be in a Players' show.' Sitting beside him in the passenger seat of his car, I stole a glance at his handsome profile. He was staring straight ahead, concentrating on over taking a slow-moving tractor that was holding up every other vehicle on the coast road, but I saw that he was smiling.

'No, I didn't,' he agreed. 'When I went to drama school, I thought I'd left South Quay behind me. I never expected to come back here. But ten years later, here I am.'

I fell for you ten years ago, I thought, and ten years later, I fell for you again. I resisted the temptation to tell him. Less than an hour before he was due to walk out on stage and perform a demanding role in a Shakespeare play, was not the time to inform a guy you'd rejected and accused of ruining your life that you were in love with him.

Unsurprisingly, given that I'd stayed in Lizzie's garden until daybreak, I'd slept on past noon. I'd woken to find a text on my phone from Jake, confirming the time he was picking me up to drive me to the Downland. I'd told myself not to make too much of it – it was only a text, for goodness' sake – but knowing that I was in his thoughts that morning had made my heart beat a little faster. There had also been an email from Henry, inviting the entire cast of *Romeo and Juliet* to an after-show party at the Moat House. I envisaged a more decorous event than those he'd held at the Wyndham's residence in Pamela and Maurice's absence when we were teenagers, and packed a sleeveless, thigh-length cotton shirt-dress suitable for a house party in my bag, along with Juliet's dresses and her flimsy nightgown. I'd also checked and re-checked to make sure I had everything I needed for the show: lipstick, dance shoes, safety pins in case of a costume malfunction. I'd had long chats on the phone with my parents and Scarlet, who'd called to wish me good luck, I'd written good luck cards for each member of the cast, and I'd read through my lines one final time, but the afternoon, the hours of waiting for the arrival of Jake's car outside the cottage, had passed very slowly.

Now, Jake turned off the coast road into the Downland's driveway, and pulled into the car park. We climbed out of the car, retrieved our costumes and bags from the boot, and headed towards the hotel's main entrance.

'What the—?' He put a hand on my arm.

I followed the direction of his gaze, and saw a van with Southcoast TV stencilled on its side, parked directly in front of the Downland. A man toting a large video camera was chatting to a woman holding a sound boom, and another woman, immaculately made up, wearing a smart blue dress, and holding a mic. As one, they saw us, and surged towards us.

'Smile, Emma,' Jake muttered. 'You're on camera.' We carried on walking, accompanied by calls for Jake to 'Look this way,' and a 'Good luck with the show, Jake.'

The woman holding the mic thrust it forward.

'So, Jake, what makes the star of *Sherwood* decide to act in an amateur production of *Romeo and Juliet*?' she said.

If Jake objected to the abruptness of her question, he didn't show it. 'I grew up in South Quay,' he said. 'I happened to be back here on holiday, when I heard that the local am dram society were in need of a director and a Romeo. I was available – the next series of *Sherwood* doesn't start shooting 'til the autumn – so I was able to help them out.'

'Are you in the show?' Suddenly the mic was in my face.

253

'I am,' I said. 'I play Juliet.'

The woman smiled encouragingly. 'And what's it like acting with a famous TV star?'

'It's great—' I'd every intention of heaping praise on my leading man, but the woman had turned back to Jake.

'And are you planning to do more theatre in future?' she said. 'Are we going to see you in the West End?'

'That rather depends on whether anyone wants to offer me a part,' Jake said. He favoured the media folk with his most charming smile. 'That's all, guys. I have a show to do. Thank you.' Placing a hand on the small of my back, he ushered me inside the Downland's reception. There we were accosted by Pamela, resplendent in silk and pearls, a lanyard declaring her to be *Chairwoman/Front of House Manager*.

'There you are at last,' she said.

'Are we late?' Jake said. 'So sorry, Pamela.'

'We'd have got here earlier but we were detained by the media,' I said. Not that we were actually late, I thought, as there was still more than half an hour to go before curtain up. If we'd had a curtain.

Pamela tutted. 'That woman with the microphone is over-zealous. I'd have thought the interview that I, the society's Chairwoman, gave her would have been ample for an item on the local news.' Recollecting herself, she added, 'You need to get backstage – many of our audience are already seated.' Her head swivelled towards the hotel entrance. 'Ah, here are Carol and her daughter.'

Leaving Chairwoman Pamela to greet Carol, her daughter Tessa, and any other members of the audience who'd yet to arrive, Jake and I made our way through the hotel to the wide corridor that ran behind the ballroom, the rest of our backstage area consisting of a small, private dining room that was standing in as the women's dressing room, and a disused office that had been given over to the men.

'A TV interview,' I said. 'Another thing you didn't expect to be doing in South Quay, I'd imagine,' I said.

'Oh, this summer in South Quay has quite confounded my expectations,' Jake said. He stepped towards me, so that we were standing close together, close enough for me to inhale the scent of his aftershave, only the costume bag clutched in my arms between us. His eyes gazed directly into mine.

'Has it?' I said. His smile melted my insides.

A male voice said, 'Evening, Jake. Emma.' For an instant, Jake held my gaze, and then he took a step away from me. Keith Preston (Gail's uncle, souvenir shop owner, and *Romeo and Juliet's* Stage Manager) was walking down the corridor towards us. He knocked on the dressing-room door and bellowed, 'This is your half-hour call, ladies.' From within, there came the sound of excited female voices and several shrieks.

'Break a leg, you two,' Keith said, and headed off towards the men's dressing room further down the corridor.

'I should—' Jake indicated vaguely.

I nodded. 'Oh – I got you a card.' I rummaged in my bag for the good luck card I'd written that afternoon.

He smiled. 'I've got something for you. That is, I found it.' He took a small object out of the pocket of his shirt and handed it to me. 'An opening-night present.'

I looked down at the smooth piece of blue glass lying in the palm of my hand.

'I remembered that you liked sea glass,' he said.

'Oh, Jake,' I said. 'It's beautiful.' My throat felt a little tight. 'Thank you.'

'Break a leg, Emma,' he said. He spun around and strode off along the corridor, vanishing inside the men's dressing room.

Jake. The look in his eyes … Suddenly, I had to put a hand on the wall to steady myself.

My phone rang, startling me. Hastily, I fished it out of my bag, and hit the answer key.

'Emma? Where are you?' It was Lizzie speaking. 'We've already had the half and you're *not here.*'

'Don't worry, I'm right outside the door,' I said. The next moment the dressing-room door was flung open and Lizzie, costumed as Lady Capulet in a silk dress she'd borrowed from her mother, was bustling me inside to a chorus of 'Hey, Emma – thought you weren't coming' from the female half of *Romeo and Juliet*'s cast. Through a fug of hairspray, I saw that the long oval oak dining table in the middle of the room was strewn with hand-mirrors, hairbrushes, mascara wands and good luck cards, while the chairs around it were piled with discarded street clothes, some neatly folded, others in careless heaps. All around the room, citizens of Verona in frayed denim shorts and skirts, strappy tops and trainers, were frenziedly checking make-up. Zoe's dancers were practising their steps one final time. In one corner, a Capulet maidservant was leafing through the script, while in another, Lady Montague was working her way through her vocal exercises. The Nurse, seated in a carver chair at the far end of the table, regarded the younger members of the cast with the benevolent expression of an experienced actress who'd seen it all many times before.

'What kept you, daughter Juliet?' Lizzie said, leading me to the chair she'd saved for me next to hers.

'The media wanted to talk to our director,' I said, peeling off my T-shirt and jeans. 'I gatecrashed his press conference.'

'Oh my goodness,' Lizzie said, 'I felt like a Hollywood star on a red carpet walking past that camera. Strangely, no one wanted to interview me or Noah.'

'Also, our director was giving me some last-minute notes.' I stepped into the red dress that Juliet would be wearing when Romeo saw her for the first time – the dress I'd worn for my school prom, when I was seventeen.

Lizzie arched her eyebrows. 'I see. And will these notes improve your performance?'

I smiled. 'I'm not *sure*,' I said. 'No one can know for sure what's going to happen in a live show. But there's every chance.'

256

Chapter Thirty-nine

A thunderous knock on the door reverberated around the dressing room. Conversation ceased. Zoe's dancers froze on the spot.

Our Stage Manager's call came to us from the corridor: 'Beginners to the stage, please.'

I placed the blue sea glass, which I'd been holding in my hand, carefully down on the table, alongside the good luck cards I'd received from other members of the cast. This is it, I thought. After months of rehearsals, three directors, and three leading men, I'm finally, at last, going to play Juliet. I made myself breathe slowly and evenly.

Lady Montague went to the door, wedging it open with a chair. Talking only in whispers if at all, the citizens of Verona in Act I, scene i started filing out into the corridor. Next to me, Lizzie pushed back her chair and stood up. She'd done a great job with Lady Capulet's make-up, I thought, making her rounded features appear harsh and angular, replacing her usual lip gloss with a slash of carmine red.

'Break a leg, Lizzie,' I said, also standing up, so that we could hug each other.

'You too, Emma.' She went out of the dressing room, leaving me alone with Phyllis, who was now reading a magazine. There were two scenes before either of us were needed on stage, but I found myself quite unable to follow her relaxed example, and went out after the others. I could almost feel the adrenaline surging through my body.

Further along the corridor, the citizens of Verona were lined up by the doors that led into the ballroom – as if in the wings at the side of a stage – about to make their entrance. Henry, dressed like all the backstage crew in the traditional black, his injured arm in a black sling, a copy of the script in his good hand, was seated on a stool, ready to prompt if needed. Jake, also not required until a later scene, was standing with his back to me, a little way behind the others. I took a moment just to look at him, drinking him in, and then went and stood beside him.

'I couldn't bear to stay in the dressing room any longer,' I said.

'You and me both,' he said, with a smile.

I became aware that the sound of the audience's voices coming to us from the auditorium had faded to silence. Light suddenly spilled into the wings from the stage. At a signal from our Stage Manager, the citizens of Verona moved forward into the performance area.

The famous first lines of the play came to me very clearly: *'Two households, both alike in dignity/In fair Verona, where we lay our scene ... A pair of star-crossed lovers ...'*

The men of the house of Capulet strolled casually onto the stage. Those of the house of Montague swaggered on after them.

'My work as director is done,' Jake said softly. 'Whatever happens out there is up to them now.'

From the stage came the sound of angry shouting, as fighting broke out among Montagues and Capulets, the voice of the furious Tybalt louder than all the rest, *'... look upon thy death ... I hate all Montagues and thee ...'*

I heard the screams of the citizens of Verona, suddenly caught up in a brawl between two armed gangs of youths. A grim-faced Prince and his guards marched out of the men's dressing room, passed by Jake and me without acknowledging our presence, and made their entrance.

On stage, the Prince declared, *'Rebellious subjects, enemies to peace ...'*

258

Beside me, Jake exhaled. 'It's going well so far,' he said. 'Much better than I expected, if I'm honest.'

I smiled. 'Amateurs who can act,' I said. 'Who'd have thought it?'

'Some of them can act,' Jake said.

'Most of them,' I said.

The Prince of Verona's voice came to us, cold as steel, and terrifying. '… *If ever you disturb our streets again/Your lives shall pay the forfeit … on pain of death, all men depart …*'

'All right,' Jake said. '*Most* of them can act. I'll give you that.'

The Prince and his retinue marched into the wings, followed by his rebellious subjects. Jake and I flattened ourselves against the wall of the corridor to allow them to dash past us to the dressing rooms, where the Capulets' guests would quickly change into their costumes – their glitziest dresses or sharpest suits – for the ball scene.

Left on stage with her son's friend, Benvolio, Lady Montague said, '*O, where is Romeo? Saw you him today?*'

'What made you do it, Jake? Why take on *a bunch of amateurs*?'

Jake angled his body towards me. 'Do you really not know?' he said.

Benvolio said, '*See here he comes …*'

Lady Montague exited the stage.

'That's my cue,' Jake said.

'Break a leg,' I said, quickly.

He spun on his heel, and strode out onto the stage.

'*Is the day so young? … Love is a smoke rais'd with the fume of sighs … a fire sparkling in lovers' eyes …*'

I stood listening to his talk of love, and the cadence of his voice rising and falling as he spoke Romeo's lines, sent shivers through my body. He's *so* good at this, I thought.

Lizzie, now attired in a long-sleeved, black lace evening gown that her mother had worn once on a cruise, and Phyllis, in a brocade ensemble that she wore fairly often, arrived in the wings, ready for the scene we were about to perform together – my first scene as Juliet.

On stage, Romeo declared his intention of gatecrashing the Capulets' ball, made his exit, and returned to stand beside me.

'You're on fire tonight,' I said.

He laughed. 'I'd forgotten the sheer *pleasure* of acting on stage in front of a live audience. Being a part of *Romeo and Juliet* has reminded me. I didn't expect that.'

'So why did you do it, Jake?' I said.

The stage lights dimmed, the fierce sunlight of Verona's marketplace becoming the warm candlelight of the Capulet's house. Lady Capulet and the Nurse entered stage right. My stomach tightened. I took a step nearer the stage, ready to make my entrance. Jake was standing behind me now. I could feel the heat and energy radiating from his body.

Lady Capulet said, '*Nurse, where's my daughter? Call her forth to me.*'

Jake put his hands on my bare shoulders, and it was as though electricity shot through me.

'I did it for you, Emma,' he said.

I gasped. 'Oh – *Oh* – Jake—' I looked back at him over my shoulder, into his grey-blue eyes.

'Focus, Emma,' he said.

The Nurse called, '*Where's this girl? What, Juliet!*'

'See you on the other side,' Jake said, giving me a gentle push towards the stage. 'Have a good one.'

I took a calming breath. '*How now, who calls? … I am here.*'

Juliet of the house of Capulet made her entrance.

260

Chapter Forty

I lay still, my eyes closed, my head resting on Jake's chest, my arm draped over his waist, his bloodied knife, with which I'd stabbed myself to death, lying beside us. The Capulets, Montagues, and citizens of Verona regarded us in grief-stricken silence.

The Prince said, '*A glooming peace this morning with it brings;/The sun for sorrow will not show his head ...*'

I could feel Jake's heart beating next to mine.

'*For never was a story of more woe/Than this of Juliet and her Romeo.*'

To the slow, solemn beat of a drum, the Prince led the citizens of Verona out of Juliet's tomb, and offstage. In the stillness and quiet that followed, I could hear the sound of sobbing, and realised it was coming from the audience. The stage lights faded to a blackout. I opened my eyes, swiftly swung my legs over the side of the bier, and with Jake close behind me, darted into the wings, where the entire cast of *Romeo and Juliet* were gathered together by the entrance, waiting to take their bow. The stage lights came up again. From the auditorium came the sound of applause, quiet at first, growing ever louder, a wave of sound, a huge breaker rolling up a beach. Jake and I hurriedly moved to one side of the corridor, standing well back, so that the citizens of Verona could get past us and return to the stage, where, as they arranged themselves into a line, they were greeted by cheers and whoops. The Montagues and Capulets followed, Mercutio and Tybalt both receiving a massive cheer, although not as deafening as the cheers and ear-piercing whistles given to the Nurse.

Jake's face broke into a broad smile. 'I think, after tonight, Master William Shakespeare may have a few new fans. Ready to take your curtain call?'

My pulse racing, breathless, too elated to speak, I nodded. Jake took hold of my hand, and together we ran out onto the brightly lit stage, to a redoubled burst of applause and cheering from the audience. Standing in front of the rest of the cast, downstage centre, Jake bowed and I curtsied. The audience applauded even louder. I looked out into the semi-darkness of the auditorium and was just able to make out the faces of my parents, and Scarlet and Nathan, sitting a couple of rows back from the front, next to Lizzie's parents, all of them smiling and clapping.

Leaning towards me so that I could hear him above the tumult, Jake said, 'Stay here, Emma.' To my surprise, he ran offstage, only to return a few seconds later with a huge bunch of my favourite yellow roses, which he gave into my hand. Overwhelmed, I felt my eyes brim with tears.

'Th-thank you so much,' I said. He kissed me on the side of my face. The audience went wild, springing to their feet, clapping so hard their palms must have stung. Jake and I both bowed again, and then, hand in hand, we left the stage, followed by the rest of the cast. Crowded together with the others in the wings, I felt light-headed, intoxicated, giddy with applause. We waited only a few seconds before all running back on stage, staying there for several minutes, until the handclapping began to die down. The citizens of Verona exited first, then the Capulets and Montagues. Jake and I waved at the audience, and then we walked slowly into the wings. The stage lights dimmed, and the house lights came on. The Players' summer show was over.

Chapter Forty-one

Raising her voice so that she could be heard above the music blasting out of Henry's speakers, Sofia said, 'I was so nervous when I was waiting to go on, but once I was out there – it felt – it was *amazing* – I can't describe it.'

'I know exactly what you mean,' I said. 'The *exhilaration* you feel when you're on stage – and afterwards, when you hear the applause – there's nothing like it.'

'You still feel like that, even after all the shows you've done?' Sofia said.

'I do,' I said. 'I can't imagine *not* feeling that way.'

'I'm going to audition for a speaking part in the next show,' Sofia said. 'I do *so* hope there *is* another Players' show.'

You and me both, I thought. I glanced over to the bar, a trestle table set up by the entrance to the poolhouse, where Maurice was pouring Keith Preston a measure of his finest whisky. The cast party, I decided, was not the time to ask our Treasurer for an update on the Players' finances – we would know soon enough if *Romeo and Juliet*'s ticket sales were enough to balance the society's books. I determinedly put my concerns about the society's future out of my mind for the rest of the night.

As soon as Jake and I'd stepped offstage and into the wings, we were enveloped by our fellow actors in a cacophony of chatter and laughter, hugs and congratulations. Back in the dressing room, I'd taken a moment to inhale the glorious scent of my roses, and then I'd thrown off Juliet's costume and put on my summer party dress. Lizzie and I'd left the dressing room together, making our way through the hotel to reception, where we'd arranged to meet our families, and where many of the audience had lingered after the show to congratulate friends and relatives in the cast. The evening became a bit of a blur at that point, with my parents, sister and brother-in-law flinging their arms round me and telling me how proud they were, Eve saying she was '*so* impressed,' Mr Gates shaking my hand, Carol informing everyone that she'd never understood Shakespeare before that night, and that the fighting had been 'as good as on TV,' Tessa admitting that she'd cried all through the play's final scene … Jake standing next to me, draping his arm loosely around my shoulders, making my whole body sing. Eventually, the crowd of well-wishers had recalled that most of them had work the next day and dispersed, leaving the cast free to relocate to the Wyndhams' garden.

Sofia said, 'Ooh, I *love* this track.' She took off, running around the swimming pool to the terrace, to join Zoe, Phyllis, Marjorie, and Zoe's dancers, who were all shimmying energetically to the summer's latest dance craze, accompanied by Eddie on air guitar. Lizzie and Noah were dancing together, swaying slowly to a rhythm only they could hear, her arms around his neck, his hands on her thickening waist. On the far side of the pool, directly opposite to where I was standing, I saw Jake talking to the sound and lighting crew. As though aware that I was looking at him, he glanced my way, and our eyes met. Not for the first time that night, a smile passed between us before he turned his attention back to whatever the soundman was saying. Henry, Gail, Shane, and other Players lounged on the floodlit lawn, talking, laughing, and drinking bottled beer; Pamela and the members of the committee sat in a circle of deckchairs, tipsily congratulating each other on *Romeo and Juliet*'s success. Fireflies and moths flitted across the grass, drawn irresistibly to the lamplight, and bats swooped overhead. I drained my wine, headed to the bar, and poured myself another. My gaze drifted back to Jake. I wondered how long he'd want to stay at the party. And what might happen after we left. My stomach clenched.

A male voice said, 'Much as I wanted to direct *Romeo and Juliet*, I have to admit that I wouldn't have done it as well as Jake Murray.' Richard was standing a few feet away from me. He, too, was looking across the pool at Jake.

'I'm sure you'd have done your best,' I said, tactfully.

'Yeah, well, it doesn't matter now,' Richard said. 'It turns out that I didn't need to direct a Shakespeare play in order to impress Zoe.'

I gaped at him. 'Zoe? You wanted to impress *Zoe*?'

He raised one eyebrow. 'Didn't I tell you I was thinking of asking her out? I know I told Henry.'

'No, you didn't tell me,' I said. He told Henry, I thought, who told Noah … and one of them got completely the wrong idea. All those times I'd avoided him, and he was interested in Zoe, not me. I resisted the urge to laugh aloud.

'Last week, I finally plucked up enough courage to ask her on a date,' Richard went on. 'I took her to the Wharf in Teymouth. Do you know it?'

'I've been there once,' I said. 'It's a fabulous restaurant.'

'Zoe and I liked it.' After a moment, he added, 'We're seeing each other.'

'That's great, Richard,' I said. 'Zoe's a nice girl.'

He looked towards the dance floor where Zoe was still dancing. 'I should probably go and join her.'

'See you later,' I said. He strutted over to Zoe and started dancing with her. Or rather, flailing around in front of her. Judging by the dreamy smile on her face, Zoe didn't appear to mind that he lacked her ability to move in perfect time with the music.

I was still watching the dancers and sipping my wine, when I sensed the presence of someone standing behind me and knew that it was Jake.

Putting his head close to mine, he said, 'Would you like to dance? Or do you think we've been at the cast party long enough?'

265

I turned around to face him. 'I would like to dance with you,' I said, 'but I'd like to leave this party with you a whole lot more.'

For a long moment, he stood quite still, looking down at me through hooded eyes. Then he took hold of my hand, lacing his fingers through mine.

'We should go,' he said.

Jake turned into his drive and brought his car smoothly to a halt. I got out, retrieved my flowers and bags from the back seat, and followed him to the door. He unlocked it, and ushered me inside.

'I've a bottle of champagne in the fridge,' he said. 'Would you like some?'

'I'd love some,' I said. I held up my roses. 'Do you have a vase? These need to go in water. I want them to last.'

'I'll see to it,' Jake said. He opened the door to the living room and switched on the light. 'You go on through.' Taking the roses with him, he vanished into the kitchen. I went into the living room, tossed my bag and costumes onto a chair, opened the French windows, and stepped out onto the veranda, into the warm summer night. As I did so, the full moon came out from behind a cloud, flooding the garden with silver light. A sea breeze stirred my hair and the skirt of my dress, and brought me the scent of brine. I heard the faint sound of waves breaking on the shore.

Jake came out of the house, without the roses, but holding an open bottle of champagne. 'Come to the beach with me, Emma?' he said, and held out his hand. I took it, and we walked across the grass, through the gate at the end of the garden, and onto the beach, and sat next to each other on the stones. He passed me the champagne bottle. I swallowed a mouthful of the deliciously cold fizzing liquid, and passed it back to him. The sea was white and silver in the moonlight, the waves rising and falling, a heavy swell, the incoming tide yet to reach the end of the breakwaters.

'You owned the stage tonight, Emma,' Jake said.

'I had a good director,' I said. 'Thank you, Jake, for directing the show, playing Romeo, for remembering about the sea glass

266

and the flowers, for all of it … For reminding me of how much I wanted to become a professional actress when I was seventeen …' I took a deep breath. 'I – I've decided I'm going to apply for drama school.'

'Oh, Emma, that's great,' Jake said.

'I know I may not get in,' I said, 'but I have to try.'

'You'll get in,' Jake said, sounding a lot more confident than I was. 'Have you chosen your audition pieces? I could help you work on them, if you like.'

'I would like,' I said. 'Thanks, Jake.'

He smiled. 'I should be thanking you,' he said.

'What for?'

'For showing me that I still love acting.' He drank more champagne and handed me the bottle. 'That play my agent wants me to do – I'm going to accept it.'

I smiled. 'Even though the money isn't right?'

'The money's dreadful,' he said, 'but the play itself and my part in it are terrific.'

'*The play's the thing*,' I said.

We fell silent, passing the champagne bottle back and forth between us. I looked up at the black velvet dome of the sky. Wisps of cloud drifted across the silver disc of the moon.

Jake said, 'Emma …' I turned my face towards him. He raised his hand and brushed a strand of hair out of my eyes. Then he trailed a finger down my arm. I thought, he's going to kiss me. My heart started beating wildly in my chest. His mouth lifted in a lazy smile.

'Fancy going for a swim?' he said.

'What, *now*?' I said.

He laughed and in one sinuous movement, stood up, reached behind his shoulders, pulled his T-shirt over his head, and tossed it onto the stones. He toed off his trainers, and then he stripped off his jeans and boxers. Without conscious thought, my gaze drifted down over his hard muscular torso. I forced myself to look back up at his face.

267

'Are you coming in?' he said. 'Don't worry – no one ever comes to this part of the beach at night.'

My pulse rate grew faster. 'I – No, I don't think – Oh, why not?' I started to undo the buttons on the front of my dress. 'You were always a bad influence on me, Jake Murray.'

He grinned and walked slowly down the slope of the stones, running across the sand and into the sea. I stood and watched him as he dived under a wave and surfaced further out.

'Is it cold?' I called out. 'I'm not coming in if it's cold.'

'It's fine,' Jake shouted back. 'Refreshing.'

I undid the last button on my dress and let it fall to the ground. Then, acutely aware that Jake was looking at me, wanting him to look at me, I peeled off my underwear. Naked, I walked daringly slowly into the shallows, gasping as the crest of a wave reached my waist. It wasn't freezing, but it wasn't warm either. Jake swam towards me, rising up out of the sea and wading once he was in his depth. His body glistening with seawater, he stood in front of me, his chest rising and falling. The sea receded, until I was standing in water that only came up to my knees. His gaze travelled over my body. Suddenly, I was trembling, and it had nothing to do with the temperature of the sea.

'I love you, Emma,' he said.

'Oh – Jake –' And then I was in his arms, and he was kissing me, tasting of champagne and moonlight, his tongue exploring my mouth, our naked bodies melding together, feeling him grow hard, the sea surging back towards the shore, swirling around our thighs, rising and falling, a wave larger than the rest breaking over our shoulders, Jake holding me, keeping me from being knocked off my feet. He lifted his mouth from mine.

'I love you,' I said.

He picked me up and carried me out of the sea, striding through the surf, and up the beach, setting me down on the sand in the shelter of a breakwater. A torrent of desire cascaded through me, passion too-long denied, and I reached for him, my arms around his neck, running my hands through his hair, my tongue in his mouth, pressing my breasts and hips against his hard body. He crushed me to him, both of us falling to the sand, limbs entangled, his kiss fierce, as he rolled me onto my back, his mouth on my throat, on my breasts, his hand sliding between my legs, pleasure intensifying ... His fingers grew still.

'Don't stop,' I gasped. 'That feels so good.'

'I need to get—If you're ready for me ...'

'Ah – yes – *yes*—'

He sat up, grasped hold of his jeans, which were lying within an arms' reach above us on the stones, and took a condom out of the pocket. I heard the sound of ripping foil, and then he was between my open thighs, thrusting himself, hard and hot, deep inside me, and I was gasping and clinging to him, digging my fingers into the muscles of his back, losing myself in him, the tang of salt on his skin, moonlight and shadow, his hand on my breast, a rising tide of pleasure, the surf pounding on the strand, Jake's body growing taut, the groan that escaped from his throat as he reached the crest of ecstasy, the wave breaking over both us and crashing on the shore ...

'Emma,' Jake whispered. 'Oh, Emma. *I do love nothing in the world so well as you.*' He eased himself out of me, and lay next to me on the sand, resting his head on his arm. '*Doubt that the stars are fire ... But never doubt that I love thee.*'

I rolled over to face him. '*I love you more than words can wield the matter.*' Sand was everywhere, in my hair, on my skin, but I really didn't care.

He reached up a hand and traced the line of my face. Then he said, 'Emma – we can't fall asleep on the beach.'

'No, we really can't,' I said. He brushed my forehead with his lips, and then he got to his feet, and pulled on his jeans. I, too, stood up, located my dress and put it on.

'You'll stay with me tonight?' Jake said. 'In my bed?'

I smiled. 'Yes.'

'Will you stay with me for the summer?'

'Yes,' I said.

'I love you, Emma.' He took both my hands in his. 'I want to be with you when the summer's over. I want us to be together. For ever.'

'I want that too,' I said.

'You'll take a chance on me?'

'Yes, I will,' I said.

Chapter Forty-two

Two Years Later …

The sea is calm, and we take a few minutes to stand at the water's edge and skim stones across its smooth mirrored surface, before making our way up the beach, along Shore Road, and into Saltwater Lane. When we reach Lizzie and Noah's cottage, she opens the front door before we're even halfway up the path.

'I was watching out for you,' she says, flinging her arms around me and Jake. 'It's so lovely to see you both.'

'It's good to see you, too, Lizzie,' I say.

We go inside. Noah comes out of the front room, carrying Lily-Mae, tow-haired, and with Lizzie's cornflower-blue eyes.

'Hello, Lily-Mae,' I say, softly. The little girl regards me suspiciously for a moment, but then, to my delight, her face breaks into a smile. I realise that it's three months since I last saw her, at Lizzie and Noah's wedding. 'Do you think she remembers me?'

'Maybe,' Lizzie says.

'Most young children of her age only recognise the faces of people they see all the time,' Noah says, 'but then, Lily-Mae is very advanced.' He kisses the top of his daughter's head.

'I can't believe how much she's grown,' Jake says.

Lizzie's mother comes out of the front room. We exchange the usual pleasantries. She congratulates Jake on the rave reviews he received for his recent performance in *Hamlet*. Since his return to the West End, he's done two more stage plays between shooting

271

his TV series and a four-part thriller for the BBC. Last week he told a journalist that while some of his best work has been on film, appearing on stage in front of a live audience never fails to remind him why he became an actor.

'I was sorry to hear that the next series of *Sherwood* is going to be the last,' Mrs Flowerdew says.

'Yeah, I'm going to miss Robert Sherwood after playing him for five years,' Jake says, 'but everyone on the show agrees that it's best that we go out on a high. There are plans for a Christmas special, though, and I'll be making the occasional guest appearance in the spin-off.'

I know that Jake's already signed the contract to play the lead in a new TV series, a historical drama about an Elizabethan spy, but we can't mention this to anyone in South Quay just yet. The production company would not be best pleased if their carefully orchestrated publicity campaign was derailed by rumours in the Armada Inn.

'Please tell me that Robert and Marion get married in the last episode,' Mrs Flowerdew says.

Jake laughs. 'I hope they do, but I won't know that myself until I get the script.'

Lily-Mae puts her thumb in her mouth, and rests her head on her father's shoulder. Her eyes close.

'She's almost asleep,' Lizzie says. 'Time we put her in her bed, Noah.'

'Shall I take her up?' Mrs Flowerdew says. 'You all need to get going. You don't want to be late.' With infinite care, Noah places Lily-Mae in her grandmother's arms. Lizzie leans forward to give her daughter a goodnight kiss.

'Night night, little one,' she says. We all smile at the sleeping child, and Mrs Flowerdew carries her upstairs to her bedroom, my old room, which Lizzie has painted to resemble a fairytale forest, with deer, rabbits, and foxes, and elves dancing among the trees.

Lizzie and Noah collect their costumes from the living room, and the four of us leave the cottage, Lizzie and I falling into step as we walk along Shore Road and turn onto the high street, edging our way through the holidaymakers returning from a day on the beach, Jake and Noah following a few paces behind. It may be nearly two years since I went to live with Jake in London, but as always when we visit South Quay, Lizzie and I pick up our conversation almost exactly from where we left off the last time we were together. I talk about my training at RoCoDa, the classes in improvisation, voice, movement, screen acting, and mic technique, and how much I'm looking forward to next term, when our projects will include a Shakespeare play, stage combat and devising our own films. Lizzie talks about Lily-Mae's delight in paddling in the sea, Noah's new-found enthusiasm for building sandcastles, and the success of the Year 6 art club she's set up at school. It strikes me forcibly, as we walk past the Armada and come in sight of the community centre, that while we don't see each other as often as we used to, though our lives are taking different paths, Lizzie and I will always be the best of friends.

We reach the community centre car park just as Sofia and Eddie are getting out of his van. Sofia comes bounding up to us, and greets us with a hug. Eddie, laden with his girlfriend's costume bag as well as his own, follows a little more slowly.

'I'm so looking forward to seeing you in your first lead role, Sofia,' I say.

Sofia beams. 'I'm super-excited,' she says. 'Eliza Doolittle is a dream of a part.'

'I don't know how she's managed to learn all those lines,' Eddie says.

'Who are you playing, Eddie?' Jake asks.

'Oh, I have several non-speaking parts,' Eddie says. 'I'm in all the crowd scenes.'

We talk about *Pygmalion* a short while longer, the fun they've had in rehearsals, how Zoe is an extremely good director, and how impressed they think Jake and I will be by Richard's impeccable comic timing in the role of the irascible male lead, Professor

273

Higgins. Jake and I wish the four of them 'good luck' and 'break a leg', and they head off to the community centre's side entrance – tonight their stage door – and the changing rooms, which Lizzie tells me are much more spacious than the ones destroyed by the storm, and with better lighting. Fond as I was of the Players' previous performance space, I have to admit that the new community centre, with its two halls – and, I'm told, enough cupboards for all the groups that use it to store their equipment – is a vast improvement on the old run-down building. Jake was immensely flattered when he was asked to open the new venue, and did so with great pleasure.

A car draws up in the space next to where Jake and I are standing, and Richard and Zoe get out.

'So glad you guys could make it for the opening night,' Richard says.

'I do hope you enjoy it,' Zoe says.

'I'm sure we will,' I say. 'Have you enjoyed directing your husband?'

'I have,' Zoe says. 'He's excellent at taking direction. I wouldn't have married him otherwise.' She adds, 'After the performance, I want to hear your notes, Jake.'

'Sure,' Jake says. 'If I have any.'

Richard and Zoe head off to the stage door. Jake and I walk up the short flight of steps to the community centre's main entrance and go inside. Henry, his lanyard proclaiming him *Front of House Manager*, is on the door. I've already congratulated him on Facebook and sent them a card, but it's the first time I've seen him since he and Gail got engaged, so I congratulate him again and Jake shakes his hand. We buy a programme.

'*Pygmalion* didn't tempt you back to the stage?' I say. The Players have put on other shows since *Romeo and Juliet* saved the society two years ago, but Henry didn't audition for any of them.

He smiles and shakes his head. 'I so much prefer working behind the scenes. I'm the Stage Manager for the panto this year.' He lowers his voice. 'Keep it to yourselves, because the candidates haven't been announced yet, but I'm planning to stand for election to the committee.'

'That's great, Henry,' I say. I decide not to tell him that I've already heard about his plans from Lizzie and Noah.

More members of the audience arrive. Henry turns to greet them and inspect their tickets. Jake and I go into the bar, which on this warm summer evening is doing a roaring trade in cold beer and wine.

Jake says, 'I reckon Henry will be Chairman of the South Quay Players one day.'

'Well, he does come from a theatrical dynasty,' I say.

I take a look at the programme, noting the number of new members of the Players in the cast list. The society really is thriving, I think. I smile when I read that they are planning to perform *A Midsummer Night's Dream* next year.

Jake says, 'I was thinking that since we've rented the villa for a whole month this summer, we could throw a house party. Or maybe a beach party. Friends, wine, music ... What do you think?'

A summer night, years ago. Me, Jake, Lizzie, Noah and Henry sitting around a driftwood fire on the beach. Noah strumming his guitar. Me telling my friends that I was going to become an actress, that I knew it was a tough profession and I might never make it, but I would never give up my dream. The taste of cider. The sound of waves breaking on the shore. Red sparks from the fire floating up into the night sky ...

'Sounds good to me,' I say.

Henry comes into the bar. 'The auditorium is now open,' he says, raising his voice above the chatter.

'We may as well go straight in,' Jake says. He smiles, leans forward and kisses me lightly on the mouth. 'I love you, Emma. We're going to have a great summer.'

My life is in London now. Jake's flat is *our* home. My first year at drama school has been everything I'd hoped, and more. But it's

275

good to be back in South Quay, knowing that Jake and I have the whole summer before us, to swim and sunbathe, to spend time with my family and our closest friends.

'I love you, Jake,' I say.

Hand in hand, we go into the theatre and take our seats for the Players' summer show.

Acknowledgements

Many thanks to Faith at Headline, and to my editor, Greg.

And to my fabulously talented and inspiring writer friends, collectively the Ten Muses, who are always ready to talk about writing and books.

And to my amazing beta readers, book-trailer makers, website designers and cheerleaders: Guy, Joanne, David, Sara, Iain, Laura, and Marc.